SHERWOOD ANDERSON'S
WINESBURG, OHIO

WITH VARIANT READINGS AND ANNOTATIONS

Winesburg, Ohio in 1919.
Wrapper of the First Edition, First Printing.

SHERWOOD ANDERSON'S
WINESBURG, OHIO

WITH VARIANT READINGS AND ANNOTATIONS

EDITED BY

RAY LEWIS WHITE

Ohio University Press

Athens

First published in the United States of America by B. W. Huebsch 1919

Copyright © 1919 by B. W. Huebsch

Copyright © 1947 by Eleanor Copenhaver Anderson

Copyright © 1997 by The Sherwood Anderson Literary Estate Trust

Introduction © 1997 by Ray Lewis White

Ohio University Press, Athens, Ohio 45701

Ohio University Press edition printed 1997

Ohio University Press books are printed on acid-free paper ∞

Some of the episodes in this book were printed
in *The Seven Arts, The Masses* and *The Little Review*
to which magazines the author makes
due acknowledgment.

Sherwood Anderson (1919)

Library of Congress Cataloging-in-Publication Data

Anderson, Sherwood, 1876–1941.

 Sherwood Anderson's Winesburg, Ohio : with variant readings and annotations /
edited by Ray Lewis White.

     p.   cm.

 Includes bibliographical references.

 ISBN 0–8214–1180–2

 1. Anderson, Sherwood, 1876–1941. Winesburg, Ohio—Criticism, Textual.
2. Ohio—Social life and customs—Fiction. 3. City and town life—Ohio—Fiction.
 I. White, Ray Lewis.   II. Title.

PS3501.N4S48   1997

813'.52—dc21

For inspiring my lifetime of
scholarly adventures, this book is dedicated to

RICHARD D. ALTICK

Ray Lewis White
1997

To the memory of my mother

EMMA SMITH ANDERSON

Whose keen observations on the life about her
first awoke in me the hunger to see beneath the surface of lives,
this book is dedicated.

Sherwood Anderson
1919

CONTENTS

List of Illustrations   ix
Preface and Acknowledgments   xi
Introduction   xv

WINESBURG, OHIO

A GROUP OF TALES OF OHIO SMALL TOWN LIFE

Foreword   The Book of the Grotesque   1

THE TALES AND THE PERSONS

Hands, *concerning Wing Biddlebaum*   5
Paper Pills, *concerning Doctor Reefy*   13
Mother, *concerning Elizabeth Willard*   17
The Philosopher, *concerning Doctor Parcival*   27
Nobody Knows, *concerning Louise Trunnion*   35
Godliness
   Part One, concerning Jesse Bentley   40
   Part Two, concerning Jesse Bentley   50
   Part Three, concerning Louise Bentley   64
   Part Four, concerning David Hardy   74
A Man of Ideas, *concerning Joe Welling*   80
Adventure, *concerning Alice Hindman*   89
Respectability, *concerning Wash Williams*   98
The Thinker, *concerning Seth Richmond*   105
Tandy, *concerning Tandy Hard*   120

Preface and Acknowledgments

The Strength of God, *concerning the Reverend Curtis Hartman*   124
The Teacher, *concerning Kate Swift*   134
Loneliness, *concerning Enoch Robinson*   143
An Awakening, *concerning Belle Carpenter*   155
"Queer," *concerning Elmer Cowley*   166
The Untold Lie, *concerning Ray Pearson*   178
Drink, *concerning Tom Foster*   185
Death, *concerning Doctor Reefy and Elizabeth Willard*   195
Sophistication, *concerning Helen White*   208
Departure, *concerning George Willard*   219

Select Bibliography   223

LIST OF ILLUSTRATIONS

frontispiece
Winesburg, Ohio in 1919.
Wrapper of the First Edition, First Printing.
Courtesy of the Sherwood Anderson Papers, the Newberry Library.

―――――――

Winesburg, Ohio. Page from the Manuscript.
"The Book of the Grotesque."
Courtesy of the Sherwood Anderson Papers, the Newberry Library.

Winesburg, Ohio. Page from the Manuscript.
"Loneliness."
Courtesy of the Sherwood Anderson Papers, the Newberry Library.

Winesburg, Ohio. Page from the Manuscript.
"The Strength of God."
Courtesy of the Sherwood Anderson Papers, the Newberry Library.

Winesburg, Ohio. Page from the Manuscript.
"Departure."
Courtesy of the Sherwood Anderson Papers, the Newberry Library.

Clyde, Ohio. Waterworks Pond.
Courtesy of John D. Maines.

List of Illustrations

Clyde, Ohio. Railroad Station.
Courtesy of John D. Maines.

Sherwood Anderson. Author of *Winesburg, Ohio.*
Courtesy of the Illinois State Historical Society.

Sherwood Anderson. Youth in Clyde, Ohio.
Courtesy of the Sherwood Anderson Papers, the Newberry Library.

Clyde, Ohio. Presbyterian Church.
Courtesy of John D. Maines.

Clyde, Ohio. Empire House Hotel.
Courtesy of John D. Maines.

Clyde, Ohio. Drawn as Winesburg by Thad Hurd.
Courtesy of John D. Maines.

Winesburg, Ohio. First-edition Endpaper.
Map Drawn by Harald Toksvig.

Clyde, Ohio. Main Street in Winter.
Courtesy of John D. Maines.

PREFACE AND ACKNOWLEDGMENTS

WINESBURG, OHIO entered my life in 1963 when I sought a research topic for a seminar in American literary naturalism. My professor encouraged me to consider writing about Sherwood Anderson, as all of the more "major authors" had been claimed by seminar students less dilatory than I. With no great enthusiasm I looked into Sherwood Anderson and into *Winesburg, Ohio;* but within a few weeks and with very great enthusiasm I decided that Anderson's life and writings should become the subject of my dissertation and the subject of some of the books that I intended to publish . . . and one of these books that I called into dreaming existence would be surely, someday, my own edition of Anderson's *Winesburg, Ohio.*

Given the unlikelihood of fulfilling these graduate-school dreams of scholarly achievement, I am yet amazed that I did manage to publish several Sherwood Anderson volumes—selected essays on the author's career, a collection of his writings for small-town newspapers, the text of an early novel, his correspondence with Gertrude Stein, editions of his three memoirs, etc.

Then, in the 1970s, having deciphered Anderson's *Winesburg* manuscripts, having collected and collated all relevant editions and printings of the work, and having readied for publication by a university press a nearly inscrutable "genetic text" edition of *Winesburg, Ohio,* I encountered for the first time the intransigence of copyright law in the form of the then-recent non-expiration of copyrighted works as dictated by the United States government: *Winesburg* would not enter public domain in 1976, as earlier law had determined, but would remain for many more years the exclusive property of its commercial publisher. And so I shelved (forever, I decided) the typescript of my finished genetic edition of *Winesburg, Ohio* but not my hope to publish someday my own non-genetic, "definitive," and clearly readable edition of that work.

From the time in 1964 when Eleanor Copenhaver Anderson, Sherwood's widow and executor, gave me my first "yellow *Winesburg*"—the B. W. Huebsch first edition of the work from 1919—I wondered how such impressive and influential words as Anderson's could have been so carelessly and unattractively presented in published form. As I came to write and publish my own books I retracted my arrogant criticism of the B. W. Huebsch staff, realizing that even this masterpiece of literature first arrived in a commercial publishing house as mere typed pages assigned to a busy editor for quick copy editing and then to a busy and perhaps untalented designer for cost-effective printing and binding, all with slight hope of modest notice and significant sales. Anderson was fortunate—given his seeming lack of promise as a middle-aged Chicago advertising writer—to publish his *Winesburg* stories at all . . . and we have shared that good fortune ever since, however imperfect the text that Ben Huebsch and his staff left to us.

I am not the first Anderson devotee to try to present *Winesburg, Ohio* in an attractive and dependable form and format, for in the late 1950s the literary enthusiast Malcolm Cowley, employed by the Viking Press, assigned members of the Viking staff to study the Huebsch/Viking text of the book in relation to the author's manuscripts, with the purpose of publishing in the Viking Compass series a new edition of the book. The new edition, which corrected several of the misprints and confusing points in the 1919 text, did appear in 1960, capably introduced by Cowley, and remained into the 1990s (under the Penguin imprint that superseded Viking) the best available version of Anderson's stories.

Then, *Winesburg, Ohio* having at last lost copyrighted status, I prepared for publication in 1996 from the W. W. Norton Company a text of the work edited according to the standards of that publisher's Critical Editions series—a text that corrected the most obvious typographical and editorial errors in the seven printings of the first edition of the book and that annotated adequately but not obtrusively several historical and cultural references made by the author. Nevertheless, *Winesburg, Ohio* was still not published in the "expert edition" that it deserved. Hence this Ohio University Press edition.

Preface and Acknowledgments

Here I present *Winesburg, Ohio* as the book should, I believe, have appeared in 1919, a text based on my study of Anderson's manuscripts, on the periodical versions of ten of the stories thus published, on the first edition in its seven printings through 1931, and on the knowledge gained from and the emotional involvement of my (soon thirty-five) years of living professionally in "Anderson Country." Here, alongside the lines of my text of *Winesburg,* are explanations of the several hundred alterations that I have made to Huebsch's first edition. Whenever cultural and historical references occur in Anderson's stories, explanations of these phenomena are to be found alongside them. Because Anderson based his created town of Winesburg, Ohio, on the very real town of his youth—Clyde, in North Central Ohio—I have provided alongside the author's fictional characters, occasions, and places my identifications of the corresponding characters, occasions, and places in Clyde and its surrounding area. Unique photographs of Clyde, Ohio, from the 1870s through the 1890s when Anderson lived among its citizens are provided.

To some experienced readers this book might not be a virtually new *Winesburg, Ohio;* but the text will be welcomed and considered, I hope, as would a centuries-old, well-loved, and newly restored painting: as a work of literary art long admired in its imperfect state and now, at last, restored and preserved for fresh and clear viewing.

Among individuals who have aided me in completing this new edition of *Winesburg, Ohio* and whom I thank for their help are David D. Anderson, Hilbert H. Campbell, Elaine Dion, Miriam Fankhauser, Jack Harrell, Diana Haskell, Kevin Jones, John D. Maines, Charles E. Modlin, Lucy Morrison, Patricia Powell, Walter B. Rideout, Carol Ruyle, William A. Sutton, Susan Swartwout, Welford D. Taylor, Timothy Twohill, Joan Winters, and William C. Woodson.

I regret that their deaths have prevented me from sharing this new edition of *Winesburg, Ohio* with several individuals, all of whom cared about my project and forwarded my progress: Eleanor Copenhaver Anderson, Michael Kaplan, Ivan Von Auw Jr., John Sherwood Anderson, and Marion Anderson Spear.

I am especially grateful to Charles E. Modlin and Hilbert H. Campbell, trustees of the Sherwood Anderson Literary Estate Trust, for recognizing my text of *Winesburg, Ohio* as officially authorized.

Introduction

ON SEPTEMBER 13, 1915, Sherwood Anderson (1876–1941) became thirty-nine years old. He was living in Chicago for the third time, writing advertising copy to support himself while trying to achieve his greatest ambition: to become a published novelist. Anderson had come to Chicago first in 1896, with only a basic grade-school education, after the death of his mother in the family hometown of Clyde, Ohio. Ambitious for great riches but able to find only dreary manual labor, probably in cold-storage warehouses, young Sherwood Anderson, a member of the Ohio National Guard, in 1898 had gladly left Chicago to serve in the United States military occupation of Cuba, and, after his military duty, to complete a high-school education at the academy of Wittenberg College, in Springfield, Ohio.[1] In 1900, armed with ambition and education and considerable new sophistication, Anderson had returned to Chicago to work prosperously in agricultural advertising, to marry the beautiful and well-educated daughter of a rich manufacturer, and to strive toward eventual ownership and control of his very own business. In 1906 he had achieved much of that very American dream: he had become president of the United Factories Company, an equipment/supplies-distribution firm in Cleveland, Ohio; and in 1907 he had headed the Anderson Manu-

1. A reliable recent biography of the writer is Kim Townsend, *Sherwood Anderson* (Boston: Houghton Mifflin, 1987).

Introduction

facturing Company, another distribution organization, in Elyria, Ohio. However, in late November 1912, succumbing to the pressure of mounting business problems and personal disillusion and mumbling to his secretary incoherent words about walking on wet feet in the bed of a stream, Sherwood Anderson had walked, dazed, out of his company office in Elyria to wander across snow-packed northern Ohio for over three days, suffering from the mental collapse of amnesia or, more likely, "fugue" (unaware and unremembered physical and mental "flight") and had come to awareness slowly in a Cleveland hospital bed.[2] By early 1913, recovering from his amnesia or fugue and feeling enabled, as a publicly acknowledged recovering invalid, to cast off the troubling social and mental constraints and financial debts of his now-unsatisfactory conventional life, Anderson had lost interest in and responsibility for his business and his lovely wife and their three handsome children, along with his dreams of the satisfactions of wealth; and he had come for the third time to Chicago, alone, ready to write advertising copy for a living and, of more importance, to make into legend the grand gesture of his middle-aged rebellion against middle-class life and commercial endeavor that he secretly knew to have been an embarrassing mental breakdown: the rebellion that he would always claim to have been the considered rejection of a potentially great career in commerce for an uncertain but far more worthwhile career in the art of literature.

Perhaps as early as 1909 Sherwood Anderson had somehow decided that he preferred to write novels instead of promotional copy, that he wanted to live in the world of artistic creation instead of the world of accountancy and country-club golf. By the time of his nervous

2. Anderson's business career and breakdown are best covered in William A. Sutton, *The Road to Winesburg* (Metuchen, N.J.: Scarecrow Press, 1972). Sutton provides fascinating documents from Anderson's breakdown, including notes that he wrote while in his fugue/flight state (pp. 552–560).

Introduction

collapse late in 1912, he had, writing at night in the attic of his home and relying on his business secretary to type his scribbled sentences, drafted parts of several novels, each with a theme of heroic worldly success and emotional despair, works then perhaps without conclusion and, if concluded, probably of no interest to publishers. Taking these manuscripts and typescripts to Chicago in 1913, Anderson had re-written them and tried to write other works of fiction, freely using much of his employers' time and probably their company secretaries whom he paid to type his manuscripts; but these unpublished literary efforts had appealed to Anderson's new "Chicago Renaissance" friends more, surely, as the surprising products of an ex-manufacturer than as the polished work of a new and gifted creative writer.

The lively artistic and intellectual atmosphere that Anderson found in Chicago in 1913 exactly suited the ex-entrepreneur, for, from around 1908 through World War I, Chicago claimed some of the most vital and innovative creative artists in America.[3] After the genteel literary realism exemplified by the aging Chicago writers Robert Herrick, Henry Blake Fuller, and Hamlin Garland, the city had become favored with exciting and liberated iconoclasts such as Harriet Monroe, who in 1912 founded *Poetry: A Magazine of Verse,* destined to bring public recognition to Robert Frost, T. S. Eliot, Ezra Pound, W. B. Yeats, E. A. Robinson, Marianne Moore, Wallace Stevens, and William Carlos Williams; Maurice Browne, who in 1912 began the Chicago Little Theatre in order to perform drama by Ibsen, Strindberg, Yeats, Wilde, Shaw, and local playwrights; Francis Hackett, Floyd Dell, Fanny Butcher, and Lucian Cary, who brought sophisticated book-reviewing to Chicago newspapers; Margaret Anderson (no relation to Sherwood),

3. The most scholarly discussion of the Chicago literary awakening is Bernard Duffey, *The Chicago Renaissance in American Letters* (East Lansing: Michigan State University Press, 1954); the broadest discussion of the arts in Chicago is Alson J. Smith, *Chicago's Left Bank* (Chicago: Regnery, 1953). Anderson's role in this Renaissance is well covered in Kenney J. Williams, *A Storyteller and a City: Sherwood Anderson's Chicago* (DeKalb: Northern Illinois University Press, 1988).

who in 1914 founded the *Little Review* in order to publish any new writing that might excite her; and the startling new authors Carl Sandburg, Edgar Lee Masters,
and Vachel Lindsay, and—soon—Sherwood Anderson,
who found easy entry into the groups of Chicago artists, bartering his story of escape from business into literature to gain admiration for his burning desire to publish great fiction. Anderson, by day cynically writing
advertising copy to sustain his simple life in rooming
houses and by night fervidly discussing freedom and
creativity and beauty to sustain his newfound emotional
life, made for himself a fresh existence as one of the
Chicago seekers of art, writers ready in the Second City,
the rough metropolis of the Midwest, to challenge the
older and more sedate accomplishments of Boston and
New York City. Thus free in early middle age from ordinary responsibilities of family, society, and commerce,
Sherwood Anderson continued to devote himself to
learning to write fiction. By the fall of 1915 he was living
alone in a rooming house on Chicago's Near North Side;
and, on some night in the winter of 1915–1916, he created his first piece of true literature.

The writing of *Winesburg, Ohio* became for Sherwood
Anderson the professional turning point of his life, the
miracle that confirmed this man's dedication to the creative act. Although Anderson always recognized the
importance to his career of *Winesburg, Ohio*, he published
relatively little about the actual composition of the work
until later in his life. Beginning in 1933, Anderson worked
on his memoirs intermittently until his death in 1941.

Perhaps the introspection and retrospection required in writing the never-finished memoirs caused Sherwood Anderson to glorify the composition of *Winesburg, Ohio* that began in 1915; or perhaps a long-promised visit, with his fourth wife, to the Chicago room where he first knew the joy of successful storytelling inspired in Anderson the many glorifications of the writing of *Winesburg, Ohio* that he thereafter made.

Soon after their marriage in 1933, Sherwood and Eleanor Copenhaver Anderson visited 735 North Cass Street (now Wabash Avenue) in Chicago, where Sherwood had lived alone in a furnished room in the winter of 1915–1916. Sherwood had, he wrote, often re-called for his Eleanor the place and "the Little Children of the Arts"—the youthful would-be artists who had then shared the rooming house with the older would-be writer:

> There were many little rooms separated by thin par-titions and they were all occupied.
>
> The occupants were all young. They were young musicians, painters, young women who aspired to be actresses. I have always wanted to write of the people of that house. They were, for the time, so close to me.
>
> I was no longer young. I was the oldest in that house. At the time the room in which I lived seemed large and later, in my thought, it kept growing larger.
>
> I often described it to my wife.
>
> "There was a great desk," I said, "as long as this room in which we now stand." I described for her my bed, the shelves built into the wall. I have always, when at work, loved to walk up and down. I am sure I gave her the impression of myself striding up and down a

Introduction

long room, grown in my imagination into something like a great hall. The council room of a king. Something of that sort.[4]

The building in 1933 "still a cheap rooming house," the room having become (or perhaps always in reality been) "a shabby little hole," Anderson quickly abandoned his romantic lover's plan to sit nostalgically with Eleanor in the room and to re-create for her the creation of *Winesburg, Ohio:*

> I had dreamed of sitting with her at the window that looked down toward the Chicago Loop in the evening, as the day faded, as the lights flashed on in the great buildings of the Loop.
>
> People passing along the street below the window, passing under the street light at a nearby corner, shabbily dressed old men, smartly dressed young women.
> . . .
> What dreams, hopes, ambitions. Sometimes it has seemed to me, when, as a young man, I sat at the window of that room, that each person who passed along the street below, under the light, shouted his secret up to me.
>
> I was myself and still I fled out of myself. It seemed to me that I went into the others.
>
> What dreams. What egotism. I had thought then, on such evenings, that I could tell all of the stories of all the people of America. I would get them all, understand them, get their stories told.
>
> And then came the night it happened.[5]

What happened was that in 1933 Anderson looked into the shabby old room that he had found and re-

4. *Sherwood Anderson's Memoirs: A Critical Edition,* edited by Ray Lewis White (Chapel Hill: University of North Carolina Press, 1969), p. 350.

5. *Sherwood Anderson's Memoirs: A Critical Edition,* edited by Ray Lewis White (Chapel Hill: University of North Carolina Press, 1969), pp. 351–352.

membered the finding there of his vocation as a writer in 1915:

> And then, on a day, late in the afternoon of a day, I had come home to that room. I sat at a desk in a corner of the room. I wrote.
>
> There was a story of another human, quite outside myself, truly told.
>
> The story was one called "Hands." It was about a poor little man beaten, pounded, frightened by the world in which he lived into something oddly beautiful.
>
> The story was written that night in one sitting. No word of it ever changed. I wrote the story and got up. I walked up and down in that little narrow room. Tears flowed from my eyes.
>
> "It is solid," I said to myself. "It is like a rock. It is there. It is put down. . . ."
>
> I am quite sure that on that night, when it happened in that room, when for the first time I dared whisper to myself, perhaps sobbing, that I had found it, my vocation, I knelt in the darkness and muttered words of gratitude to God.[6]

6. *Sherwood Anderson's Memoirs: A Critical Edition*, edited by Ray Lewis White (Chapel Hill: University of North Carolina Press, 1969), pp. 352–353.

Sherwood Anderson told this story of the writing of the first *Winesburg, Ohio* tale in not only his memoirs but also in letters to correspondents in the 1930s. In April 1935, he advised an aspiring young author:

> . . . if you are ever to be a real writer, your moment comes. I remember mine. I walked along a city street in the snow. I was working at work I hated. . . . I was ill, discouraged, broke. I was living in a cheap rooming house. I remember that I went upstairs and into

the room. It was very shabby. I had no relatives in the city and few enough friends. I remember how cold the room was. On that afternoon I had heard that I was to lose my job.

I grew desperate, went and threw up a window. I sat by the open window. It began to snow. "I'll catch cold sitting here."

"What do I care?" There was some paper on a small kitchen table I had bought and had brought up into the room. I turned on a light and began to write. I wrote, without looking up—I never changed a word of it afterwards—a story called "Hands." It was and is a very beautiful story.

I wrote the story and then got up from the table at which I had been sitting, I do not know how long, and went down into the city street. I thought that the snow had suddenly made the city very beautiful. There were people in the street, all sorts of people, shabby ones, brisk young ones, old discouraged ones. I went along wanting to hug people, to shout.

"I've done it. At last, after all these years I've done something." How did I know I had? I did know. I was drunk with a new drunkenness. I cannot remember all of the absurd, foolish things I did that evening. I had a little money in my pocket and went into saloons. I called men up to the bar. "Drink. Drink to me, men." I remember that a prostitute accosted me and that I threw some money toward her and ran away laughing. It must have been several hours before I got the courage to return to my room and read my own story.

It was all right. It was sound. It was real. I went to sit by my desk. A great many others have had such

Introduction

moments. I wonder what they did. I sat there and cried. For the moment I thought the world very wonderful, and I thought also that there was a great deal of wonder in me. [7]

And in late May 1935, Anderson in a letter to a very close friend re-told the composition of the first *Winesburg, Ohio* story:

7. *Letters of Sherwood Anderson,* edited by Howard Mumford Jones in association with Walter B. Rideout (Boston: Little Brown, 1953), pp. 314–315.

. . . on this day I had come home from the place where I was employed very tired. My room was small and cheerless enough. I was discouraged and blue, hating the work by which I made a living.

I sat there at my desk and suddenly picked up my pen. I think every man must be filled with a thousand impressions, feelings, impulses that never get expressed.

Suddenly I began to write as I had never written. It did not seem to be me sitting there holding the pen. There was no me. It was as though some mysterious force outside myself had taken possession of me.

There were people everywhere, thousands, millions of people wanting their stories told. They didn't want it glossed over, made glamorous. That, in the end, only hurt and made life more difficult.

"If you knew my story, you might like, even love me a little."

That seemed to be the cry.

It was as though one of these began to speak through me. The pen began to run over the paper. I did not seek for words. They were there. They seemed to leap out from my hand to the paper.

Now there was no such thing as time, no little

Introduction

shabby room, no rainy street outside the window. Life was there on the sheets of paper, word[s] marching, sentences marching.

I don't know how long I sat that day. When my tale was finished, I got up and stood. Tears came. I cried because I was happy. I had written something that was solid and true. There was no fakiness, no false glamour. There was a beauty that perhaps few people would find or understand. I think I must have felt as a woman feels after a birth, when she has her first babe in her arms. I kept saying words to myself. "It's there. It's solid. It will stand there like a rock. If no one else knows, I know."

I was both humble and proud. It was almost as though God had reached a hand down out of the sky and touched me. [8]

In his *Memoirs,* Sherwood Anderson completed his story of the composition of *Winesburg, Ohio:*

The tales were all written in a few months, one following the other, a kind of joyous time for me, the words and ideas flowing freely, very little revision to be done. I had set upon an idea and am quite sure the idea had come out of a certain rather fine feeling, toward myself, by the people about me. . . .

The idea I had was to take them, just as they were, as I felt them, and transfer them from the city rooming house to an imagined small town, the physical aspects of the town having, let us say, been picked up from my living in several such towns. . . .

And so the stories came, in this rather strange way, into existence. I had, in relation to them, a somewhat new feeling. It was as though I had little or nothing

8. *Letters of Sherwood Anderson,* edited by Howard Mumford Jones in association with Walter B. Rideout (Boston: Little Brown, 1953), p. 317.

Introduction

to do with the writing. It was as though the people of that house, all of them wanting so much, none of them really equipped to wrestle with life as it was, had, in this odd way, used me as an instrument. They had got, I felt, through me, their stories told, and not in their own persons but, in a much more real and satisfactory way, through the lives of these queer small town people of the book.[9]

9. *Sherwood Anderson's Memoirs: A Critical Edition,* edited by Ray Lewis White (Chapel Hill: University of North Carolina Press, 1969), p. 348.

One of Sherwood Anderson's younger friends in the Chicago Renaissance group of writers has described Anderson at the time when he was composing *Winesburg, Ohio.* In *Letters from Bohemia,* Ben Hecht colorfully recounted one of Anderson's more dramatic re-creations of his (by now crafty) rejection in Ohio of a career in business and then recalled:

I had sat in his Cass Street room with a half-dozen others and listened to him read from his frequently rejected and as yet unpublished manuscripts, *Windy McPherson's Son, Marching Men,* and *Winesburg, Ohio.*

The writing held us but it was the voice that sold us its greatness. Sherwood read his writings like a preacher offering revelations.

He was in many ways like a preacher who had found God. The God was himself.[10]

10. Ben Hecht, *Letters from Bohemia* (Garden City: Doubleday, 1964), p. 88.

And in *A Child of the Century,* Hecht described in greater detail Sherwood Anderson, visited by friends in his rooming house on Cass Street, reading an unpublished *Winesburg* story:

The candles continued to light up our host, and eventually the guests became silent and sat looking at him

Introduction

as if he were an actor on a stage. His rugged-looking face with its wide mouth and glowing black eyes smiled at the shadowed figures in his room. Under its wing of flat black hair, it looked like an Italian face, the kind you saw behind barber chairs. It was odd that such a face should be called Sherwood Anderson.

Our host addressed us and I became aware that this rugged-seeming man was a gentle, almost womanish fellow. There was a tremor to his lips, and his large, handsome face seemed to flutter when he spoke, as did his voice. He changed as he spoke from a barber into a swami. One hand reached out and waved rhythmically at us, in a gentle, patronizing fashion. His voice caressed us and I heard a fine writer speak for the first time.

"I was going to read you a book I've written called *Windy McPherson's Son,*" he said, "but it's a very long manuscript and kind of heavy to hold. So I'll read you some stories I've written about a town called Winesburg, Ohio. They're not really stories. They're just people."

We waited silently as our host moved a candle nearer his pen-written pages.

"Down the street ran George . . ." Sherwood Anderson began reading.[11]

11. Ben Hecht, *A Child of the Century* (New York: Simon and Schuster, 1954), pp. 224–225. Hecht recalled Anderson's *Winesburg, Ohio* character George Willard wrongly as "George Hadley."

No matter how ecstatic for Sherwood Anderson was the moment of creation of the first *Winesburg, Ohio* story, "Hands" did not come perfect and without preparation from the mind of an inexperienced writer, for Anderson had since 1900 made his living by writing words on paper. Even though writing advertising and promotional copy had lost its satisfaction and even though his labors over long novels had not resulted in the great fiction that he longed to publish, Anderson had begun in 1914, about the time that he moved alone into his rented room at 735 North Cass Street, to write essays on the purpose and method of the would-be artist. Near Cass Street in Chicago was the office of a new magazine, the *Little Review,* founded and edited by Margaret Anderson (again, friend but not relative to Sherwood). In this innovative new journal of the arts Sherwood Anderson published early in 1914 two essays on being or becoming an artist in words. In "The New Note" he defined his new goal in writing:

> Simply stated, it is a cry for the reinjection of truth and honesty into the craft; it is an appeal from the standards set up by money-making magaziners and book publishers in Europe and America to the older, sweeter standards of the craft itself, it is the voice of the new man, come into a new world, proclaiming his right to speak out of the body and soul of youth, rather than through the bodies and souls of the master craftsmen who are gone.[12]

And in "More About the New Note," Anderson recommended to other writers (as though he were a master teacher and they were the needful pupils), the keeping of an honest diary or journal to record and analyze the innermost thoughts and emotions—all this to lead to a new fidelity and depth in American writing.[13] Then, in a series of fictionalized musings about the difficulty of achieving good writing, Anderson continued his efforts at esthetic self-definition.

In "Sister," published late in 1915, Anderson wrote al-

12. "The New Note," *Little Review* I (March 1914): 23. In *Sherwood Anderson: Early Writings,* edited by Ray Lewis White (Kent: Kent State University Press, 1989), pp. 120–122.

13. "More About the New Note," *Little Review* I (April 1914): 16–17. In *Sherwood Anderson: Early Writings,* edited by Ray Lewis White (Kent: Kent State University Press, 1989), pp. 122–124.

Introduction

legorically of himself as an artist and his imagined sister as Art itself. Rejected by family and society for daring to live in social and sexual freedom, the sister inspires the writer to imagine the inner life and ". . . I begin to understand my sister. She is the artist right to adventure in the world, to be destroyed in the adventure, if that be necessary, and I, on my couch, am the worker in the world, blinking up at the stars that can be seen from my window when my couch is properly arranged."[14]

In "The Story Writers," published by H. L. Mencken in his magazine *Smart Set*, Anderson even more clearly allegorized about writing and subject matter. Two would-be writers, one a lawyer and the other a grocer, together rent and furnish a special room where, away from their families and their businesses, they can write fine fiction. While the accidents of life and the unpleasantnesses of experience go on just outside their window and around them even in the city streets, however, these two figures find themselves unable to come up with anything at all worth writing about, for in seeking exotically romantic stories they cannot see all about them the real lives of sorrow and hurt and desperation.[15]

In "The Novelist," published in the *Little Review*, Anderson imagined himself a writer who imagines writing a novel about a woman: "What a multitude of words: For hours he will sit perfectly still, writing madly and throwing the sheets about. That is a happy time. The madness has possession of him. . . ."[16]

Finally, in "Blackfoot's Masterpiece," published in *Forum* in 1916, Anderson wrote of a painter of other-worldly genius and achievement who, because of the needs of his many children for this-worldly food, is forced to sell his paintings to a rich but heartless collector who bargains the prices down to the minimum, even-

14. *Little Review* 2 (December 1915): 3–4. In *Sherwood Anderson: Early Writings,* edited by Ray Lewis White (Kent: Kent State University Press, 1989), p. 140.

15. "The Story Writers," *Smart Set* 48 (January 1916): 243–248. In *Sherwood Anderson: Early Writings,* edited by Ray Lewis White (Kent: Kent State University Press, 1989), pp. 141–150.

16. "The Novelist," *Little Review* 2 (January–February 1916): 12–14. In *Sherwood Anderson: Early Writings,* edited by Ray Lewis White (Kent: Kent State University Press, 1989), pp. 151–154.

Introduction

tually driving the painter insane enough to be committed to an asylum for those sensitive people maddened by this money-oriented world.[17]

17. "Blackfoot's Masterpiece," *Forum* 55 (June 1916): 679–683. In *Sherwood Anderson: Early Writings,* edited by Ray Lewis White (Kent: Kent State University Press, 1989), pp. 164–168.

Just when Sherwood Anderson was publishing his essays or parables about the right subject matter and method for good writing, the good writing that he himself had not yet done, external events occurred to encourage the aspiring artist to be receptive, that bleak winter evening in his cold rented room in Cass Street, to the honest telling of an unhappy but beautiful life.

In the spring of 1915, a best-selling poetry volume had shocked American readers with its over three hundred ironic and scandalous imagined epitaphs from a typical Midwestern small-town cemetery. *Spoon River Anthology,* by Anderson's Chicago acquaintance Edgar Lee Masters, revealed the American town as not the place of complete virtue and quiet joy that Americans believed in but as instead a place of greed, indifference, cruelty, and repression never before honestly exposed to view in print. Not a writer later to admit literary influence, Sherwood Anderson steadfastly denied the obvious inspiration of *Spoon River Anthology,* with its imagined and literally buried Illinois lives, upon his own upcoming stories of small-town metaphorically buried Ohio lives; but Anderson did indeed borrow a copy of Masters's book from a fellow-roomer in Cass Street and read late into a night the short and bitter free-verse epitaphs spoken from the unquiet graves of Central Illinois.

Other events occurred in Chicago to bring Anderson closer to writing his first *Winesburg* story, for in November 1915, Cloyd Head's experimental drama *Grotesques*

Introduction

was performed at the Chicago Little Theatre. This one-act free-verse expressionistic tragedy of psychological repression and liberation was described by Harriet Monroe in *Poetry* as "life as a shadow-play, men and women as puppets moved by a master-experimentalist."[18] And Arthur Davison Ficke's poems "Ten Grotesques," published in the *Little Review*,[19] where Anderson was publishing some of his own essays on writing, brought to Anderson the concept of the "grotesque" in art.[20]

Then Sherwood Anderson, surrounded in Chicago by reference to and example of the artistic grotesque and driven to strive in essays toward definition of just what he wanted to do or ought to do in writing, in the autumn of 1915 produced one more notable meditation on the art of fiction. In "The Book of the Grotesque," probably written in November, Anderson created an old would-be writer who lived in a rented room and who had his bed raised so that he could at night look out at city lights and who then, near uneasy sleep in his old age and ill health, envisioned a procession of figures passing before him, figures somehow formed or reformed or deformed by their experience of life into physically grotesque people who were, to the careful observer, nevertheless beautiful in character . . . and here, finally, in the concept of the literary "pathetic grotesque," Sherwood Anderson had in place the theory of character in fiction that had so long eluded him.[21]

Thus infused with the goal of revealing the concealed or buried inner human life in short revelations instead of in the epical novels that Anderson had attempted and, then, with his idea of human beings as grotesque characters in place, the author lacked only the right subject matter and setting for the stories that he felt able now to compose; and he found the right subject

18. "Editorial Comment," *Poetry* 7 (January 1916): 194.

19. "Ten Grotesques," *Little Review* 2 (March 1915): 31–35.

20. Regarding "grotesques," the word and the concept were not uncommon ca. 1913–1916, witnessed by these occurrences and by James Huneker, *Old Fogy: His Musical Opinions and Grotesques* (Philadelphia: Theodore Presser, 1913). Huneker commented on love of "the fantastic, the bizarre, the grotesque . . ." (p. 7).

21. "The Book of the Grotesque," *Masses* 8 (February 1916): 1.

matter and setting close at hand: in the lodgers at 735 North Cass Street; in people silently beheld everywhere by Sherwood Anderson the careful and empathetic observer; and in the novels that Anderson had begun in Ohio and perhaps completed in Chicago, where he had used Clyde, the small Ohio town of his boyhood, as the fictional background from which his imagined youths, maturing and ready for adventures in life, had to escape to find their business or social success. To give texture and color to the youths in these novels that he had been drafting since perhaps 1909, Anderson had in short sketches limned around these main characters in their small towns many secondary or minor characters who were memorable for their physical differences, their mental quirks, and their frequent inability to fit comfortably into mainstream life . . . in other words, "grotesques." Therefore, with his purpose changed, late in 1915, from writing epical novels of small-town youths who emerged heroically to confront and reform the greater world, to detailing now in miniature the lives of the unimportant, the ill-formed, the reprobate, and the often unhappy small-town inhabitants who never left their towns, who never fitted into their towns, and who were alone in misery in their towns, Anderson found, ready-made in his mind, the subjects for the great fiction that he wanted to write.

It is not possible, given the documents that have survived from Sherwood Anderson's life as an author, to reconstruct exactly the circumstances and dates of the writing of every one of the *Winesburg, Ohio* stories; but much can be learned or assumed from the extant com-

Introduction

ments that Anderson made in letters to friends, magazine editors, and book publishers from late 1915, when the stories were conceived, into early 1919, when they were published as a book.

In November 1915, soon after writing "The Book of the Grotesque," Anderson wrote "Hands," the story that later in letters and memoirs he described elatedly as his first great creation. "Hands" was published in March 1916, in *Masses*, a New York City magazine of radical politics and opinion.[22] Anderson must have written as his second *Winesburg* story "'Queer,'" in December 1915, because on January 4, 1916, he wrote to H. L. Mencken, editor of the magazine *Smart Set*, that he regretted Mencken's rejection of "the Elmer Cowley story" but that he had feared that this story might not fit that magazine's needs.

Anderson must have written "Paper Pills," regarding Dr. Reefy, early in 1916, for the story was published (entitled "The Philosopher") in the June–July issue of *Little Review*.[23] In the spring or early summer of 1916 he wrote "The Strength of God," which appeared in *Masses* in August of that year.[24] And then, with his first novel, *Windy McPherson's Son*, published in September by the London-based publisher John Lane,[25] Anderson in an October 24 letter to a friend wrote his first extant (and revealing) comment on how the plot of a *Winesburg* story came to him, as he was riding aboard a train in the American Midwest:

> Here before me is a long stretch of fields and in the distance a town. I put down my pencil and immediately a scene is enacted. Across the fields tramps a man in boots that are heavy with mud. He has a beard and wears an overcoat that is torn at the pockets. He is

22. "Hands," *Masses* 8 (March 1916): 5, 7.

23. "Paper Pills" (published as "The Philosopher") *Little Review* 8 (June–July 1916): 7-9.

24. "The Strength of God," *Masses* 8 (August 1918): 12–13.

25. *Windy McPherson's Son* (New York: John Lane, 1916).

Introduction

going to town to buy meat and has $3. Suddenly an impulse comes to him. He begins to run. Tears come into his eyes and he runs harder and harder. He is fifty years old and has been married thirty years. He is a farm hand. He has made up his mind to desert his wife and family and run away. He runs so hard across the field because he wants to get into town and board the train before his courage fails.

What an intense study the mind of the man running in the field. My mind can play with it for hours. I should be able to pick a thousand varieties of scenes like that from every field.[26]

Here, nearly complete, is the plot of "The Untold Lie," one of the few *Winesburg* stories for which Anderson recorded an exact origin and which he must have written soon after this letter about seeing the running man, because the story appeared in December in *Seven Arts*.[27] Salvaging the story "'Queer'" after its rejection by Mencken, Anderson wrote from Chicago to Waldo Frank, editor in New York City of the recently founded *Seven Arts*, who was going to publish "'Queer'" in his December issue, offering more of the stories:

I made last year a series of intensive studies of people of my home town, Clyde, Ohio. In the book I called the town Winesburg, Ohio. Some of the studies you may think pretty raw, and there is a sad note running through them. One or two of them get pretty closely down to ugly things of life. However, I put a good deal into the writing of them, and I believe they, as a whole, come a long step toward achieving what you are asking for . . . in *Seven Arts*.

Some of these things have been used. *Masses* ran a

26. *Letters to Bab: Sherwood Anderson to Marietta D. Finley, 1916–33*, edited by William A. Sutton (Urbana: University of Illinois Press, 1985), p. 6.

27. "The Untold Lie," *Seven Arts* 1 (December 1916): 215–221.

story called "Hands," from this series. Two or three also appeared in a little magazine out here called the *Little Review*. The story called "'Queer'" you are using in December is one of them. [28]

This thought occurs to me. There are or will be seventeen of these studies. Fifteen are, I believe, completed. If you have the time and the inclination, I might send the lot to you to be looked over. [29]

Assuming that Anderson was asking that the stories appear all together in one issue of *Seven Arts*, Frank replied that he preferred to publish the stories as a series over several issues of his magazine and that Anderson should continue mailing the pieces to Frank. [30] Thus, on November 20, Anderson wrote to Frank to acknowledge the latter's acceptance of the story "The Untold Lie" ("Thanks for ... liking the story of the farm hands") and submitting two new stories, "Mother" and "Loneliness." About "Loneliness" Anderson told Frank: "Personally I like the Enoch Robinson thing better than anything else I have ever done." [31]

On November 23, 1916, Anderson mentioned in a letter that he was writing a book about a character named Tandy:

As you well enough know I have on now a big piece of work. It can only be completed now in a twisted, distorted way. I shall just write it blindly, pouring myself and my character Tandy into it when I can. Then when I have leisure I will go back at it, eliminating, changing, trying to make a book of it. [32]

But on December 6 of that year, while visiting Clyde, Ohio, for three hours, in the midst of a business trip,

28. "'Queer,'" *Seven Arts* 1 (December 1916): 97–108.

29. *Letters of Sherwood Anderson,* edited by Howard Mumford Jones in association with Walter B. Rideout (Boston: Little Brown, 1953), p. 4.

30. William Bittner, *The Novels of Waldo Frank* (Philadelphia: University of Pennsylvania Press, 1958), p. 21.

31. Information and quotations from unpublished letters written by and to Anderson are from the Anderson Papers, the Newberry Library, Chicago.

32. *Letters to Bab: Sherwood Anderson to Marietta D. Finley 1916–33,* edited by William A. Sutton (Urbana: University of Illinois Press, 1985), p. 9.

Introduction

Anderson wrote movingly about the background of the quite personal stories that he had been writing:

I am sitting in the little hotel office writing. I have hardly gone to see anyone and have only walked through two or three streets. Why?—well, because what I have already seen has awakened such a flood of memories that I am overwhelmed. I realize as I sit here that I could sit thus for hours—as long as life remained in me, writing of my people and the strange things that have happened to them. What real and living people they are to me. Even Jerry Donlin, the baggage man who I am told dropped dead of heart failure and who has just by chance come into my mind. His life is a living thing to me. I could write long novels concerning this sweet-hearted, profane Irishman and the wonderful things my imagination helps me to believe went on in his head while he outwardly did no more than push baggage trucks up and down this station platform here. [33]

33. *Letters to Bab: Sherwood Anderson to Marietta D. Finley, 1916–33,* edited by William A. Sutton (Urbana: University of Illinois Press, 1985), p. 24.

On December 14, Anderson wrote to Waldo Frank of his pleasure that "Mother" would appear in *Seven Arts,* adding that he had completed "another fine story about the same woman's death" and that he regretted the editor's reaction to "Loneliness":

. . . I wanted you to like the story about Enoch Robinson and the woman who came into his room and was too big for the room.

There is a story every critic is bound to dislike. I can remember reading it to Floyd Dell and it made him hopping mad. "It's damn rot," says Floyd. "It does not get anywhere."

Introduction

"It gets there but you are not at the station," I replied to Floyd and I think I was right.

Why do I try to convince you of this story? Well I want it in print in *Seven Arts*. A writer knows when a story is good and that story is good.

Sometime when I am in New York, I'll bring that story in, and I'll make you see it.[34]

34. *Letters of Sherwood Anderson,* edited by Howard Mumford Jones in association with Walter B. Rideout (Boston: Little Brown, 1953), p. 5.

Sherwood Anderson ended the year 1916 with a brave note to Waldo Frank, telling the editor that for any further *Winesburg* stories submitted for publication in *Seven Arts* Anderson expected a competitive offer, for he no longer thought that mere publication at whatever payment Frank offered was enough reward for his works. Yet on January 2, 1917, Anderson quickly retreated from his demand, writing to Frank that he would accept for the *Winesburg* stories whatever money the editor felt able to pay.

"The Untold Lie" then appeared in the January *Seven Arts,* followed by quick submission of the story "Death." Anderson wrote, "I am sending you another *Winesburg* story and hope you will like it. The other story concerning the death of George Willard's mother should not, I believe, be published too closely on the heels of the first story about her." "Death" never appeared in any periodical, but in February of 1917 Anderson found his chance to meet Waldo Frank in person and perhaps to follow through on the kindly threat to explain the rejected "Loneliness" until Frank bought it. Whatever else the author and the editor talked of when Anderson visited the offices of *Seven Arts* in New York City in February, Frank did not accept "Loneliness"; and he apparently did not decide to bid competitively for Anderson's

Introduction

stories. On March 2, Anderson wrote his strongest objection about low pay from *Seven Arts:*

> I'm damned, Frank, if I am going to let you pull and haul among my stories, taking the cream at $40 per. It isn't fair, and you know it. I will send you the stories one at a time, and you accept or reject. Forget the notion that there is no other market for these things. I've got offers on my desk for them now. I believe in *Seven Arts* and want to swim with you, but there is no reason why I should give you this unseemly privilege. You may consider this an overt act, but I'm going to stand on it. Now, damn it, man, behave.[35]

Frank's response is not recorded, but he never behaved any better, according to Anderson, declining other *Winesburg* stories as they were mailed from Chicago. For example, on April 5, Anderson submitted "the little piece of rather colorful writing called 'Tandy Hard' and would like to have your opinion of it." And probably on the same day Anderson wrote Frank about the rejection of "Drink":

> Wish you had liked my story of the drunken boy. I liked it fine. It was true as hell. I'll stir the pot again soon.
>
> Please don't always apply your reason to these things. They are to my mind fragments that will be more keenly realized in the minds of the reader than you fellows think.[36]

But Frank did reject "Tandy," a move that Anderson must have taken in stride considering the difficulty of

35. *Letters of Sherwood Anderson,* edited by Howard Mumford Jones in association with Walter B. Rideout (Boston: Little Brown, 1953), pp. 9–10.

36. *Letters of Sherwood Anderson,* edited by Howard Mumford Jones in association with Walter B. Rideout (Boston: Little Brown, 1953), p. 11.

Introduction

that story, for he had personal matters to attend to. In January 1917, he had decided that he probably would soon move from 735 North Cass Street, where he had lived since 1914 and where he had happily conceived and carried out "Hands" and successive *Winesburg* stories. As Anderson wrote about the rooming house, whose tenants he had nicknamed "The Little Children of the Arts" because of their hope for careers in music and sculpture and painting and dance (and, in his own case, writing) and on whose failures and frustrations he might have modeled some of the grotesques in *Winesburg*, he declared:

> In the house then to dream a thing was to have it become an actuality. Every one had a dream and talked of it as though it were a fact already achieved. In the evening the house reeked of dreams. . . .
> The place has become slipshod and it is hard to keep alive the spirit of my room. Presently I shall move away. [37]

37. *Letters to Bab: Sherwood Anderson to Marietta D. Finley, 1916–33,* edited by William A. Sutton (Urbana: University of Illinois Press, 1985), pp. 47, 48.

Soon, in May, Anderson did move in Chicago, to 12 East Division Street; but the fresh surroundings did not keep him permanently in Chicago, for he spent the summer of 1917 at a health ("eurhythmics") camp operated by Alys Bentley near Upper Chateaugay Lake, in New York State, near Canada. He apparently kept writing stories while learning breathing and relaxation exercises . . . and setting an accidental fire in his tent, for he had to ask a friend in Indiana to lend him as replacement copies the stories that he had read to and then left with her.[38] In July he mailed to Waldo Frank "The Thinker," apologizing for the scorched edges of the pages and asking for fifty dollars for the piece, which did appear soon

38. William A. Sutton, *The Road to Winesburg* (Metuchen, N.J.: Scarecrow Press, 1972), p. 429.

Introduction

in *Seven Arts*.[39] Then, back at work writing advertisements in Chicago, Anderson, while awaiting publication of his second novel, *Marching Men*,[40] began writing a new long work "starting with life on a big farm in Ohio" and about "a delightful old man, Joseph Bentley by name, who is full of old Bible thoughts and impulses."[41] Early in September, Anderson again wrote to Frank about the enthusiasm that he felt for his new project: "The theme is intense and the distractions continuous. I write in restaurants, in my office between interviews with men and while I am not writing advertisements." Soon Anderson expanded even more fully for Frank the joy that literary creation was bringing him amidst the hated drudgery of living upon advertising:

> In self defense one is compelled to create and sustain in his own mind a world of people who have significance. Day by day as he goes on this created world becomes a thing more definite. It comes to have height, breadth and thickness. . . .
>
> I am beginning again to live in a wonderful world. Things march in long processions past me. I wake and sleep and dream in a world full of significance. All the weary trivialities with which my hours in the office are occupied count as nothing.

As far as the composition of the *Winesburg, Ohio* stories is concerned, little more can be learned from Anderson's extant comments. Two other stories appeared in periodical form but not in *Seven Arts,* for that magazine died in October 1917; and Anderson turned back to his Chicago friend Margaret Anderson to publish in her *Little Review* "The Man of Ideas" and "An Awakening."[42] And, clearly, the Bentley novel of Ohio farm life

39. "The Thinker," *Seven Arts* 2 (September 1917): 584–597.

40. *Marching Men* (New York: John Lane, 1917).

41. *Letters of Sherwood Anderson,* edited by Howard Mumford Jones in association with Walter B. Rideout (Boston: Little Brown, 1953), p. 15.

42. "The Man of Ideas," *Little Review* 5 (June 1918): 22–28; "An Awakening," *Little Review* 5 (December 1918): 13–21.

of which Anderson had written at least five chapters had changed into the four-part story "Godliness," the longest of the *Winesburg* stories, although the tone had certainly been transformed from "delightful" to downright somber when the piece appeared in the completed volume. To round out his stories about Ohio village life, Anderson wrote "Sophistication" and "Departure," although the dates of their composition cannot now be determined. One must assume that, by the beginning of 1918, *Winesburg, Ohio* was substantially completed, although many of the stories had not appeared in periodicals. Then publication of the stories as a volume became Anderson's goal, a goal that was to prove more difficult than Anderson had assumed.

But first the individual stories had to be organized into a unified whole, a cycle equivalent to a composite novel; and surviving evidence reveals the difficulty that Anderson faced in unifying his volume. It is not possible now to discover Anderson's final organization of his *Winesburg, Ohio* stories for their appearance in book form except from the book itself, for the table of contents pages which he included with the publisher's typescript have not survived. It is possible, however, to reconstruct from two documents some early versions of the arrangement of *Winesburg, Ohio.* The first document is an original contents page owned by the Newberry Library of Chicago, a typescript bearing revisions in Anderson's hand. The second document, a carbon copy of this typescript page located at one time in the library of the University of North Carolina at Chapel Hill and

Introduction

preserved now on a microfilm in that library, carries revisions by Anderson that differ from the author's changes on the original page. Study of these original, revised, and final tables of contents prepared by Anderson provides this schema of the orderings of the *Winesburg* stories:

Original

1 Hands, 2 Paper Pills, 3 Mother, 4 The Philosopher, 5 Nobody Knows, 6 A Man of Ideas, 7 Respectability, 8 The Thinker,[43] 9 Godliness, 10 Loneliness,[44] 11 "Queer," 12 The Strength of God, 13 The Teacher, 14 The Untold Lie, 15 An Awakening, 16 Drink, 17 Death, 18 Sophistication,[45] 19 Departure

43. Untitled but concerning Seth Richmond.
44. Here called "The Lonely Man" but concerning Enoch Robinson.
45. Here called "Adolescence" but concerning Helen White.

Original Revised

1 Hands, 2 Paper Pills, 3 Mother, 4 The Philosopher, 5 Nobody Knows, 6 A Man of Ideas, 7 Respectability, 8 The Thinker, 9 Godliness, 10 Loneliness, 11 "Queer," 12 The Strength of God, 13 The Teacher, 14 The Untold Lie, 15 Drink, 16 Death, 17 Sophistication, 18 An Awakening, 19 Departure

Carbon Revised

The Book of the Grotesque

1 Hands, 2 Paper Pills, 3 Mother, 4 The Philosopher, 5 Nobody Knows, 6 Godliness, 7 A Man of Ideas, 8 Respectability, 9 The Thinker, 10 Loneliness, 11 "Queer," 12 The Strength of God, 13 The Teacher, 14 The Untold Lie, 15 An Awakening, 16 Drink, 17 Death, 18 Sophistication, 19 Departure, 20 Adventure, 21 Tandy[46]

46. Untitled but concerning Tandy Hard.

47. Another title for "The Book of the Grotesque."

Carbon Again Revised

Foreword[47]

1 Hands, 2 Paper Pills, 3 Mother, 4 The Philosopher, 5 Nobody Knows, 6 Godliness, 7 A Man of Ideas, 8 Respectability, 9 The Thinker, 10 Adventure, 11 Loneliness, 12 "Queer," 13 The Strength of God, 14 The Teacher, 15 The Untold Lie, 16 An Awakening, 17 Drink, 18 Death, 19 Sophistication, 20 Adventure

Book

The Book of the Grotesque

1 Hands, 2 Paper Pills, 3 Mother, 4 The Philosopher, 5 Nobody Knows, 6 Godliness, 7 A Man of Ideas, 8 Adventure, 9 Respectability, 10 The Thinker, 11 Tandy, 12 The Strength of God, 13 The Teacher, 14 Loneliness, 15 An Awakening, 16 "Queer," 17 The Untold Lie, 18 Drink, 19 Death, 20 Sophistication, 21 Departure

According to the earliest extant table of contents, *Winesburg, Ohio* thus first consisted of nineteen stories, arranged from "Hands" through "Departure." When Anderson revised the original contents page, he made one tentative modification, moving "An Awakening" from its place after "The Untold Lie" to a new position as the penultimate story in the cycle. The effect of this alteration would be to interrupt the final three stories ("Death," "Sophistication," and "Departure"), likely written after Anderson had realized his conception of the life of young George Willard and his small Midwestern town. In this tentative revision, George in his attempted seduction of Belle Carpenter suffers humiliation and defeat—just after his moment of communication with the chaste Helen White in "Sophistication."

Then the young newspaperman with dreams of becoming a writer escapes from Winesburg in "Departure," possibly wiser in the ways of women and possibly more callused than Anderson had intended in the first contents plan. This revision did not hold.

Comparison of the original table of contents with the revised carbon of the same page reveals that Anderson made three changes. First, he moved the longest *Winesburg* story, "Godliness"—the four-part history of the Bentley family and of Northern Ohio from settlement toward the end of the nineteenth century—so that it follows the first five stories and is no longer ninth in the overall order. The effect of this shift is immediately to remove the reader's attention from George Willard for almost one-quarter of Anderson's book—not necessarily a wise strategy by the author. More important here is the addition of two new *Winesburg* stories—"Adventure" and "Tandy." Loss of "Tandy"—the shortest and most unsatisfying (and seemingly incomplete) story of the whole cycle—would not be thought disastrous by most readers of Anderson's book; but loss of "Adventure"—apotheosis of Anderson's theory and demonstration of pathetic grotesquerie and sexual frustration—would seriously harm *Winesburg, Ohio*. (The placement of "Adventure" and "Tandy" last on Anderson's revised carbon should not indicate that he ever intended to end his book with these stories; rather, he placed the stories thus to incorporate them and to remind himself to find later the best placement for these two fictions.) Most intriguing of these three changes in *Winesburg* is the addition of an introduction called "The Book of the Grotesque," Anderson's oblique, mystical semi-story and exposition of his theory of human personality, his theory of the "grotesque." In Anderson's earliest plan there was

Introduction

to be no such introduction.

The second revision of the carbon copy of the table of contents reveals two additional changes by Anderson. First, the introductory "Book of the Grotesque" is now called "Foreword," revealing the writer's intention that this short piece be thought an introduction to the *Winesburg* stories that follow it. Second, "Adventure" has been moved from its temporary place near the end of the revised carbon and made tenth in the collection, ahead of "Loneliness" and "'Queer.'" Noteworthy is the fact that there is no inclusion of "Tandy," implying again that Anderson doubted the merit of this story. This revision of the contents of *Winesburg, Ohio* thus gives Anderson a collection of twenty stories, preceded by a "Foreword." [48]

But comparison of this revision with the contents of the book as read since 1919 reveals several more alterations by Anderson. Major changes are the re-naming of the introduction as "The Book of the Grotesque" and the decision to include "Tandy" midway through the series. Last shifts, such as the movement of "Loneliness" and "'Queer'" to make them appear later in the collection, the two then becoming separated by "An Awakening," are probably of subtle thematic result.

Anderson throughout these five stages of ordering the *Winesburg* stories kept intact the first five narratives and the general order of the last three stories, suggesting that, by the time he came to attempt a table of contents, he had clearly in mind the order for his stories in book form. The observer has learned, however, that "Loneliness" was once called "The Lonely Man," that "Sophistication" was once called "Adolescence," [49] that "Adventure" and "Tandy" might be latecomers to the series, that the volume originally lacked any introduction or

48. See Ray Lewis White, *"Winesburg, Ohio:* The Table of Contents," *Notes on Modern American Literature* 8 (Autumn 1984): [1–4].

49. See Ray Lewis White, *"Winesburg, Ohio:* The Story Titles," *Winesburg Eagle: The Official Publication of the Sherwood Anderson Society* 10 (November 1984): 6–7.

Introduction

foreword, and that Anderson struggled several times to make his completed stories fit into a well-planned sequence.

One of the *Seven Arts* advisory editors whom Anderson had come to admire in New York City was Van Wyck Brooks, to whom Anderson wrote early in April 1918, that, after the John Lane Company would publish a third one of his volumes—the poetry that Anderson had recently been writing—"Then I am going to publish the Winesburg tales, some two dozen of them, in a book under the title *Winesburg.* . . ."[50] A few days later, on April 10, he continued to Frank, "Winesburg will come along in the fall." *Mid-American Chants* was published on April 12, 1918,[51] and Anderson worked until summer preparing the *Winesburg* stories for Lane, because in late May or early June he wrote to Waldo Frank of the completed project: "Winesburg has gone off to Lane. I wonder if the public will really take that book."

The public reaction to the *Winesburg* stories would be denied to Anderson for some time, however, for the Lane company was not under contract to publish or interested in publishing a fourth volume by the writer, as the two novels and the verse that they published had been neither profitable nor popular enough to encourage a new gamble. Anderson therefore traveled to New York City again, late in the summer of 1918, having arranged to work there for a film company (probably writing advertising instead of scenarios) while he sought a publisher for the collected *Winesburg* stories. Just which publishers turned down *Winesburg* is unclear, but in New York City Anderson had important friends to further

50. *Letters of Sherwood Anderson,* edited by Howard Mumford Jones in association with Walter B. Rideout (Boston: Little Brown, 1953), p. 31.

51. *Mid-American Chants* (New York: John Lane, 1918).

his career. Van Wyck Brooks, Waldo Frank, Francis Hackett, and Theodore Dreiser contributed their good will and good influence to Anderson's cause, for around August 20 Anderson wrote to a well-respected publisher named Benjamin W. Huebsch, whom he hoped to meet soon: "So many of the fellows I know have spoken to me of you that I would like to come and call on you." In recent years Huebsch had published such important literary volumes as James Joyce's *Dubliners, A Portrait of the Artist as a Young Man, Chamber Music,* and *Exiles;* D. H. Lawrence's *The Rainbow, The Prussian Officer,* and *Twilight in Italy;* Van Wyck Brooks's *America's Coming of Age* and *Letters and Leadership;* and Francis Hackett's *The Riddle of Ireland* and *Horizons.* Ben Huebsch graciously responded on August 21 to Anderson's overture: "The same friends who spoke to you about me are probably the ones who spoke to me about you. Since learning that you were in town I have hoped to meet you."[52]

Within a month of their first meeting Huebsch and Anderson were well enough acquainted to visit socially; and Huebsch agreed to look over the completed *Winesburg* stories, which Anderson might have been trying to market as *The Book of the Grotesque,* so named for the essay-story that he had written in November 1915 and which he was thinking of using as a foreword to *Winesburg.*

Whether Huebsch sought advice from any readers in his company or from his circle of advisors is unclear, but by December he had expressed willingness to publish the new volume. Anderson wrote to Huebsch near the first of December, "I am glad you liked *Winesburg.* From the first I have had a hunch that you are the man to publish my stuff. It is so delightful to have a publisher you can have as a friend also." And around a week

52. The career of Ben Huebsch and his relationship with Anderson are well presented in Catherine McCullough, "A History of B. W. Huebsch, Publisher," Dissertation, University of Wisconsin, 1979. Passages from unpublished letters written by Anderson and by Huebsch not otherwise cited are taken from this dissertation; from Barbara Murel Gage, "Correspondence: Sherwood Anderson and Benjamin W. Huebsch, 1918–1925," Thesis, George Washington University, 1968; and from the Anderson Papers at the Newberry Library.

later: "I can't tell you how glad I am that you are to be my publisher." When Huebsch much later in life recalled his reaction to the *Winesburg* stories, he remembered receiving *Winesburg, Ohio* "simply as a group of stories without any over-all name (not even *The Book of the Grotesque*"); that he "looked at the stories, saw 'what they were about,' and gave the book its name"; and that, noting the geographical centrality of the collection, he suggested that Anderson work with Francis Hackett's brother-in-law, a Danish-born artist named Harald Toksvig, to supply a map of the imaginary town for the front endpaper of the book.[53]

53. Notes from Huebsch interview with Walter B. Rideout, December 6, 1960. (But note earlier references by Anderson to the collection as *Winesburg* and that Huebsch might have worked with Anderson on the final arrangement of the *Winesburg* stories.)

On December 18, 1918, Huebsch and Anderson met in New York City to sign a standard contract to publish a literary work entitled *Winesburg*, a work already in hand, with the author to receive 10% of catalogue/retail price up to 2500 copies; then 12% from 2500 to 5000 copies; and then 15% exceeding 5000 copies and 5% for copies sold in Canada. Anderson's stay in New York thus personally successful but film work as a career proving unsatisfactory, Anderson by the end of 1918 returned to life in Chicago and to his job in an advertising agency; and he ended the year by writing to friends that he should have proofs of the *Winesburg* tales at any time, with publication perhaps as early as March. When the author completed proofreading is unsure but likely in January 1919; and in March 1919, Huebsch released publicity for the upcoming volume:

Sherwood Anderson, in his new book, whimsically titled "Winesburg, Ohio," lays bare the hearts and minds of the inhabitants of a typical American village. The revelation is as simple and earnest and truly dramatic as if it were the work of a great Russian in-

Introduction

stead of a Chicago advertising man. It is the psycho-analytic method applied to literature. This is more nearly an approach to *the* American work of fiction than even Mr. Anderson's two novels that were so widely acclaimed.[54]

Printing was completed on April 28 by the Van Rees Press of New York City, from plates for 303 pages made by the Plimpton Press of Norwood, Massachusetts; and with binding in yellow (sometimes orange-yellow) cloth by the H. Wolff Estate of New York City, *Winesburg, Ohio: A Group of Tales of Ohio Small Town Life* was officially published in a run of 1800 copies on May 8, 1919.[55] The handsome white wrapper of the book, bearing the logo menorah cartouche of the B. W. Huebsch Company, asked the potential reader (in words possibly written by Sherwood Anderson): "What is the fiction that you remember—that sticks for years after reading it? The mystery story? The swashbuckler story? The motor-car romance? The propaganda novel?" The wrapper text answered:

> No, to all, except for the rare achievements by masters in those fields.
>
> What stories do you remember? Is it not those in which people's very souls are bared, in which their heart-beats are almost heard, in which life is not described but revealed.
>
> Such a book is this one: a book to be read, reread and given away because it is too good to keep; a masterly work—perhaps a masterwork.

Sales at $1.50 proving moderately respectable for a collection of short stories, Huebsch reprinted *Winesburg,*

54. See Ray Lewis White, "*Winesburg* in 1919: The Publisher's Catalog Copy." *Winesburg Eagle: The Official Publication of the Sherwood Anderson Society* 3 (April 1978): 3–4.

55. The first British edition of *Winesburg, Ohio* appeared in 1922 from Jonathan Cape of London, with the intriguing and attractive subtitle *Intimate Histories of Every-day People.*

Ohio in December of 1919, again in January of 1921, again in December of 1921, and finally in March of 1922. Then, merging the B. W. Huebsch Company with the Viking Press, Ben Huebsch published two more printings of Anderson's volume under the Viking imprint—once in March 1927, and, finally, in June 1931. All of the seven printings would have been small pressruns, and copies from all of the printings have become treasured rare books.

No sooner was *Winesburg, Ohio* in print than Sherwood Anderson wanted to correct the text of his published volume, for on June 14, 1919, the author wrote to Ben Huebsch that he would send a list of errors to be corrected in any possible second printing and that he had learned, to his total surprise, that there was indeed in Ohio a place called "Weinsburg," a village where people might not be happy with the implications cast over their locale and their families by what some readers would consider to be the scandalous fictional characters in Anderson's stories.[56] Anderson's list of errata to be corrected in the Huebsch printing plates does not survive; but the writer would for years be irritated by charges that he had misused the good name of the real Winesburg, Ohio, a community in Holmes County, southeast of Clyde, an area settled and yet populated, some claim, solely by peaceful and pious farming folk.

In justification for having accidentally borrowed the name of an actual town, Anderson claimed to remember that, when he was seeking a name for his fictional town, he had consulted a list of Ohio communities to prevent use in his fictions of a real place but that, as the list contained names of towns and cities served by rail-

56. See Ray Lewis White, "Sherwood Anderson and the Real Winesburg, Ohio." *Winesburg Eagle: The Official Publication of the Sherwood Anderson Society* 12 (April 1987): 1–4. It should be noted that examination of a directory of all of the post offices ever located in the state of Ohio reveals that Anderson might have borrowed more than one town's name. In fact, he might have peopled *Winesburg* with Ohio place-names used as character names: *Alice, Beebe, Belle Center, Bentley, Carpenter, Daugherty, Ebenezer, Elizabeth, Enoch, Foster, George, Green, Griffith, Handley, Handy, Hard, Hardy, Harriet, Henby, Herrick, Jesse, King, Paris, Pearson, Port William, Ray, Richmond, Turner, Washington, Wesley, White, Willard, Williams, Wilson, Winters Station, Wood,* and *Woods Mills.* (Yet, to urge caution in implications of borrowing, note that there are in Ohio also the towns of *Sherwood* and *Anderson.*) See John S. Gallagher and Alan Patera, *The Post Offices of Ohio* (Burtonsville, Md.: Depot, 1979).

Introduction

roads and as the real Winesburg had no train service, the list did not carry that town's name.

There is no evidence that Anderson and Huebsch ever considered changing the name of Anderson's imagined town or of Huebsch's book in response to discontent in Holmes County, Ohio. The textual changes which Anderson and Huebsch did make within *Winesburg, Ohio*, however, require more discussion.

On August 23, 1919, Sherwood Anderson mailed to Ben Huebsch his changes for the text of *"Wiensburg"* (the author could indeed misspell the name of his town); but this list of changes and any lists made by Huebsch and his editors do not exist, and only these few changes (beyond mending broken type) were made to the printing plates for the second and subsequent five pressruns:

- Hundreds and hundreds of were the truths and they were all beautiful. *became* Hundreds and hundreds were the truths and they were all beautiful.
- . . . threatening us if we dared so much as touch the money that sometimes laid on the table three days. *became* . . . threatening us if we dared so much as touch the money that sometimes lay on the table three days.
- . . . sickening dread that he thought must have laid heavy on the heart of Saul . . . *became* . . . sickening dread that he thought must have lain heavy on the heart of Saul . . .
- In the woods an intense silence seemed to lay over everything . . . *became* In the woods an intense silence seemed to lie over everything . . .

Introduction

- Sometimes the lights were turned low and young man and woman embraced. *became* Sometimes the lights were turned low and the young man and woman embraced.
- It's rust you see. *became* It rusts, you see.
- . . . my mind thinking of the shoulders and the neck of a woman . . . *became* . . . my mind thinking of the shoulders and neck of a woman . . .
- . . . the two sat down on a grassy bank to talk. *became* . . . the two sat on a grassy bank and talked.
- They think that it matters much more than it does. *became* They think it matters much more than it does.
- . . . their tales of thieving, drunkenness unmoved and strangely unaffected. *became* . . . their tales of thieving and drunkenness unmoved and strangely unaffected.
- Now I know that you won't . . . *became* Now I know you won't . . .

It seems unlikely that these eleven emendations to the first edition of *Winesburg, Ohio* were the changes that would have constituted for Anderson and Huebsch a supposedly noteworthy list, as some of the changes are of dubious merit and were made, clearly, to please someone's particular preference in rhythm, style, or logic. Perhaps, given the expense of correcting printing plates even in Anderson's day, more corrections were listed and considered but not actually made. Nevertheless, a new edition of *Winesburg, Ohio* must take account of these few changes and corrections, discovered through collation of the seven printings of the first edition of the book, and, following bibliographical theory, incorporate them into a new text.[57] But preparing a new text of *Winesburg,*

57. An admirable statement of bibliographical theory and practice in editing modern literary texts is given in *The Great Gatsby* by F. Scott Fitzgerald, edited by Matthew J. Bruccoli, with textual consultant Fredson Bowers (Cambridge: Cambridge University Press, 1991). Bruccoli's edition of *Gatsby* serves in most ways as the model for the present edition of the text of *Winesburg.*

Introduction

Ohio requires further exploration of the 1919 publication, beginning with Sherwood Anderson's method of composing and the actions that the offices of Ben Huebsch as publisher performed in readying Anderson's text for printing.

Sherwood Anderson wrote and corrected the *Winesburg, Ohio* stories in pencil and in ink, copying text from his early (occasionally, perhaps, his first) draft of each story onto verso sheets of his own discarded typescript or manuscript or onto fresh sheets of the cheap unlined paper used in the advertising office where he worked.[58] Contrary to the author's memory of the perfection with which "Hands," the first of the *Winesburg* stories, late in 1915 came to him, the surviving manuscript of that story reveals that, although Anderson probably did conceive of the story suddenly and write it through quickly, he indeed made many changes to the text of this story, as he did make a multitude of changes to the texts of all of the subsequent stories before having them typed, probably by his secretary at the advertising office (for a few dollars in extra pay) and by a freelance typist who would come to Anderson's room at 735 North Cass Street (to type for money for food). Not a single one of the typescripts thus produced survives, unfortunately, so that today an accurate new text of *Winesburg, Ohio* must depend on (1) the manuscripts of all of the stories; on (2) the periodical texts of the ten pieces that Anderson placed with the *Little Review, Masses,* and *Seven Arts;* and on (3) the first edition of the book published by Huebsch in its seven printings from 1919 through 1931.[59]

The basis of a new text of *Winesburg, Ohio* must be

58. For a technical description of the manuscripts, see Ray Lewis White, "The Manuscripts of *Winesburg, Ohio*," *Winesburg Eagle: The Official Publication of the Sherwood Anderson Society* 11 (November 1985): 4–10.

59. William Louis Phillips, in "Sherwood Anderson's *Winesburg, Ohio*: Its Origins, Composition, Technique, and Reception," Dissertation, University of Chicago, 1949; and in his often-reprinted article "How Sherwood Anderson Wrote *Winesburg, Ohio*," *American Literature* 23 (March 1951): 7–30 stated that he could determine, from a study of the discarded matter that Anderson had written earlier on the obverse pages of some *Winesburg, Ohio* stories, the order of composition of the stories. Recent study of the manuscripts

Introduction

the words of the first edition of the book published in 1919, with incorporation of the eleven corrections made with Anderson's approval or at least without his known objection in the second through seventh printings (1919–1931); and such is the basis of this new text of Anderson's masterpiece. Nevertheless, mere reproduction here of the 1919 text of *Winesburg, Ohio* would be totally unacceptable to readers who require carefully edited books, for the B. W. Huebsch offices did not serve literary history well in the production of their published volume.

To the now unknown, probably overworked, and surely underpaid copy editor of 1918 who was handed Anderson's typescript, the stories were just another 71,100 or so words to be marked hastily for decent spelling and punctuation and, perhaps, for the occasional niceties of house style. And haste seems to have been the major factor in the copyediting, for there are grammar and logic and printing errors that were never corrected in the work and—most noticeable and most irritating of all flaws—there are scores and scores of inconsistencies in the spelling and punctuation of Anderson's text. Variant (sometimes multiply variant) forms are omnipervasive in the text, occurring often within a distance of mere words or lines or paragraphs from one another. Among them are:

reveals that Phillips's idea does not yield useful results in regard to the order of writing of the stories. For example, Phillips assumed that only one copy of each story ever existed; and the existence in the Newberry Library of an alternate manuscript of "Nobody Knows," as well as the necessary (and now lost) typescripts of the stories submitted to at least four periodicals, argues against his conclusion. Further, Phillips's idea that Anderson wrote each *Winesburg* story only once and then corrected it is not defensible. Of the stories, only "The Book of the Grotesque" and "Tandy" might exist in first-draft form.

- any one / anyone
- baggage master / baggageman
- Biff Carter's Lunch Room / Biff Carter's lunch room
- broad shouldered / broad-shouldered
- businesslike / childlike / shed-like
- Callie / Sallie
- door knob / doorknob

Introduction

- down stairs / downstairs
- Ed Griffith's Saloon / Ed Griffith's saloon
- every one / everyone
- Ed Hanby / Ed Handby
- Fair / fair
- Fair Ground / Fair Grounds / fair ground
- fierce looking / wicked-looking
- grand-stand / grandstand
- half forgotten / half insane / half-formed / half-witted
- Hearn's Grocery / Hern's grocery
- hotel keeper / housekeeper
- lamp post / lamp-post
- Main street / Main Street
- Nate / Kate
- Nature / nature
- New Willard House / new Willard House / old Willard House
- night-robe / nightdress
- nursery man / nurseryman
- O / Oh
- Paris Dry Goods Co. / Paris Dry Goods Store / Paris Dry Goods Store Co.
- plead / pleaded
- pocket-book / pocketbook
- print shop / printshop
- residence streets / resident streets
- reawaken / re-echoed
- re-rented / rearranged
- saloon keeper / storekeeper
- school-master / schoolmaster
- show case / showcase
- Sinning's / Sinnings
- Smollet / Smallet

- some time / sometime
- some one / someone
- South / south
- tired out / tired-out
- tonight / to-night
- toward / towards
- town people / townsmen / trainsmen
- railroad track / railroad tracks
- trouser / trousers
- Wacker's Cigar Store / Wracker's tobacco store
- Wesley / Westley
- Wesley Moyer's livery barn / Westley Moyer's livery barn / Moyer's Livery
- Winney's store / Winny's Dry Goods Store / Winney's Dry Goods Store
- Winter's barn / Winters family
- wood / woods

Given these (and other) inconsistencies and errors in the Huebsch text of *Winesburg, Ohio,* corrections made for this text must be explained and exemplified in several stages. First, some once-separable or once-hyphenated forms favored by the Huebsch copy editor in 1919 are herein unified and modernized: *anyone, someone, downstairs, today, tomorrow.* Next, given the prevalence of varying compound forms used in *Winesburg,* preference here has been accorded to separation of the forms, a practice that seems preferred by Anderson in his manuscripts, although his practice was mixed. For example, these forms are herein adopted as standard: *barn yard, battle ground, birth mark, corn field, fair grounds, door knob, farm house, lamp light, print shop, school room.* Consistency and smoothness in reading have been the goal of the present edition.

Next, discrepancies in the naming of businesses or people are resolved herein by choosing and capitalizing the most common usages of Anderson himself. Thus, from the previous list, forms regularized in this text include: *Biff Carter's Lunch Room, Hern's Grocery, Ed Griffith's Saloon, the New Willard House, Winney's Dry Goods Store.* Similarly, names of characters (even Anderson sometimes misnamed his characters or misspelled their names) are herein regularized. For example, from the previous list: *Callie, Handby, Nate, Hern, Smollet, Wacker, Winney, Winters, Sinnings, Wesley.*

The unfamiliarity of Ben Huebsch's copy editor of *Winesburg, Ohio* with Sherwood Anderson's informal and almost-colloquial usage brought on unwise word-form choices in the Huebsch text. For example, the editor did not always recognize Anderson's usage of singular forms for repeated action—hence, herein, such times as *evening, afternoon,* and *morning* are kept when clear in context. And Anderson's preference is herein maintained for such forms as *woods, trousers, fair grounds,* and *railroad tracks* instead of the forms seemingly (but inconsistently) preferred by a New York City editor.

A few typographical errors not corrected when Huebsch/Viking Press reprinted *Winesburg* from 1919 through 1931 are corrected in this new text. For example, *you-ve* becomes *you've, track's* becomes *tracks, bead* becomes *head, murmer* becomes *murmur;* and an ungrammatical form *who/whom* is repaired. A few antique spellings are modernized: *clew* becomes *clue,* and *phantasies* becomes *fantasies* (but Anderson's preferred spelling *grey* is maintained).

A few tenses are herein altered to the form that clarifies their action: *had* becomes *has* and *achieved* becomes *has achieved.* Paragraphing is restored to that of Anderson's manuscript (only a few such restorations are necessary). And, finally, a few errors of fact or reference are corrected. For example, Dr. Reefy's horse, which Anderson makes *grey* and then *white*, is herein made *white*. The Ohio State University that Seth Richmond might attend is either *up* (north) from Winesburg or *down* (south) from Winesburg; herein it is *down*, because Clyde, Ohio, is north of Columbus, Ohio. A character cleans snow from his feet by tapping the *heel* (not the *toe*) of one boot against the *heel* of another boot (Anderson in his manuscript had this maneuver right). One *sheet*, not multiple *sheets*, covers the body of the dead Elizabeth Willard. And Sherwood Anderson's correct opposition of *carefulness and abandon* in his manuscript instead of *carelessness and abandon* in the first edition is here restored to its place.

In the matter of punctuation, Sherwood Anderson's manuscripts and typescripts always caused problems for the editors of magazines and books who were publishing his writings. (Some editors thought that Anderson simply cast an endless supply of commas randomly about.) For Anderson did not write to the rules of the formal punctuation of his day or of any other day; he wrote instead to the *sound of the text* as he heard himself *in his mind* rhythmically writing and slowly and solemnly reading and re-reading his own words as if aloud.

Hence, compound sentences may or may not be marked with separating commas (or, rarely, semicolons). Anderson composed in phrases and clauses that frequently interrupt the flow of his otherwise uncomplicated sentences, and he intended that many such phrases and clauses be marked off by paired commas (even if, as frequently happened, he forgot—in his intensity or haste—to write in one of the commas for a pair). Fur-

Introduction

ther, Anderson did not often end his sentences with marks of emotion or tone such as exclamation marks or questions marks, preferring to let his words carry the intended emotion or tone and to let periods close the sentences. In sum, the punctuation in this text relies, whenever possible, on the punctuation found in Anderson's carefully drafted manuscripts of his stories, as this punctuation, one can be certain, is the author's own.

Additionally, because Anderson's carefully copied manuscripts, prepared for his typist(s) to transform into fair copy for a publisher, do not in a new edition require re-ordering or re-titling of the *Winesburg* stories, the only necessary such change to the contents made herein is the re-titling of the introductory "The Book of the Grotesque" to make that prolegomenon bear prominently the writer's earlier (and clearer) designation: "Foreword."

The most important aspect of this text of *Winesburg, Ohio* is that it is a virtually *new* text, one with at least seven hundred emendations and corrections, and that it is an *expert* text, meaning that the editor has relied on many years of experience in reading and editing Sherwood Anderson material and has enjoyed access to all of the extant manuscripts and typescripts and relevant letters and diaries and all printings of the work under study. The result is this text that is modified by a knowledgeable editor who documents every modification made and reveals the original published reading and the reason for the modification or the authority for the modification.

Thus this expert text of *Winesburg, Ohio* documents

Introduction

marginally, in bold type, every reading in the 1919 B. W. Huebsch first edition of Anderson's book that is herein changed, with a mark < to indicate the change made and with the authority for the change attributed to the manuscript, to the periodical text of the stories, or to the judgment of the editor. The eleven changes made by Anderson or Huebsch or the publisher's staff are shown with the authority for *printing number(s)* as in *Pr 2* or *Pr 2–Pr 7*.

The second major aspect of this expert edition is the nontextual annotations, for never before has the text of *Winesburg, Ohio* received the explanations that it needs. Even the curious and aware reader of Anderson's work no longer can be depended on always to understand allusions to *Andersonville Prison, William McKinley and Mark Hanna, Socrates and Plato, Standard Oil, Cedar Point, the Epworth League, Charles Lamb and Benvenuto Cellini,* and *"Pop" Geers* and references to even the once most commonly known biblical myths. Such allusions and references are clarified herein marginally, each annotation appearing in the margin beside or near the line(s) of text in which the allusion or reference occurs. Likewise, numerous social customs and artifacts of small-town existence that have perished or changed over the past century would, without explanation, merely puzzle today's reader; hence, the editor explains marginally the use that Anderson made of *horse blocks, town blocks, railroad-yard trucks, kerosene, dry-goods stores* and *notions stores, livery stables, women riding bicycles,* etc.

Another innovative aspect of the annotations to this new text of *Winesburg, Ohio* is reference to the possible or probable originals for Anderson's characters, when such originals (or originating circumstances) can be determined with any degree of likelihood. Thus, the reader

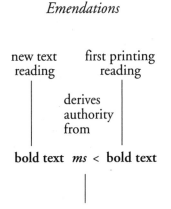

Key to Textual Emendations

new text   first printing
reading   reading

derives
authority
from

bold text *ms* < **bold text**

manuscript
or *ed* = editor
or *per* = periodical
or *Pr* = printings 2–7

will find occasional explanations when Anderson is for
his fictional characters almost definitely referring to or
drawing on his parents, on newspaper editors or business men whom he knew, or on one of his teachers or
advertising friends; and, when Anderson commented
elsewhere on the significance of his individual fictional
characters, those comments are noted herein.

But most innovative of the background annotations
in this re-newed edition of *Winesburg, Ohio* is the identification of the references to the state of Ohio and to
Anderson's hometown of Clyde. Readers have tended
to forget or to ignore the prominent and very important subtitle of the work—*A Group of Tales of Ohio Small
Town Life*—along with the map of "Winesburg" that
Anderson coached Harald Toksvig to draw for Ben
Huebsch's first edition. Although *Winesburg, Ohio* is not
geographically so dependent on intimate knowledge of
city maps as might be Charles Dickens's London, England, James Joyce's Dublin, Ireland, or Thomas Wolfe's
Asheville, North Carolina, it is yet possible to identify
and indicate on maps of Clyde, Ohio, the actual build-
ings and areas of the town referred to in Anderson's stories. Such identification, along with rare (often unique)
photographs of Clyde, Ohio, from the years when
Anderson lived in the town, here professionally published for the first time, are intended not to narrow the
appreciation of *Winesburg* as a work of multiple mean-
ings and universal appeal, but instead to deepen the
reader's knowledge of and feeling for the actual town
and the time—the geographical and social contexts—
from which Anderson drew his setting and his characters.
With this edition, *Winesburg* is thus revealed to be,
unexpectedly to even most long-abiding admirers, an
intensely local narrative and very much an "Ohio" book

Introduction

. . . but a book that has deserved and found worldwide fame.[60]

Yet despite the vibrant historical and geographical contexts of *Winesburg, Ohio,* the book will properly remain a fictional literary work of careful construction and profound inspiration and not a primarily autobiographical work and must not be read as a primarily autobiographical work, for the circumstances of Sherwood Anderson's early life differed greatly from those of his fictional George Willard: for example, Anderson was a poor boy with many siblings, one who did not share the relative wealth and comfort of George Willard; a boy who did not finish high school or plan a life in journalism; and a boy who might have sold copies of newspapers for pennies but who in his early manhood had nothing to do with writing and printing newspaper copy. It is probable that young Sherwood Anderson shared George Willard's fascination with the suffering grotesque characters of his hometown, but it is unlikely that the youthful Sherwood Anderson was so naive or so pleasant or so authorially inclined as his recurring character George Willard.

60. A partial list of the non-English editions is given in Ray Lewis White, *"Winesburg* in Translation," *Ohioana Quarterly* 19 (Summer 1976): 58–60. Among these are translations into Russian, Italian, Spanish, Danish, German, Portuguese, Swedish, Finnish, French, Bulgarian, Japanese, Chinese, Czech, Polish, Korean, Hebrew, Hungarian, Greek, Romanian, and Dutch.

But Sherwood "Jobby" Anderson, the hard-working, highly observant, and empathetic youth of Clyde, Ohio, did indeed grow up to write, as he declared in his letter of early 1916, "a series of intensive studies of people of my home town, Clyde, Ohio. . . ."

And *Winesburg, Ohio: A Group of Tales of Ohio Small Town Life* is presented at last in this new Ohio University Press edition in the state of textual clarity and rich contextual reference that the book has needed and deserved since its initial appearance, in May 1919, as Ben Huebsch's and Sherwood Anderson's little yellow-orange book in its plain white wrapper.

FOREWORD

The Book of the Grotesque

THE WRITER, AN old man with a white mustache, had some difficulty in getting into bed. The windows of the house in which he lived were high and he wanted to look at the trees when he awoke in the morning. A carpenter came to fix the bed so that it would be on a level with the window.

Quite a fuss was made about the matter. The carpenter, who had been a soldier in the Civil War, came into the writer's room and sat down to talk of building a platform for the purpose of raising the bed. The writer had cigars lying about and the carpenter smoked.

For a time the two men talked of the raising of the bed and then they talked of other things. The soldier got on the subject of the war. The writer, in fact, led him to that subject. The carpenter had once been a prisoner in Andersonville Prison and had lost a brother. The brother had died of starvation, and whenever the carpenter got upon that subject he cried. He, like the old writer, had a white mustache, and when he cried he puckered up his lips and the mustache bobbed up and down. The weeping old man with the cigar in his mouth was ludicrous. The plan the writer had for the raising of his bed was forgotten and later the carpenter did it in

Sherwood Anderson, in the rented room at 735 North Cass Street in Chicago where he wrote most of Winesburg, Ohio, *raised his own bed to window-ledge height in order to look at the bright nighttime lights of the city.*

Prison *ms* < prison

During the American Civil War, Confederate military forces imprisoned thousands of captured Union soldiers near Andersonville, Georgia. In 1864–1865, over 13,000 of these prisoners died from starvation and brutality.

Foreword

his own way and the writer, who was past sixty, had to help himself with a chair when he went to bed at night.

In his bed the writer rolled over on his side and lay quite still. For years he had been beset with notions concerning his heart. He was a hard smoker and his heart fluttered. The idea had got into his mind that he would sometime die unexpectedly and always when he got into bed he thought of that. It did not alarm him. The effect in fact was quite a special thing and not easily explained. It made him more alive, there in bed, than at any other time. Perfectly still he lay and his body was old and not of much use anymore but something inside him was altogether young. He was like a pregnant woman, only that the thing inside him was not a baby but a youth. No, it wasn't a youth, it was a woman, young, and wearing a coat of mail like a knight. It is absurd, you see, to try to tell what was inside the old writer as he lay on his high bed and listened to the fluttering of his heart. The thing to get at is what the writer, or the young thing within the writer, was thinking about.

The old writer, like all of the people in the world, had got, during his long life, a great many notions in his head. He had once been quite handsome and a number of women had been in love with him and then, of course, he had known people, many people, known them in a peculiarly intimate way that was different from the way in which you and I know people. At least that is what the writer thought and the thought pleased him. Why quarrel with an old man concerning his thoughts?

In the bed the writer had a dream that was not a dream. As he grew somewhat sleepy but was still conscious, figures began to appear before his eyes. He imagined the young indescribable thing within himself was driving a long procession of figures before his eyes.

sometime *ms* < some time

anymore *ed* < any more
more *ms* < more,

him and *ms* < him. And

Anderson himself suffered from such nights when faces appeared in the "half dream state" of his near-sleeping mind . . . exhausting experiences that he dreaded but that likely inspired his fiction, especially stories like these about Winesburg.

The Book of the Grotesque

You see the interest in all this lies in the figures that went before the eyes of the writer. They were all grotesques. All of the men and women the writer had ever known had become grotesques.

The grotesques were not all horrible. Some were amusing, some almost beautiful, and one, a woman all drawn out of shape, hurt the old man by her grotesqueness. When she passed he made a noise like a small dog whimpering. Had you come into the room you might have supposed the old man had unpleasant dreams or perhaps indigestion.

For an hour the procession of grotesques passed before the eyes of the old man, and then, although it was a painful thing to do, he crept out of bed and began to write. Some one of the grotesques had made a deep impression on his mind and he wanted to describe it.

At his desk the writer worked for an hour. In the end he wrote a book which he called "The Book of the Grotesque." It was never published, but I saw it once and it made an indelible impression on my mind. The book had one central thought that is very strange and has always remained with me. By remembering it I have been able to understand many people and things that I was never able to understand before. The thought was involved but a simple statement of it would be something like this:

That in the beginning when the world was young there were a great many thoughts but no such thing as a truth. Man made the truths himself and each truth was a composite of a great many vague thoughts. All about in the world were the truths and they were all beautiful.

The old man had listed hundreds of the truths in his book. I will not try to tell you of all of them. There was the truth of virginity and the truth of passion, the truth

"Grotesque" derives from "grotto," because on the walls of grottos or caves ancient artists sometimes drew human figures that were distorted, exaggerated, or ugly, at least by later standards.

No such old writer or book ever existed to impress Anderson, who invents them here to serve as the implied inspiration for his theory of human character and imaginative writing.

Foreword

(carefulness *ms*
(< carelessness
(hundreds were *ms, Pr*
(2–*Pr 7* < hundreds of
(were

of wealth and of poverty, of thrift and of profligacy, of carefulness and abandon. Hundreds and hundreds were the truths and they were all beautiful.

And then the people came along. Each as he appeared snatched up one of the truths and some who were quite strong snatched up a dozen of them.

It was the truths that made the people grotesques. The old man had quite an elaborate theory concerning the matter. It was his notion that the moment one of the people took one of the truths to himself, called it his truth, and tried to live his life by it, he became a grotesque and the truth he embraced became a falsehood.

You can see for yourself how the old man, who had spent all of his life writing and was filled with words, would write hundreds of pages concerning this matter. The subject would become so big in his mind that he himself would be in danger of becoming a grotesque. He didn't, I suppose, for the same reason that he never published the book. It was the young thing inside him that saved the old man.

The weeping old carpenter may be based on a Civil War veteran whom Anderson remembered as Jim Lane, native of Clyde, Ohio, who had seen his brother starve to death in Andersonville Prison and who later wept when he saw Sherwood Anderson and other young men of Ohio march away to take part in the Spanish-American War.

Concerning the old carpenter who fixed the bed for the writer, I only mentioned him because he, like many of what are called very common people, became the nearest thing to what is understandable and lovable of all the grotesques in the writer's book.

A GROUP OF TALES OF OHIO
SMALL TOWN LIFE

HANDS

Concerning Wing Biddlebaum

UPON THE HALF decayed veranda of a small frame house that stood near the edge of a ravine near the town of Winesburg, Ohio, a fat little old man walked nervously up and down. Across a long field that had been seeded for clover but that had produced only a dense crop of yellow mustard weeds, he could see the public highway along which went a wagon filled with berry pickers returning from the fields. The berry pickers, youths and maidens, laughed and shouted boisterously. A boy, clad in a blue shirt, leaped from the wagon and attempted to drag after him one of the maidens who screamed and protested shrilly. The feet of the boy in the road kicked up a cloud of dust that floated across the face of the departing sun. Over the long field came a thin girlish voice. "Oh, you Wing Biddlebaum, comb your hair, it's falling into your eyes," commanded the voice to the man, who was bald and whose nervous little hands fiddled about the bare white forehead as though arranging a mass of tangled locks.

Wing Biddlebaum, forever frightened and beset by a ghostly band of doubts, did not think of himself as in

had *ed* < has

boy, *ms* < boy
shirt, *ms* < shirt

The public highway in Winesburg is Trunion Pike, based on the Western Reserve and Maumee Turnpike that transverses Clyde, Ohio, and that in Clyde was called the McPherson Highway (now U.S. 20).

Hands

New *ed* < new

any way a part of the life of the town where he had lived for twenty years. Among all the people of Winesburg but one had come close to him. With George Willard, son of Tom Willard, the proprietor of the New Willard House, he had formed something like a friendship. George Willard was the reporter on the *Winesburg Eagle* and sometimes in the evening he walked out along the highway to Wing Biddlebaum's house. Now, as the old man walked up and down on the veranda, his hands moving nervously about, he was hoping that George Willard would come and spend the evening with him. After the wagon containing the berry pickers had passed, he went across the field through the tall mustard weeds and climbing a rail fence peered anxiously along the road to the town. For a moment he stood thus, rubbing his hands together and looking up and down the road, and then, fear overcoming him, ran back to walk again upon the porch of his own house.

(evening *ms*
< evenings
Now, *ed* < Now

of *ed* < on

In the presence of George Willard, Wing Biddlebaum, who for twenty years had been the town mystery, lost something of his timidity, and his shadowy personality, submerged in a sea of doubts, came forth to look at the world. With the young reporter at his side, he ventured in the light of day into Main Street or strode up and down on the rickety front porch of his own house talking excitedly. The voice that had been low and trembling became shrill and loud. The bent figure straightened. With a kind of wriggle, like a fish returned to the brook by the fisherman, Biddlebaum the silent began to talk, striving to put into words the ideas that had been accumulated by his mind during long years of silence.

house *ms* < house,

Wing Biddlebaum talked much with his hands. The slender expressive fingers, forever active, forever striv-

Concerning Wing Biddlebaum

ing to conceal themselves in his pockets or behind his back, came forth and became the piston rods of his machinery of expression.

The story of Wing Biddlebaum is a story of hands. Their restless activity, like unto the beating of the wings of an imprisoned bird, had given him his name. Some obscure "poet" of the town had thought of it. The hands alarmed their owner. He wanted to keep them hidden away and looked with amazement at the quiet inexpressive hands of other men who worked beside him in the fields, or passed driving sleepy teams on country roads.

When he talked to George Willard, Wing Biddlebaum closed his fists and beat with them upon a table or on the walls of his house. The action made him more comfortable. If the desire to talk came to him when the two were walking in the fields, he sought out a stump or the top board of a fence and with his hands pounding busily talked with renewed ease.

The story of Wing Biddlebaum's hands is worth a book in itself. Sympathetically set forth it would tap many strange, beautiful qualities in obscure men. It is a job for a poet. In Winesburg the hands had attracted attention merely because of their activity. With them Wing Biddlebaum had picked as high as a hundred and forty quarts of strawberries in a day. They became his distinguishing feature, the source of his fame. Also they made more grotesque an already grotesque and elusive individuality. Winesburg was proud of the hands of Wing Biddlebaum in the same spirit in which it was proud of Banker White's new stone house and Wesley Moyer's bay stallion, Tony Tip, that had won the two-fifteen trot at the fall races in Cleveland.

As for George Willard, he had many times wanted to ask about the hands. At times an almost overwhelming

By "poet" Anderson does not here or hereafter in Winesburg refer to a creative writer of verse but instead to some ordinary person gifted with close observation and the use of imaginative language.

"poet" *ed < poet*

passed *ms < passed,*

The rich land surrounding Clyde, Ohio, produced huge amounts of strawberries and raspberries (and other fruits and vegetables) that in Anderson's day accounted for much local income when the crops were shipped to market by railroads.

Anderson places the fictional house of Banker White at the location of the actual Emmons D. Harkness house, at 136 West Buckeye Street, in Clyde.

Hands

curiosity had taken hold of him. He felt that there must be a reason for their strange activity and their inclination to keep hidden away and only a growing respect for Wing Biddlebaum kept him from blurting out the questions that were often in his mind.

Once he had been on the point of asking. The two were walking in the fields on a summer afternoon and had stopped to sit upon a grassy bank. All afternoon Wing Biddlebaum had talked as one inspired. By a fence he had stopped and beating like a giant woodpecker upon the top board had shouted at George Willard, condemning his tendency to be too much influenced by the people about him. "You are destroying yourself," he cried. "You have the inclination to be alone and to dream and you are afraid of dreams. You want to be like others in town here. You hear them talk and you try to imitate them."

On the grassy bank Wing Biddlebaum had tried again to drive his point home. His voice became soft and reminiscent, and with a sigh of contentment he launched into a long rambling talk, speaking as one lost in a dream.

Out of the dream Wing Biddlebaum made a picture for George Willard. In the picture men lived again in a kind of pastoral golden age. Across a green open country came clean-limbed young men, some afoot, some mounted upon horses. In crowds the young men came to gather about the feet of an old man who sat beneath a tree in a tiny garden and who talked to them.

Wing Biddlebaum became wholly inspired. For once he forgot the hands. Slowly they stole forth and lay upon George Willard's shoulders. Something new and bold came into the voice that talked. "You must try to forget all you have learned," said the old man. "You must be-

The unnamed teacher of young men whom Biddlebaum describes is either Socrates (470–399 B.C.), the Greek philosopher who suffered death for questioning the basis of Athenian society, or Plato (427–347 B.C.), student of Socrates who established the idea of a college or a university through teaching young Greek men in a grove of trees in Athens.

Concerning Wing Biddlebaum

gin to dream. From this time on you must shut your ears to the roaring of the voices."

Pausing in his speech, Wing Biddlebaum looked long and earnestly at George Willard. His eyes glowed. Again he raised the hands to caress the boy and then a look of horror swept over his face.

With a convulsive movement of his body Wing Biddlebaum sprang to his feet and thrust his hands deep into his trousers pockets. Tears came to his eyes. "I must be getting along home. I can talk no more with you," he said nervously.

Without looking back, the old man had hurried down the hillside and across a meadow, leaving George Willard perplexed and frightened upon the grassy slope. With a shiver of dread the boy arose and went along the road toward town. "I'll not ask him about his hands," he thought, touched by the memory of the terror he had seen in the man's eyes. "There's something wrong, but I don't want to know what it is. His hands have something to do with his fear of me and of everyone."

And George Willard was right. Let us look briefly into the story of the hands. Perhaps our talking of them will arouse the poet who will tell the hidden wonder story of the influence for which the hands were but fluttering pennants of promise.

In his youth Wing Biddlebaum had been a school teacher in a town in Pennsylvania. He was not then known as Wing Biddlebaum but went by the less euphonic name of Adolph Myers. As Adolph Myers he was much loved by the boys of his school.

Adolph Myers was meant by nature to be a teacher of youth. He was one of those rare little-understood men who rule by a power so gentle that it passes as a lovable

body *ms* < body,

(Biddlebaum *ms*
< Biddlebaum,

rare *ms* < rare,

Hands

weakness. In their feeling for the boys under their charge such men are not unlike the finer sort of women in their love of men.

And yet that is but crudely stated. It needs the poet there. With the boys of his school, Adolph Myers had walked in the evening or had sat talking until dusk upon the school house steps, lost in a kind of dream. Here and there went his hands, caressing the shoulders of the boys, playing about the tousled heads. As he talked his voice became soft and musical. There was a caress in that also. In a way the voice and the hands, the stroking of the shoulders and the touching of the hair was a part of the school master's effort to carry a dream into the young minds. By the caress that was in his fingers he expressed himself. He was one of those men in whom the force that creates life is diffused, not centralized. Under the caress of his hands doubt and disbelief went out of the minds of the boys and they began also to dream.

And then the tragedy. A half witted boy of the school became enamored of the young master. In his bed at night he imagined unspeakable things and in the morning went forth to tell his dreams as facts. Strange hideous accusations fell from his loose-hung lips. Through the Pennsylvania town went a shiver. Hidden shadowy doubts that had been in men's minds concerning Adolph Myers were galvanized into beliefs.

The tragedy did not linger. Trembling lads were jerked out of bed and questioned. "He put his arms about me," said one. "His fingers were always playing in my hair," said another.

One afternoon a man of the town, Henry Bradford, who kept a saloon, came to the school house door. Calling Adolph Myers into the school yard he began to beat

school house *ed*
(< schoolhouse
steps, *ms* < steps

school master's *ed*
(< school-master's

half *ed* < half-

Strange *ms* < Strange,

Hidden *ms* < Hidden,

school house *ed*
(< schoolhouse

Concerning Wing Biddlebaum

him with his fists. As his hard knuckles beat down into the frightened face of the school master, his wrath became more and more terrible. Screaming with dismay, the children ran here and there like disturbed insects. "I'll teach you to put your hands on my boy, you beast," roared the saloon keeper, who, tired of beating the master, had begun to kick him about the yard.

> school master *ed*
> < schoolmaster

Adolph Myers was driven from the Pennsylvania town in the night. With lanterns in their hands a dozen men came to the door of the house where he lived alone and commanded that he dress and come forth. It was raining and one of the men had a rope in his hands. They had intended to hang the school master, but something in his figure, so small, white, and pitiful, touched their hearts and they let him escape. As he ran away into the darkness they repented of their weakness and ran after him, swearing and throwing sticks and great balls of soft mud at the figure that screamed and ran faster and faster into the darkness.

> school master *ed*
> < schoolmaster

For twenty years Adolph Myers had lived alone in Winesburg. He was but forty but looked sixty-five. The name of Biddlebaum he got from a box of goods seen at a freight station as he hurried through an eastern Ohio town. He had an aunt in Winesburg, a black-toothed old woman who raised chickens, and with her he lived until she died. He had been ill for a year after the experience in Pennsylvania, and after his recovery worked as a day laborer in the fields, going timidly about and striving to conceal his hands. Although he did not understand what had happened he felt that the hands must be to blame. Again and again the fathers of the boys had talked of the hands. "Keep your hands to yourself," the saloon keeper had roared, dancing with fury in the school house yard.

> school house *ed*
> < schoolhouse

Hands

Upon the veranda of his house by the ravine, Wing Biddlebaum continued to walk up and down until the sun had disappeared and the road beyond the field was lost in the grey shadows. Going into his house he cut slices of bread and spread honey upon them. When the rumble of the evening train that took away the express cars loaded with the day's harvest of berries had passed and restored the silence of the summer night, he went again to walk upon the veranda. In the darkness he could not see the hands and they became quiet. Although he still hungered for the presence of the boy, who was the medium through which he expressed his love of man, the hunger became again a part of his loneliness and his waiting. Lighting a lamp Wing Biddlebaum washed the few dishes soiled by his simple meal and, setting up a folding cot by the screen door that led to the porch, prepared to undress for the night. A few stray white bread crumbs lay on the cleanly washed floor by the table; putting the lamp upon a low stool he began to pick up the crumbs, carrying them to his mouth one by one with unbelievable rapidity. In the dense blotch of light beneath the table, the kneeling figure looked like a priest engaged in some service of his church. The nervous expressive fingers, flashing in and out of the light, might well have been mistaken for the fingers of the devotee going swiftly through decade after decade of his rosary.

lamp *ms* < lamp,

PAPER PILLS

Concerning Doctor Reefy

HE WAS AN old man with a white beard and huge nose and hands. Long before the time during which we will know him, he was a doctor and drove a jaded white horse from house to house through the streets of Winesburg. Later he married a girl who had money. She had been left a large fertile farm when her father died. The girl was quiet, tall and dark, and to many people she seemed very beautiful. Everyone in Winesburg wondered why she married the doctor. Within a year after the marriage she died.

The knuckles of the doctor's hands were extraordinarily large. When the hands were closed they looked like clusters of unpainted wooden balls as large as walnuts fastened together by steel rods. He smoked a cob pipe and after his wife's death sat all day in his empty office close by a window that was covered with cobwebs. He never opened the window. Once on a hot day in August he tried but found it stuck fast and after that he forgot all about it.

Winesburg had forgotten the old man, but in Doctor Reefy there were the seeds of something very fine. Alone in his musty office in the Heffner Block above the Paris

tall ms < tall,

hands ms < hand

A "block" referred to a long building two or three stories high, with spaces to be rented to offices or retail stores; a "dry goods" store sold merchandise such as cloth and light-duty home furnishings and decorations—items that were neither food nor hardware. The fictional Heffner Block is based on the Richards Block at 112–124 South Main Street, in Clyde.

Paper Pills

Dry Goods Company, he worked ceaselessly, building up something that he himself destroyed. Little pyramids of truth he erected and after erecting knocked them down again that he might have the truth to erect other pyramids.

Doctor Reefy was a tall man who had worn one suit of clothes for ten years. It was frayed at the sleeves and little holes had appeared at the knees and elbows. In the office he wore also a linen duster with huge pockets into which he continually stuffed scraps of paper. After some weeks the scraps of paper became little hard round balls, and when the pockets were filled he dumped them out upon the floor. For ten years he had but one friend, another old man named John Spaniard who owned a tree nursery. Sometimes, in a playful mood, old Doctor Reefy took from his pockets a handful of the paper balls and threw them at the nursery man. "That is to confound you, you blithering old sentimentalist," he cried, shaking with laughter.

The story of Doctor Reefy and his courtship of the tall dark girl who became his wife and left her money to him is a very curious story. It is delicious like the twisted little apples that grow in the orchards of Winesburg. In the fall one walks in the orchards and the ground is hard with frost underfoot. The apples have been taken from the trees by the pickers. They have been put in barrels and shipped to the cities where they will be eaten in apartments that are filled with books, magazines, furniture and people. On the trees are only a few gnarled apples that the pickers have rejected. They look like the knuckles of Doctor Reefy's hands. One nibbles at them and they are delicious. Into a little round place at the side of the apple has been gathered all of its sweetness. One runs from tree to tree over the frosted ground pick-

Concerning Doctor Reefy

ing the gnarled twisted apples and filling his pockets with them. Only the few know the sweetness of the twisted apples.

The girl and Doctor Reefy began their courtship on a summer afternoon. He was forty-five then and already he had begun the practice of filling his pockets with the scraps of paper that became hard balls and were thrown away. The habit had been formed as he sat in his buggy behind the jaded white horse and went slowly along country roads. On the papers were written thoughts, ends of thoughts, beginnings of thoughts.

white *ed* < grey

One by one the mind of Doctor Reefy had made the thoughts. Out of many of them he formed a truth that arose gigantic in his mind. The truth clouded the world. It became terrible and then faded away and the little thoughts began again.

The tall dark girl came to see Doctor Reefy because she was in the family way and had become frightened. She was in that condition because of a series of circumstances also curious.

The death of her father and mother and the rich acres of land that had come down to her had set a train of suitors on her heels. For two years she saw suitors almost every evening. Except two they were all alike. They talked to her of passion and there was a strained eager quality in their voices and in their eyes when they looked at her. The two who were different were much unlike each other. One of them, a slender young man with white hands, the son of a jeweler in Winesburg, talked continually of virginity. When he was with her he was never off the subject. The other, a black-haired boy with large ears, said nothing at all but always managed to get her into the darkness where he began to kiss her.

For a time the tall dark girl thought she would marry

Paper Pills

the jeweler's son. For hours she sat in silence listening as he talked to her and then she began to be afraid of something. Beneath his talk of virginity she began to think there was a lust greater than in all the others. At times it seemed to her that as he talked he was holding her body in his hands. She imagined him turning it slowly about in the white hands and staring at it. At night she dreamed that he had bitten into her body and that his jaws were dripping. She had the dream three times, then she became in the family way to the one who said nothing at all but who in the moment of his passion actually did bite her shoulder so that for days the marks of his teeth showed.

After the tall dark girl came to know Doctor Reefy it seemed to her that she never wanted to leave him again. She went into his office one morning and without her saying anything he seemed to know what had happened to her.

In the office of the doctor there was a woman, the wife of the man who kept the book store in Winesburg. Like all old-fashioned country practitioners, Doctor Reefy pulled teeth, and the woman who waited held a handkerchief to her teeth and groaned. Her husband was with her and when the tooth was taken out they both screamed and blood ran down on the woman's white dress. The tall dark girl did not pay any attention. When the woman and the man had gone the doctor smiled. "I will take you driving into the country with me," he said.

For several weeks the tall dark girl and the doctor were together almost every day. The condition that had brought her to him passed in an illness, but she was like one who has discovered the sweetness of the twisted

book store *ed*
(< bookstore

Dr. Reefy's office is re-created by Anderson from memories of the office of Dr. Stephen T. Finch (and, later, of Dr. A. R. Lord), on the second floor of 112 South Main Street, in Clyde. There was a Heffner Block in Clyde at 217–225 North Main Street.

apples. She could not get her mind fixed again upon the round perfect fruit that is eaten in the city apartments. In the fall, after the beginning of her acquaintanceship with him, she married Doctor Reefy and in the following spring she died. During the winter he read to her all of the odds and ends of thoughts he had scribbled on the bits of paper. After he had read them he laughed and stuffed them away in his pockets to become round hard balls.

apples. She *ms* < apples, she

fall, *ms* < fall
him, *ed* < him

MOTHER

Concerning Elizabeth Willard

ELIZABETH WILLARD, the mother of George Willard, was tall and gaunt and her face was marked with smallpox scars. Although she was but forty-five, some obscure disease had taken the fire out of her figure. Listlessly she went about the disorderly old hotel looking at the faded wall paper and the ragged carpets and, when she was able to be about, doing the work of a chambermaid among beds soiled by the slumbers of fat traveling men. Her husband Tom Willard, a slender, graceful man, with square shoulders, a quick military step, and a black mustache, trained to turn sharply up at the ends, tried to put the wife out of his mind. The presence of the tall ghostly figure, moving slowly through the halls, he took as a reproach to himself. When he thought of her he grew angry and swore. The hotel was

wall paper *ed* < wall-paper

husband *ms* < husband,

man, *ms* < man

Mother

unprofitable and forever on the edge of failure and he wished himself out of it. He thought of the old house and the woman who lived there with him as things defeated and done for. The hotel in which he had begun life so hopefully was now a mere ghost of what a hotel should be. As he went spruce and business-like through the streets of Winesburg, he sometimes stopped and turned quickly about as though fearing that the spirit of the hotel and of the woman would follow him even into the streets. "Damn such a life, damn it!" he sputtered aimlessly.

Tom Willard had a passion for village politics and for years had been the leading Democrat in a strongly Republican community. Someday, he told himself, the tide of things political will turn in my favor and the years of ineffectual service count big in the bestowal of rewards. He dreamed of going to congress and even of becoming governor. Once, when a younger member of the party arose at a political conference and began to boast of his faithful service, Tom Willard grew white with fury. "Shut up, you," he roared, glaring about. "What do you know of service? What are you but a boy? Look at what I've done here. I was a Democrat here in Winesburg when it was a crime to be a Democrat. In the old days they fairly hunted us with guns."

Between Elizabeth and her one son George there was a deep unexpressed bond of sympathy, based on a girlhood dream that had long ago died. In the son's presence she was timid and reserved, but sometimes while he hurried about town, intent upon his duties as a reporter, she went into his room and closing the door knelt by a little desk, made of a kitchen table, that sat near a window. In the room by the desk, she went through a ceremony that was half a prayer, half a demand addressed

business-like *ed* < businesslike

The Republican political party, organized in 1854 to oppose admitting new slaveholding states to the Union, elected Abraham Lincoln president in 1860 and, victorious in the (cont'd below)

Someday *ed* < Some day

congress *ms* < Congress

Once, *ed* < Once

Civil War, tried to dominate postwar politics so that Democrats (organized in 1792) would long remain in minority status.

here. *ms* < here!

town, *ms* < town

desk, *ms* < desk

demand *ms* < demand,

Concerning Elizabeth Willard

to the skies. In the boyish figure she yearned to see something half forgotten that had once been a part of herself recreated. The prayer concerned that. "Even though I die, I will in some way keep defeat from you," she cried and so deep was her determination that her whole body shook. Her eyes glowed and she clenched her fists. "If I am dead and see him becoming a meaningless drab figure like myself, I will come back," she declared. "I ask God now to give me that privilege. I demand it. I will pay for it. God may beat me with his fists. I will take any blow that may befall if but this my boy be allowed to express something for us both." Pausing uncertainly, the woman stared about the boy's room. "And do not let him become smart and successful either," she added vaguely.

The communion between George Willard and his mother was outwardly a formal thing without meaning. When she was ill and sat by the window in her room he sometimes went in the evening to make her a visit. They sat by a window that looked over the roof of a small frame building into Main Street. By turning their heads they could see, through another window, along an alleyway that ran behind the Main Street stores and into the back door of Abner Groff's Bakery. Sometimes as they sat thus a picture of village life presented itself to them. At the back door of his shop appeared Abner Groff with a stick or an empty milk bottle in his hand. For a long time there was a feud between the baker and a grey cat that belonged to Sylvester West, the druggist. The boy and his mother saw the cat creep into the door of the bakery and presently emerge followed by the baker who swore and waved his arms about. The baker's eyes were small and red and his black hair and beard were filled with flour dust. Sometimes he was so angry that, although the cat had disappeared, he hurled sticks, bits

cried *ms* < cried,

The New Willard House Hotel is based on the Empire House Hotel in Clyde, which stood north of the Lake Shore Railroad tracks, west of North Main Street, and opposite the railroad depot. Anderson's parents had nothing to do with owning or operating any hotel in Clyde; but in his youth Sherwood knew Maria Welling, who moved with her husband from Sandusky to Clyde to operate a hotel and its bar and dining room. Yet Anderson's parents are reflected in the fictional suffering mother and the talkative, never-do-well father.

Bakery *ed* < bakery

The Abner Groff Bakery is drawn from the C. D. Arnold Bakery, at 109 North Main Street, in Clyde. The fictional Sinnings' Hardware Store would be at 105 North Main Street, in Clyde, where Miller's Tailor Shop was located; but a real Sinnings' Hardware Store stood in Clyde, at 122 South Main Street.

Mother

of broken glass, and even some of the tools of his trade about. Once he broke a window at the back of Sinnings' Hardware Store. In the alley the grey cat crouched behind barrels filled with torn papers and broken bottles above which flew a black swarm of flies. Once when she was alone, and after watching a prolonged and ineffectual outburst on the part of the baker, Elizabeth Willard put her head down on her long white hands and wept. After that she did not look along the alleyway anymore, but tried to forget the contest between the bearded man and the cat. It seemed like a rehearsal of her own life, terrible in its vividness.

In the evening, when the son sat in the room with his mother, the silence made them both feel awkward. Darkness came on and the evening train came in at the station. In the street below feet tramped up and down upon a board sidewalk. In the station yard, after the evening train had gone, there was a heavy silence. Perhaps Skinner Leason, the express agent, moved a truck the length of the station platform. Over on Main Street sounded a man's voice, laughing. The door of the express office banged. George Willard arose and crossing the room fumbled for the door knob. Sometimes he knocked against a chair making it scrape along the floor. By the window sat the sick woman, perfectly still, listless. Her long hands, white and bloodless, could be seen, drooping over the ends of the arms of the chair. "I think you had better be out among the boys. You are too much indoors," she said striving to relieve the embarrassment of the departure. "I thought I would take a walk," replied George Willard, who felt awkward and confused.

One evening in July, when the transient guests who made the New Willard House their temporary homes had become scarce, and the hallways, lighted only by

Concerning Elizabeth Willard

kerosene lamps, turned low, were plunged in gloom, Elizabeth Willard had an adventure. She had been ill in bed for several days and her son had not come to visit her. She was alarmed. The feeble blaze of life that remained in her body was blown into a flame by her anxiety and she crept out of bed, dressed and hurried along the hallway toward her son's room, shaking with exaggerated fears. As she went along she steadied herself with her hand, slipped along the papered wall of the hall, and breathed with difficulty. The air whistled through her teeth. As she hurried forward she thought how foolish she was. "He is concerned with boyish affairs," she told herself. "Perhaps he has now begun to walk about in the evening with girls."

Elizabeth Willard had a dread of being seen by guests in the hotel that had once belonged to her father and the ownership of which still stood recorded in her name in the county court house. The hotel was continually losing patronage because of its shabbiness and she thought of herself as also shabby. Her own room was in an obscure corner and when she felt able to work she voluntarily worked among the beds, preferring the labor that could be done when the guests were abroad seeking trade among the merchants of Winesburg.

By the door of her son's room the mother knelt upon the floor and listened for some sound from within. When she heard the boy moving about and talking in low tones a smile came to her lips. George Willard had a habit of talking aloud to himself and to hear him doing so had always given his mother a peculiar pleasure. The habit in him, she felt, strengthened the secret bond that existed between them. A thousand times she had whispered to herself of the matter. "He is groping about, trying to find himself," she thought. "He is not a dull

lamps, *ms* < lamps

wall *ms* < walls
hall, *ed* < hall

(court house *ms*
< courthouse

Mother

clod, all words and smartness. Within him there is a secret something that is striving to grow. It is the thing I let be killed in myself."

In the darkness in the hallway by the door the sick woman arose and started again toward her own room. She was afraid that the door would open and the boy come upon her. When she had reached a safe distance and was about to turn a corner into a second hallway she stopped and, bracing herself with her hands, waited, thinking to shake off a trembling fit of weakness that had come upon her. The presence of the boy in the room had made her happy. In her bed during the long hours alone the little fears that had visited her had become giants. Now they were all gone. "When I get back to my room I shall sleep," she murmured gratefully.

But Elizabeth Willard was not to return to her bed and to sleep. As she stood trembling in the darkness, the door of her son's room opened and the boy's father, Tom Willard, stepped out. In the light that streamed out at the door he stood with the knob in his hand and talked. What he said infuriated the woman.

Tom Willard was ambitious for his son. He had always thought of himself as a successful man although nothing he had ever done had turned out successfully. However, when he was out of sight of the New Willard House and had no fear of coming upon his wife, he swaggered and began to dramatize himself as one of the chief men of the town. He wanted his son to succeed. He it was who had secured for the boy the position on the *Winesburg Eagle*. Now, with a ring of earnestness in his voice, he was advising concerning some course of conduct. "I tell you what, George, you've got to wake up," he said sharply. "Will Henderson has spoken to me three times concerning the matter. He says you go

and, *ed* < and
hands, *ms* < hands

bed *ms* < bed,
alone *ms* < alone,

darkness, *ms* < darkness

man *ms* < man,

Concerning Elizabeth Willard

along for hours not hearing when you are spoken to and acting like a gawky girl. What ails you?" Tom Willard laughed good-naturedly. "Well, I guess you'll get over it," he said. "I told Will that. You're not a fool and you're not a woman. You're Tom Willard's son and you'll wake up. I'm not afraid. What you say clears things up. If being a newspaper man has put the notion of becoming a writer into your mind that's all right. Only I guess you'll have to wake up to do that too, eh?"

Tom Willard went briskly along the hallway and down a flight of stairs to the office. The woman in the darkness could hear him laughing and talking with a guest who was striving to wear away a dull evening by dozing in a chair by the office door. She returned to the door of her son's room. The weakness had passed from her body as by a miracle and she stepped boldly along. A thousand ideas raced through her head. When she heard the scraping of a chair and the sound of a pen scratching upon paper, she again turned and went back along the hallway to her own room.

A definite determination had come into the mind of the defeated wife of the Winesburg hotel keeper. The determination was the result of long years of quiet and rather ineffectual thinking. "Now," she told herself, "I will act. There is something threatening my boy and I will ward it off." The fact that the conversation between Tom Willard and his son had been rather quiet and natural, as though an understanding existed between them, maddened her. Although for years she had hated her husband, her hatred had always before been a quite impersonal thing. He had been merely a part of something else that she hated. Now, and by the few words at the door, he had become the thing personified. In the darkness of her own room she clenched her fists and

has *ms* < had

hotel *ed* < Hotel

Mother

glared about. Going to a cloth bag that hung on a nail by the wall she took out a long pair of sewing scissors and held them in her hand like a dagger. "I will stab him," she said aloud. "He has chosen to be the voice of evil and I will kill him. When I have killed him something will snap within myself and I will die also. It will be a release for all of us."

In her girlhood and before her marriage with Tom Willard, Elizabeth had borne a somewhat shaky reputation in Winesburg. For years, she had been what is called "stage-struck" and had paraded through the streets with traveling men guests at her father's hotel, wearing loud clothes and urging them to tell her of life in the cities out of which they had come. Once she startled the town by putting on men's clothes and riding a bicycle down Main Street.

In her own mind the tall dark girl had been in those days much confused. A great restlessness was in her and it expressed itself in two ways. First there was an uneasy desire for change, for some big definite movement to her life. It was this feeling that had turned her mind to the stage. She dreamed of joining some company and wandering over the world, seeing always new faces and giving something out of herself to all people.

Sometimes at night she was quite beside herself with the thought, but, when she tried to talk of the matter to the members of the theatrical companies that came to Winesburg and stopped at her father's hotel, she got nowhere. They did not seem to know what she meant, or if she did get something of her passion expressed they only laughed. "It's not like that," they said. "It's as dull and uninteresting as this here. Nothing comes of it."

With the traveling men when she walked about with them and later with Tom Willard, it was quite different.

years, *ms* < years

For a young woman to wear men's clothing or to ride a bicycle in the late nineteenth century would startle spectators and bring disgrace to the woman.

([new ¶] *ms* < [no new ¶]

but, *ed* < but

(expressed *ms* < expressed,

them *ms* < them,

Concerning Elizabeth Willard

Always they seemed to understand and sympathize with her. On the side streets of the village, in the darkness under the trees, they took hold of her hand and she thought that something unexpressed in herself came forth and became a part of an unexpressed something in them.

And then there was the second expression of her restlessness. When that came she felt for a time released and happy. She did not blame the men who walked with her and later she did not blame Tom Willard. It was always the same, beginning with kisses and ending, after strange wild emotions, with peace and then sobbing repentance. When she sobbed she put her hand upon the face of the man and had always the same thought. Even though he were large and bearded she thought he had become suddenly a little boy. She wondered why he did not sob also.

In her room, tucked away in a corner of the New Willard House, Elizabeth Willard lighted a lamp and put it on a dressing table that stood by the door. A thought had come into her mind and she went to a closet and brought out a small square box and set it on the table. The box contained material for make-up and had been left with other things by a theatrical company that had once been stranded in Winesburg. Elizabeth Willard had decided that she would be beautiful. Her hair was still black and there was a great mass of it braided and coiled about her head. The scene that was to take place in the office below began to grow in her mind. No ghostly worn-out figure should confront Tom Willard, but something quite unexpected and startling. Tall and with dusky cheeks and hair that fell in a mass from her shoulders, a figure should come striding down the stairway before the startled loungers in the hotel office. The

New *ed* < old

Mother

figure would be silent—it would be swift and terrible. As a tigress whose cub had been threatened would she appear, coming out of the shadows, stealing noiselessly along and holding the long wicked scissors in her hand.

With a little broken sob in her throat, Elizabeth Willard blew out the light that stood upon the table and stood weak and trembling in the darkness. The strength that had been as a miracle in her body left and she half reeled across the floor, clutching at the back of the chair in which she had spent so many long days staring out over the tin roofs into the main street of Winesburg. In the hallway there was the sound of footsteps and George Willard came in at the door. Sitting in a chair beside his mother he began to talk. "I'm going to get out of here," he said. "I don't know where I shall go or what I shall do but I am going away."

The woman in the chair waited and trembled. An impulse came to her. "I suppose you had better wake up," she said. "You think that? You will go to the city and make money, eh? It will be better for you, you think, to be a business man, to be brisk and smart and alive?" She waited and trembled.

The son shook his head. "I suppose I can't make you understand, but oh, I wish I could," he said earnestly. "I can't even talk to father about it. I don't try. There isn't any use. I don't know what I shall do. I just want to go away and look at people and think."

Silence fell upon the room where the boy and woman sat together. Again, as on the other evenings, they were embarrassed. After a time the boy tried again to talk. "I suppose it won't be for a year or two but I've been thinking about it," he said, rising and going toward the door. "Something father said makes it sure that I shall have to go away." He fumbled with the door knob. In the room

Concerning Elizabeth Willard

the silence became unbearable to the woman. She wanted to cry out with joy because of the words that had come from the lips of her son, but the expression of joy had become impossible to her. "I think you had better go out among the boys. You are too much indoors," she said. "I thought I would go for a little walk," replied the son stepping awkwardly out of the room and closing the door.

THE PHILOSOPHER

Concerning Doctor Parcival

DOCTOR PARCIVAL was a large man with a drooping mouth covered by a yellow mustache. He always wore a dirty white waistcoat out of the pockets of which protruded a number of the kind of black cigars known as stogies. His teeth were black and irregular and there was something strange about his eyes. The lid of the left eye twitched; it fell down and snapped up; it was exactly as though the lid of the eye were a window shade and someone stood inside the doctor's head playing with the cord.

Doctor Parcival had a liking for the boy George Willard. It began when George had been working for a year on the *Winesburg Eagle* and the acquaintanceship was entirely a matter of the doctor's own making.

In the late afternoon Will Henderson, owner and editor of the *Eagle*, went over to Tom Willy's Saloon. Along an alleyway he went and slipping in at the back door of the saloon began drinking a drink made of a combina-

boy *ed* < boy,

Saloon *ed* < saloon

The Philosopher

tion of sloe gin and soda water. Will Henderson was a sensualist and had reached the age of forty-five. He imagined the gin renewed the youth in him. Like most sensualists he enjoyed talking of women, and for an hour he lingered about gossiping with Tom Willy. The saloon keeper was a short broad-shouldered man with peculiarly marked hands. That flaming kind of birth mark that sometimes paints with red the faces of men and women had touched with red Tom Willy's fingers and the backs of his hands. As he stood by the bar talking to Will Henderson he rubbed the hands together. As he grew more and more excited the red of his fingers deepened. It was as though the hands had been dipped in blood that had dried and faded.

short *ms* < short,
(birth mark *ed* < birthmark

As Will Henderson stood at the bar looking at the red hands and talking of women, his assistant, George Willard, sat in the office of the *Winesburg Eagle* and listened to the talk of Doctor Parcival.

Anderson based the Willy saloon on the Louis Hock Saloon, at 103 North Main Street, in Clyde.

Doctor Parcival appeared immediately after Will Henderson had disappeared. One might have supposed that the doctor had been watching from his office window and had seen the editor going along the alleyway. Coming in at the front door and finding himself a chair he lighted one of the stogies and crossing his legs began to talk. He seemed intent upon convincing the boy of the advisability of adopting a line of conduct that he was himself unable to define.

chair *ms* < chair,

"If you have your eyes open you will see that although I call myself a doctor I have mighty few patients," he began. "There is a reason for that. It is not an accident and it is not because I do not know as much of medicine as anyone here. I do not want patients. The reason, you see, does not appear on the surface. It lies in fact in my character, which has, if you think about it, many

Concerning Doctor Parcival

strange turns. Why I want to talk to you of the matter I don't know. I might keep still and get more credit in your eyes. I have a desire to make you admire me, that's a fact. I don't know why. That's why I talk. It's very amusing, eh?"

Sometimes the doctor launched into long tales concerning himself. To the boy the tales were very real and full of meaning. He began to admire the fat unclean-looking man and, in the afternoon when Will Henderson had gone, looked forward with keen interest to the doctor's coming.

Doctor Parcival had been in Winesburg about five years. He came from Chicago and when he arrived was drunk and got into a fight with Albert Longworth, the baggage man. The fight concerned a trunk and ended by the doctor's being escorted to the village lockup. When he was released he rented a room above a shoe-repairing shop at the lower end of Main Street and put out the sign that announced himself as a doctor. Although he had but few patients and these of the poorer sort who were unable to pay, he seemed to have plenty of money for his needs. He slept in the office that was unspeakably dirty and dined at Biff Carter's Lunch Room in a small frame building opposite the railroad station. In the summer the lunch room was filled with flies and Biff Carter's white apron was more dirty than his floor. Doctor Parcival did not mind. Into the lunch room he stalked and deposited twenty cents upon the counter. "Feed me what you wish for that," he said laughing. "Use up food that you wouldn't otherwise sell. It makes no difference to me. I am a man of distinction, you see. Why should I concern myself with what I eat."

The tales that Doctor Parcival told George Willard began nowhere and ended nowhere. Sometimes the boy

baggage man *ed*
< baggageman

The actual baggage man of Clyde, Ohio, known to Anderson was Jerry Donlin, dead when the author revisited the town while writing the Winesburg tales.

Lunch Room *ed*
< lunch room

Biff Carter's Lunch Room is located where Mrs. Henry Baker's Restaurant and Bakery stood, at 109 Railroad Street, in Clyde.

The Philosopher

thought they must all be inventions, a pack of lies. And then again he was convinced that they contained the very essence of truth.

"I was a reporter, like you here," Doctor Parcival began. "It was in a town in Iowa—or was it in Illinois? I don't remember and anyway it makes no difference. Perhaps I am trying to conceal my identity and don't want to be very definite. Have you never thought it strange that I have money for my needs although I do nothing? I may have stolen a great sum of money or been involved in a murder before I came here. There is food for thought in that, eh? If you were a really smart newspaper reporter you would look me up. In Chicago there was a Doctor Cronin who was murdered. Have you heard of that? Some men murdered him and put him in a trunk. In the early morning they hauled the trunk across the city. It sat on the back of an express wagon and they were on the seat as unconcerned as anything. Along they went through quiet streets where everyone was asleep. The sun was just coming up over the lake. Funny, eh—just to think of them smoking pipes and chattering as they drove along as unconcerned as I am now. Perhaps I was one of those men. That would be a strange turn of things, now wouldn't it, eh?" Again Doctor Parcival began his tale. "Well, anyway there I was, a reporter on a paper just as you are here, running about and getting little items to print. My mother was poor. She took in washing. Her dream was to make me a Presbyterian minister and I was studying with that end in view.

"My father had been insane for a number of years. He was in an asylum over at Dayton, Ohio. There, you see, I have let it slip out. All of this took place in Ohio, right here in Ohio. There is a clue if you ever get the notion of looking me up.

reporter, *ms* < reporter

never *ms* < ever

Dr. Patrick Cronin of Chicago, associated with one of the Irish immigrant clans or secret societies, was killed in May, 1889, by members of a rival clan; one suspect in his murder escaped from Chicago before trial could be held.

tale. *ms* < tale:

(There, you see,
  ed < There you see
out. *ms* < out!
clue *ed* < clew

Concerning Doctor Parcival

"I was going to tell you of my brother. That's the object of all this. That's what I'm getting at. My brother was a railroad painter and had a job on the Big Four. You know that road runs through Ohio here. With other men he lived in a box car and away they went from town to town painting the railroad property—switches, crossing gates, bridges and stations.

"The Big Four paints its stations a nasty orange color. How I hated that color! My brother was always covered with it. On pay days he used to get drunk and come home wearing his paint-covered clothes and bringing his money with him. He did not give it to mother but laid it in a pile on our kitchen table.

"About the house he went in the clothes covered with the nasty orange colored paint. I can see the picture. My mother, who was small and had red, sad-looking eyes, would come into the house from a little shed at the back. That's where she spent her time over the wash tub scrubbing people's dirty clothes. In she would come and stand by the table, rubbing her eyes with her apron that was covered with soap suds.

"'Don't touch it! Don't you dare touch that money,' my brother roared and then he himself took five or ten dollars and went tramping off to the saloons. When he had spent what he had taken he came back for more. He never gave my mother any money at all but stayed about until he had spent it all, a little at a time. Then he went back to his job with the painting crew on the railroad. After he had gone things began to arrive at our house, groceries and such things. Sometimes there would be a dress for mother or a pair of shoes for me.

"Strange, eh? My mother loved my brother much more than she did me, although he never said a kind word to either of us and always raved up and down threatening

bridges ms < bridges,

The late-nineteenth-century Vanderbilt railroad holdings included the Big Four Railroads, made up of systems that served Cleveland and Cincinnati, Ohio; Chicago, Illinois; and St. Louis, Missouri.

wash tub *ed* < washtub

soap suds *ed* < soap-suds

roared *ms* < roared,

Anderson often wrote about his long-suffering and emotionally exhausted mother, Emma Smith Anderson, who did take in washing for residents of Clyde, Ohio . . . and to whom he dedicated his Winesburg stories.

The Philosopher

lay *ms, Pr 5–Pr 7* < laid

us if we dared so much as touch the money that sometimes lay on the table three days.

"We got along pretty well. I studied to be a minister and prayed. I was a regular ass about saying prayers. You should have heard me. When my father died I prayed all night, just as I did sometimes when my brother was in town drinking and going about buying the things for us. In the evening after supper I knelt by the table where the money lay and prayed for hours. When no one was looking I stole a dollar or two and put it in my pocket. That makes me laugh now but then it was terrible. It was on my mind all the time. I got six dollars a week from my job on the paper and always took it straight home to mother. The few dollars I stole from my brother's pile I spent on myself, you know, for trifles, candy and cigarettes and such things.

"When my father died at the asylum over at Dayton, I went over there. I borrowed some money from the man for whom I worked and went on the train at night. It was raining. In the asylum they treated me as though I were a king.

"The men who had jobs in the asylum had found out I was a newspaper reporter. That made them afraid. There had been some negligence, some carelessness, you see, when father was ill. They thought perhaps I would write it up in the paper and make a fuss. I never intended to do anything of the kind.

"Anyway, in I went to the room where my father lay dead and blessed the dead body. I wonder what put that notion into my head. Wouldn't my brother, the painter, have laughed, though. There I stood over the dead body and spread out my hands. The superintendent of the asylum and some of his helpers came in and stood about

The impetuous but good-hearted older Reefy brother is probably based on "Mac," a young baker of Clyde, Ohio, who worked steadily to save money for an occasional debauch, after which he returned to bakery work and, later, railroad labor.

Concerning Doctor Parcival

looking sheepish. It was very amusing. I spread out my hands and said, 'Let peace brood over this carcass.' That's what I said."

Jumping to his feet and breaking off the tale, Doctor Parcival began to walk up and down in the office of the *Winesburg Eagle* where George Willard sat listening. He was awkward and, as the office was small, continually knocked against things. "What a fool I am to be talking," he said. "That is not my object in coming here and forcing my acquaintanceship upon you. I have something else in mind. You are a reporter just as I was once and you have attracted my attention. You may end by becoming just such another fool. I want to warn you and keep on warning you. That's why I seek you out."

Doctor Parcival began talking of George Willard's attitude toward men. It seemed to the boy that the man had but one object in view, to make everyone seem despicable. "I want to fill you with hatred and contempt so that you will be a superior being," he declared. "Look at my brother. There was a fellow, eh? He despised everyone, you see. You have no idea with what contempt he looked upon mother and me. And was he not our superior? You know he was. You have not seen him and yet I have made you feel that. I have given you a sense of it. He is dead. Once when he was drunk he lay down on the tracks and the car in which he lived with the other painters ran over him."

———

One day in August Doctor Parcival had an adventure in Winesburg. For a month George Willard had been going each morning to spend an hour in the doctor's office. The visits came about through a desire on the part of the doctor to read to the boy from the pages of a

The Philosopher

book he was in the process of writing. To write the book Doctor Parcival declared was the object of his coming to Winesburg to live.

On the morning in August, before the coming of the boy, an incident had happened in the doctor's office. There had been an accident on Main Street. A team of horses had been frightened by a train and had run away. A little girl, the daughter of a farmer, had been thrown from a buggy and killed.

On Main Street everyone had become excited and a cry for doctors had gone up. All three of the active practitioners of the town had come quickly but had found the child dead. From the crowd someone had run to the office of Doctor Parcival who had bluntly refused to go down out of his office to the dead child. The useless cruelty of his refusal had passed unnoticed. Indeed, the man who had come up the stairway to summon him had hurried away without hearing the refusal.

All of this Doctor Parcival did not know and when George Willard came to his office he found the man shaking with terror. "What I have done will arouse the people of this town," he declared excitedly. "Do I not know human nature? Do I not know what will happen? Word of my refusal will be whispered about. Presently men will get together in groups and talk of it. They will come here. We will quarrel and there will be talk of hanging. Then they will come again bearing a rope in their hands."

Doctor Parcival shook with fright. "I have a presentiment," he declared emphatically. "It may be that what I am talking about will not occur this morning. It may be put off until tonight but I will be hanged. Everyone will get excited. I will be hanged to a lamp post on Main Street."

August, *ed* < August

In Clyde, Ohio, Main Street runs north and south and is divided by East Buckeye Street and West Buckeye Street.

this *ms* < this,

tonight *ms* < to-night

(**lamp post** *ms* < lamp-post

Page from the Manuscript.
"The Book of the Grotesque."

Page from the Manuscript.
"Loneliness."

Page from the Manuscript.
"The Strength of God"

Page from the Manuscript.
"Departure"

Clyde, Ohio. Waterworks Pond.

Clyde, Ohio. Railroad Station.

Sherwood Anderson.
Author of *Winesburg, Ohio.*

Sherwood Anderson.
Youth in Clyde, Ohio.

(right)
Clyde, Ohio.
Presbyterian Church.

(below)
Clyde, Ohio.
Empire House Hotel.

Clyde, Ohio. Drawn as Winesburg by Thad Hurd.

Map by Harald Toksvig for the First Edition.

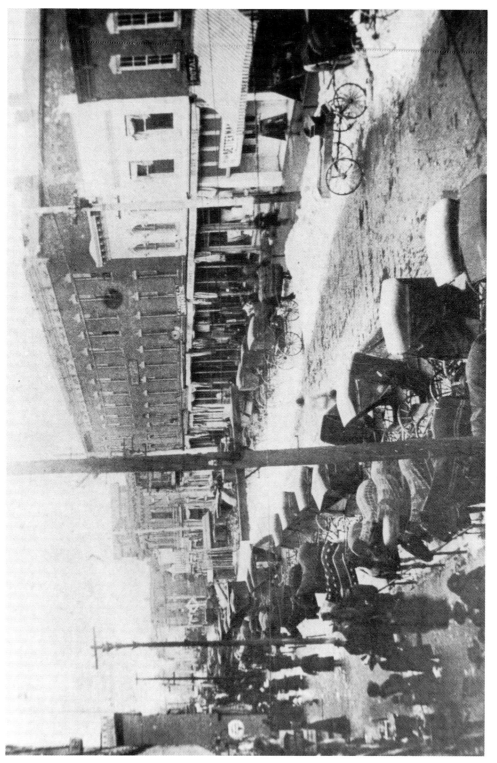

Clyde, Ohio. Main Street in Winter.

Concerning Doctor Parcival

Going to the door of his dirty little office, Doctor Parcival looked timidly down the stairway leading to the street. When he returned the fright that had been in his eyes was beginning to be replaced by doubt. Coming on tiptoe across the room he tapped George Willard on the shoulder. "If not now, sometime," he whispered, shaking his head. "In the end I will be crucified, uselessly crucified."

Doctor Parcival began to plead with George Willard. "You must pay attention to me," he urged. "If something happens perhaps you will be able to write the book that I may never get written. The idea is very simple, so simple that if you are not careful you will forget it. It is this—that everyone in the world is Christ and they are all crucified. That's what I want to say. Don't you forget that. Whatever happens, don't you dare let yourself forget."

tiptoe *ed* < tip-toe

NOBODY KNOWS

Concerning Louise Trunnion

LOOKING CAUTIOUSLY about, George Willard arose from his desk in the office of the *Winesburg Eagle* and went hurriedly out at the back door. The night was warm and cloudy and although it was not yet eight o'clock the alleyway back of the *Eagle* office was pitch dark. A team of horses tied to a post somewhere in the darkness stamped on the hard-baked ground. A cat sprang from under George Willard's feet and

o'clock *ms* < o'clock,

Nobody Knows

ran away into the night. The young man was nervous. All day he had gone about his work like one dazed by a blow. In the alleyway he trembled as though with fright.

In the darkness George Willard walked along the alleyway, going carefully and cautiously. The back doors of the Winesburg stores were open and he could see men sitting about under the store lamps. In Myerbaum's Notion Store Mrs. Willy, the saloon keeper's wife, stood by the counter with a basket on her arm. Sid Green, the clerk, was waiting on her. He leaned over the counter and talked earnestly.

George Willard crouched and then jumped through the path of light that came out at the door. He began to run forward in the darkness. Behind Ed Griffith's Saloon old Jerry Bird, the town drunkard, lay asleep on the ground. The runner stumbled over the sprawling legs. He laughed brokenly.

George Willard had set forth upon an adventure. All day he had been trying to make up his mind to go through with the adventure and now he was acting. In the office of the *Winesburg Eagle* he had been sitting since six o'clock trying to think.

There had been no decision. He had just jumped to his feet, hurried past Will Henderson who was reading proof in the print shop and started to run along the alleyway.

Through street after street went George Willard, avoiding the people who passed. He crossed and recrossed the road. When he passed a street lamp he pulled his hat down over his face. He did not dare think. In his mind there was a fear but it was a new kind of fear. He was afraid the adventure on which he had set out would be spoiled, that he would lose courage and turn back.

Similar to a dry-goods store, a "notion" store sold textile and decorative items not related to groceries or machinery.

Mrs. Willy, *ed* < Willy
wife, *ed* < wife
Green, *ed* < Green
clerk, *ed* < clerk

Saloon *ed* < saloon
Bird, *ed* < Bird
drunkard, *ed* < drunkard

Ed Griffith's Saloon is based on John Surbeck's Saloon, at 103 South Main Street in Clyde.

In Clyde, Ohio, the office of the Clyde Enterprise *was on the second floor of 101 North Main Street, above the Jackson Hardware Store.*

Concerning Louise Trunnion

George Willard found Louise Trunnion in the kitchen of her father's house. She was washing dishes by the light of a kerosene lamp. There she stood behind the screen door in the little shed-like kitchen at the back of the house. George Willard stopped by a picket fence and tried to control the shaking of his body. Only a narrow potato patch separated him from the adventure. Five minutes passed before he felt sure enough of himself to call to her. "Louise! Oh Louise!" he called. The cry stuck in his throat. His voice became a hoarse whisper.

Louise Trunnion, resident of the poorer district of Winesburg, is not related to the dignitary for whom Trunion Pike, a major Winesburg area thoroughfare, is named.

Louise Trunnion came out across the potato patch holding the dish cloth in her hand. "How do you know I want to go out with you?" she said sulkily. "What makes you so sure?"

you? *ms* < you,

George Willard did not answer. In silence the two stood in the darkness with the fence between them. "You go on along," she said. "Pa's in there. I'll come along. You wait by Williams' barn."

Williams' *ed* < William's

The young newspaper reporter had received a letter from Louise Trunnion. It had come that morning to the office of the *Winesburg Eagle*. The letter was brief. "I'm yours if you want me," it said. He thought it annoying that in the darkness by the fence she had pretended there was nothing between them. "She has a nerve. Well, gracious sakes, she has a nerve," he muttered as he went along the street and passed a row of vacant lots where corn grew. The corn was shoulder high and had been planted right down to the sidewalk.

nerve. *ms* < nerve!

This adventure may be based on the author's memory of a young but experienced girl from Castalia, Ohio, visiting Clyde and seducing the youthful Sherwood Anderson in perhaps his first sexual adventure.

When Louise Trunnion came out of the front door of her house she still wore the gingham dress in which she had been washing dishes. There was no hat on her head. The boy could see her standing with the door knob in her hand talking to someone within, no doubt to old

door knob *ed* < doorknob

Nobody Knows

Jake Trunnion, her father. Old Jake was half deaf and she shouted. The door closed and everything was dark and silent in the little side street. George Willard trembled more violently than ever.

In the shadows by Williams' barn George and Louise stood, not daring to talk. She was not particularly comely and there was a black smudge on the side of her nose. George thought she must have rubbed her nose with her finger after she had been handling some of the kitchen pots.

The young man began to laugh nervously. "It's warm," he said. He wanted to touch her with his hand. "I'm not very bold," he thought. Just to touch the folds of the soiled gingham dress would, he decided, be an exquisite pleasure. She began to quibble. "You think you're better than I am. Don't tell me, I guess I know," she said drawing closer to him.

A flood of words burst from George Willard. He remembered the look that had lurked in the girl's eyes when they had met on the streets and thought of the note she had written. Doubt left him. The whispered tales concerning her that had gone about town gave him confidence. He became wholly the male, bold and aggressive. In his heart there was no sympathy for her. "Ah, come on, it'll be all right. There won't be anyone know anything. How can they know?" he urged.

They began to walk along a narrow brick sidewalk between the cracks of which tall weeds grew. Some of the bricks were missing and the sidewalk was rough and irregular. He took hold of her hand that was also rough and thought it delightfully small. "I can't go far," she said and her voice was quiet, unperturbed.

They crossed a bridge that ran over a tiny stream and passed another vacant lot in which corn grew. The street

Williams' *ed* < William's

Concerning Louise Trunnion

ended. In the path at the side of the road they were compelled to walk one behind the other. Will Overton's berry field lay beside the road and there was a pile of boards. "Will is going to build a shed to store berry crates here," said George and they sat down upon the boards.

When George Willard got back into Main Street it was past ten o'clock and had begun to rain. Three times he walked up and down the length of Main Street. Sylvester West's Drug Store was still open and he went in and bought a cigar. When Shorty Crandall, the clerk, came out at the door with him he was pleased. For five minutes the two stood in the shelter of the store awning and talked. George Willard felt satisfied. He had wanted more than anything else to talk to some man. Around a corner toward the New Willard House he went whistling softly.

On the sidewalk at the side of Winney's Dry Goods Store where there was a high board fence covered with circus pictures he stopped whistling and stood perfectly still in the darkness, attentive, listening as though for a voice calling his name. Then again he laughed nervously. "She hasn't got anything on me. Nobody knows," he muttered doggedly and went on his way.

Crandall, the clerk, *ed* < Crandall the clerk

West's Drug Store is located where the H. H. Rabe Drug Store stood in Clyde, at 107 North Main Street. Winney's Dry Goods Store is (con't below)

Winney's *ed* < Winny's

pictures *ms* < pictures,

based on the Henry ("Penny") Weissert Notion Store, at 111 North Main Street, in Clyde.

GODLINESS—A TALE IN FOUR PARTS

PART ONE

Concerning Jesse Bentley

THERE WERE ALWAYS three or four old people sitting on the front porch of the house or puttering about the garden of the Bentley farm. Three of the old people were women and sisters to Jesse. They were a colorless, soft-voiced lot. Then there was a silent old man with thin white hair who was Jesse's uncle.

The farm house was built of wood, a board outer-covering over a framework of logs. It was in reality not one house but a cluster of houses joined together in a rather haphazard manner. Inside, the place was full of surprises. One went up steps from the living room into the dining room and there were always steps to be ascended or descended in passing from one room to another. At meal times the place was like a beehive. At one moment all was quiet, then doors began to open, feet clattered on stairs, a murmur of soft voices arose and people appeared from a dozen obscure corners.

Besides the old people, already mentioned, many others lived in the Bentley house. There were four hired men, a woman named Aunt Callie Beebe, who was in charge of the house keeping, a dull-witted girl named

farm house *ms*
< farmhouse

The fictional Bentley farm is based on the William E. Lay farm of Anderson's youth, three miles south of Clyde. Jesse's name may come from that of Jesse Benton, the first white settler in the area, who by 1820 had built a cabin near the later Spring Avenue in Clyde.

Besides *ed* < Beside

house keeping *ed*
< housekeeping

Concerning Jesse Bentley

Eliza Stoughton, who made beds and helped with the milking, a boy who worked in the stables, and Jesse Bentley himself, the owner and overlord of it all.

By the time the American Civil War had been over for twenty years that part of Northern Ohio where the Bentley farms lay had begun to emerge from pioneer life. Jesse then owned machinery for harvesting grain. He had built modern barns and most of his land was drained with carefully laid tile drain, but in order to understand the man we will have to go back to an earlier day.

The Bentley family had been in Northern Ohio for several generations before Jesse's time. They came from New York State and took up land when the country was new and land could be had at a low price. For a long time they, in common with all the other Middle Western people, were very poor. The land they had settled upon was heavily wooded and covered with fallen logs and underbrush. After the long hard labor of clearing these away and cutting the timber, there were still the stumps to be reckoned with. Plows run through the fields caught on hidden roots, stones lay all about, on the low places water gathered and the young corn turned yellow, sickened and died.

When Jesse Bentley's father and brothers had come into their ownership of the place, much of the harder part of the work of clearing had been done, but they clung to old traditions and worked like driven animals. They lived as practically all of the farming people of the time lived. In the spring and through most of the winter the highways leading into the town of Winesburg were a sea of mud. The four young men of the family worked hard all day in the fields, they ate heavily of coarse greasy food, and at night slept like tired beasts on beds

years ms < years,

Originally "black swamp" land, flooded several months of each year, the Clyde area became agriculturally rich only when settlers learned to tile and drain the flood-prone soil.

gathered ms < gathered,

coarse ms < coarse,

Godliness, Part One

of straw. Into their lives came little that was not coarse and brutal and outwardly they were themselves coarse and brutal. On Saturday afternoon they hitched a team of horses to a three-seated wagon and went off to town. In town they stood about the stoves in the stores talking to other farmers or to the store keepers. They were dressed in overalls and in the winter wore heavy coats that were flecked with mud. Their hands as they stretched them out to the heat of the stoves were cracked and red. It was difficult for them to talk and so they for the most part kept silent. When they had bought meat, flour, sugar and salt, they went into one of the Winesburg saloons and drank beer. Under the influence of drink the naturally strong lusts of their natures, kept suppressed by the heroic labor of breaking up new ground, were released. A kind of crude and animal-like poetic fervor took possession of them. On the road home they stood up on the wagon seats and shouted at the stars. Sometimes they fought long and bitterly and at other times they broke forth into songs. Once Enoch Bentley, the oldest one of the boys, struck his father, old Tom Bentley, with the butt of a teamster's whip and the old man seemed likely to die. For days Enoch lay hid in the straw in the loft of the stable ready to flee if the result of his momentary passion turned out to be murder. He was kept alive with food brought by his mother who also kept him informed of the injured man's condition. When all turned out well he emerged from his hiding place and went back to the work of clearing land as though nothing had happened.

The Civil War brought a sharp turn to the fortunes of the Bentleys and was responsible for the rise of the youngest son, Jesse. Enoch, Edward, Harry, and Will

afternoon *ms* < afternoons

sugar *ms* < sugar,

oldest *ed* < older

whip *ms* < whip,

Concerning Jesse Bentley

Bentley all enlisted and before the long war ended they were all killed. For a time after they went away to the south old Tom tried to run the place but he was not successful. When the last of the four had been killed he sent word to Jesse that he would have to come home.

south *ed* < South
south *ms* < South,
place *ms* < place,

Then the mother, who had not been well for a year, died suddenly and the father became altogether discouraged. He talked of selling the farm and moving into town. All day he went about shaking his head and muttering. The work in the fields was neglected and weeds grew high in the corn. Old Tom hired men but he did not use them intelligently. When they had gone away to the fields in the morning he wandered into the woods and sat down on a log. Sometimes he forgot to come home at night and one of the daughters had to go in search of him.

suddenly *ms* < suddenly,

When Jesse Bentley came home to the farm and began to take charge of things he was a slight, sensitive-looking man of twenty-two. At eighteen he had left home to go to school to become a scholar and eventually to become a minister of the Presbyterian Church. All through his boyhood he had been what in our country was called an "odd sheep" and had not got on with his brothers. Of all the family only his mother had understood him and she was now dead. When he came home to take charge of the farm that had at that time grown to more than six hundred acres, everyone on the farms about and in the nearby town of Winesburg smiled at the idea of his trying to handle the work that had been done by his four strong brothers.

farm *ms* < farm,

There was indeed good cause to smile. By the standards of his day Jesse did not look like a man at all. He was small and very slender and womanish of body and, true to the traditions of young ministers, wore a long

Godliness, Part One

black coat and a narrow black string tie. The neighbors were amused when they saw him, after the years away, and they were even more amused when they saw the woman he had married in the city.

As a matter of fact Jesse's wife did soon go under. That was perhaps Jesse's fault. A farm in Northern Ohio in the hard years after the Civil War was no place for a delicate woman, and Katherine Bentley was delicate. Jesse was hard with her as he was with everybody about him in those days. She tried to do such work as all the neighbor women about her did and he let her go on without interference. She helped to do the milking and did part of the housework; she made the beds for the men and prepared their food. For a year she worked every day from sunrise until late at night and then after giving birth to a child she died.

As for Jesse Bentley—although he was a delicately built man there was something within him that could not easily be killed. He had brown curly hair and grey eyes that were at times hard and direct, at times wavering and uncertain. Not only was he slender but he was also short of stature. His mouth was like the mouth of a sensitive and very determined child. Jesse Bentley was a fanatic. He was a man born out of his time and place and for this he suffered and made others suffer. Never did he succeed in getting what he wanted out of life and he did not know what he wanted. Within a very short time after he came home to the Bentley farm he made everyone there a little afraid of him, and his wife, who should have been close to him as his mother had been, was afraid also. At the end of two weeks after his coming, old Tom Bentley made over to him the entire ownership of the place and retired into the background.

fact *ms* < fact,

Concerning Jesse Bentley

Everyone retired into the background. In spite of his youth and inexperience, Jesse had the trick of mastering the souls of his people. He was so in earnest in everything he did and said that no one understood him. He made everyone on the farm work as they had never worked before and yet there was no joy in the work. If things went well they went well for Jesse and never for the people who were his dependents. Like a thousand other strong men who have come into the world here in America in these later times, Jesse was but half strong. He could master others but he could not master himself. The running of the farm as it had never been run before was easy for him. When he came home from Cleveland where he had been in school he shut himself off from all of his people and began to make plans. He thought about the farm night and day and that made him successful. Other men on the farms about him worked too hard and were too tired to think, but to think of the farm and to be everlastingly making plans for its success was a relief to Jesse. It partially satisfied something in his passionate nature. Immediately after he came home he had a wing built onto the old house and in a large room facing the west he had windows that looked into the barn yard and other windows that looked off across the fields. By the window he sat down to think. Hour after hour and day after day he sat and looked over the land and thought out his new place in life. The passionate burning thing in his nature flamed up and his eyes became hard. He wanted to make the farm produce as no farm in his state had ever produced before and then he wanted something else. It was the indefinable hunger within that made his eyes waver and that kept him always more and more silent before people.

school *ms* < school,

onto *ed* < on to

barn yard *ed* < barnyard

Godliness, Part One

He would have given much to achieve peace and in him was a fear that peace was the thing he could not achieve.

All over his body Jesse Bentley was alive. In his small frame was gathered the force of a long line of strong men. He had always been extraordinarily alive when he was a small boy on the farm and later when he was a young man in school. In the school he had studied and thought of God and the bible with his whole mind and heart. As time passed and he grew to know people better he began to think of himself as an extraordinary man, one set apart from his fellows. He wanted terribly to make his life a thing of great importance, and as he looked about at his fellow men and saw how like clods they lived it seemed to him that he could not bear to become also such a clod. Although in his absorption in himself and in his own destiny he was blind to the fact that his young wife was doing a strong woman's work even after she had become large with child and that she was killing herself in his service, he did not intend to be unkind to her. When his father, who was old and twisted with toil, made over to him the ownership of the farm and seemed content to creep away to a corner and wait for death, he shrugged his shoulders and dismissed the old man from his mind.

In the room by the window overlooking the land that had come down to him sat Jesse thinking of his own affairs. In the stables he could hear the tramping of his horses and the restless movement of his cattle. Away in the fields he could see other cattle wandering over green hills. The voices of men, his men who worked for him, came in to him through the window. From the milk house there was the steady thump, thump of a churn being manipulated by the half witted girl, Eliza Stoughton. Jesse's mind went back to the men of Old

bible *ed* < Bible
better *ms* < better,

half *ed* < half-

Concerning Jesse Bentley

Testament days who had also owned lands and herds. He remembered how God had come down out of the skies and talked to these men and he wanted God to notice and to talk to him also. A kind of feverish boyish eagerness to in some way achieve in his own life the flavor of significance that had hung over these men took possession of him. Being a prayerful man he spoke of the matter aloud to God and the sound of his own words strengthened and fed his eagerness.

"I am a new kind of man come into possession of these fields," he declared. "Look upon me, oh God, and look thou also upon my neighbors and all the men who have gone before me here. Oh God, create in me another Jesse, like that one of old, to rule over men and to be the father of sons who shall be rulers!" Jesse grew excited as he talked aloud and jumping to his feet walked up and down in the room. In fancy he saw himself living in old times and among old peoples. The land that lay stretched out before him became of vast significance, a place peopled by his fancy with a new race of men sprung from himself. It seemed to him that in his day, as in those other and older days, kingdoms might be created and new impulses given to the lives of men by the power of God speaking through a chosen servant. He longed to be such a servant. "It is God's work I have come to the land to do," he declared in a loud voice and his short figure straightened and he thought that something like a halo of godly approval hung over him.

oh *ed* < O
thou *ed* < Thou
here. *ms* < here!
Oh *ed* < O

Jesse fathered David, who became champion warrior and monarch of the Hebrews. (See 1 Samuel 16.)

day, *ed* < day

godly *ed* < Godly

———————

It will perhaps be somewhat difficult for the men and women of a later day to understand Jesse Bentley. In the last fifty years a vast change has taken place in the lives of our people. A revolution has in fact taken place. The coming of industrialism, attended by all the roar and

Godliness, Part One

overseas *ed* < over seas

(farm houses *ed*
< farmhouses
(automobile *ms*
< automobiles

child-like *ed* < childlike

vague *ms* < vague,
half *ed* < half-

rattle of affairs, the shrill cries of millions of new voices that have come among us from overseas, the going and coming of trains, the growth of cities, the building of the interurban car lines that weave in and out of towns and past farm houses, and now in these later days the coming of the automobile has worked a tremendous change in the lives and in the habits of thought of our people of Mid-America. Books, badly imagined and written though they may be in the hurry of our times, are in every household, magazines circulate by the millions of copies, newspapers are everywhere. In our day a farmer standing by the stove in the store in his village has his mind filled to overflowing with the words of other men. The newspapers and the magazines have pumped him full. Much of the old brutal ignorance that had in it also a kind of beautiful child-like innocence is gone forever. The farmer by the stove is brother to the men of the cities, and if you listen you will find him talking as glibly and as senselessly as the best city man of us all.

In Jesse Bentley's time and in the country districts of the whole Middle West in the years after the Civil War it was not so. Men labored too hard and were too tired to read. In them was no desire for words printed upon paper. As they worked in the fields, vague half formed thoughts took possession of them. They believed in God and in God's power to control their lives. In the little Protestant churches they gathered on Sunday to hear of God and his works. The churches were the center of the social and intellectual life of the times. The figure of God was big in the hearts of men.

And so, having been born an imaginative child and having within him a great intellectual eagerness, Jesse

Concerning Jesse Bentley

Bentley had turned wholeheartedly toward God. When the war took his brothers away, he saw the hand of God in that. When his father became ill and could no longer attend to the running of the farm, he took that also as a sign from God. In the city, when the word came to him, he walked about at night through the streets thinking of the matter and, when he had come home and had got the work on the farm well under way, he went again at night to walk through the forests and over the low hills and to think of God.

As he walked the importance of his own figure in some divine plan grew in his mind. He grew avaricious and was impatient that the farm contained only six hundred acres. Kneeling in a fence corner at the edge of some meadow, he sent his voice abroad into the silence and looking up he saw the stars shining down at him.

One evening, some months after his father's death, and when his wife Katherine was expecting at any moment to be laid abed of childbirth, Jesse left his house and went for a long walk. The Bentley farm was situated in a tiny valley watered by Wine Creek and Jesse walked along the bank of the stream to the end of his own land and on through the fields of his neighbors. As he walked the valley broadened and then narrowed again. Great open stretches of fields and woods lay before him. The moon came out from behind clouds, and, climbing a low hill, he sat down to think.

Jesse thought that as the true servant of God the entire stretch of country through which he had walked should have come into his possession. He thought of his dead brothers and blamed them that they had not worked harder and achieved more. Before him in the moonlight the tiny stream ran down over stones, and

and, *ed* < and

Creek *ms* < Creek, (
bank *ms* < banks

(fields and woods *ms*
(< field and wood

Godliness, Part One

he began to think of the men of old times who like himself had owned flocks and lands.

A fantastic impulse, half fear, half greediness, took possession of Jesse Bentley. He remembered how in the old bible story the Lord had appeared to that other Jesse and told him to send his son David to where Saul and the men of Israel were fighting the Philistines in the Valley of Elah. Into Jesse's mind came the conviction that all of the Ohio farmers who owned land in the valley of Wine Creek were Philistines and enemies of God. "Suppose," he whispered to himself, "there should come from among them one who, like Goliath the Philistine of Gath, could defeat me and take from me my possessions." In fancy he felt the sickening dread that he thought must have lain heavy on the heart of Saul before the coming of David. Jumping to his feet, he began to run through the night. As he ran he called to God. His voice carried far over the low hills. "Jehovah of Hosts," he cried, "send to me this night out of the womb of Katherine a son. Let thy grace alight upon me. Send me a son to be called David who shall help me to pluck at last all of these lands out of the hands of the Philistines and turn them to thy service and to the building of thy kingdom on earth."

PART TWO

Concerning Jesse Bentley

DAVID HARDY OF Winesburg, Ohio, was the grandson of Jesse Bentley, the owner of Bentley farms. When he was twelve years old he went to the old Bentley place to live. His mother, Louise Bentley, the girl who came into the world on that night when Jesse ran through the

---

greediness, *ed* < greediness

bible *ed* < Bible

Saul, the first king of Old Testament Israel, was summoned by the prophet Samuel to battle the enemy Philistines in the Valley of Elah for control of central Israel. (See 1 Samuel 9–29.) Jesse sent his youngest son, David, who would much later (con't below)

lain *ms, Pr 5–Pr 7* < laid

become king of Israel, to lead Israelite forces under Saul to conquer the enemy Philistines.

Katherine *ms* < Katherine,

thy *ed* < Thy
thy *ed* < Thy

Ohio, *ed* < Ohio

Concerning Jesse Bentley

fields crying to God that he be given a son, had grown to womanhood on the farm and had married young John Hardy of Winesburg who became a banker. Louise and her husband did not live happily together and everyone agreed that she was to blame. She was a small woman with sharp grey eyes and black hair. From childhood she had been inclined to fits of temper and when not angry she was often morose and silent. In Winesburg it was said that she drank. Her husband, the banker, who was a careful shrewd man, tried hard to make her happy. When he began to make money he bought for her a large brick house on Elm Street in Winesburg and he was the first man in that town to keep a manservant to drive his wife's carriage.

careful *ms* < careful,

Elm Street in Winesburg is based on East Forest Street in Clyde; and Banker White's house is based on Clyde's Rader family house, at 117 East Forest Street.

But Louise could not be made happy. She flew into half insane fits of temper during which she was sometimes silent, sometimes noisy and quarrelsome. She swore and cried out in her anger. She got a knife from the kitchen and threatened her husband's life. Once she deliberately set fire to the house, and often she hid herself away for days in her own room and would see no one. Her life, lived as a half recluse, gave rise to all sorts of stories concerning her. It was said that she took drugs and that she hid herself away from people because she was often so under the influence of drink that her condition could not be concealed. Sometimes on summer afternoons she came out of the house and got into her carriage. Dismissing the driver she took the reins in her own hands and drove off at top speed through the streets. If a pedestrian got in her way she drove straight ahead and the frightened citizen had to escape as best he could. To the people of the town it seemed as though she wanted to run them down. When she had driven through several streets, tearing around corners and beat-

Godliness, Part Two

ing the horses with the whip, she drove off into the country. On the country roads after she had gotten out of sight of the houses she let the horses slow down to a walk and her wild, reckless mood passed. She became thoughtful and muttered words. Sometimes tears came into her eyes. And then when she came back into town she again drove furiously through the quiet streets. But for the influence of her husband and the respect he inspired in people's minds she would have been arrested more than once by the town marshal.

Young David Hardy grew up in the house with this woman and as can well be imagined there was not much joy in his childhood. He was too young then to have opinions of his own about people, but at times it was difficult for him not to have very definite opinions about the woman who was his mother. David was always a quiet orderly boy and for a long time was thought by the people of Winesburg to be something of a dullard. His eyes were brown and as a child he had a habit of looking at things and people a long time without appearing to see what he was looking at. When he heard his mother spoken of harshly or when he overheard her berating his father, he was frightened and ran away to hide. Sometimes he could not find a hiding place and that confused him. Turning his face toward a tree or if he were indoors toward the wall, he closed his eyes and tried not to think of anything. He had a habit of talking aloud to himself, and early in life a spirit of quiet sadness often took possession of him.

On the occasions when David went to visit his grandfather on the Bentley farm, he was altogether contented and happy. Often he wished that he would never have to go back to town and once, when he had come home from the farm after a long visit, something happened that had a lasting effect on his mind.

David had come back into town with one of the hired

once, *ms* < once

Concerning Jesse Bentley

men. The man was in a hurry to go about his own affairs and left the boy at the head of the street in which the Hardy house stood. It was early dusk of a fall evening and the sky was overcast with clouds. Something happened to David. He could not bear to go into the house where his mother and father lived, and on an impulse he decided to run away from home. He intended to go back to the farm and to his grandfather, but lost his way and for hours he wandered weeping and frightened on country roads. It started to rain and lightning flashed in the sky. The boy's imagination was excited and he fancied that he could see and hear strange things in the darkness. Into his mind came the conviction that he was walking and running in some terrible void where no one had ever been before. The darkness about him seemed limitless. The sound of the wind blowing in trees was terrifying. When a team of horses approached along the road in which he walked he was frightened and climbed a fence. Through a field he ran until he came into another road and getting upon his knees felt of the soft ground with his fingers. But for the figure of his grandfather, whom he was afraid he would never find in the darkness, he thought the world must be altogether empty. When his cries were heard by a farmer who was walking home from town and he was brought back to his father's house, he was so tired and excited that he did not know what was happening to him.

By chance David's father knew that he had disappeared. On the street he had met the farm hand from the Bentley place and knew of his son's return to town. When the boy did not come home an alarm was set up and John Hardy, with several men of the town, went to search the country. The report that David had been kidnapped ran about through the streets of Winesburg. When he came home there were no lights in the house, but his mother appeared and clutched him eagerly in

Hardy, *ms* < Hardy town, *ed* < town

Godliness, Part Two

her arms. David thought she had suddenly become another woman. He could not believe that so delightful a
thing had happened. With her own hands Louise Hardy
bathed his tired young body and cooked him food. She
would not let him go to bed but, when he had put on
his night gown, blew out the lights and sat down in a
chair to hold him in her arms. For an hour the woman
sat in the darkness and held her boy. All the time she
kept talking in a low voice. David could not understand
what had so changed her. Her habitually dissatisfied face
had become, he thought, the most peaceful and lovely
thing he had ever seen. When he began to weep she
held him more and more tightly. On and on went her
voice. It was not harsh or shrill as when she talked to
her husband, but was like rain falling on trees. Presently
men began coming to the door to report that he had
not been found, but she made him hide and be silent
until she had sent them away. He thought it must be a
game his mother and the men of the town were playing
with him and laughed joyously. Into his mind came the
thought that his having been lost and frightened in the
darkness was an altogether unimportant matter. He
thought that he would have been willing to go through
the frightful experience a thousand times to be sure of
finding at the end of the long black road a thing so lovely
as his mother had suddenly become.

*(night gown ed
< nightgown*

During the last years of young David's boyhood he
saw his mother but seldom and she became for him just
a woman with whom he had once lived. Still he could
not get her figure out of his mind and as he grew older
it became more definite. When he was twelve years old

Concerning Jesse Bentley

he went to the Bentley farm to live. Old Jesse came into town and fairly demanded that he be given charge of the boy. The old man was excited and determined on having his own way. He talked to John Hardy in the office of the Winesburg Savings Bank and then the two men went to the house on Elm Street to talk with Louise. They both expected her to make trouble but were mistaken. She was very quiet and, when Jesse had explained his mission and had gone on at some length about the advantages to come through having the boy out of doors and in the quiet atmosphere of the old farm house, she nodded her head in approval. "It is an atmosphere not corrupted by my presence," she said sharply. Her shoulders shook and she seemed about to fly into a fit of temper. "It is a place for a man child, although it was never a place for me," she went on. "You never wanted me there and of course the air of your house did me no good. It was like poison in my blood but it will be different with him."

Louise turned and went out of the room leaving the two men to sit in embarrassed silence. As very often happened she later stayed in her room for days. Even when the boy's clothes were packed and he was taken away she did not appear. The loss of her son made a sharp break in her life and she seemed less inclined to quarrel with her husband. John Hardy thought it had all turned out very well indeed.

And so young David went to live in the Bentley farm house with Jesse. Two of the old farmer's sisters were alive and still lived in the house. They were afraid of Jesse and rarely spoke when he was about. One of the women who had been noted for her flaming red hair when she was younger was a born mother and became the boy's caretaker. Every night when he had gone to

In Clyde, the People's Banking Company (later the Clyde Savings Bank) was located on the first floor of 106 South Main Street.

and, *ms* < and

(farm house *ed*
  < farmhouse

room *ms* < room,

(farm house *ed*
  < farmhouse

Godliness, Part Two

bed she went into his room and sat on the floor until he fell asleep. When he became drowsy she became bold and whispered things that he later thought he must have dreamed.

Her soft low voice called him endearing names and he dreamed that his mother had come to him and that she had changed so that she was always as she had been that time after he ran away. He also grew bold and reaching out his hand stroked the face of the woman on the floor so that she was ecstatically happy. Everyone in the old house became happy after the boy went there. The hard insistent thing in Jesse Bentley that had kept the people in the house silent and timid and that had never been dispelled by the presence of the girl Louise was apparently swept away by the coming of the boy. It was as though God had relented and sent a son to the man.

The man who had proclaimed himself the only true servant of God in all the valley of Wine Creek and who had wanted God to send him a sign of approval by way of a son out of the womb of Katherine began to think that at last his prayers had been answered. Although he was at that time only fifty-five years old he looked seventy and was worn out with much thinking and scheming. The efforts he had made to extend his land holdings had been successful and there were few farms in the valley that did not belong to him, but until David came he was a bitterly disappointed man.

There were two influences at work in Jesse Bentley and all his life his mind had been a battle ground for these influences. First there was the old thing in him. He wanted to be a man of God and a leader among men of God. His walking in the fields and through the forests at night had brought him close to nature and there were forces in the passionately religious man that

Creek *ms* < Creek,

(Katherine *ed*
< Katherine,

efforts *ms* < effort

(battle ground *ed*
< battleground

Concerning Jesse Bentley

ran out to the forces in nature. The disappointment that had come to him when a daughter and not a son had been born to Katherine had fallen upon him like a blow struck by some unseen hand and the blow had somewhat softened his egotism. He still believed that God might at any moment make himself manifest out of the winds or the clouds, but he no longer demanded such recognition. Instead he prayed for it. Sometimes he was altogether doubtful and thought God had deserted the world. He regretted the fate that had not let him live in a simpler and sweeter time when at the beckoning of some strange cloud in the sky men left their lands and houses and went forth into the wilderness to create new races. While he worked night and day to make his farms more productive and to extend his holdings of land, he regretted that he could not use his own restless energy in the building of temples, the slaying of unbelievers and in general in the work of glorifying God's name on earth.

That is what Jesse hungered for and then also he hungered for something else. He had grown into maturity in America in the years after the Civil War and he, like all men of his time, had been touched by the deep influences that were at work in the country during those years when modern industrialism was being born. He began to buy machines that would permit him to do the work of the farms while employing fewer men and he sometimes thought that if he were a younger man he would give up farming altogether and start a factory in Winesburg for the making of machinery. Jesse formed the habit of reading newspapers and magazines. He invented a machine for the making of fence out of wire. Faintly he realized that the atmosphere of old times and places that he had always cultivated in his own mind

Godliness, Part Two

Anderson might have based Jesse Bentley partly on Joseph F. Glidden (1813–1906) of DeKalb, Illinois, who owned amounts of land similar to Bentley's and who did patent a barbed-wire machine.

son-in-law, *ms*
< son-in-law
Hardy, *ms* < Hardy

was strange and foreign to the thing that was growing up in the minds of others. The beginning of the most materialistic age in the history of the world, when wars would be fought without patriotism, when men would forget God and only pay attention to moral standards, when the will to power would replace the will to serve and beauty would be well-nigh forgotten in the terrible headlong rush of mankind toward the acquiring of possessions, was telling its story to Jesse the man of God as it was to the men about him. The greedy thing in him wanted to make money faster than it could be made by tilling the land. More than once he went into Winesburg to talk with his son-in-law, John Hardy, about it. "You are a banker and you will have chances I never had," he said and his eyes shone. "I am thinking about it all the time. Big things are going to be done in the country and there will be more money to be made than I ever dreamed of. You get into it. I wish I were younger and had your chance." Jesse Bentley walked up and down in the bank office and grew more and more excited as he talked. At one time in his life he had been threatened with paralysis and his left side remained somewhat weakened. As he talked his left eyelid twitched. Later when he drove back home and when night came on and the stars came out it was harder to get back the old feeling of a close and personal God who lived in the sky overhead and who might at any moment reach out his hand, touch him on the shoulder, and appoint for him some heroic task to be done. Jesse's mind was fixed upon the things read in newspapers and magazines, on fortunes to be made almost without effort by shrewd men who bought and sold. For him the coming of the boy David did much to bring back with renewed force the old faith

Concerning Jesse Bentley

and it seemed to him that God had at last looked with favor upon him.

As for the boy on the farm, life began to reveal itself to him in a thousand new and delightful ways. The kindly attitude of all about him expanded his quiet nature and he lost the half timid, hesitating manner he had always had with his people. At night when he went to bed after a long day of adventures in the stables, in the fields, or driving about from farm to farm with his grandfather he wanted to embrace everyone in the house. If Sherley Bentley, the woman who came each night to sit on the floor by his bedside, did not appear at once, he went to the head of the stairs and shouted, his young voice ringing through the narrow halls where for so long there had been a tradition of silence. In the morning when he awoke and lay still in bed, the sounds that came in to him through the windows filled him with delight. He thought with a shudder of the life in the house in Winesburg and of his mother's angry voice that had always made him tremble. There in the country all sounds were pleasant sounds. When he awoke at dawn the barn yard back of the house also awoke. In the house people stirred about. Eliza Stoughton, the half witted girl, was poked in the ribs by a farm hand and giggled noisily, in some distant field a cow bawled and was answered by the cattle in the stables, and one of the farm hands spoke sharply to the horse he was grooming by the stable door. David leaped out of bed and ran to a window. All of the people stirring about excited his mind, and he wondered what his mother was doing in the house in town.

From the window of his own room he could not see directly into the barn yard where the farm hands had now all assembled to do the morning chores, but he

barn yard *ed* < barnyard

(Stoughton, *ed*
 < Stoughton
half *ms* < half-
girl, *ed* < girl

window *ms* < windows
(barn yard *ms*
 < barnyard

Godliness, Part Two

could hear the voices of the men and the neighing of the horses. When one of the men laughed, he laughed also. Leaning out at the open window, he looked into an orchard where a fat sow wandered about with a litter of tiny pigs at her heels. Every morning he counted the pigs. "Four, five, six, seven," he said slowly, wetting his finger and making straight up and down marks on the window ledge. David ran to put on his trousers and shirt. A feverish desire to get out of doors took possession of him. Every morning he made such a noise coming downstairs that Aunt Callie, the house keeper, declared he was trying to tear the house down. When he had run through the long old house, shutting doors behind him with a bang, he came into the barn yard and looked about with an amazed air of expectancy. It seemed to him that in such a place tremendous things might have happened during the night. The farm hands looked at him and laughed. Henry Strader, an old man who had been on the farm since Jesse came into possession and who before David's time had never been known to make a joke, made the same joke every morning. It amused David so that he laughed and clapped his hands. "See, come here and look," cried the old man, "Grandfather Jesse's white mare has torn the black stocking she wears on her foot."

Day after day through the long summer Jesse Bentley drove from farm to farm up and down the valley of Wine Creek, and his grandson went with him. They rode in a comfortable old phaeton drawn by the white horse. The old man scratched his thin white beard and talked to himself of his plans for increasing the productiveness of the fields they visited and of God's part in the plans all men made. Sometimes he looked at David and smiled happily and then for a long time he appeared to forget

(downstairs *ed* < down stairs
Callie *ed* < Sallie
(house keeper *ed* < housekeeper
(barn yard *ed* < barnyard

summer *ms* < summer,

A "phaeton" is a light-duty horse-drawn four-wheeled carriage, usually topless and fitted with two forward-facing seats.

Concerning Jesse Bentley

the boy's existence. More and more every day now his mind turned back again to the dreams that had filled his mind when he had first come out of the city to live on the land. One afternoon he startled David by letting his dreams take entire possession of him. With the boy as a witness, he went through a ceremony and brought about an accident that nearly destroyed the companionship that was growing up between them.

Jesse and his grandson were driving in a distant part of the valley some miles from home. A forest came down to the road and through the forest Wine Creek wriggled its way over stones toward a distant river. All the afternoon Jesse had been in a meditative mood and now he began to talk. His mind went back to the night when he had been frightened by thoughts of a giant that might come to rob and plunder him of his possessions, and again, as on that night when he had run through the fields crying for a son, he became excited to the edge of insanity. Stopping the horse he got out of the buggy and asked David to get out also. The two climbed over a fence and walked along the bank of the stream. The boy paid no attention to the muttering of his grandfather, but ran along beside him and wondered what was going to happen. When a rabbit jumped up and ran away through the woods, he clapped his hands and danced with delight. He looked at the tall trees and was sorry that he was not a little animal to climb high in the air without being frightened. Stooping, he picked up a small stone and threw it over the head of his grandfather into a clump of bushes. "Wake up, little animals. Go and climb to the top of the trees," he shouted in a shrill voice.

Jesse Bentley went along under the trees with his head bowed and with his mind in a ferment. His earnestness

The fictional Wine Creek resembles Raccoon Creek, which flows from the south through west Clyde, into Waterworks Pond.

again, *ed* < again

animals *ms* < animal

head *ms* < bead

Godliness, Part Two

affected the boy who presently became silent and a little alarmed. Into the old man's mind had come the notion that now he could bring from God a word or a sign out of the sky, that the presence of the boy and man on their knees in some lonely spot in the forest would make the miracle he had been waiting for almost inevitable. "It was in just such a place as this that other David tended the sheep when his father came and told him to go down unto Saul," he muttered.

Taking the boy rather roughly by the shoulder, he climbed over a fallen log and, when he had come to an open place among the trees, he dropped upon his knees and began to pray in a loud voice.

A kind of terror he had never known before took possession of David. Crouching beneath a tree he watched the man on the ground before him and his own knees began to tremble. It seemed to him that he was in the presence not only of his grandfather, but of someone else, someone who might hurt him, someone who was not kindly but dangerous and brutal. He began to cry and reaching down picked up a small stick which he held tightly gripped in his fingers. When Jesse Bentley, absorbed in his own idea, suddenly arose and advanced toward him, his terror grew until his whole body shook. In the woods an intense silence seemed to lie over everything and suddenly out of the silence came the old man's harsh and insistent voice. Gripping the boy's shoulders, Jesse turned his face to the sky and shouted. The whole left side of his face twitched and his hand on the boy's shoulder twitched also. "Make a sign to me, God," he cried, "here I stand with the boy David. Come down to me out of the sky and make thy presence known to me."

and, *ed* < and

presence *ed* < presence,
(grandfather, *ms*
< grandfather

lie *ms, Pr 2–Pr 7* < lay

thy *ed* < Thy

Concerning Jesse Bentley

With a cry of fear David turned and, shaking himself loose from the hands that held him, ran away through the forest. He did not believe that the man who turned up his face and in a harsh voice shouted at the sky was his grandfather at all. The man did not look like his grandfather. The conviction that something strange and terrible had happened, that by some miracle a new and dangerous person had come into the body of the kindly old man, took possession of him. On and on he ran down the hillside sobbing as he ran. When he fell over the roots of a tree and in falling struck his head, he arose and tried to run on again. His head hurt so that presently he fell down and lay still, but it was only after Jesse had carried him to the buggy and he awoke to find the old man's hand stroking his head tenderly that the terror left him. "Take me away. There is a terrible man back there in the woods," he declared firmly while Jesse looked away over the tops of the trees and again his lips cried out to God. "What have I done that thou dost not approve of me," he whispered softly, saying the words over and over as he drove rapidly along the road with the boy's cut and bleeding head held tenderly against his shoulder.

fear *ms* < fear,
and, *ed* < and

sky *ed* < sky,

man, *ed* < man

tenderly *ed* < tenderly,

firmly *ms* < firmly,

thou *ed* < Thou
dost *ed* < doest

PART THREE—SURRENDER

Concerning Louise Bentley

THE STORY OF Louise Bentley, who became Mrs. John Hardy and lived with her husband in a brick house on Elm Street in Winesburg, is a story of misunderstanding.

Before such women as Louise can be understood and their lives made livable, much will have to be done. Thoughtful books will have to be written and thoughtful lives lived by people about them.

mother *ed* < mother,
father *ms* < father,
world *ms* < world,
⎧ oversensitive *ed*
⎩ < over-sensitive

Born of a delicate and overworked mother and an impulsive, hard, imaginative father who did not look with favor upon her coming into the world Louise was from childhood a neurotic, one of the race of oversensitive women that in later days industrialism was to bring in such great numbers into the world.

During her early years she lived on the Bentley farm, a silent, moody child, wanting love more than anything else in the world and not getting it. When she was fifteen she went to live in Winesburg with the family of Albert Hardy who had a store for the sale of buggies and wagons, and who was a member of the town board of education.

Louise went into town to be a student in the

Concerning Louise Bentley

Winesburg High School and she went to live at the Hardys' because Albert Hardy and her father were friends.

Hardy, the vehicle merchant of Winesburg, like thousands of other men of his times, was an enthusiast on the subject of education. He had made his own way in the world without learning got from books but he was convinced that had he but known books things would have gone better with him. To everyone who came into his shop he talked of the matter, and in his own household he drove his family distracted by his constant harping on the subject.

He had two daughters and one son, John Hardy, and more than once the daughters threatened to leave school altogether. As a matter of principle they did just enough work in their classes to avoid punishment. "I hate books and I hate anyone who likes books," Harriet, the younger of the two girls, declared passionately.

In Winesburg as on the farm Louise was not happy. For years she had dreamed of the time when she could go forth into the world, and she looked upon the move into the Hardy household as a great step in the direction of freedom. Always when she had thought of the matter it had seemed to her that in town all must be gaiety and life, that there men and women must live happily and freely giving and taking friendship and affection as one takes the feel of a wind on the cheek. After the silence and the cheerlessness of life in the Bentley house, she dreamed of stepping forth into an atmosphere that was warm and pulsating with life and reality. And in the Hardy household Louise might have got something of the thing for which she so hungered but for a mistake she made when she had just come to town.

Louise won the disfavor of the two Hardy girls, Mary

Hardys' *ed* < Hardy's
The Union (High) School was constructed at 521 Vine Street, in Clyde, Ohio, in 1870.

books *ms* < books,

matter *ms* < matter,

freely *ms* < freely,

Godliness, Part Three

and Harriet, by her application to her studies in school. She did not come to the house until the day when school was to begin and knew nothing of the feeling they had in the matter. She was timid and during the first month made no acquaintances. Every Friday afternoon one of the hired men from the farm drove into Winesburg and took her home for the week-end, so that she did not spend the Saturday holiday with the townspeople. Because she was embarrassed and lonely she worked constantly at her studies. To Mary and Harriet, it seemed as though she tried to make trouble for them by her proficiency. In her eagerness to appear well Louise wanted to answer every question put to the class by the teacher. She jumped up and down and her eyes flashed. Then, when she had answered some question the others in the class had been unable to answer, she smiled happily. "See, I have done it for you," her eyes seemed to say. "You need not bother about the matter. I will answer all questions. For the whole class it will be easy while I am here."

In the evening, after supper in the Hardy house, Albert Hardy began to praise Louise. One of the teachers had spoken highly of her and he was delighted. "Well, again I have heard of it," he began, looking hard at his daughters and then turning to smile at Louise. "Another of the teachers has told me of the good work Louise is doing. Everyone in Winesburg is telling me how smart she is. I am ashamed that they do not speak so of my own girls." Arising, the merchant marched about the room and lighted his evening cigar.

The two girls looked at each other and shook their heads wearily. Seeing their indifference the father became angry. "I tell you it is something for you two to be thinking about," he cried, glaring at them. "There is a

townspeople *ed* < town people

Then, *ed* < Then

evening, *ed* < evening

Concerning Louise Bentley

big change coming here in America and in learning is the only hope of the coming generations. Louise is the daughter of a rich man but she is not ashamed to study. It should make you ashamed to see what she does."

The merchant took his hat from a rack by the door and prepared to depart for the evening. At the door he stopped and glared back. So fierce was his manner that Louise was frightened and ran upstairs to her own room. The daughters began to speak of their own affairs. "Pay attention to me," roared the merchant. "Your minds are lazy. Your indifference to education is affecting your characters. You will amount to nothing. Now mark what I say—Louise will be so far ahead of you that you will never catch up."

The distracted man went out of the house and into the street shaking with wrath. He went along muttering words and swearing but when he got into Main Street *swearing ms < swearing,* his anger passed. He stopped to talk of the weather or the crops with some other merchant or with a farmer who had come into town and forgot his daughters altogether or, if he thought of them, only shrugged his shoulders. "Oh, well, girls will be girls," he muttered philosophically.

In the house, when Louise came down into the room *house, ed < house* where the two girls sat, they would have nothing to do with her. One evening, after she had been there for more *evening, ed < evening* than six weeks and was heartbroken because of the continued air of coldness with which she was always greeted, she burst into tears. "Shut up your crying and go back to your own room and to your books," Mary Hardy said sharply.

———————

The room occupied by Louise was on the second floor of the Hardy house, and her window looked out upon

Godliness, Part Three

an orchard. There was a stove in the room and every evening young John Hardy carried up an armful of wood and put it in a box that stood by the wall. During the second month after she came to the house Louise gave up all hope of getting on a friendly footing with the Hardy girls and went to her own room as soon as the evening meal was at an end.

Her mind began to play with thoughts of making friends with John Hardy. When he came into the room with the wood in his arms, she pretended to be busy with her studies but watched him eagerly. When he had put the wood in the box and turned to go out, she put down her head and blushed. She tried to make talk but could say nothing, and after he had gone she was angry at herself for her stupidity.

The mind of the country girl became filled with the idea of drawing close to the young man. She thought that in him might be found the quality she had all her life been seeking in people. It seemed to her that, between herself and all the other people in the world, a wall had been built up and that she was living just on the edge of some warm inner circle of life that must be quite open and understandable to others. She became obsessed with the thought that it wanted but a courageous act on her part to make all of her associations with people something quite different, and that it was possible by such an act to pass into a new life as one opens a door and goes into a room. Day and night she thought of the matter, but although the thing she wanted so earnestly was something very warm and close it had as yet no conscious connection with sex. It had not become that definite, and her mind had only alighted upon the person of John Hardy because he was at hand and unlike his sisters had not been unfriendly to her.

house *ms* < house,

that, *ed* < that

(associations *ms*
(< association

Concerning Louise Bentley

The Hardy sisters, Mary and Harriet, were both older than Louise. In a certain kind of knowledge of the world they were years older. They lived as all of the young women of Middle Western towns lived. In those days young women did not go out of our towns to eastern colleges and ideas in regard to social classes had hardly begun to exist. A daughter of a laborer was in much the same social position as a daughter of a farmer or a merchant, and there were no leisure classes. A girl was "nice" or she was "not nice." If a nice girl she had a young man who came to her house to see her on Sunday and on Wednesday evenings. Sometimes she went with her young man to a dance or a church social. At other times she received him at the house and was given the use of the parlor for that purpose. No one intruded upon her. For hours the two sat behind closed doors. Sometimes the lights were turned low and the young man and woman embraced. Cheeks became hot and hair disarranged. After a year or two, if the impulse within them became strong and insistent enough, they married.

One evening during her first winter in Winesburg, Louise had an adventure that gave a new impulse to her desire to break down the wall that she thought stood between her and John Hardy. It was Wednesday and immediately after the evening meal Albert Hardy put on his hat and went away. Young John brought the wood and put it in the box in Louise's room. "You do work hard, don't you?" he said awkwardly, and then, before she could answer, he also went away.

Louise heard him go out of the house and had a mad desire to run after him. Opening her window she leaned out and called softly. "John, dear John, come back, don't go away." The night was cloudy and she could not see far into the darkness, but as she waited she fancied she

girl *ms* < girl,

(the young *ms, Pr 2–*
  Pr 7 < young

then, *ed* < then
answer, *ms* < answer

Godliness, Part Three

could hear a soft little noise as of someone going on tiptoe through the trees in the orchard. She was frightened and closed the window quickly. For an hour she moved about the room trembling with excitement and when she could no longer bear the waiting, she crept into the hall and down the stairs into a closet-like room that opened off the parlor.

Louise had decided that she would perform the courageous act that had for weeks been in her mind. She was convinced that John Hardy had concealed himself in the orchard beneath her window and she was determined to find him and tell him that she wanted him to come close to her, to hold her in his arms, to tell her of his thoughts and dreams and to listen while she told him her thoughts and dreams. "In the darkness it will be easier to say things," she whispered to herself, as she stood in the little room groping for the door.

And then suddenly Louise realized that she was not alone in the house. In the parlor on the other side of the door a man's voice spoke softly and the door opened. Louise just had time to conceal herself in a little opening beneath the stairway when Mary Hardy, accompanied by her young man, came into the little dark room.

For an hour Louise sat on the floor in the darkness and listened. Without words Mary Hardy, with the aid of the man who had come to spend the evening with her, brought to the country girl a knowledge of men and women. Putting her head down until she was curled into a little ball she lay perfectly still. It seemed to her that, by some strange impulse of the gods, a great gift had been brought to Mary Hardy and she could not understand the older woman's determined protest.

The young man took Mary Hardy into his arms and kissed her. When she struggled and laughed, he but held

tiptoe *ed* < tiptoes

no *ms* < not

that, *ed* < that

Concerning Louise Bentley

her the more tightly. For an hour the contest between them went on and then they went back into the parlor and Louise escaped up the stairs. "I hope you were quiet out there. You must not disturb the little mouse at her studies," she heard Harriet saying to her sister as she stood by her own door in the hallway above.

Louise wrote a note to John Hardy and late that night, when all in the house were asleep, she crept downstairs and slipped it under his door. She was afraid that if she did not do the thing at once her courage would fail. In the note she tried to be quite definite about what she wanted. "I want someone to love me and I want to love someone," she wrote. "If you are the one for me I want you to come into the orchard at night and make a noise under my window. It will be easy for me to crawl down over the shed and come to you. I am thinking about it all the time, so if you are to come at all you must come soon."

For a long time Louise did not know what would be the outcome of her bold attempt to secure for herself a lover. In a way she still did not know whether or not she wanted him to come. Sometimes it seemed to her that to be held tightly and kissed was the whole secret of life and then a new impulse came and she was terribly afraid. The age-old woman's desire to be possessed had taken possession of her but so vague was her notion of life that it seemed to her just the touch of John Hardy's hand upon her own hand would satisfy. She wondered if he would understand that. At the table next day, while Albert Hardy talked and the two girls whispered and laughed, she did not look at John but at the table and as soon as possible escaped. In the evening she went out of the house until she was sure he had taken the wood to her room and gone away. When after several evenings

night, *ed* < night

life *ms* < life,

her *ms* < her,

day, *ed* < day

Godliness, Part Three

of intense listening she heard no call from the darkness in the orchard, she was half beside herself with grief and decided that for her there was no way to break through the wall that had shut her off from the joy of life.

And then on a Monday evening, two or three weeks after the writing of the note, John Hardy came for her. Louise had so entirely given up the thought of his coming that for a long time she did not hear the call that came up from the orchard. On the Friday evening before, as she was being driven back to the farm for the week-end by one of the hired men, she had on an impulse done a thing that had startled her, and, as John Hardy stood in the darkness below and called her name softly and insistently, she walked about in her room and wondered what new impulse had led her to commit so ridiculous an act.

The farm hand, a young fellow with black curly hair, had come for her somewhat late on that Friday evening and they drove home in the darkness. Louise, whose mind was filled with thoughts of John Hardy, tried to make talk but the country boy was embarrassed and would say nothing. Her mind began to review the loneliness of her childhood and she remembered with a pang the sharp new loneliness that had just come to her. "I hate everyone," she cried suddenly, and then broke forth into a tirade that frightened her escort. "I hate father and old man Hardy too," she declared vehemently. "I get my lessons there in the school in town but I hate that also."

Louise frightened the farm hand still more by turning and putting her cheek down upon his shoulder. Vaguely she hoped that he like that young man who had stood in the darkness with Mary would put his arms about her and kiss her, but the country boy was only alarmed.

evening, *ed* < evening

and, *ed* < and

Hardy *ms* < Hardy,

Concerning Louise Bentley

He struck the horse with the whip and began to whistle. "The road is rough, eh?" he said loudly. Louise was so angry that reaching up she snatched his hat from his head and threw it into the road. When he jumped out of the buggy and went to get it, she drove off and left him to walk the rest of the way back to the farm.

Louise Bentley took John Hardy to be her lover. That was not what she wanted but it was so the young man had interpreted her approach to him, and so anxious was she to achieve something else that she made no resistance. When after a few months they were both afraid that she was about to become a mother, they went one evening to the county seat and were married. For a few months they lived in the Hardy house and then took a house of their own. All during the first year Louise tried to make her husband understand the vague and intangible hunger that had led to the writing of the note and that was still unsatisfied. Again and again she crept into his arms and tried to talk of it, but always without success. Filled with his own notions of love between men and women, he did not listen but began to kiss her upon the lips. That confused her so that in the end she did not want to be kissed. She did not know what she wanted.

When the alarm that had tricked them into marriage proved to be groundless, she was angry and said bitter, hurtful things. Later, when her son David was born, she could not nurse him and did not know whether she wanted him or not. Sometimes she stayed in the room with him all day, walking about and occasionally creeping close to touch him tenderly with her hands, and then other days came when she did not want to see or be near the tiny bit of humanity that had come into the house. When John Hardy reproached her for her cru-

Anderson never in Winesburg *names his fictional county or its county seat; but the county seat for Clyde, in Sandusky County, Ohio, is Fremont, eight miles east of Clyde on the McPherson Highway, named thus in honor of General James B. McPherson (1828–1864), Clyde native, killed near Atlanta in the Civil War.*

Later, *ed* < Later

Godliness, Part Three

elty, she laughed. "It is a man child and will get what it wants anyway," she said sharply. "Had it been a woman child there is nothing in the world I would not have done for it."

PART FOUR—TERROR

Concerning David Hardy

WHEN DAVID HARDY was a tall boy of fifteen, he, like his mother, had an adventure that changed the whole current of his life and sent him out of his quiet corner into the world. The shell of the circumstances of his life was broken and he was compelled to start forth. He left Winesburg and no one there ever saw him again. After his disappearance, his mother and grandfather both died and his father became very rich. He spent much money in trying to locate his son, but that is no part of this story.

It was in the late fall of an unusual year on the Bentley farms. Everywhere the crops had been heavy. That spring, Jesse had bought part of a long strip of black swamp land that lay in the valley of Wine Creek. He got the land at a low price but had spent a large sum of money to improve it. Great ditches had to be dug and thousands of tile laid. Neighboring farmers shook their heads over the expense. Some of them laughed and hoped that Jesse would lose heavily by the venture, but the old man went silently on with the work and said nothing.

When the land was drained he planted it to cabbages and onions, and again the neighbors laughed. The crop was, however, enormous and brought high prices. In

In the 1890s, Clyde, Ohio, boasted of being the location of the Clyde Kraut Plant, then the largest in the nation.

Concerning David Hardy

the one year Jesse made enough money to pay for all the cost of preparing the land and had a surplus that enabled him to buy two more farms. He was exultant and could not conceal his delight. For the first time in all the history of his ownership of the farms he went among his men with a smiling face.

farms *ms* < farms,

Jesse bought a great many new machines for cutting down the cost of labor and all of the remaining acres in the strip of black fertile swamp land. One day he went into Winesburg and bought a bicycle and a new suit of clothes for David and he gave his two sisters money with which to go to a religious convention at Cleveland, Ohio.

In the fall of that year, when the frost came and the trees in the forests along Wine Creek were golden brown, David spent every moment, when he did not have to attend school, out in the open. Alone or with other boys he went every afternoon into the woods to gather nuts. The other boys of the countryside, most of them sons of laborers on the Bentley farms, had guns with which they went hunting rabbits and squirrels, but David did not go with them. He made himself a sling with rubber bands and a forked stick and went off by himself to gather nuts. As he went about thoughts came to him. He realized that he was almost a man and wondered what he would do in life but, before they came to anything, the thoughts passed and he was a boy again. One day he killed a squirrel that sat on one of the lower branches of a tree and chattered at him. Home he ran with the squirrel in his hand. One of the Bentley sisters cooked the little animal and he ate it with great gusto. The skin he tacked on a board and suspended the board by a string from his bedroom window.

year, *ed* < year

moment, *ed* < moment

life *ms* < life,
but, *ms* < but

That gave his mind a new turn. After that he never went into the woods without carrying the sling in his

Godliness, Part Four

pocket and he spent hours shooting at imaginary animals concealed among the brown leaves in the trees. Thoughts of his coming manhood passed and he was content to be a boy with a boy's impulses.

One Saturday morning, when he was about to set off for the woods with the sling in his pocket and a bag for nuts on his shoulder, his grandfather stopped him. In the eyes of the old man was the strained serious look that always a little frightened David. At such times Jesse Bentley's eyes did not look straight ahead but wavered and seemed to be looking at nothing. Something like an invisible curtain appeared to have come between the man and all the rest of the world. "I want you to come with me," he said briefly and his eyes looked over the boy's head into the sky. "We have something important to do today. You may bring the bag for nuts if you wish. It does not matter and anyway we will be going into the woods."

Jesse and David set out from the Bentley farm house in the old phaeton that was drawn by the white horse. When they had gone along in silence for a long way they stopped at the edge of a field where a flock of sheep were grazing. Among the sheep was a lamb that had been born out of season, and this David and his grandfather caught and tied so tightly that it looked like a little white ball. When they drove on again Jesse let David hold the lamb in his arms. "I saw it yesterday and it put me in mind of what I have long wanted to do," he said, and again he looked away over the head of the boy with the wavering, uncertain stare in his eyes.

After the feeling of exaltation that had come to the farmer as a result of his successful year, another mood had taken possession of him. For a long time he had

morning, *ed* < morning

briefly *ms* < briefly,

today *ms* < to-day

(farm house *ed* < farmhouse

Because lambs are usually born in late winter or early spring and grow rapidly to become sheep, this lamb had to be born untimely in summer or early autumn to remain of suitable small size and young age for sacrifice.

Concerning David Hardy

been going about feeling very humble and prayerful. Again he walked alone at night thinking of God and as he walked he again connected his own figure with the figures of old days. Under the stars he knelt on the wet grass and raised up his voice in prayer. Now he had decided that, like the men whose stories filled the pages of the bible, he would make a sacrifice to God. "I have been given these abundant crops and God has also sent me a boy who is called David," he whispered to himself. "Perhaps I should have done this thing long ago." He was sorry the idea had not come into his mind in the days before his daughter Louise had been born and thought that surely now, when he had erected a pile of burning sticks in some lonely place in the woods and had offered the body of a lamb as a burnt offering, God would appear to him and give him a message.

that, *ed* < that
bible *ed* < Bible

now, *ed* < now

More and more as he thought of the matter he thought also of David and his passionate self love was partially forgotten. "It is time for the boy to begin thinking of going out into the world and the message will be one concerning him," he decided. "God will make a pathway for him. He will tell me what place David is to take in life and when he shall set out on his journey. It is right that the boy should be there. If I am fortunate and an angel of God should appear, David will see the beauty and glory of God made manifest to man. It will make a true man of God of him also."

matter *ms* < matter,

In silence Jesse and David drove along the road until they came to that place where Jesse had once before appealed to God and had frightened his grandson. The morning had been bright and cheerful, but a cold wind now began to blow and clouds hid the sun. When David saw the place to which they had come he began to

Godliness, Part Four

tremble with fright, and, when they stopped by the bridge where the creek came down from among the trees, he wanted to spring out of the phaeton and run away.

A dozen plans for escape ran through David's head, but when Jesse stopped the horse and climbed over the fence into the woods he followed. "It is foolish to be afraid. Nothing will happen," he told himself as he went along with the lamb in his arms. There was something in the helplessness of the little animal, held so tightly in his arms, that gave him courage. He could feel the rapid beating of the beast's heart and that made his own heart beat less rapidly. As he walked swiftly along behind his grandfather, he untied the string with which the four legs of the lamb were fastened together. "If anything happens we will run away together," he thought.

In the woods, after they had gone a long way from the road, Jesse stopped in an opening among the trees where a clearing, overgrown with small bushes, ran up from the creek. He was still silent but began at once to erect a heap of dry sticks which he presently set afire. The boy sat on the ground with the lamb in his arms. His imagination began to invest every movement of the old man with significance and he became every moment more afraid. "I must put the blood of the lamb on the head of the boy," Jesse muttered when the sticks had begun to blaze greedily, and taking a long knife from his pocket he turned and walked rapidly across the clearing toward David.

Terror seized upon the soul of the boy. He was sick with it. For a moment he sat perfectly still and then his body stiffened and he sprang to his feet. His face became as white as the fleece of the lamb that, now finding itself suddenly released, ran down the hill. David ran also. Fear made his feet fly. Over the low bushes and

woods *ed* < wood
woods *ms* < wood,

arms, *ed* < arms

Abraham, patriarch of the Israelites, was willing to kill his son Isaac to demonstrate his faith in God; Abraham's faith tested satisfactorily, God provided in time an animal to substitute for Isaac in the ceremony. (See Genesis 22.)

lamb *ed* < lamb,
that, *ed* < that

Concerning David Hardy

logs he leaped frantically. As he ran he put his hand into his pocket and took out the branched stick from which the sling for shooting squirrels was suspended. When he came to the creek that was shallow and splashed down over the stones, he dashed into the water and turned to look back, and when he saw his grandfather still running toward him with the long knife held tightly in his hand he did not hesitate but, reaching down, selected a stone and put it in the sling. With all his strength he drew back the heavy rubber band and the stone whistled through the air. It hit Jesse, who had entirely forgotten the boy and was pursuing the lamb, squarely in the head. With a groan he pitched forward and fell almost at the boy's feet. When David saw that he lay still and that he was apparently dead, his fright increased immeasurably. It became an insane panic.

With a cry he turned and ran off through the woods, weeping convulsively. "I don't care—I killed him but I don't care," he sobbed. As he ran on and on he decided suddenly that he would never go back again to the Bentley farms or to the town of Winesburg. "I have killed the man of God and now I will myself be a man and go into the world," he said stoutly as he stopped running and walked rapidly down a road that followed the windings of Wine Creek as it ran through fields and forests into the west.

On the ground by the creek Jesse Bentley moved uneasily about. He groaned and opened his eyes. For a long time he lay perfectly still and looked at the sky. When at last he got to his feet his mind was confused and he was not surprised by the boy's disappearance. By the roadside he sat down on a log and began to talk about God. That is all they ever got out of him. Whenever David's name was mentioned he looked vaguely at

but, *ed* < but

band *ms* < bands

The Philistine giant Goliath, who had defeated the Israelite army, was killed by the boy David, who shot one rock from his sling into the forehead of the giant. (See 1 Samuel 17.)

woods, *ms* < woods

him *ms* < him,

feet *ms* < feet,

Godliness, Part Four

the sky and said that a messenger from God had taken the boy. "It happened because I was too greedy for glory," he declared, and would have no more to say in the matter.

A MAN OF IDEAS

Concerning Joe Welling

HE LIVED WITH his mother, a grey, silent woman with a peculiar ashy complexion. The house in which they lived stood in a little grove of trees beyond where the main street of Winesburg crossed Wine Creek. His name was Joe Welling, and his father had been a man of some dignity in the community, a lawyer and a member of the state legislature at Columbus. Joe himself was small of body and in his character unlike anyone else in town. He was like a tiny little volcano that lies silent for days and then suddenly spouts fire. No, he wasn't like that—he was like a man who is subject to fits, one who walks among his fellow men inspiring fear because a fit may come upon him suddenly and blow him away into a strange uncanny physical state in which his eyes roll and his legs and arms jerk. He was like that, only that the visitation that descended upon Joe Welling was a mental and not a physical thing. He was beset by ideas and in the throes of one of his ideas was uncontrollable. Words rolled and tumbled from his mouth. A peculiar smile came upon his lips. The edges of his teeth that were tipped with gold glistened in the light. Pouncing

The character Joe Welling is apparently not to be taken as related to Winesburg's third physician, Dr. Welling.

Joe Welling may be modeled on a friend whom Anderson knew in Elyria, Ohio, when he lived there, from 1907 to 1913. Perry Williams, editor of the Elyria Republican, *printed materials for Anderson's company and resembled Joe Welling in action and looks.*

Concerning Joe Welling

upon a bystander he began to talk. For the bystander there was no escape. The excited man breathed into his face, peered into his eyes, pounded upon his chest with a shaking forefinger, demanded, compelled attention.

In those days the Standard Oil Company did not deliver oil to the consumer in big wagons and motor trucks as it does now, but delivered instead to retail grocers, hardware stores and the like. Joe was the Standard Oil agent in Winesburg and in several towns up and down the railroad that went through Winesburg. He collected bills, booked orders, and did other things. His father, the legislator, had secured the job for him.

In and out of the stores of Winesburg went Joe Welling—silent, excessively polite, intent upon his business. Men watched him with eyes in which lurked amusement tempered by alarm. They were waiting for him to break forth, preparing to flee. Although the seizures that came upon him were harmless enough, they could not be laughed away. They were overwhelming. Astride an idea, Joe was overmastering. His personality became gigantic. It overrode the man to whom he talked, swept him away, swept all away, all who stood within sound of his voice.

In Sylvester West's Drug Store stood four men who were talking of horse racing. Wesley Moyer's stallion, Tony Tip, was to race at the June meeting at Tiffin, Ohio, and there was a rumor that he would meet the stiffest competition of his career. It was said that Pop Geers, the great racing driver, would himself be there. A doubt of the success of Tony Tip hung heavy in the air of Winesburg.

Into the drug store came Joe Welling, brushing the screen door violently aside. With a strange absorbed light

The entrepreneur John D. Rockefeller (1839–1937) in 1870 organized in Cleveland, Ohio, the Standard Oil Company of Ohio, the first giant American business trust. In preautomobile Winesburg, Joe Welling would be selling not gasoline but instead kerosene for lamps and stoves or lubricants for machinery.

Tiffin, Ohio, the seat of Seneca County, is seventeen miles southwest of Clyde. Edward Franklin Geers (1851–1924), called "Pop," expert rider and trainer of race horses, was known to Anderson, a fan of horse-racing, by reputation and through Ed Geers' Experience with Trotters and Pacers *(1901).*

A Man of Ideas

in his eyes he pounced upon Ed Thomas, he who knew Pop Geers and whose opinion of Tony Tip's chances was worth considering.

"The water is up in Wine Creek," cried Joe Welling with the air of Pheidippides bringing news of the victory of the Greeks in the struggle at Marathon. His finger beat a tattoo upon Ed Thomas' broad chest. "By Trunion bridge it is within eleven and a half inches of the flooring," he went on, the words coming quickly and with a little whistling noise from between his teeth. An expression of helpless annoyance crept over the faces of the four.

"I have my facts correct. Depend upon that. I went to Sinnings' Hardware Store and got a rule. Then I went back and measured. I could hardly believe my own eyes. It hasn't rained, you see, for ten days. At first I didn't know what to think. Thoughts rushed through my head. I thought of subterranean passages and springs. Down under the ground went my mind, delving about. I sat on the floor of the bridge and rubbed my head. There wasn't a cloud in the sky, not one. Come out into the street and you'll see. There wasn't a cloud. There isn't a cloud now. Yes, there was a cloud. I don't want to keep back any facts. There was a cloud in the west down near the horizon, a cloud no bigger than a man's hand.

"Not that I think that has anything to do with it. There it is, you see. You understand how puzzled I was.

"Then an idea came to me. I laughed. You'll laugh too. Of course it rained over in Medina County. That's interesting, eh? If we had no trains, no mails, no tele-graph, we would know that it rained over in Medina County. That's where Wine Creek comes from. Every-one knows that. Little old Wine Creek brought us the

Concerning Joe Welling

news. That's interesting. I laughed. I thought I'd tell you—it's interesting, eh?"

Joe Welling turned and went out at the door. Taking a book from his pocket, he stopped and ran a finger down one of the pages. Again he was absorbed in his duties as agent of the Standard Oil Company. "Hern's Grocery will be getting low on coal oil. I'll see them," he muttered, hurrying along the street and bowing politely to the right and left at the people walking past.

When George Willard went to work for the *Winesburg Eagle* he was besieged by Joe Welling. Joe envied the boy. It seemed to him that he was meant by nature to be a reporter on a newspaper. "It is what I should be doing. There is no doubt of that," he declared, stopping George Willard on the sidewalk before Daugherty's Feed Store. His eyes began to glisten and his forefinger to tremble. "Of course I make more money with the Standard Oil Company and I'm only telling you," he added. "I've got nothing against you, but I should have your place. I could do the work at odd moments. Here and there I would run finding out things you'll never see."

Becoming more excited Joe Welling crowded the young reporter against the front of the feed store. He appeared to be lost in thought, rolling his eyes about and running a thin nervous hand through his hair. A smile spread over his face and his gold teeth glittered. "You get out your note book," he commanded. "You carry a little pad of paper in your pocket, don't you? I knew you did. Well, you set this down. I thought of it the other day. Let's take decay. Now what is decay? It's fire. It burns up wood and other things. You never thought of that. Of course not. This sidewalk here and this feed store, the trees down the street there—they're

Anderson maintained a life-long fondness for Herman Hurd (1877–1963), probably his closest boyhood chum, whose father and grandfather owned a grocery store in Clyde, at 124 South Main Street, and who devoted himself to preserving Clyde history.
street *ms* < street,

nature *ed* < Nature
(doing. There *ms* < doing, there

Daugherty's Feed Store is probably named humorously for George Daugherty, who worked in Chicago in advertising with Anderson.

that. *ms* < that?

A Man of Ideas

Decay, *ed* < Decay
see, *ed* < see
{ It rusts, you see. *ms,*
{ *Pr 2–Pr 7* < It's rust
{ you see.
fire *ms* < fire,
piece *ms* < pieces

all on fire. They're burning up. Decay, you see, is always going on. It don't stop. Water and paint can't stop it. If a thing is iron, then what? It rusts, you see. That's fire too. The world is on fire. Start your piece in the paper that way. Just say in big letters *'The World Is On Fire.'* That will make 'em look up. They'll say you're a smart one. I don't care. I don't envy you. I just snatched that idea out of the air. I would make a newspaper hum. You got to admit that."

Turning quickly, Joe Welling walked rapidly away. When he had taken several steps he stopped and looked back. "I'm going to stick to you," he said. "I'm going to make you a regular hummer. I should start a newspaper myself, that's what I should do. I'd be a marvel. Everybody knows that."

When George Willard had been for a year on the *Winesburg Eagle,* four things happened to Joe Welling. His mother died, he came to live at the New Willard House, he became involved in a love affair, and he organized the Winesburg Baseball Club.

Joe organized the baseball club because he wanted to be a coach and in that position he began to win the respect of his townsmen. "He is a wonder," they declared after Joe's team had whipped the team from Medina County. "He gets everybody working together. You just watch him."

Upon the baseball field Joe Welling stood by first base, his whole body quivering with excitement. In spite of themselves all of the players watched him closely. The opposing pitcher became confused.

"Now! Now! Now! Now!" shouted the excited man. "Watch me! Watch me! Watch my fingers! Watch my hands! Watch my feet! Watch my eyes! Let's work together here! Watch me! In me you see all the movements

Concerning Joe Welling

of the game! Work with me! Work with me! Watch me! Watch me! Watch me!"

With runners of the Winesburg team on bases, Joe Welling became as one inspired. Before they knew what had come over them, the base runners were watching the man, edging off the bases, advancing, retreating, held as by an invisible cord. The players of the opposing team also watched Joe. They were fascinated. For a moment they watched and then as though to break a spell that hung over them they began hurling the ball wildly about, and amid a series of fierce animal-like cries from the coach the runners of the Winesburg team scampered home.

Joe Welling's love affair set the town of Winesburg on edge. When it began everyone whispered and shook his head. When people tried to laugh, the laughter was forced and unnatural. Joe fell in love with Sarah King, a lean, sad-looking woman who lived with her father and brother in a brick house that stood opposite the gate leading to the Winesburg Cemetery.

The two Kings, Edward the father and Tom the son, were not popular in Winesburg. They were called proud and dangerous. They had come to Winesburg from someplace in the south and ran a cider mill on the Trunion Pike. Tom King was reported to have killed a man before he came to Winesburg. He was twenty-seven years old and rode about town on a grey pony. Also he had a long yellow mustache that drooped down over his teeth and always carried a heavy, wicked-looking walking stick in his hand. Once he killed a dog with the stick. The dog belonged to Win Pawsey, the shoe merchant, and stood on the sidewalk wagging its tail. Tom King killed it with one blow. He was arrested and paid a fine of ten dollars.

them *ms* < them,

coach *ms* < coach,

McPherson Cemetery lies in the northeast part of Clyde.
father *ms* < father,

(someplace *ed*
(< some place
south *ed* < South

drooped *ed* < dropped

teeth *ed* < teeth,

In Clyde, on the first floor of 114 South Main Street, Alfred Pawsey operated a shoe store.

A Man of Ideas

Old Edward King was small of stature and when he passed people in the street laughed a queer unmirthful laugh. When he laughed he scratched his left elbow with his right hand. The sleeve of his coat was almost worn through from the habit. As he walked along the street, looking nervously about and laughing, he seemed more dangerous than his silent, fierce-looking son.

fierce-looking ed
< fierce looking

When Sarah King began walking out in the evening with Joe Welling, people shook their heads in alarm. She was tall and pale and had dark rings under her eyes. The couple looked ridiculous together. Under the trees they walked and Joe talked. His passionate eager protestations of love, heard coming out of the darkness by the cemetery wall, or from the deep shadows of the trees on the hill that ran up to the Fair Grounds from Waterworks Pond, were repeated in the stores. Men stood by the bar in the New Willard House laughing and talking of Joe's courtship. After the laughter came silence. The Winesburg baseball team, under his management, was winning game after game, and the town had begun to respect him. Sensing a tragedy, they waited, laughing nervously.

The community Waterworks and its reservoir pond, established in 1883, and the Fair Grounds were located in southeast Clyde; the Fair Grounds, developed in 1870, centered around a one-half-mile race track.

Late on a Saturday afternoon the meeting between Joe Welling and the two Kings, the anticipation of which had set the town on edge, took place in Joe Welling's room in the New Willard House. George Willard was a witness to the meeting. It came about in this way:

When the young reporter went to his room after the evening meal he saw Tom King and his father sitting in the half darkness in Joe's room. The son had the heavy walking stick in his hand and sat near the door. Old Edward King walked nervously about, scratching his left elbow with his right hand. The hallways were empty and silent.

Concerning Joe Welling

George Willard went to his own room and sat down at his desk. He tried to write but his hand trembled so that he could not hold the pen. He also walked nervously up and down. Like the rest of the town of Winesburg he was perplexed and knew not what to do.

It was seven-thirty and fast growing dark when Joe Welling came along the station platform toward the New Willard House. In his arms he held a bundle of weeds and grasses. In spite of the terror that made his body shake, George Willard was amused at the sight of the small spry figure holding the grasses and half running along the platform.

Shaking with fright and anxiety, the young reporter lurked in the hallway outside the door of the room in which Joe Welling talked to the two Kings. There had been an oath, the nervous giggle of old Edward King and then silence. Now the voice of Joe Welling, sharp and clear, broke forth. George Willard began to laugh. He understood. As he had swept all men before him, so now Joe Welling was carrying the two men in the room off their feet with a tidal wave of words. The listener in the hall walked up and down, lost in amazement.

King *ms* < King,

Inside the room Joe Welling had paid no attention to the grumbled threat of Tom King. Absorbed in an idea he closed the door and, lighting a lamp, spread the handful of weeds and grasses upon the floor. "I've got something here," he announced solemnly. "I was going to tell George Willard about it, let him make a piece out of it for the paper. I'm glad you're here. I wish Sarah were here also. I've been going to come to your house and tell you of some of my ideas. They're interesting. Sarah wouldn't let me. She said we'd quarrel. That's foolish."

and, *ed* < and

Running up and down before the two perplexed men,

A Man of Ideas

Joe Welling began to explain. "Don't you make a mistake now," he cried. "This is something big." His voice was shrill with excitement. "You just follow me, you'll be interested. I know you will. Suppose this—suppose all of the wheat, the corn, the oats, the peas, the potatoes were all by some miracle swept away. Now here we are, you see, in this county. There is a high fence built all around us. We'll suppose that. No one can get over the fence and all the fruits of the earth are destroyed, nothing left but these wild things, these grasses. Would we be done for? I ask you that. Would we be done for?" Again Tom King growled and for a moment there was silence in the room. Then again Joe plunged into the exposition of his idea. "Things would go hard for a time. I admit that. I've got to admit that. No getting around it. We'd be hard put to it. More than one fat stomach would cave in. But they couldn't down us. I should say not."

Tom King laughed good-naturedly and the shivery, nervous laugh of Edward King rang through the house. Joe Welling hurried on. "We'd begin, you see, to breed up new vegetables and fruits. Soon we'd regain all we had lost. Mind, I don't say the new things would be the same as the old. They wouldn't. Maybe they'd be better, maybe not so good. That's interesting, eh? You can think about that. It starts your mind working, now don't it?"

In the room there was silence and then again old Edward King laughed nervously. "Say, I wish Sarah was here," cried Joe Welling. "Let's go up to your house. I want to tell her of this."

There was a scraping of chairs in the room. It was then that George Willard retreated to his own room. Leaning out at the window he saw Joe Welling going

potatoes *ed* < potatoes,

(good-naturedly *ed*
 < good naturedly

Concerning Joe Welling

along the street with the two Kings. Tom King was forced to take extraordinary long strides to keep pace with the little man. As he strode along, he leaned over, listening—absorbed, fascinated. Joe Welling again talked excitedly. "Take milk weed now," he cried. "A lot might be done with milk weed, eh? It's almost unbelievable. I want you to think about it. I want you two to think about it. There would be a new vegetable kingdom, you see. It's interesting, eh? It's an idea. Wait till you see Sarah, she'll get the idea. She'll be interested. Sarah is always interested in ideas. You can't be too smart for Sarah, now can you? Of course you can't. You know that."

milk weed *ed* < milkweed

milk weed *ed* < milkweed

kingdom, *ed* < kingdom

ADVENTURE

Concerning Alice Hindman

ALICE HINDMAN, a woman of twenty-seven when George Willard was a mere boy, had lived in Winesburg all her life. She clerked in Winney's Dry Goods Store and lived with her mother who had married a second husband.

Alice's step-father was a carriage painter and given to drink. His story is an odd one. It will be worth telling someday.

painter *ms* < painter,

someday *ed* < some day

At twenty-seven Alice was tall and somewhat slight. Her head was large and overshadowed her body. Her shoulders were a little stooped and her hair and eyes brown. She was very quiet but beneath a placid exterior a continual ferment went on.

Adventure

When she was a girl of sixteen and before she began to work in the store, Alice had an affair with a young man. The young man, named Ned Currie, was older than Alice. He, like George Willard, was employed on the *Winesburg Eagle* and for a long time he went to see Alice almost every evening. Together the two walked under the trees through the streets of the town and talked of what they would do with their lives. Alice was then a very pretty girl and Ned Currie took her into his arms and kissed her. He became excited and said things he did not intend to say and Alice, betrayed by her desire to have something beautiful come into her rather narrow life, also grew excited. She also talked. The outer crust of her life, all of her natural diffidence and reserve, was torn away and she gave herself over to the emotions of love. When, late in the fall of her sixteenth year, Ned Currie went away to Cleveland, where he hoped to get a place on a city newspaper and rise in the world, she wanted to go with him. With a trembling voice she told him what was in her mind. "I will work and you can work," she said. "I do not want to harness you to a needless expense that will prevent your making progress. Don't marry me now. We will get along without that and we can be together. Even though we live in the same house no one will say anything. In the city we will be unknown and people will pay no attention to us."

Ned Currie was puzzled by the determination and abandon of his sweetheart and was also deeply touched. He had wanted the girl to become his mistress but changed his mind. He wanted to protect and care for her. "You don't know what you're talking about," he said sharply. "You may be sure I'll let you do no such thing. As soon as I get a good job I'll come back. For the present you'll have to stay here. It's the only thing we can do."

Cleveland, *ed*
< Cleveland

sharply. "You *ms*
< sharply; "you

Concerning Alice Hindman

On the evening before he left Winesburg to take up his new life in the city, Ned Currie went to call on Alice. They walked about through the streets for an hour and then got a rig from Wesley Moyer's Livery and went for a drive in the country. The moon came up and they found themselves unable to talk. In his sadness the young man forgot the resolutions he had made regarding his conduct with the girl.

They got out of the buggy at a place where a long meadow ran down to the bank of Wine Creek and there in the dim light became lovers. When at midnight they returned to town they were both glad. It did not seem to them that anything that could happen in the future could blot out the wonder and beauty of the thing that had happened. "Now we will have to stick to each other, whatever happens we will have to do that," Ned Currie said as he left the girl at her father's door.

The young newspaper man did not succeed in getting a place on a Cleveland paper and went west to Chicago. For a time he was lonely and wrote to Alice almost every day. Then he was caught up by the life of the city; he began to make friends and found new interests in life. In Chicago he boarded at a house where there were several women. One of them attracted his attention and he forgot Alice in Winesburg. At the end of a year he had stopped writing letters, and only once in a long time, when he was lonely or when he went into one of the city parks and saw the moon shining on the grass as it had shone that night on the meadow by Wine Creek, did he think of her at all.

In Winesburg the girl who had been loved grew to be a woman. When she was twenty-two years old her father, who owned a harness repair shop, died suddenly. The harness maker was an old soldier, and after a few

Livery *ms* < livery

Harvey & Whitaker Livery Stable, in Clyde, was located at 114 Railroad Street. Horses could be boarded, fed, and cared for at livery stables, establishments where people could in preautomobile days also rent horses and vehicles.

Adventure

months his wife received a widow's pension. She used the first money she got to buy a loom and became a weaver of carpets, and Alice got a place in Winney's Store. For a number of years nothing could have induced her to believe that Ned Currie would not in the end return to her.

She was glad to be employed because the daily round of toil in the store made the time of waiting seem less long and uninteresting. She began to save money, thinking that when she had saved two or three hundred dollars she would follow her lover to the city and try if her presence would not win back his affections.

Alice did not blame Ned Currie for what had happened, in the moonlight in the field, but felt that she could never marry another man. To her the thought of giving to another what she still felt could belong only to Ned seemed monstrous. When other young men tried to attract her attention she would have nothing to do with them. "I am his wife and shall remain his wife whether he comes back or not," she whispered to herself and for all of her willingness to support herself could not have understood the growing modern idea of a woman's owning herself and giving and taking for her own ends in life.

Alice worked in the dry goods store from eight in the morning until six at night and on three evenings a week went back to the store to stay from seven until nine. As time passed and she became more and more lonely she began to practice the devices common to lonely people. When at night she went upstairs into her own room she knelt on the floor to pray and in her prayers whispered things she wanted to say to her lover. She became attached to inanimate objects, and, because it was her own, could not bear to have anyone touch the furniture of

Store *ed* < store

(**happened,** *ed* < happened

herself *ms* < herself,

and, *ed* < and

Concerning Alice Hindman

her room. The trick of saving money, begun for a purpose, was carried on after the scheme of going to the
city to find Ned Currie had been given up. It became a
fixed habit, and when she needed new clothes she did
not get them. Sometimes on rainy afternoons in the store   them. *ms* < them
she got out her bank book and, letting it lie open before
her, spent hours dreaming impossible dreams of saving
money enough so that the interest would support both
herself and her future husband.

"Ned always liked to travel about," she thought. "I'll
give him the chance. Someday, when we are married   Someday, *ed* < Some day
and I can save both his money and my own, we will be
rich. Then we can travel together all over the world."

In the dry goods store weeks ran into months and
months into years as Alice waited and dreamed of her
lover's return. Her employer, a grey old man with false
teeth and a thin grey mustache that drooped down over
his mouth, was not given to conversation and some-   conversation *ms*
times, on rainy days and in the winter when a storm   < conversation,
raged in Main Street, long hours passed when no cus-
tomers came in. Alice arranged and re-arranged the stock.   re-arranged *ed*
She stood near the front window where she could look   < rearranged
down the deserted street and thought of the evenings
when she had walked with Ned Currie and of what he
had said. "We will have to stick to each other now." The
words echoed and re-echoed through the mind of the
maturing woman. Tears came into her eyes. Sometimes
when her employer had gone out and she was alone in
the store she put her head on the counter and wept.
"Oh, Ned, I am waiting," she whispered over and over,
and all the time the creeping fear that he would never
come back grew stronger within her.

In the spring, when the rains have passed and before   spring, *ed* < spring
the long hot days of summer have come, the country

Adventure

passes *ms* < passes,

woods *ms* < wood

(Sunday. But *ms*
  < Sunday, but
day, *ms* < day

fields *ms* < fields,

(never-ceasing *ed*
  < never ceasing

knees *ms* < knees,

about Winesburg is delightful. The town lies in the midst of open fields, but beyond the fields are pleasant patches of woodlands. In the wooded places are many little cloistered nooks, quiet places where lovers go to sit on Sunday afternoons. Through the trees they look out across the fields and see farmers at work about the barns or people driving up and down on the roads. In the town bells ring and occasionally a train passes looking like a toy thing in the distance.

For several years after Ned Currie went away Alice did not go into the woods with other young people on Sunday. But one day, after he had been gone for two or three years and when her loneliness seemed unbearable, she put on her best dress and set out. Finding a little sheltered place from which she could see the town and a long stretch of the fields she sat down. Fear of age and ineffectuality took possession of her. She could not sit still, and arose. As she stood looking out over the land something, perhaps the thought of never-ceasing life as it expresses itself in the flow of the seasons, fixed her mind on the passing years. With a shiver of dread, she realized that for her the beauty and freshness of youth had passed. For the first time she felt that she had been cheated. She did not blame Ned Currie and did not know what to blame. Sadness swept over her. Dropping to her knees she tried to pray, but instead of prayers words of protest came to her lips. "It is not going to come to me. I will never find happiness. Why do I tell myself lies?" she cried, and an odd sense of relief came with this, her first bold attempt to face the fear that had become a part of her everyday life.

In the year when Alice Hindman became twenty-five two things happened to disturb the dull uneventfulness

Concerning Alice Hindman

of her days. Her mother married Bush Milton, the carriage painter of Winesburg, and she herself became a member of the Winesburg Methodist Church. Alice joined the church because she had become frightened by the loneliness of her position in life. Her mother's second marriage had emphasized her isolation. "I am becoming old and queer. If Ned comes he will not want me. In the city where he is living men are perpetually young. There is so much going on that they do not have time to grow old," she told herself, with a grim little smile, and went resolutely about the business of becoming acquainted with people. Every Thursday evening when the store had closed she went to a prayer meeting in the basement of the church and on Sunday evening attended a meeting of an organization called the Epworth League.

When Will Hurley, a middle-aged man who clerked in a drug store and who also belonged to the church, offered to walk home with her she did not protest. "Of course I will not let him make a practice of being with me, but if he comes to see me once in a long time there can be no harm in that," she told herself, still determined in her loyalty to Ned Currie.

Without realizing what was happening, Alice was trying feebly at first, but with growing determination, to get a new hold upon life. Beside the drug clerk she walked in silence, but sometimes in the darkness as they went stolidly along she put out her hand and touched softly the folds of his coat. When he left her at the gate before her mother's house she did not go indoors, but stood for a moment by the door. She wanted to call to the drug clerk, to ask him to sit with her in the darkness on the porch before the house, but was afraid he would not

In Clyde the First United Methodist Church, built in 1851, stood at 160 West Buckeye Street.

herself, *ed* < herself

the *ed* < The
The Epworth League to encourage upright living and social service was a Methodist youth fellowship, named for the rectory in Lincolnshire, England, where a youthful John Wesley (1703–1791), founder of Methodism, served as his father's aide.

Adventure

understand. "It is not him that I want," she told herself; "I want to avoid being so much alone. If I am not careful I will grow unaccustomed to being with people."

During the early fall of her twenty-seventh year a passionate restlessness took possession of Alice. She could not bear to be in the company of the drug clerk and when, in the evening, he came to walk with her she sent him away. Her mind became intensely active and when, weary from the long hours of standing behind the counter in the store, she went home and crawled into bed, she could not sleep. With staring eyes she looked into the darkness. Her imagination, like a child awakened from long sleep, played about the room. Deep within her there was something that would not be cheated by fantasies and that demanded some definite answer from life.

Alice took a pillow into her arms and held it tightly against her breasts. Getting out of bed she arranged a blanket so that in the darkness it looked like a form lying between the sheets and, kneeling beside the bed, she caressed it, whispering words over and over, like a refrain. "Why doesn't something happen? Why am I left here alone?" she muttered. Although she sometimes thought of Ned Currie, she no longer depended on him. Her desire had grown vague. She did not want Ned Currie or any other man. She wanted to be loved, to have something answer the call that was growing louder and louder within her.

And then one night when it rained Alice had an adventure. It frightened and confused her. She had come home from the store at nine and found the house empty. Bush Milton had gone off to town and her mother to the house of a neighbor. Alice went upstairs to her room

clerk *ms* < clerk,

⎧ fantasies *ed*
⎩ < phantasies

bed *ms* < bed,

Concerning Alice Hindman

and undressed in the darkness. For a moment she stood by the window hearing the rain beat against the glass and then a strange desire took possession of her. Without stopping to think of what she intended to do, she ran downstairs through the dark house and out into the rain. As she stood on the little grass plot before the house and felt the cold rain on her body a mad desire to run naked through the streets took possession of her.

She thought that the rain would have some creative and wonderful effect on her body. Not for years had she felt so full of youth and courage. She wanted to leap and run, to cry out, to find some other lonely human and embrace him. On the brick sidewalk before the house a man stumbled homeward. Alice started to run. A wild, desperate mood took possession of her. "What do I care who it is? He is alone and I will go to him," she thought; and then, without stopping to consider the possible result of her madness, called softly. "Wait," she cried. "Don't go away. Whoever you are you must wait."

is? *ms* < is.
alone *ms* < alone,
then, *ed* < then

"Wait," *ms* < "Wait!"

are *ms* < are,

The man on the sidewalk stopped and stood listening. He was an old man and somewhat deaf. Putting his hand to his mouth, he shouted. "What? What say?" he called.

shouted. *ed* < shouted:

Alice dropped to the ground and lay trembling. She was so frightened at the thought of what she had done that when the man had gone on his way she did not dare get to her feet, but crawled on hands and knees through the grass to the house. When she got to her own room she bolted the door and drew her dressing table across the doorway. Her body shook as with a chill and her hands trembled so that she had difficulty getting into her night dress. When she got into bed she buried her face in the pillow and wept broken-heartedly. "What is the matter with me? I will do something dread-

night dress *ed* < nightdress

Adventure

ful if I am not careful," she thought, and, turning her face to the wall, began trying to force herself to face bravely the fact that many people must live and die alone, even in Winesburg.

RESPECTABILITY

Concerning Wash Williams

IF YOU HAVE lived in cities and have walked in the park on a summer afternoon, you have perhaps seen, blinking in a corner of his iron cage, a huge, grotesque kind of monkey, a creature with ugly, sagging hairless skin below his eyes and a bright purple underbody. This monkey is a true monster. In the completeness of his ugliness he has achieved a kind of perverted beauty. Children stopping before the cage are fascinated, men turn away with an air of disgust, and women linger for a moment, trying perhaps to remember which one of their male acquaintances the thing in some faint way resembles.

Had you been in the earlier years of your life a citizen of the village of Winesburg, Ohio, there would have been for you no mystery in regard to the beast in his cage. "It is like Wash Williams," you would have said. "As he sits in the corner there, the beast is exactly like old Wash sitting on the grass in the station yard on a summer evening after he has closed his office for the night."

Wash Williams, the telegraph operator of Winesburg, was the ugliest thing in town. His girth was immense,

Concerning Wash Williams

his neck thin, his legs feeble. He was dirty. Everything about him was unclean. Even the whites of his eyes looked soiled.

I go too fast. Not everything about Wash was unclean. He took care of his hands. His fingers were fat, but there was something sensitive and shapely in the hand that lay on the table by the instrument in the telegraph office. In his youth Wash Williams had been called the best telegraph operator in the state, and in spite of his degradement to the obscure office at Winesburg, he was still proud of his ability.

Wash Williams did not associate with the men of the town in which he lived. "I'll have nothing to do with them," he said, looking with bleary eyes at the men who walked along the station platform past the telegraph office. Up along Main Street he went in the evening to Ed Griffith's Saloon, and after drinking unbelievable quantities of beer staggered off to his room in the New Willard House and to his bed for the night.

Saloon *ed* < saloon

Wash Williams was a man of courage. A thing had happened to him that made him hate life and he hated it whole-heartedly, with the abandon of a poet. First of all he hated women. "Bitches," he called them. His feeling toward men was somewhat different. He pitied them. "Does not every man let his life be managed for him by some bitch or another?" he asked.

life *ms* < life,

all *ms* < all,

In Winesburg no attention was paid to Wash Williams and his hatred of his fellows. Once Mrs. White, the banker's wife, complained to the telegraph company, saying that the office in Winesburg was dirty and smelled abominably, but nothing came of her complaint. Here and there a man respected the operator. Instinctively the man felt in him a glowing resentment of something he had not the courage to resent. When Wash walked

The Clyde, Ohio, telegraph office was located in the northwest corner of the train depot, the business center of the town, developed after the Lake Shore and the Big Four Railroads came in the 1850s.

Respectability

through the streets such a one had an instinct to pay him homage, to raise his hat or to bow before him. The superintendent who had supervision over the telegraph operators on the railroad that went through Winesburg felt that way. He had put Wash into the obscure office at Winesburg to avoid discharging him, and he meant to keep him there. When he received the letter of complaint from the banker's wife he tore it up and laughed unpleasantly. For some reason he thought of his own wife as he tore up the letter.

Wash Williams once had a wife. When he was still a young man he married a woman at Dayton, Ohio. The woman was tall and slender and had blue eyes and yellow hair. Wash was himself a comely youth. He loved the woman with a love as absorbing as the hatred he later felt for all women.

In all of Winesburg there was but one person who knew the story of the thing that had made ugly the person and the character of Wash Williams. He once told the story to George Willard and the telling of the tale came about in this way:

George Willard went one evening to walk with Belle Carpenter, a trimmer of women's hats who worked in a millinery shop kept by Mrs. Nate McHugh. The young man was not in love with the woman, who, in fact, had a suitor who worked as bartender in Ed Griffith's Saloon, but as they walked about under the trees they occasionally embraced. The night and their own thoughts had aroused something in them. As they were returning to Main Street they passed the little lawn beside the railroad station and saw Wash Williams apparently asleep on the grass beneath a tree. On the next evening the operator and George Willard walked out together. Down the railroad they went and sat on a pile of decaying rail-

wife *ms* < wife,

Nate *ed* < Kate

Saloon *ed* < saloon

In an age when all respectable women wore hats or bonnets whenever out of their homes, hat or millinery shops that existed in every town and city provided many women with commercial employment.

Concerning Wash Williams

road ties beside the tracks. It was then that the operator told the young reporter his story of hate.

Perhaps a dozen times George Willard and the strange, shapeless man who lived at his father's hotel had been on the point of talking. The young man looked at the hideous, leering face staring about the hotel dining room and was consumed with curiosity. Something he saw lurking in the staring eyes told him that the man who had nothing to say to others had nevertheless something to say to him. On the pile of railroad ties, on the summer evening, he waited expectantly. When the operator remained silent and seemed to have changed his mind about talking, he tried to make conversation. "Were you ever married, Mr. Williams?" he began. "I suppose you were and your wife is dead, is that it?"

Wash Williams spat forth a succession of vile oaths. "Yes, she is dead," he agreed. "She is dead as all women are dead. She is a living-dead thing, walking in the sight of men and making the earth foul by her presence." Staring into the boy's eyes, the man became purple with rage. "Don't have fool notions in your head," he commanded. "My wife, she is dead; yes, surely. I tell you, all women are dead, my mother, your mother, that tall dark woman who works in the millinery store and with whom I saw you walking about yesterday—all of them, they are all dead. I tell you there is something rotten about them. I was married, sure. My wife was dead before she married me, she was a foul thing come out of a woman more foul. She was a thing sent to make life unbearable to me. I was a fool, do you see, as you are now, and so I married this woman. I would like to see men a little begin to understand women. They are sent to prevent men's making the world worthwhile. It is a trick in nature. Ugh! They are creeping, crawling, squirming things,

ties, *ed* < ties

(yesterday— *ed*
(< yesterday, —

men's *ms* < men
(worthwhile *ed*
(< worth while
nature *ed* < Nature

Respectability

they with their soft hands and their blue eyes. The sight of a woman sickens me. Why I don't kill every woman I see I don't know."

Half frightened and yet fascinated by the light burning in the eyes of the hideous old man, George Willard listened, afire with curiosity. Darkness came on and he leaned forward trying to see the face of the man who talked. When, in the gathering darkness, he could no longer see the purple, bloated face and the burning eyes, a curious fancy came to him. Wash Williams talked in low even tones that made his words seem the more terrible. In the darkness the young reporter found himself imagining that he sat on the railroad ties beside a comely young man with black hair and black shining eyes. There was something almost beautiful in the voice of Wash Williams, the hideous, telling his story of hate.

The telegraph operator of Winesburg, sitting in the darkness on the railroad ties, had become a poet. Hatred had raised him to that elevation. "It is because I saw you kissing the lips of that Belle Carpenter that I tell you my story," he said. "What happened to me may next happen to you. I want to put you on your guard. Already you may be having dreams in your head. I want to destroy them."

Wash Williams began telling the story of his married life with the tall blonde girl with blue eyes whom he had met when he was a young operator at Dayton, Ohio. Here and there his story was touched with moments of beauty intermingled with strings of vile curses. The operator had married the daughter of a dentist who was the youngest of three sisters. On his marriage day, because of his ability, he was promoted to a position as dispatcher at an increased salary and sent to an office at Columbus, Ohio. There he settled down with his young wife and began buying a house on the installment plan.

Concerning Wash Williams

The young telegraph operator was madly in love. With a kind of religious fervor he had managed to go through the pitfalls of his youth and to remain virginal until after his marriage. He made for George Willard a picture of his life in the house at Columbus, Ohio, with the young wife. "In the garden back of our house we planted vegetables," he said, "you know, peas and corn and such things. We went to Columbus in early March and as soon as the days became warm I went to work in the garden. With a spade I turned up the black ground while she ran about laughing and pretending to be afraid of the worms I uncovered. Late in April came the planting. In the little paths among the seed beds she stood holding a paper bag in her hand. The bag was filled with seeds. A few at a time she handed me the seeds that I might thrust them into the warm, soft ground."

For a moment there was a catch in the voice of the man talking in the darkness. "I loved her," he said. "I don't claim not to be a fool. I love her yet. There in the dusk in the spring evening I crawled along the black ground to her feet and groveled before her. I kissed her shoes and the ankles above her shoes. When the hem of her garment touched my face I trembled. When after two years of that life I found she had managed to acquire three other lovers who came regularly to our house when I was away at work, I didn't want to touch them or her. I just sent her home to her mother and said nothing. There was nothing to say. I had four hundred dollars in the bank and I gave her that. I didn't ask her reasons. I didn't say anything. When she had gone I cried like a silly boy. Pretty soon I had a chance to sell the house and I sent that money to her."

Wash Williams and George Willard arose from the pile of railroad ties and walked along the tracks toward town. The operator finished his tale quickly, breathlessly.

Respectability

"Her mother sent for me," he said. "She wrote me a letter and asked me to come to their house at Dayton. When I got there it was evening about this time."

Wash Williams' voice rose to a half scream. "I sat in the parlor of that house two hours. Her mother took me in there and left me. Their house was stylish. They were what is called respectable people. There were plush chairs and a couch in the room. I was trembling all over. I hated the men I thought had wronged her. I was sick of living alone and wanted her back. The longer I waited the more raw and tender I became. I thought that if she came in and just touched me with her hand I would perhaps faint away. I ached to forgive and forget."

Wash Williams stopped and stood staring at George Willard. The boy's body shook as from a chill. Again the man's voice became soft and low. "She came into the room naked," he went on. "Her mother did that. While I sat there she was taking the girl's clothes off, perhaps coaxing her to do it. First I heard voices at the door that led into a little hallway and then it opened softly. The girl was ashamed and stood perfectly still staring at the floor. The mother didn't come into the room. When she had pushed the girl in through the door she stood in the hallway waiting, hoping we would—well, you see—waiting."

George Willard and the telegraph operator came into the main street of Winesburg. The lights from the store windows lay bright and shining on the sidewalks. People moved about laughing and talking. The young reporter felt ill and weak. In imagination he also became old and shapeless. "I didn't get the mother killed," said Wash Williams, staring up and down the street. "I struck her once with a chair and then the neighbors came in and took it away. She screamed so loud, you see. I won't ever

imagination *ms*
< imagination,

loud, *ms* < loud

have a chance to kill her now. She died of a fever a month after that happened."

THE THINKER

Concerning Seth Richmond

THE HOUSE IN which Seth Richmond of Winesburg lived with his mother had been at one time the show place of the town, but when young Seth lived there its glory had become somewhat dimmed. The huge brick house which Banker White had built on Buckeye Street had overshadowed it. The Richmond place was in a little valley far out at the end of Main Street. Farmers coming into town by a dusty road from the south passed by a grove of walnut trees, skirted the Fair Grounds with its high board fence covered with advertisements, and trotted their horses down through the valley past the Richmond place into town. As much of the country north and south of Winesburg was devoted to fruit and berry raising, Seth saw wagon-loads of berry pickers—boys, girls, and women—going to the fields in the morning and returning covered with dust in the evening. The chattering crowd, with their rude jokes cried out from wagon to wagon, sometimes irritated him sharply. He regretted that he also could not laugh boisterously, shout meaningless jokes and make of himself a figure in the endless stream of moving, giggling activity that went up and down the road.

The Richmond house was built of limestone and, although it was said in the village to have become run

The fictional stone Richmond house was modeled on the brick Michael Kiefer house, at 522 South Main Street in Clyde.

Grounds *ed* < Ground

limestone *ms* < limestone, and, *ms* < and

The Thinker

down, had in reality grown more beautiful with every passing year. Already time had begun a little to color the stone, lending a golden richness to its surface and in the evening or on dark days touching the shaded places beneath the eaves with wavering patches of browns and blacks.

The house had been built by Seth's grandfather, a stone quarryman, and it, together with the stone quarries on Lake Erie, eighteen miles to the north, had been left to his son, Clarence Richmond, Seth's father. Clarence Richmond, a quiet passionate man extraordinarily admired by his neighbors, had been killed in a street fight with the editor of a newspaper in Toledo, Ohio. The fight concerned the publication of Clarence Richmond's name coupled with that of a woman school teacher, and as the dead man had begun the row by firing upon the editor, the effort to punish the slayer was unsuccessful. After the quarryman's death it was found that much of the money left to him had been squandered in speculation and in insecure investments made though the influence of friends.

Left with but a small income, Virginia Richmond had settled down to a retired life in the village and to the raising of her son. Although she had been deeply moved by the death of the husband and father, she did not at all believe the stories concerning him that ran about after his death. To her mind the sensitive, boyish man, whom all had instinctively loved, was but an unfortunate, a being too fine for everyday life. "You'll be hearing all sorts of stories but you are not to believe what you hear," she said to her son. "He was a good man, full of tenderness for everyone, and should not have tried to be a man of affairs. No matter how much I were to plan and dream of your future, I could not imagine anything

Erie, *ms* < Erie

mind *ms* <mind,
man, *ed* < man

stories *ms* < stories,

Concerning Seth Richmond

better for you than that you turn out as good a man as your father."

Several years after the death of her husband, Virginia Richmond had become alarmed at the growing demands upon her income and had set herself to the task of increasing it. She had learned stenography and through the influence of her husband's friends got the position of court stenographer at the county seat. There she went by train each morning during the sessions of the court and, when no court sat, spent her days working among the rose bushes in her garden. She was a tall, straight figure of a woman with a plain face and a great mass of brown hair.

and, *ed* < and

rose bushes *ms* < rosebushes

In the relationship between Seth Richmond and his mother, there was a quality that even at eighteen had begun to color all of his traffic with men. An almost unhealthy respect for the youth kept the mother for the most part silent in his presence. When she did speak sharply to him he had only to look steadily into her eyes to see dawning there the puzzled look he had already noticed in the eyes of others when he looked at them.

The truth was that the son thought with remarkable clearness and the mother did not. She expected from all people certain conventional reactions to life. A boy was your son, you scolded him and he trembled and looked at the floor. When you had scolded enough he wept and all was forgiven. After the weeping and when he had gone to bed, you crept into his room and kissed him.

Virginia Richmond could not understand why her son did not do these things. After the severest reprimand, he did not tremble and look at the floor but instead looked steadily at her, causing uneasy doubts to invade her mind. As for creeping into his room—after Seth

The Thinker

had passed his fifteenth year, she would have been half afraid to do anything of the kind.

Once, when he was a boy of sixteen, Seth, in company with two other boys, ran away from home. The three boys climbed into the open door of an empty freight car and rode some forty miles to a town where a fair was being held. One of the boys had a bottle filled with a combination of whiskey and blackberry wine, and the three sat with legs dangling out of the car door drinking from the bottle. Seth's two companions sang and waved their hands to idlers about the stations of the towns through which the train passed. They planned raids upon the baskets of farmers who had come with their families to the fair. "We will live like kings and won't have to spend a penny to see the fair and horse races," they declared boastfully.

After the disappearance of Seth, Virginia Richmond walked up and down the floor of her home—filled with vague alarms. Although on the next day she discovered, though an inquiry made by the town marshal, on what adventure the boys had gone, she could not quiet herself. All through the night she lay awake hearing the clock tick and telling herself that Seth, like his father, would come to a sudden and violent end. So determined was she that the boy should this time feel the weight of her wrath that, although she would not allow the marshal to interfere with his adventure, she got out pencil and paper and wrote down a series of sharp, stinging reproofs she intended to pour out upon him. The reproofs she committed to memory, going about the garden and saying them aloud like an actor memorizing his part.

And when, at the end of the week, Seth returned, a little weary and with coal soot in his ears and about his

Once, *ms* < Once
Seth, *ms* < Seth

(home—filled *ms*
(< home filled

Concerning Seth Richmond

eyes, she again found herself unable to reprove him. Walking into the house he hung his cap on a nail by the kitchen door and stood looking steadily at her. "I wanted to turn back within an hour after we had started," he explained. "I didn't know what to do. I knew you would be bothered, but I knew also that if I didn't go on I would be ashamed of myself. I went through with the thing for my own good. It was uncomfortable, sleeping on wet straw, and two drunken negroes came and slept with us. When I stole a lunch basket out of a farmer's wagon I couldn't help thinking of his children going all day without food. I was sick of the whole affair, but I was determined to stick it out until the other boys were ready to come back."

"I'm glad you did stick it out," replied the mother, half resentfully, and kissing him upon the forehead pretended to busy herself with the work about the house.

On a summer evening Seth Richmond went to the New Willard House to visit his friend George Willard. It had rained during the afternoon, but, as he walked through Main Street, the sky had partially cleared and a golden glow lit up the west. Going around a corner, he turned in at the door of the hotel and began to climb the stairway leading up to his friend's room. In the hotel office the proprietor and two traveling men were engaged in a discussion of politics.

friend *ed* < friend, but, *ed* < but

On the stairway Seth stopped and listened to the voices of the men below. They were excited and talked rapidly. Tom Willard was berating the traveling men. "I am a Democrat but your talk makes me sick," he said. "You don't understand McKinley. McKinley and Mark Hanna are friends. It is impossible perhaps for your mind to grasp that. If anyone tells you that a friendship can be deeper and bigger and more worthwhile than dollars

worthwhile *ed* < worth while

The Thinker

worthwhile *ed*
< worth while

and cents, or even more worthwhile than state politics, you snicker and laugh."

The landlord was interrupted by one of the guests, a tall grey-mustached man who worked for a wholesale grocery house. "Do you think that I've lived in Cleveland all these years without knowing Mark Hanna?" he demanded. "Your talk is piffle. Hanna is after money and nothing else. This McKinley is his tool. He has McKinley bluffed and don't you forget it."

Mark Hanna (1837–1904), Republican Ohio businessman, spent and worked to have his friend William McKinley (1843–1901) elected Republican governor of Ohio (1892–1896) and president (1897–1901).

The young man on the stairs did not linger to hear the rest of the discussion, but went on up the stairway and into a little dark hall. Something in the voices of the men talking in the hotel office started a chain of thoughts in his mind. He was lonely and had begun to think that loneliness was a part of his character, something that would always stay with him. Stepping into a side hall he stood by a window that looked into an alleyway. At the back of his shop stood Abner Groff, the town baker. His tiny blood-shot eyes looked up and down the alleyway. In his shop someone called the baker who pretended not to hear. The baker had an empty milk bottle in his hand and an angry sullen look in his eyes.

blood-shot *ms*
< bloodshot

In Winesburg, Seth Richmond was called the "deep one." "He's like his father," men said as he went through the streets. "He'll break out some of these days. You wait and see."

The talk of the town and the respect with which men and boys instinctively greeted him, as all men greet silent people, had affected Seth Richmond's outlook on life and on himself. He, like most boys, was deeper than boys are given credit for being, but he was not what the men of the town, and even his mother, thought him to be. No great underlying purpose lay back of his habitual

Concerning Seth Richmond

silence, and he had no definite plan for his life. When the boys with whom he associated were noisy and quarrelsome, he stood quietly at one side. With calm eyes he watched the gesticulating lively figures of his companions. He wasn't particularly interested in what was going on, and sometimes wondered if he would ever be particularly interested in anything. Now, as he stood in the half darkness by the window watching the baker, he wished that he himself might become thoroughly stirred by something, even by the fits of sullen anger for which Baker Groff was noted. "It would be better for me if I could become excited and wrangle about politics like windy old Tom Willard," he thought as he left the window and went again along the hallway to the room occupied by his friend George Willard.

half *ms* < half-

thought *ms* < thought,

friend *ms* < friend,
but, *ed* < but

George Willard was older than Seth Richmond, but, in the rather odd friendship between the two, it was he who was forever courting and the younger boy who was being courted. The paper on which George worked had one policy. It strove to mention by name, in each issue, as many as possible of the inhabitants of the village. Like an excited dog, George Willard ran here and there, noting on his pad of paper who had gone on business to the county seat or had returned from a visit to a neighboring village. All day he wrote little facts upon the pad. "A. P. Wringlet has received a shipment of straw hats. Ed Byerbaum and Tom Marshall were in Cleveland Friday. Uncle Tom Sinnings is building a new barn on his place on the Valley Road."

name, *ed* < name

The idea that George Willard would someday become a writer had given him a place of distinction in Winesburg, and to Seth Richmond he talked continually of the matter. "It's the easiest of all lives to live," he declared, becoming excited and boastful. "Here and there

someday *ed* < some day

The Thinker

you go and there is no one to boss you. Though you are in India or in the South Seas in a boat, you have but to write and there you are. Wait till I get my name up and then see what fun I shall have."

In George Willard's room, which had a window looking down into an alleyway and one that looked across railroad tracks to Biff Carter's Lunch Room facing the railroad station, Seth Richmond sat in a chair and looked at the floor. George Willard, who had been sitting for an hour idly playing with a lead pencil, greeted him effusively. "I've been trying to write a love story," he explained, laughing nervously. Lighting a pipe he began walking up and down the room. "I know what I'm going to do. I'm going to fall in love. I've been sitting here and thinking it over and I'm going to do it."

As though embarrassed by his declaration, George went to a window and turning his back to his friend leaned out. "I know who I'm going to fall in love with," he said sharply. "It's Helen White. She is the only girl in town with any get-up to her."

Struck with a new idea, young Willard turned and walked toward his visitor. "Look here," he said. "You know Helen White better than I do. I want you to tell her what I said. You just get to talking to her and say that I'm in love with her. See what she says to that. See how she takes it and then you come and tell me."

Seth Richmond arose and went toward the door. The words of his comrade irritated him unbearably. "Well, good-by," he said briefly.

George was amazed. Running forward he stood in the darkness trying to look into Seth's face. "What's the matter? What are you going to do? You stay here and let's talk," he urged.

A wave of resentment directed against his friend, the

tracks *ed* < track's

Willard, *ed* < Willard

get-up *ms* < 'get up'

toward *ms* < towards

it *ms* < it,
toward *ms* < towards

good-by *ms*
< good-bye,"

Concerning Seth Richmond

men of the town who were, he thought, perpetually talking of nothing, and, most of all, against his own habit of silence made Seth half desperate. "Aw, speak to her yourself," he burst forth and then, going quickly through the door, slammed it sharply in his friend's face. "I'm going to find Helen White and talk to her but not about him," he muttered.

Seth went down the stairway and out at the front door of the hotel muttering with wrath. Crossing a little dusty street and climbing a low iron railing, he went to sit upon the grass in the station yard. George Willard he thought a profound fool, and he wished that he had said so more vigorously. Although his acquaintanceship with Helen White, the banker's daughter, was outwardly but casual, she was often the subject of his thoughts and he felt that she was something private and personal to himself. "The busy fool with his love stories," he muttered, staring back over his shoulder at George Willard's room, "why does he never tire of his eternal talking."

It was berry harvest time in Winesburg and upon the station platform men and boys loaded the boxes of red, fragrant berries into two express cars that stood upon the siding. A June moon was in the sky, although in the west a storm threatened and no street lamps were lighted. In the dim light the figures of the men standing upon the express trucks and pitching the boxes in at the doors of the cars were but dimly discernible. Upon the iron railing that protected the station lawn sat other men. Pipes were lighted. Village jokes went back and forth. Away in the distance a train whistled and the men loading the boxes into the cars worked with renewed activity.

Seth arose from his place on the grass and went silently past the men perched upon the railing and into Main Street. He had come to a resolution. "I'll get out

and, *ed* < and

silence *ed* < silence,

then, *ed* < then

her *ms* < her,

(threatened *ms* < threatened,

trucks *ms* < truck

The Thinker

here. *ms* < here?

(tomorrow *ms*
(< to-morrow

Tobacco *ed* < Cigar
*In Clyde, the S. R. Hart-
zel Cigar Store stood at
101 South Main Street.
The town hall, the Clyde
Village Hall, at 131 South
Main Street, was con-
structed in 1882.*

half *ed* < half-

and, *ed* < and
*Dr. Welling's house repre-
sents the Dr. J. F. Whitte-
more house and office in
Clyde, at 133 West Buck-
eye Street, later the house
and office of Dr. James
E. Ott.*

of here," he told himself. "What good am I here. I'm
going to some city and go to work. I'll tell mother about
it tomorrow."

Seth Richmond went slowly along Main Street, past
Wacker's Tobacco Store and the Town Hall, and into
Buckeye Street. He was depressed by the thought that
he was not a part of the life in his own town, but the
depression did not cut deeply as he did not think of
himself as at fault. In the heavy shadows of a big tree
before Dr. Welling's house, he stopped and stood watching half witted Turk Smollet, who was pushing a wheelbarrow in the road. The old man with his absurdly boyish mind had a dozen long boards on the wheelbarrow,
and, as he hurried along the road, balanced the load
with extreme nicety. "Easy there, Turk! Steady now, old
boy!" the old man shouted to himself, and laughed so
that the load of boards rocked dangerously.

Seth knew Turk Smollet, the half dangerous old wood
chopper whose peculiarities added so much of color to
the life of the village. He knew that when Turk got into
Main Street he would become the center of a whirlwind
of cries and comments, that in truth the old man was
going far out of his way in order to pass through Main
Street and exhibit his skill in wheeling the boards. "If
George Willard were here, he'd have something to say,"
thought Seth. "George belongs to this town. He'd shout
at Turk and Turk would shout at him. They'd both be
secretly pleased by what they had said. It's different with
me. I don't belong. I'll not make a fuss about it, but I'm
going to get out of here."

Seth stumbled forward through the half darkness, feeling himself an outcast in his own town. He began to
pity himself, but a sense of the absurdity of his thoughts
made him smile. In the end he decided that he was sim-

Concerning Seth Richmond

ply old beyond his years and not at all a subject for self pity. "I'm made to go to work. I may be able to make a place for myself by steady working, and I might as well be at it," he decided.

Seth went to the house of Banker White and stood in the darkness by the front door. On the door hung a heavy brass knocker, an innovation introduced into the village by Helen White's mother, who had also organized a women's club for the study of poetry. Seth raised the knocker and let it fall. Its heavy clatter sounded like a report from distant guns. "How awkward and foolish I am," he thought. "If Mrs. White comes to the door, I won't know what to say."

It was Helen White who came to the door and found Seth standing at the edge of the porch. Blushing with pleasure, she stepped forward, closing the door softly. "I'm going to get out of town. I don't know what I'll do but I'm going to get out of here and go to work. I think I'll go to Columbus," he said. "Perhaps I'll get into the State University down there. Anyway, I'm going. I'll tell mother tonight." He hesitated and looked doubtfully about. "Perhaps you wouldn't mind coming to walk with me."

Seth and Helen walked through the streets beneath the trees. Heavy clouds had drifted across the face of the moon, and before them in the deep twilight went a man with a short ladder upon his shoulder. Hurrying forward, the man stopped at the street crossings and, putting the ladder against the wooden lamp posts, lighted the village lights so that their way was half lighted, half darkened by the lamps and by the deepening shadows cast by the low-branched trees. In the tops of the trees the wind began to play, disturbing the sleeping birds so that they flew about calling plaintively. In the

self pity *ed* < self-pity

women's *ed* < woman's

do *ms* < do,
The Ohio State University, at Columbus, lies south of Clyde; Anderson later erred in referring to it as "up" (north) from the village.
tonight *ms* < to-night

me. *ms* < me?

crossings *ms* < crossing

posts *ms* < post

darkened *ed* < darkened,

The Thinker

lighted space before one of the lamps, two bats wheeled and circled, pursuing the gathering swarm of night flies.

Since Seth had been a boy in knee trousers there had been a half expressed intimacy between him and the maiden who now for the first time walked beside him. For a time she had been beset with a madness for writing notes which she addressed to Seth. He had found them concealed in his books at school and one had been given him by a child met in the street, while several had been delivered through the village post office.

The notes had been written in a round, boyish hand and had reflected a mind inflamed by novel reading. Seth had not answered them, although he had been moved and flattered by some of the sentences scrawled in pencil upon the stationery of the banker's wife. Putting them into the pocket of his coat, he went through the street or stood by the fence in the school yard with something burning at his side. He thought it fine that he should be thus selected as the favorite of the richest and most attractive girl in town.

Helen and Seth stopped by a fence near where a low dark building faced the street. The building had once been a factory for the making of barrel staves but was now vacant. Across the street upon the porch of a house a man and woman talked of their childhood, their voices coming clearly across to the half embarrassed youth and maiden. There was the sound of scraping chairs and the man and woman came down the gravel path to a wooden gate. Standing outside the gate the man leaned over and kissed the woman. "For old times' sake," he said and, turning, walked rapidly away along the sidewalk.

"That's Belle Turner," whispered Helen, and put her hand boldly into Seth's hand. "I didn't know she had a fellow. I thought she was too old for that." Seth laughed

half *ed* < half-

gate *ms* < gate,

Concerning Seth Richmond

uneasily. The hand of the girl was warm and a strange, dizzy feeling crept over him. Into his mind came a desire to tell her something he had been determined not to tell. "George Willard's in love with you," he said, and in spite of his agitation his voice was low and quiet. "He's writing a story and he wants to be in love. He wants to know how it feels. He wanted me to tell you and see what you said."

story ms < story,

Again Helen and Seth walked in silence. They came to the garden surrounding the old Richmond place and going through a gap in the hedge sat on a wooden bench beneath a bush.

On the street as he walked beside the girl new and daring thoughts had come into Seth Richmond's mind. He began to regret his decision to get out of town. "It would be something new and altogether delightful to remain and walk often through the streets with Helen White," he thought. In imagination he saw himself putting his arm about her waist and feeling her arms clasped tightly about his neck. One of those odd combinations of events and places made him connect the idea of love-making with this girl and a spot he had visited some days before. He had gone on an errand to the house of a farmer who lived on a hillside beyond the Fair Grounds and had returned by a path through a field. At the foot of the hill below the farmer's house Seth had stopped beneath a sycamore tree and looked about him. A soft humming noise had greeted his ears. For a moment he had thought the tree must be the home of a swarm of bees.

Grounds ed < Ground

And then, looking down, Seth had seen the bees everywhere all about him in the long grass. He stood in a mass of weeds that grew waist-high in the field that ran away from the hillside. The weeds were abloom with

The Thinker

tiny purple blossoms and gave forth an overpowering fragrance. Upon the weeds the bees were gathered in armies, singing as they worked.

Seth imagined himself lying on a summer evening, buried deep among the weeds beneath the tree. Beside him, in the scene built in his fancy, lay Helen White, her hand lying in his hand. A peculiar reluctance kept him from kissing her lips, but he felt he might have done that if he wished. Instead, he lay perfectly still, looking at her and listening to the army of bees that sang the sustained masterful song of labor above his head.

On the bench in the garden Seth stirred uneasily. Releasing the hand of the girl he thrust his hands into his trousers pockets. A desire to impress the mind of his companion with the importance of the resolution he had made came over him and he nodded his head toward the house. "Mother'll make a fuss, I suppose," he whispered. "She hasn't thought at all about what I'm going to do in life. She thinks I'm going to stay on here forever just being a boy."

Seth's voice became charged with boyish earnestness. "You see, I've got to strike out. I've got to get to work. It's what I'm good for."

Helen White was impressed. She nodded her head and a feeling of admiration swept over her. "This is as it should be," she thought. "This boy is not a boy at all, but a strong, purposeful man." Certain vague desires that had been invading her body were swept away and she sat up very straight on the bench. The thunder continued to rumble and flashes of heat lightning lit up the eastern sky. The garden that had been so mysterious and vast, a place that with Seth beside her might have become the background for strange and wonderful adven-

girl *ms* < girl,
trousers *ed* < trouser

Concerning Seth Richmond

tures, now seemed no more than an ordinary Winesburg back yard, quite definite and limited in its outlines.

"What will you do down there?" she whispered.

Seth turned half around on the bench, striving to see her face in the darkness. He thought her infinitely more sensible and straight-forward than George Willard, and was glad he had come away from his friend. A feeling of impatience with the town that had been in his mind returned, and he tried to tell her of it. "Everyone talks and talks," he began. "I'm sick of it. I'll do something, get into some kind of work where talk don't count. Maybe I'll just be a mechanic in a shop. I don't know. I guess I don't care much. I just want to work and keep quiet. That's all I've got in my mind."

Seth arose from the bench and put out his hand. He did not want to bring the meeting to an end but could not think of anything more to say. "It's the last time we'll see each other," he whispered.

A wave of sentiment swept over Helen. Putting her hand upon Seth's shoulder, she started to draw his face down toward her own upturned face. The act was one of pure affection and cutting regret that some vague adventure that had been present in the spirit of the night would now never be realized. "I think I'd better be going along," she said, letting her hand fall heavily to her side. A thought came to her. "Don't you go with me; I want to be alone," she said. "You go and talk with your mother. You'd better do that now."

Seth hesitated and, as he stood waiting, the girl turned and ran away through the hedge. A desire to run after her came to him, but he only stood staring, perplexed and puzzled by her action as he had been perplexed and puzzled by all of the life of the town out of which she

down *ed* < up

straight-forward *ms* < straightforward

toward *ms* < towards

The Thinker

had come. Walking slowly toward the house, he stopped in the shadow of a large tree and looked at his mother sitting by a lighted window busily sewing. The feeling of loneliness that had visited him earlier in the evening returned and colored his thoughts of the adventure through which he had just passed. "Huh!" he exclaimed, turning and staring in the direction taken by Helen White. "That's how things'll turn out. She'll be like the rest. I suppose she'll begin now to look at me in a funny way." He looked at the ground and pondered this thought. "She'll be embarrassed and feel strange when I'm around," he whispered to himself. "That's how it'll be. That's how everything'll turn out. When it comes to loving someone, it won't never be me. It'll be someone else—some fool—someone who talks a lot—someone like that George Willard."

someone *ms*
(< some one,
(someone *ms*
 < some one
(someone *ms*
 < some one
someone *ms*
(< some one

TANDY

Concerning Tandy Hard

UNTIL SHE WAS seven years old she lived in an old unpainted house on an unused road that led off Trunion Pike. Her father gave her but little attention and her mother was dead. The father spent his time talking and thinking of religion. He proclaimed himself an agnostic and was so absorbed in destroying the ideas of God that had crept into the minds of his neighbors that he never saw God manifesting himself in the little child that, half forgotten, lived here and there on the bounty of her dead mother's relatives.

Concerning Tandy Hard

A stranger came to Winesburg and saw in the child what the father did not see. He was a tall, red-haired young man who was almost always drunk. Sometimes he sat in a chair before the New Willard House with Tom Hard, the father. As Tom talked, declaring there could be no God, the stranger smiled and winked at the bystanders. He and Tom became friends and were much together.

The stranger was the son of a rich merchant of Cleveland and had come to Winesburg on a mission. He wanted to cure himself of the habit of drink and thought that by escaping from his city associates and living in a rural community he would have a better chance in the struggle with the appetite that was destroying him.

His sojourn in Winesburg was not a success. The dullness of the passing hours led to his drinking harder than ever. But he did succeed in doing something. He gave a name rich with meaning to Tom Hard's daughter.

One evening when he was recovering from a long debauch the stranger came reeling along the main street of the town. Tom Hard sat in a chair before the New Willard House with his daughter, then a child of five, on his knees. Beside him on the board sidewalk sat young George Willard. The stranger dropped into a chair beside them. His body shook and when he tried to talk his voice trembled.

It was late evening and darkness lay over the town and over the railroad that ran along the foot of a little incline before the hotel. Somewhere in the distance, off to the west, there was a prolonged blast from the whistle of a passenger engine. A dog that had been sleeping in the roadway arose and barked. The stranger began to babble and made a prophecy concerning the child that lay in the arms of the agnostic.

Anderson claimed to have written this story to help him seduce a blonde woman resistant to his charms or (another explanation) perhaps to reflect on the unfulfilled life of his brother Earl.

drink *ms* < drink,

that *ed* < than

Tandy

"I came here to quit drinking," he said, and tears began to run down his cheeks. He did not look at Tom Hard but leaned forward and stared into the darkness as though seeing a vision. "I ran away to the country to be cured, but I am not cured. There is a reason." He turned to look at the child who sat up very straight on her father's knee and returned the look.

Hard *ms* < Hard,

The stranger touched Tom Hard on the arm. "Drink is not the only thing to which I am addicted," he said. "There is something else. I am a lover and have not found my thing to love. That is a big point if you know enough to realize what I mean. It makes my destruction inevitable, you see. There are few who understand that."

The stranger became silent and seemed overcome with sadness, but another blast from the whistle of the passenger engine aroused him. "I have not lost faith. I proclaim that. I have only been brought to the place where I know my faith will not be realized," he declared hoarsely. He looked hard at the child and began to address her, paying no more attention to the father. "There is a woman coming," he said, and his voice was now sharp and earnest. "I have missed her, you see. She did not come in my time. You may be the woman. It would be like fate to let me stand in her presence once, on such an evening as this, when I have destroyed myself with drink and she is as yet only a child."

The shoulders of the stranger shook violently, and when he tried to roll a cigarette the paper fell from his trembling fingers. He grew angry and scolded. "They

woman *ms* < woman,

think it's easy to be a woman to be loved, but I know better," he declared. Again he turned to the child. "I understand," he cried. "Perhaps of all men I alone understand."

His glance again wandered away to the darkened street.

Concerning Tandy Hard

"I know about her although she has never crossed my path," he said softly. "I know about her struggles and her defeats. It is because of her defeats that she is to me the lovely one. Out of her defeats has been born a new quality in woman. I have a name for it. I call it Tandy. I made up the name when I was a true dreamer and before my body became vile. It is the quality of being strong to be loved. It is something men need from women and that they do not get."

The stranger arose and stood before Tom Hard. His body rocked back and forth and he seemed about to fall, but instead he dropped to his knees on the sidewalk and raised the hands of the little girl to his drunken lips. He kissed them ecstatically. "Be Tandy, little one," he pleaded. "Dare to be strong and courageous. That is the road. Venture anything. Be brave enough to dare to be loved. Be something more than man or woman. Be Tandy."

The stranger arose and staggered off down the street. A day or two later he got aboard a train and returned to his home in Cleveland. On the summer evening, after the talk before the hotel, Tom Hard took the girl child to the house of a relative where she had been invited to spend the night. As he went along in the darkness under the trees he forgot the babbling voice of the stranger and his mind returned to the making of arguments by which he might destroy men's faith in God. He spoke his daughter's name and she began to weep.

"I don't want to called that," she declared. "I want to be called Tandy—Tandy Hard." The child wept so bitterly that Tom Hard was touched and tried to comfort her. He stopped beneath a tree and, taking her into his arms, began to caress her. "Be good, now," he said sharply; but she would not be quieted. With childish

---

her *ms* < her,

pleaded *ed* < plead

Tandy

abandon she gave herself over to grief, her voice breaking the evening stillness of the street. "I want to be Tandy.
I want to be Tandy. I want to be Tandy Hard," she cried,
shaking her head and sobbing as though her young
strength were not enough to bear the vision the words
of the drunkard had brought to her.

THE STRENGTH OF GOD

Concerning the Reverend Curtis Hartman

THE REVEREND Curtis Hartman was pastor of the
Presbyterian Church of Winesburg, and had been in
that position ten years. He was forty years old, and by
his nature very silent and reticent. To preach, standing
in the pulpit before the people, was always a hardship
for him and from Wednesday morning until Saturday
evening he thought of nothing but the two sermons that
must be preached on Sunday. Early on Sunday morning he went into a little room called a study in the bell
tower of the church and prayed. In his prayers there was
one note that always predominated. "Give me strength
and courage for thy work, oh Lord!" he pleaded, kneeling on the bare floor and bowing his head in the presence of the task that lay before him.

The Reverend Hartman was a tall man with a brown
beard. His wife, a stout, nervous woman, was the daughter of a manufacturer of underwear at Cleveland, Ohio.
The minister himself was rather a favorite in the town.
The elders of the church liked him because he was quiet

thy *ed* < Thy
oh *ed* < O
pleaded *ed* < plead

Concerning the Reverend Curtis Hartman

and unpretentious and Mrs. White, the banker's wife, thought him scholarly and refined.

The Presbyterian Church held itself somewhat aloof from the other churches of Winesburg. It was larger and more imposing and its minister was better paid. He even had a carriage of his own and on summer evenings sometimes drove about town with his wife. Through Main Street and up and down Buckeye Street he went, bowing gravely to the people, while his wife, afire with secret pride, looked at him out of the corners of her eyes and worried lest the horse become frightened and run away.

In Clyde, the Presbyterian Church, built in 1869, stood at 113 West Forest Street.

For a good many years after he came to Winesburg things went well with Curtis Hartman. He was not one to arouse keen enthusiasm among the worshippers in his church but on the other hand he made no enemies. In reality he was much in earnest and sometimes suffered prolonged periods of remorse because he could not go crying the word of God in the highways and byways of the town. He wondered if the flame of the spirit really burned in him and dreamed of a day when a strong sweet new current of power would come like a great wind into his voice and his soul and the people would tremble before the spirit of God made manifest in him. "I am a poor stick and that will never really happen to me," he mused dejectedly and then a patient smile lit up his features. "Oh well, I suppose I'm doing well enough," he added philosophically.

The room in the bell tower of the church, where on Sunday mornings the minister prayed for an increase in him of the power of God, had but one window. It was long and narrow and swung outward on a hinge like a door. On the window, made of little leaded panes, was a

The Strength of God

design showing the Christ laying his hand upon the head of a child. One Sunday morning in the summer as he sat by his desk in the room with a large bible opened before him, and the sheets of his sermon scattered about, the minister was shocked to see, in the upper room of the house next door, a woman lying in her bed and smoking a cigarette while she read a book. Curtis Hartman went on tiptoe to the window and closed it softly. He was horror stricken at the thought of a woman smoking and trembled also to think that his eyes, just raised from the pages of the book of God, had looked upon the bare shoulders and white throat of a woman. With his brain in a whirl he went down into the pulpit and preached a long sermon without once thinking of his gestures or his voice. The sermon attracted unusual attention because of its power and clearness. "I wonder if she is listening, if my voice is carrying a message into her soul," he thought and began to hope that on future Sunday mornings he might be able to say words that would touch and awaken the woman apparently far gone in secret sin.

The house next door to the Presbyterian Church, through the window of which the minister had seen the sight that had so upset him, was occupied by two women. Aunt Elizabeth Swift, a grey competent-looking widow with money in the Winesburg National Bank, lived there with her daughter Kate Swift, a school teacher. The school teacher was thirty years old and had a neat trim-looking figure. She had few friends and bore a reputation of having a sharp tongue. When he began to think about her, Curtis Hartman remembered that she had been to Europe and had lived for two years in New York City. "Perhaps after all her smoking means nothing," he thought. He began to remember that, when he was a

---

bible *ed* < Bible

Although this woman may offend the minister by lying late abed, by not preparing to attend church, and by reading probably nonreligious writing, it is most of all her smoking cigarettes, a habit in women completely unacceptable to the small-town man of the 1890s, that shocks him.

The Swift house represents the Dr. E. D. Cooper house and office in Clyde, at 137 South Main Street.

window *ms* < windows

Respected older women were often addressed by nonrelatives honorifically as "aunt"; Elizabeth Swift is thus "Aunt" to others but "Mother" to Kate. The Winesburg National Bank is modeled on the First National Bank (later the Clyde Savings Bank), at 108 South Main Street.

that, *ed* < that

Concerning the Reverend Curtis Hartman

student in college and occasionally read novels, good
although somewhat worldly women had smoked
through the pages of a book that had once fallen into
his hands. With a rush of new determination he worked
on his sermons all through the week and forgot, in his
zeal to reach the ears and the soul of this new listener,
both his embarrassment in the pulpit and the necessity
of prayer in the study on Sunday mornings.

Reverend Hartman's experience with women had been
somewhat limited. He was the son of a wagon maker
from Muncie, Indiana, and had worked his way through
college. The daughter of the underwear manufacturer
had boarded in a house where he lived during his school
days and he had married her after a formal and prolonged courtship, carried on for the most part by the
girl herself. On his marriage day the underwear
manufacturer had given his daughter five thousand dollars and he promised to leave her at least twice that
amount in his will. The minister had thought himself
fortunate in marriage and had never permitted himself
to think of other women. He did not want to think of
other women. What he wanted was to do the work of
God quietly and earnestly.

In the soul of the minister a struggle awoke. From
wanting to reach the ears of Kate Swift, and through his
sermons to delve into her soul, he began to want also to
look again at the figure lying white and quiet in the
bed. On a Sunday morning when he could not sleep
because of his thoughts he arose and went to walk in
the streets. When he had gone along Main Street almost to the old Richmond place he stopped and pick-
ing up a stone rushed off to the room in the bell tower.
With the stone he broke out a corner of the window
and then locked the door and sat down at the desk be-

good *ed* < good,
women *ed* < women,

The Strength of God

fore the open bible to wait. When the shade of the window to Kate Swift's room was raised he could see, through the hole, directly into her bed, but she was not there. She also had arisen and had gone for a walk and the hand that raised the shade was the hand of Aunt Elizabeth Swift.

The minister almost wept with joy at this deliverance from the carnal desire to "peep" and went back to his own house praising God. In an ill moment he forgot, however, to stop the hole in the window. The piece of glass broken out at the corner of the window just nipped off the bare heel of the boy standing motionless and looking with rapt eyes into the face of the Christ.

Curtis Hartman forgot his sermon on that Sunday morning. He talked to his congregation and in his talk said that it was a mistake for people to think of their minister as a man set aside and intended by nature to lead a blameless life. "Out of my own experience I know that we, who are the ministers of God's word, are beset by the same temptations that assail you," he declared. "I have been tempted and have surrendered to temptation. It is only the hand of God, placed beneath my head, that has raised me up. As he has raised me so also will he raise you. Do not despair. In your hour of sin raise your eyes to the skies and you will be again and again saved."

Resolutely the minister put the thoughts of the woman in the bed out of his mind and began to be something like a lover in the presence of his wife. One evening when they drove out together he turned the horse out of Buckeye Street and in the darkness on Gospel Hill, above Waterworks Pond, put his arm about Sarah Hartman's waist. When he had eaten breakfast in the morning and was ready to retire to his study at the back

The counterpart to Winesburg's Piety Hill was Clyde's Gospel Hill (thus called, although flat), west of Waterworks Pond.

Concerning the Reverend Curtis Hartman

of his house he went around the table and kissed his wife on the cheek. When thoughts of Kate Swift came into his head he smiled and raised his eyes to the skies. "Intercede for me, Master," he muttered, "keep me in the narrow path intent on thy work."

And now began the real struggle in the soul of the brown-bearded minister. By chance he discovered that Kate Swift was in the habit of lying in her bed in the evening and reading a book. A lamp stood on a table by the side of the bed and the light streamed down upon her white shoulders and bare throat. On the evening when he made the discovery the minister sat at the desk in the study from nine until after eleven and when her light was put out stumbled out of the church to spend two more hours walking and praying in the streets. He did not want to kiss the shoulders and the throat of Kate Swift and had not allowed his mind to dwell on such thoughts. He did not know what he wanted. "I am God's child and he must save me from myself," he cried, in the darkness under the trees as he wandered in the streets. By a tree he stood and looked at the sky that was covered with hurrying clouds. He began to talk to God intimately and closely. "Please, Father, do not forget me. Give me power to go tomorrow and repair the hole in the window. Lift my eyes again to the skies. Stay with me, thy servant, in his hour of need."

Up and down through the silent streets walked the minister and for days and weeks his soul was troubled. He could not understand the temptation that had come to him nor could he fathom the reason for its coming. In a way he began to blame God, saying to himself that he had tried to keep his feet in the true path and had not run about seeking sin. "Through my days as a young man and all through my life here I have gone quietly

head *ms* < head,

thy *ed* < Thy

evening *ms* < evenings

tomorrow *ed* < to-morrow

thy *ed* < Thy

The Strength of God

about my work," he declared. "Why now should I be tempted? What have I done that this burden should be laid on me?"

Three times during the early fall and winter of that year Curtis Hartman crept out of his house to the room in the bell tower to sit in the darkness looking at the figure of Kate Swift lying in her bed and later went to walk and pray in the streets. He could not understand himself. For weeks he would go along scarcely thinking of the school teacher and telling himself that he had conquered the carnal desire to look at her body. And then something would happen. As he sat in the study of his own house, hard at work on a sermon, he would become nervous and begin to walk up and down the room. "I will go out into the streets," he told himself and even as he let himself in at the church door he persistently denied to himself the cause of his being there. "I will not repair the hole in the window and I will train myself to come here at night and sit in the presence of this woman without raising my eyes. I will not be defeated in this thing. The Lord has devised this temptation as a test of my soul and I will grope my way out of darkness into the light of righteousness."

One night in January when it was bitter cold and snow lay deep on the streets of Winesburg Curtis Hartman paid his last visit to the room in the bell tower of the church. It was past nine o'clock when he left his own house and he set out so hurriedly that he forgot to put on his overshoes. In Main Street no one was abroad but Hop Higgins, the night watchman, and in the whole town no one was awake but the watchman and young George Willard, who sat in the office of the *Winesburg Eagle* trying to write a story. Along the street to the church went the minister, plowing through the drifts

Higgins, *ed* < Higgins
watchman, *ed*
(< watchman

Concerning the Reverend Curtis Hartman

and thinking that this time he would utterly give way to sin. "I want to look at the woman and to think of kissing her shoulders and I am going to let myself think what I choose," he declared bitterly and tears came into his eyes. He began to think that he would get out of the ministry and try some other way of life. "I shall go to some city and get into business," he declared. "If my nature is such that I cannot resist sin, I shall give myself over to sin. At least I shall not be a hypocrite, preaching the word of God with my mind thinking of the shoulders and neck of a woman who does not belong to me."

and neck *ms, Pr 2–Pr 7* < and the neck

It was cold in the room of the bell tower of the church on that January night and almost as soon as he came into the room Curtis Hartman knew that if he stayed he would be ill. His feet were wet from tramping in the snow and there was no fire. In the room in the house next door Kate Swift had not yet appeared. With grim determination the man sat down to wait. Sitting in the chair and gripping the edge of the desk on which lay the bible he stared into the darkness thinking the blackest thoughts of his life. He thought of his wife and for the moment almost hated her. "She has always been ashamed of passion and has cheated me," he thought. "Man has a right to expect living passion and beauty in a woman. He has no right to forget that he is an animal and in me there is something that is Greek. I will throw off the woman of my bosom and seek other women. I will besiege this school teacher. I will fly in the face of all men and if I am a creature of carnal lusts I will live then for my lusts."

bible *ed* < Bible

The desperate Reverend Hartman decides that his life of denial and repression (Hebraic or Old Testament qualities) must give way to a new life of expression and fulfillment (classic Greek qualities).

The distracted man trembled from head to foot, partly from cold, partly from the struggle in which he was engaged. Hours passed and a fever assailed his body. His throat began to hurt and his teeth chattered. His feet on

The Strength of God

the study floor felt like two cakes of ice. Still he would not give up. "I will see this woman and will think the thoughts I have never dared to think," he told himself, gripping the edge of the desk and waiting.

Curtis Hartman came near dying from the effects of that night of waiting in the church, and also he found in the thing that happened what he took to be the way of life for him. On other evenings when he had waited he had not been able to see, through the little hole in the glass, any part of the school teacher's room except that occupied by her bed. In the darkness he had waited until the woman suddenly appeared sitting in the bed in her white night robe. When the light was turned up she propped herself up among the pillows and read a book. Sometimes she smoked one of the cigarettes. Only her bare shoulders and throat were visible.

On the January night, after he had come near dying with cold and after his mind had two or three times actually slipped away into an odd land of fantasy so that he had by an exercise of will power to force himself back into consciousness, Kate Swift appeared. In the room next door a lamp was lighted and the waiting man stared into an empty bed. Then upon the bed before his eyes a naked woman threw herself. Lying face downward she wept and beat with her fists upon the pillow. With a final outburst of weeping she half arose, and in the presence of the man who had waited to look and to think thoughts the woman of sin began to pray. In the lamp light her figure, slim and strong, looked like the figure of the boy in the presence of the Christ on the leaded window.

Curtis Hartman never remembered how he got out of the church. With a cry he arose, dragging the heavy desk along the floor. The bible fell making a great clat-

(night robe *ed*
< night-robe

(lamp light *ed*
< lamplight

bible *ed* < Bible
fell *ms* < fell,

Concerning the Reverend Curtis Hartman

ter in the silence. When the light in the house next door went out he stumbled down the stairway and into the street. Along the street he went and ran in at the door of the *Winesburg Eagle.* To George Willard, who was tramping up and down in the office undergoing a struggle of his own, he began to talk half incoherently. "The ways of God are beyond human understanding," he cried, running in quickly and closing the door. He began to advance upon the young man his eyes glowing and his voice ringing with fervor. "I have found the light," he cried. "After ten years in this town, God has manifested himself to me in the body of a woman." His voice dropped and he began to whisper. "I did not understand," he said. "What I took to be a trial of my soul was only a preparation for a new and more beautiful fervor of the spirit. God has appeared to me in the person of Kate Swift, the school teacher, kneeling naked on a bed. Do you know Kate Swift? Although she may not be aware of it, she is an instrument of God, bearing the message of truth."

Reverend Curtis Hartman turned and ran out of the office. At the door he stopped, and, after looking up and down the deserted street, turned again to George Willard. "I am delivered. Have no fear." He held up a bleeding fist for the young man to see. "I smashed the glass of the window," he cried. "Now it will have to be wholly replaced. The strength of God was in me and I broke it with my fist."

man *ms* < man,

and, *ed* < and

THE TEACHER

Concerning Kate Swift

SNOW LAY DEEP in the streets of Winesburg. It had begun to snow about ten o'clock in the morning and a wind sprang up and blew the snow in clouds along Main Street. The frozen mud roads that led into town were fairly smooth and in places ice covered the mud. "There will be good sleighing," said Will Henderson, standing by the bar in Ed Griffith's Saloon. Out of the saloon he went and met Sylvester West, the druggist, stumbling along in the kind of heavy overshoes called arctics. "Snow will bring the people into town on Saturday," said the druggist. The two men stopped and discussed their affairs. Will Henderson, who had on a light overcoat and no overshoes, kicked the heel of his left foot with the heel of the right. "Snow will be good for the wheat," observed the druggist sagely.

Young George Willard, who had nothing to do, was glad because he did not feel like working that day. The weekly paper had been printed and taken to the post office on Wednesday evening and the snow began to fall on Thursday. At eight o'clock, after the morning train had passed, he put a pair of skates in his pocket and went up to Waterworks Pond but did not go skating.

Saloon *ed* < saloon

West, *ed* < West
(druggist, *ed*
< druggist

heel *ms* < toe

The post office in Clyde, Ohio, was at 100 North Main Street.

Concerning Kate Swift

Past the pond and along a path that followed Wine Creek he went until he came to a grove of beech trees. There he built a fire against the side of a log and sat down at the end of the log to think. When the snow began to fall and the wind to blow he hurried about getting fuel for the fire.

The young reporter was thinking of Kate Swift who had once been his school teacher. On the evening before he had gone to her house to get a book she wanted him to read and had been alone with her for an hour. For the fourth or fifth time the woman had talked to him with great earnestness and he could not make out what she meant by her talk. He began to believe she might be in love with him and the thought was both pleasing and annoying.

Up from the log he sprang and began to pile sticks on the fire. Looking about to be sure he was alone he talked aloud pretending he was in the presence of the woman. "Oh, you're just letting on, you know you are," he declared. "I am going to find out about you. You wait and see."

The young man got up and went back along the path toward town leaving the fire blazing in the woods. As he went through the streets the skates clanked in his pocket. In his own room in the New Willard House he built a fire in the stove and lay down on top of the bed. He began to have lustful thoughts and pulling down the shade of the window closed his eyes and turned his face to the wall. He took a pillow into his arms and embraced it thinking first of the school teacher, who by her words had stirred something within him, and later of Helen White, the slim daughter of the town banker, with whom he had been for a long time half in love.

By nine o'clock of that evening snow lay deep in the

woods *ed* < wood

him, *ed* < him

The Teacher

streets and the weather had become bitter cold. It was difficult to walk about. The stores were dark and the people had crawled away to their houses. The evening train from Cleveland was very late but nobody was interested in its arrival. By ten o'clock all but four of the eighteen hundred citizens of the town were in bed.

Hop Higgins, the night watchman, was partially awake. He was lame and carried a heavy stick. On dark nights he carried a lantern. Between nine and ten o'clock he went his rounds. Up and down Main Street he stumbled through the drifts trying the doors of the stores. Then he went into alleyways and tried the back doors. Finding all tight he hurried around the corner to the New Willard House and beat on the door. Through the rest of the night he intended to stay by the stove. "You go to bed. I'll keep the stove going," he said to the boy who slept on a cot in the hotel office.

Hop Higgins sat down by the stove and took off his shoes. When the boy had gone to sleep he began to think of his own affairs. He intended to paint his house in the spring and sat by the stove calculating the cost of paint and labor. That led him into other calculations. The night watchman was sixty years old and wanted to retire. He had been a soldier in the Civil War and drew a small pension. He hoped to find some new method of making a living and aspired to become a professional breeder of ferrets. Already he had four of the strangely shaped savage little creatures, that are used by sportsmen in the pursuit of rabbits, in the cellar of his house. "Now I have one male and three females," he mused. "If I am lucky by spring I shall have twelve or fifteen. In another year I shall be able to begin advertising ferrets for sale in the sporting papers."

The night watchman settled into his chair and his

Concerning Kate Swift

mind became a blank. He did not sleep. By years of practice he had trained himself to sit for hours through the long nights neither asleep nor awake. In the morning he was almost as refreshed as though he had slept.

With Hop Higgins safely stowed away in the chair behind the stove only three people were awake in Winesburg. George Willard was in the office of the *Eagle* pretending to be at work on the writing of a story but in reality continuing the mood of the morning by the fire in the woods. In the bell tower of the Presbyterian Church the Reverend Curtis Hartman was sitting in the darkness preparing himself for a revelation from God, and Kate Swift, the school teacher, was leaving her house for a walk in the storm.

woods *ed* < wood

It was past ten o'clock when Kate Swift set out and the walk was unpremeditated. It was as though the man and the boy, by thinking of her, had driven her forth into the wintry streets. Aunt Elizabeth Swift had gone to the county seat concerning some business in connection with mortgages in which she had money invested and would not be back until the next day. By a huge stove, called a base burner, in the living room of the house sat the daughter reading a book. Suddenly she sprang to her feet and, snatching a cloak from a rack by the front door, ran out of the house.

Before the age of central heating, many well-off people kept in their living rooms large coal- or wood-burning stoves, "base burners," that in some designs could refill their fire-boxes from attached hoppers.

At the age of thirty Kate Swift was not known in Winesburg as a pretty woman. Her complexion was not good and her face was covered with blotches that indicated ill health. Alone in the night in the winter streets she was lovely. Her back was straight, her shoulders square and her features were as the features of a tiny goddess on a pedestal in a garden in the dim light of a summer evening.

During the afternoon the school teacher had been to

The Teacher

see Dr. Welling concerning her health. The doctor had scolded her and had declared she was in danger of losing her hearing. It was foolish for Kate Swift to be abroad in the storm, foolish and perhaps dangerous.

The woman in the streets did not remember the words of the doctor and would not have turned back had she remembered. She was very cold but after walking for five minutes no longer minded the cold. First she went to the end of her own street and then across a pair of hay scales set in the ground before a feed barn and into Trunion Pike. Along Trunion Pike she went to Ned Winters' barn and turning east followed a street of low frame houses that led over Gospel Hill and into Sucker Road that ran down a shallow valley past Ike Smead's chicken farm to Waterworks Pond. As she went along the bold, excited mood that had driven her out of doors passed and then returned again.

There was something biting and forbidding in the character of Kate Swift. Everyone felt it. In the school room she was silent, cold and stern, and yet in an odd way very close to her pupils. Once in a long while something seemed to have come over her and she was happy. All of the children in the school room felt the effect of her happiness. For a time they did not work but sat back in their chairs and looked at her.

With hands clasped behind her back the school teacher walked up and down in the school room and talked very rapidly. It did not seem to matter what subject came into her mind. Once she talked to the children of Charles Lamb and made up strange intimate little stories concerning the life of the dead writer. The stories were told with the air of one who had lived in a house with Charles Lamb and knew all the secrets of his private life. The children were somewhat confused, thinking Charles

Winters' *ms* < Winter's

along *ms* < along,

(school room *ed* < schoolroom
cold *ms* < cold,

(school room *ed* < schoolroom

(school room *ed* < schoolroom

Charles Lamb (1775–1834) was an English Romantic essayist whose personal and nostalgic writings as "Elia" endeared him to escapist readers.

Concerning Kate Swift

Lamb must be someone who had once lived in Winesburg.

On another occasion the teacher talked to the children of Benvenuto Cellini. That time they laughed. What a bragging, blustering, brave, lovable fellow she made of the old artist. Concerning him also she invented anecdotes. There was one of a German music teacher who had a room above Cellini's lodgings in the city of Milan that made the boys guffaw. Sugars McNutts, a fat boy with red cheeks, laughed so hard that he became dizzy and fell off his seat and Kate Swift laughed with him. Then suddenly she became again cold and stern.

On the winter night when she walked through the deserted snow-covered streets, a crisis had come into the life of the school teacher. Although no one in Winesburg would have suspected it, her life had been very adventurous. It was still adventurous. Day by day as she worked in the school room or walked in the streets, grief, hope, and desire fought within her. Behind a cold exterior the most extraordinary events transpired in her mind. The people of the town thought of her as a confirmed old maid and because she spoke sharply and went her own way thought her lacking in all the human feelings that did so much to make and mar their own lives. In reality she was the most eagerly passionate soul among them, and more than once, in the five years since she had come back from her travels to settle in Winesburg and become a school teacher, had been compelled to go out of the house and walk half through the night fighting out some battle raging within. Once on a night when it rained she had stayed out six hours and when she came home had a quarrel with Aunt Elizabeth Swift. "I am glad you're not a man," said the mother sharply. "More than once I've waited for your father to

artist. ms < artist!

Benvenuto Cellini (1500–1571), a sculptor and metalsmith and a lustful, brawling genius, recounted many adventures in his Vita, *begun in 1558 and completed in 1562; Cellini was, however, more closely associated with the cities of Rome, Florence, and Paris than with the city of Milan.*

⎧ **school room** *ed*
⎨ < **schoolroom**

feelings *ms* < **feeling**

Kate Swift may be modeled on Trillena White, a teacher in Springfield, Ohio, whom Anderson met while he was attending Wittenberg Academy (1899–1900) for his high-school-equivalent education. Miss White introduced Anderson to good literature, and he wrote to her faithfully until her death in 1940.

The Teacher

come home, not knowing what new mess he had got into. I've had my share of uncertainty and you cannot blame me if I do not want to see the worst side of him reproduced in you."

———————

Kate Swift's mind was ablaze with thoughts of George Willard. In something he had written as a school boy she thought she had recognized the spark of genius and wanted to blow on the spark. One day in the summer she had gone to the *Eagle* office and finding the boy unoccupied had taken him out Main Street to the Fair Grounds, where the two sat on a grassy bank to talk. The school teacher tried to bring home to the mind of the boy some conception of the difficulties he would have to face as a writer. "You will have to know life," she declared, and her voice trembled with earnestness. She took hold of George Willard's shoulders and turned him about so that she could look into his eyes. A passer-by might have thought them about to embrace. "If you are to become a writer you'll have to stop fooling with words," she explained. "It would be better to give up the notion of writing until you are better prepared. Now it's time to be living. I don't want to frighten you, but I would like to make you understand the import of what you think of attempting. You must not become a mere peddler of words. The thing to learn is to know what people are thinking about, not what they say."

On the evening before that stormy Thursday night, when the Reverend Curtis Hartman sat in the bell tower of the church waiting to look at her body, young Willard had gone to visit the teacher and to borrow a book. It was then the thing happened that confused and puzzled the boy. He had the book under his arm and was preparing to depart. Again Kate Swift talked with great ear-

(Fair Grounds
  ed < fair ground
(sat on *ms, Pr 2–Pr 7*
  < sat down on
(to talk < *Pr 2–Pr 7*
  < and talked

Concerning Kate Swift

nestness. Night was coming on and the light in the room grew dim. As he turned to go she spoke his name softly and with an impulsive movement took hold of his hand. Because the reporter was rapidly becoming a man something of his man's appeal, combined with the winsomeness of the boy, stirred the heart of the lonely woman. A passionate desire to have him understand the import of life, to learn to interpret it truly and honestly, swept over her. Leaning forward, her lips brushed his cheek. At the same moment he for the first time became aware of the marked beauty of her features. They were both embarrassed, and to relieve her feelings she became harsh and domineering. "What's the use? It will be ten years before you begin to understand what I mean when I talk to you," she cried passionately.

feelings *ms* < feeling

On the night of the storm and while the minister sat in the church waiting for her, Kate Swift went to the office of the *Winesburg Eagle*, intending to have another talk with the boy. After the long walk in the snow, she was cold, lonely, and tired. As she came through Main Street she saw the light from the print shop window shining on the snow and on an impulse opened the door and went in. For an hour she sat by the stove in the office talking of life. She talked with passionate earnestness. The impulse that had driven her out into the snow poured itself out into talk. She became inspired as she sometimes did in the presence of the children in school. A great eagerness to open the door of life to the boy, who had been her pupil and who she thought might possess a talent for the understanding of life, had possession of her. So strong was her passion that it became something physical. Again her hands took hold of his shoulders and she turned him about. In the dim light

snow, *ms* < snow

who *ed* < whom

The Teacher

her eyes blazed. She arose and laughed, not sharply as was customary with her, but in a queer, hesitating way. "I must be going," she said. "In a moment, if I stay, I'll be wanting to kiss you."

In the newspaper office a confusion arose. Kate Swift turned and walked to the door. She was a teacher but she was also a woman. As she looked at George Willard, the passionate desire to be loved by a man, that had a thousand times before swept like a storm over her body, took possession of her. In the lamp light George Willard looked no longer a boy, but a man ready to play the part of a man.

The school teacher let George Willard take her into his arms. In the warm little office the air became suddenly heavy and the strength went out of her body. Leaning against a low counter by the door she waited. When he came and put a hand on her shoulder she turned and let her body fall heavily against him. For George Willard the confusion was immediately increased. For a moment he held the body of the woman tightly against his body and then it stiffened. Two sharp little fists began to beat on his face. When the school teacher had run away and left him alone, he walked up and down in the office swearing furiously.

It was into this confusion that the Reverend Curtis Hartman protruded himself. When he came in George Willard thought the town had gone mad. Shaking a bleeding fist in the air, the minister proclaimed the woman George had only a moment before held in his arms an instrument of God bearing a message of truth.

George blew out the lamp by the window and locking the door of the print shop went home. Through the hotel office, past Hop Higgins lost in his dream of the

(lamp light *ed*
< lamplight

Concerning Kate Swift

raising of ferrets, he went and up into his own room. The fire in the stove had gone out and he undressed in the cold. When he got into bed the sheets were like blankets of dry snow.

George Willard rolled about in the bed on which he had lain in the afternoon hugging the pillow and thinking thoughts of Kate Swift. The words of the minister, who he thought had gone suddenly insane, rang in his ears. His eyes stared about the room. The resentment, natural to the baffled male, passed and he tried to understand what had happened. He could not make it out. Over and over he turned the matter in his mind. Hours passed and he began to think it must be time for another day to come. At four o'clock he pulled the covers up about his neck and tried to sleep. When he became drowsy and closed his eyes, he raised a hand and with it groped about in the darkness. "I have missed something. I have missed something Kate Swift was trying to tell me," he muttered sleepily. Then he slept and in all Winesburg he was the last soul on that winter night to go to sleep.

LONELINESS

Concerning Enoch Robinson

HE WAS THE son of Mrs. Al Robinson who once owned a farm on a side road leading off Trunion Pike, east of Winesburg and two miles beyond the town limits. The farm house was painted brown and the blinds to all of the windows facing the road were kept closed.

(farm house *ed*
< farm-house

Loneliness

In the road before the house a flock of chickens, accompanied by two guinea hens, lay in the deep dust. Enoch lived in the house with his mother in those days and when he was a young boy went to school at the Winesburg High School. Old citizens remembered him as a quiet, smiling youth inclined to silence. He walked in the middle of the road when he came into town and sometimes read a book. Drivers of teams had to shout and swear to make him realize where he was so that he would turn out of the beaten track and let them pass.

When he was twenty-one years old Enoch went to New York City and was a city man for fifteen years. He studied French and went to an art school, hoping to develop a faculty he had for drawing. In his own mind he planned to go to Paris and to finish his art education among the masters there, but that never turned out.

Nothing ever turned out for Enoch Robinson. He could draw well enough and he had many odd delicate thoughts hidden away in his brain that might have expressed themselves through the brush of a painter, but he was always a child and that was a handicap to his worldly development. He never grew up and of course he couldn't understand people and he couldn't make people understand him. The child in him kept bumping against things, against actualities like money and sex and opinions. Once he was hit by a street car and thrown against an iron post. That made him lame. It was one of the many things that kept things from turning out for Enoch Robinson.

In New York City, when he first went there to live and before he became confused and disconcerted by the facts of life, Enoch went about a good deal with young men. He got into a group of other young artists, both men

Concerning Enoch Robinson

and women, and in the evening they sometimes came to visit him in his room. Once he got drunk and was taken to a police station where a police magistrate frightened him horribly, and once he tried to have an affair with a woman of the town met on the sidewalk before his lodging house. The woman and Enoch walked together three blocks and then the young man grew afraid and ran away. The woman had been drinking and the incident amused her. She leaned against the wall of a building and laughed so heartily that another man stopped and laughed with her. The two went away together, still laughing, and Enoch crept off to his room trembling and vexed.

The room in which young Robinson lived in New York faced Washington Square and was long and narrow like a hallway. It is important to get that fixed in your mind. The story of Enoch is in fact the story of a room almost more than it is the story of a man.

And so into the room in the evening came young Enoch's friends. There was nothing particularly striking about them except that they were artists of the kind that talk. Everyone knows of the talking artists. Throughout all of the known history of the world they have gathered in rooms and talked. They talk of art and are passionately, almost feverishly, in earnest about it. They think it matters much more than it does.

And so these people gathered and smoked cigarettes and talked and Enoch Robinson, the boy from the farm near Winesburg, was there. He stayed in a corner and for the most part said nothing. How his big blue child-like eyes stared about! On the walls were pictures he had made, crude things, half finished. His friends talked of these. Leaning back in their chairs, they talked and

evening ms < *evenings*

Bordered by 14th Street, Spring Street, Brooklyn, and the Hudson River, Greenwich Village in New York City was in the late nineteenth century becoming a bohemian artistic district centered around Washington Square.

(*think it* ms, Pr 2–Pr 7
  < *think that it*

child-like ed < *childlike*
In art discourse, "line" is the drawn or painted mark that shows the contours of an object or form; "value" is the

Loneliness

talked with their heads rocking from side to side. Words were said about line and values and composition, lots of words, such as are always being said.

Enoch wanted to talk too but he didn't know how. He was too excited to talk coherently. When he tried he sputtered and stammered and his voice sounded strange and squeaky to him. That made him stop talking. He knew what he wanted to say. But he knew also that he could never by any possibility say it. When a picture he had painted was under discussion, he wanted to burst out with something like this: "You don't get the point," he wanted to explain; "the picture you see doesn't consist of the things you see and say words about. There is something else, something you don't see at all, something you aren't intended to see. Look at this one over here, by the door here, where the light from the window falls on it. The dark spot by the road that you might not notice at all is, you see, the beginning of everything. There is a clump of elders there such as used to grow beside the road before our house back in Winesburg, Ohio, and in among the elders there is something hidden. It is a woman, that's what it is. She has been thrown from a horse and the horse has run away out of sight. Do you not see how the old man who drives a cart looks anxiously about? That is Thad Grayback who has a farm up the road. He is taking corn to Winesburg to be ground into meal at Comstock's Mill. He knows there is something in the elders, something hidden away, and yet he doesn't quite know.

"It's a woman you see, that's what it is! It's a woman and, oh, she is lovely! She is hurt and is suffering but she makes no sound. Don't you see how it is? She lies quite still, white and still, and the beauty comes out from her and spreads over everything. It is in the sky back there

Concerning Enoch Robinson

and all around everywhere. I didn't try to paint the woman, of course. She is too beautiful to be painted. How dull to talk of composition and such things. Why do you not look at the sky and then run away as I used to do when I was a boy back there in Winesburg, Ohio?"

That is the kind of thing young Enoch Robinson trembled to say to the guests who came into his room when he was a young fellow in New York City, but he always ended by saying nothing. Then he began to doubt his own mind. He was afraid the things he felt were not getting expressed in the pictures he painted. In a half indignant mood he stopped inviting people into his room and presently got into the habit of locking the door. He began to think that enough people had visited him, that he did not need people anymore. With quick imagination he began to invent his own people to whom he could really talk and to whom he explained the things he had been unable to explain to living people. His room began to be inhabited by the spirits of men and women among whom he went, in his turn saying words. It was as though everyone Enoch Robinson had ever seen had left with him some essence of himself, something he could mould and change to suit his own fancy, something that understood all about such things as the wounded woman behind the elders in the pictures.

The mild, blue-eyed young Ohio boy was a complete egotist, as all children are egotists. He did not want friends for the quite simple reason that no child wants friends. He wanted most of all the people of his own mind, people with whom he could really talk, people he could harangue and scold by the hour, servants, you see, to his fancy. Among these people he was always self-confident and bold. They might talk, to be sure, and even have opinions of their own, but always he talked

things. *ms* < things!

everyone *ed* < every one

Loneliness

last and best. He was like a writer busy among the figures of his brain, a kind of tiny blue-eyed king he was, in a six-dollar room facing Washington Square in the city of New York.

Then Enoch Robinson got married. He began to get lonely and to want to touch actual flesh and bone people with his hands. Days passed when his room seemed empty. Lust visited his body and desire grew in his mind. At night strange fevers, burning within, kept him awake. He married a girl who sat in a chair next to his own in the art school and went to live in an apartment house in Brooklyn. Two children were born to the woman he married, and Enoch got a job in a place where illustrations are made for advertisements.

That began another phase of Enoch's life. He began to play at a new game. For a while he was very proud of himself in the rôle of producing citizen of the world. He dismissed the essence of things and played with realities. In the fall he voted at an election and he had a newspaper thrown on his porch each morning. When in the evening he came home from work he got off a street car and walked sedately along behind some business man, striving to look very substantial and important. As a payer of taxes he thought he should post himself on how things are run. "I'm getting to be of some moment, a real part of things, of the state and the city and all that," he told himself with an amusing miniature air of dignity. Once, coming home from Philadelphia, he had a discussion with a man met on a train. Enoch talked about the advisability of the government's owning and operating the railroads and the man gave him a cigar. It was Enoch's notion that such a move on the part of the government would be a good thing, and

Once, *ed* < Once

Concerning Enoch Robinson

he grew quite excited as he talked. Later he remembered his own words with pleasure. "I gave him something to think about, that fellow," he muttered to himself as he climbed the stairs to his Brooklyn apartment.

To be sure, Enoch's marriage did not turn out. He himself brought it to an end. He began to feel choked and walled in by the life in the apartment and to feel toward his wife and even toward his children as he had felt concerning the friends who once came to visit him. He began to tell little lies about business engagements that would give him freedom to walk alone in the streets at night and, the chance offering, he secretly re-rented the room facing Washington Square. Then Mrs. Al Robinson died on the farm near Winesburg, and he got eight thousand dollars from the bank that acted as trustee of her estate. That took Enoch out of the world of men altogether. He gave the money to his wife and told her he could not live in the apartment anymore. She cried and was angry and threatened, but he only stared at her and went his own way. In reality the wife did not care much. She thought Enoch slightly insane and was a little afraid of him. When it was quite sure that he would never come back, she took the two children and went to a village in Connecticut where she had lived as a girl. In the end she married a man who bought and sold real estate and was contented enough.

And so Enoch Robinson stayed in the New York room among the people of his fancy, playing with them, talking to them, happy as a child is happy. They were an odd lot, Enoch's people. They were made, I suppose, out of real people he had seen and who had for some obscure reason made an appeal to him. There was a woman with a sword in her hand, an old man with a

apartment *ms* < apartment,

streets *ms* < street

anymore *ed* < any more

Loneliness

long white beard who went about followed by a dog, a young girl whose stockings were always coming down and hanging over her shoe tops. There must have been two dozen of the shadow people, invented by the child-mind of Enoch Robinson, who lived in the room with him.

And Enoch was happy. Into the room he went and locked the door. With an absurd air of importance he talked aloud, giving instructions, making comments on life. He was happy and satisfied to go on making his living in the advertising place until something happened. Of course something did happen. That is why he went back to live in Winesburg and why we know about him. The thing that happened was a woman. It would be that way. He was too happy. Something had to come into his world. Something had to drive him out of the New York room to live out his life, an obscure, jerky little figure, bobbing up and down on the streets of an Ohio town at evening when the sun was going down behind the roof of Wesley Moyer's Livery.

About the thing that happened. Enoch told George Willard about it one night. He wanted to talk to some-one, and he chose the young newspaper reporter be-cause the two happened to be thrown together at a time when the younger man was in a mood to understand.

Youthful sadness, young man's sadness, the sadness of a growing boy in a village at the year's end, opened the lips of the old man. The sadness was in the heart of George Willard and was without meaning but it ap-pealed to Enoch Robinson.

It rained on the evening when the two met and talked, a drizzly wet October rain. The fruition of the year had come and the night should have been fine with a moon in the sky and the crisp sharp promise of frost in the air,

Livery *ed* < livery barn

end, *ms* < end

(meaning *ms*
(< meaning,

Concerning Enoch Robinson

but it wasn't that way. It rained and little puddles of water shone under the street lamps on Main Street. In the woods in the darkness beyond the Fair Grounds water dripped from the black trees. Beneath the trees wet leaves were pasted against tree roots that protruded from the ground. In gardens back of houses in Winesburg dry shriveled potato vines lay sprawling on the ground. Men who had finished the evening meal and who had planned to go uptown to talk the evening away with other men at the back of some store changed their minds. George Willard tramped about in the rain and was glad that it rained. He felt that way. He was like Enoch Robinson on the evenings when the old man came down out of his room and wandered alone in the streets. He was like that only that George Willard had become a tall young man and did not think it manly to weep and carry on. For a month his mother had been very ill and that had something to do with his sadness, but not much. He thought about himself and to the young that always brings sadness.

Enoch Robinson and George Willard met beneath a wooden awning that extended out over the sidewalk before Voight's Wagon Shop on Maumee Street just off the main street of Winesburg. They went together from there through the rain-washed streets to the older man's room on the third floor of the Heffner Block. The young reporter went willingly enough. Enoch Robinson asked him to go after the two had talked for ten minutes. The boy was a little afraid but had never been more curious in his life. A hundred times he had heard the old man spoken of as a little off his head and he thought himself rather brave and manly to go at all. From the very beginning, in the street in the rain, the old man talked in a queer way, trying to tell the story of the room in Wash-

Grounds *ms* < Ground

(Wagon Shop *ed*
< wagon shop

Loneliness

ington Square and of his life in the room. "You'll understand if you try hard enough," he said conclusively. "I have looked at you when you went past me on the street and I think you can understand. It isn't hard. All you have to do is to believe what I say, just listen and believe, that's all there is to it."

It was past eleven o'clock that evening when Old Enoch, talking to George Willard in the room in the Heffner Block, came to the vital thing, the story of the woman and of what drove him out of the city to live out his life alone and defeated in Winesburg. He sat on a cot by the window with his head in his hand and George Willard was in a chair by a table. A kerosene lamp sat on the table and the room, although almost bare of furniture, was scrupulously clean. As the man talked George Willard began to feel that he would like to get out of the chair and sit on the cot also. He wanted to put his arms about the little old man. In the half darkness the man talked and the boy listened, filled with sadness.

"She got to coming in there after there hadn't been anyone in the room for years," said Enoch Robinson. "She saw me in the hallway of the house and we got acquainted. I don't know just what she did in her own room. I never went there. I think she was a musician and played a violin. Every now and then she came and knocked at the door and I opened it. In she came and sat down beside me, just sat and looked about and said nothing. Anyway she said nothing that mattered." The old man arose from the cot and moved about the room. The overcoat he wore was wet from the rain and drops of water kept falling with a soft little thump on the floor. When he again sat upon the cot George Willard got out of the chair and sat beside him.

Although Vogt Brothers' Wagon Shop was at 111 Duane Street, in Clyde, Anderson uses for Voight's Wagon Shop in Winesburg the George Adams Carriage Shop, at 119 East Buckeye Street. Maumee Street was in reality East Buckeye Street.

Anyway *ms* < Anyway,
(mattered." [no ¶] *ms*
(< mattered." [¶]

Concerning Enoch Robinson

"I had a feeling about her. She sat there in the room with me and she was too big for the room. I felt that she was driving everything else away. We just talked of little things, but I couldn't sit still. I wanted to touch her with my fingers and to kiss her. Her hands were so strong and her face was so good and she looked at me all the time."

The trembling voice of the old man became silent and his body shook as from a chill. "I was afraid," he whispered. "I was terribly afraid. I didn't want to let her come in when she knocked at the door but I couldn't sit still. 'No, no,' I said to myself, but I got up and opened the door just the same. She was so grown up, you see. She was a woman. I thought she would be bigger than I was there in that room."

Enoch Robinson stared at George Willard, his child-like blue eyes shining in the lamp light. Again he shivered. "I wanted her and all the time I didn't want her," he explained. "Then I began to tell her about my people, about everything that meant anything to me. I tried to keep quiet, to keep myself to myself, but I couldn't. I felt just as I did about opening the door. Sometimes I ached to have her go away and never come back anymore."

The old man sprang to his feet and his voice shook with excitement. "One night something happened. I became mad to make her understand me and to know what a big thing I was in that room. I wanted her to see how important I was. I told her over and over. When she tried to go away, I ran and locked the door. I followed her about. I talked and talked and then all of a sudden things went to smash. A look came into her eyes and I knew she did understand. Maybe she had understood all the time. I was furious. I couldn't stand it. I

child-like *ed* < childlike

lamp light *ed* < lamplight

anymore *ed* < any more

Loneliness

wanted her to understand but, don't you see, I couldn't let her understand. I felt that then she would know everything, that I would be submerged, drowned out, you see. That's how it is. I don't know why."

The old man dropped into a chair by the lamp and the boy listened, filled with awe. "Go away, boy," said the man. "Don't stay here with me anymore. I thought it might be a good thing to tell you but it isn't. I don't want to talk anymore. Go away."

George Willard shook his head and a note of command came into his voice. "Don't stop now. Tell me the rest of it," he commanded sharply. "What happened? Tell me the rest of the story."

Enoch Robinson sprang to his feet and ran to the window that looked down into the deserted main street of Winesburg. George Willard followed. By the window the two stood, the tall awkward boy-man and the little wrinkled man-boy. The childish, eager voice carried forward the tale. "I swore at her," he explained. "I said vile words. I ordered her to go away and not to come back. Oh, I said terrible things. At first she pretended not to understand but I kept at it. I screamed and stamped on the floor. I made the house ring with my curses. I didn't want ever to see her again and I knew, after some of the things I said, that I never would see her again."

The old man's voice broke and he shook his head. "Things went to smash," he said quietly and sadly. "Out she went through the door and all the life there had been in the room followed her out. She took all of my people away. They all went out through the door after her. That's the way it was."

George Willard turned and went out of Enoch Robinson's room. In the darkness by the window, as he

anymore *ed* < any more

anymore *ed* < any more

Concerning Enoch Robinson

went through the door, he could hear the thin old voice whimpering and complaining. "I'm alone, all alone here," said the voice. "It was warm and friendly in my room but now I'm all alone."

AN AWAKENING

Concerning Belle Carpenter

BELLE CARPENTER had a dark skin, grey eyes and thick lips. She was tall and strong. When black thoughts visited her she grew angry and wished she were a man and could fight someone with her fists. She worked in the millinery shop kept by Mrs. Nate McHugh and during the day sat trimming hats by a window at the rear of the store. She was the daughter of Henry Carpenter, book keeper in the First National Bank of Winesburg, and lived with him in a gloomy old house far out at the end of Buckeye Street. The house was surrounded by pine trees and there was no grass beneath the trees. A rusty tin eaves-trough had slipped from its fastenings at the back of the house and when the wind blew it beat against the roof of a small shed, making a dismal drumming noise that sometimes persisted all through the night.

book keeper *ed*
< bookkeeper

When she was a young girl Henry Carpenter made life almost unbearable for Belle, but as she emerged from girlhood into womanhood he lost his power over her. The book keeper's life was made up of innumerable little pettinesses. When he went to the bank in the morning he stepped into a closet and put on a black alpaca coat

book keeper's *ed*
< bookkeeper's

An Awakening

that had become shabby with age. At night when he returned to his home he donned another black alpaca coat. Every evening he pressed the clothes worn in the streets. He had invented an arrangement of boards for the purpose. The trousers to his street suit were placed between the boards and the boards were clamped together with heavy screws. In the morning he wiped the boards with a damp cloth and stood them upright behind the dining room door. If they were moved during the day he was speechless with anger and did not recover his equilibrium for a week.

The bank cashier was a little bully and was afraid of his daughter. She, he realized, knew the story of his brutal treatment of her mother and hated him for it. One day she went home at noon and carried a handful of soft mud, taken from the road, into the house. With the mud she smeared the face of the boards used for the pressing of trousers and then went back to her work feeling relieved and happy.

Belle Carpenter occasionally walked out in the evening with George Willard. Secretly she loved another man, but her love affair, about which no one knew, caused her much anxiety. She was in love with Ed Handby, bartender in Ed Griffith's Saloon, and went about with the young reporter as a kind of relief to her feelings. She did not think that her station in life would permit her to be seen in the company of the bartender and walked about under the trees with George Willard and let him kiss her to relieve a longing that was very insistent in her nature. She felt that she could keep the younger man within bounds, about Ed Handby she was somewhat uncertain.

bounds, about *ms* < bounds. About

Handby, the bartender, was a tall, broad-shouldered man of thirty who lived in a room upstairs above

Concerning Belle Carpenter

Griffith's Saloon. His fists were large and his eyes unusually small, but his voice, as though striving to conceal the power back of his fists, was soft and quiet.

At twenty-five the bartender had inherited a large farm from an uncle in Indiana. When sold, the farm brought in eight thousand dollars which Ed spent in six months. Going to Sandusky, on Lake Erie, he began an orgy of dissipation, the story of which afterwards filled his home town with awe. Here and there he went throwing the money about, driving carriages through the streets, giving wine parties to crowds of men and women, playing cards for high stakes and keeping mistresses whose wardrobes cost him hundreds of dollars. One night at a resort called Cedar Point he got into a fight and ran amuck like a wild thing. With his fist he broke a large mirror in the wash room of a hotel and later went about smashing windows and breaking chairs in dance halls for the joy of hearing the glass rattle on the floor and seeing the terror in the eyes of clerks who had come from Sandusky to spend the evening at the resort with their sweethearts.

The affair between Ed Handby and Belle Carpenter on the surface amounted to nothing. He had succeeded in spending but one evening in her company. On that evening he hired a horse and buggy at Wesley Moyer's Livery and took her for a drive. The conviction that she was the woman his nature demanded and that he must get her settled upon him and he told her of his desires.

The bartender was ready to marry and to begin trying to earn money for the support of his wife, but so simple was his nature that he found it difficult to explain his intentions. His body ached with physical longing and with his body he expressed himself. Taking the milliner into his arms and holding her tightly in spite of her struggles, he kissed her until she became helpless.

Saloon *ed* < saloon

afterwards *ms* < afterward

Point *ms* < Point,
A huge amusement park at Cedar Point peninsula, on the Sandusky Bay of Lake Erie, eight miles north of Clyde, has been in operation since the mid-1890s.

Livery *ed* < livery barn

desires. [¶] *ms* < desires. [no ¶]

An Awakening

Then he brought her back to town and let her out of the buggy. "When I get hold of you again I'll not let you go. You can't play with me," he declared as he turned to drive away. Then, jumping out of the buggy, he gripped her shoulders with his strong hands. "I'll keep you for good the next time," he said. "You might as well make up your mind to that. It's you and me for it and I'm going to have you before I get through."

One night in January when there was a new moon George Willard, who was in Ed Handby's mind the only obstacle to his getting Belle Carpenter, went for a walk. Early that evening George went into Ransom Surbeck's Pool Room with Seth Richmond and Art Wilson, son of the town butcher. Seth Richmond stood with his back against the wall and remained silent, but George Willard talked. The pool room was filled with Winesburg boys and they talked of women. The young reporter got into that vein. He said that women should look out for themselves, that the fellow who went out with a girl was not responsible for what happened. As he talked he looked about, eager for attention. He held the floor for five minutes and then Art Wilson began to talk. Art was learning the barber's trade in Cal Prouse's shop and already began to consider himself an authority in such matters as baseball, horse racing, drinking and going about with women. He began to tell of a night when he with two men from Winesburg went into a house of prostitution at the county seat. The butcher's son held a cigar in the side of his mouth and as he talked spat on the floor. "The women in the place couldn't embarrass me although they tried hard enough," he boasted. "One of the girls in the house tried to get fresh, but I fooled her. As soon as she began to talk I went and sat in her

Pool Room *ed*
< pool room

In Clyde, the C. J. Miller Billiard and Pool Room was located at 210 North Main Street.

drinking *ms* < drinking,

Concerning Belle Carpenter

lap. Everyone in the room laughed when I kissed her. I taught her to let me alone."

George Willard went out of the pool room and into Main Street. For days the weather had been bitter cold with a high wind blowing down on the town from Lake Erie, eighteen miles to the north, but on that night the wind had died away and a new moon made the night unusually lovely. Without thinking where he was going or what he wanted to do, George went out of Main Street and began walking in dimly lighted streets filled with frame houses.

Out of doors, under the black sky filled with stars, he forgot his companions of the pool room. Because it was dark and he was alone he began to talk aloud. In a spirit of play he reeled along the street imitating a drunken man and then imagined himself a soldier clad in shining boots that reached to the knees and wearing a sword that jingled as he walked. As a soldier he pictured himself as an inspector, passing before a long line of men who stood at attention. He began to examine the accouterments of the men. Before a tree he stopped and began to scold. "Your pack is not in order," he said sharply. "How many times will I have to speak of this matter? Everything must be in order here. We have a difficult task before us and no difficult task can be done without order."

Hypnotized by his own words, the young man stumbled along the board sidewalk saying more words. "There is a law for armies and for men too," he muttered, lost in reflection. "The law begins with little things and spreads out until it covers everything. In every little thing there must be order, in the place where men work, in their clothes, in their thoughts. I myself must be or-

doors, *ed* < doors
stars, *ms* < stars

(accouterments *ms*
(< accoutrements

An Awakening

derly. I must learn that law. I must get myself into touch with something orderly and big that swings through the night like a star. In my little way I must begin to learn something, to give and swing and work with life, with the law."

George Willard stopped by a picket fence near a street lamp and his body began to tremble. He had never before thought such thoughts as had just come into his head and he wondered where they had come from. For the moment it seemed to him that some voice outside of himself had been talking as he walked. He was amazed and delighted with his own mind and when he walked on again spoke of the matter with fervor. "To come out of Ransom Surbeck's Pool Room and think things like that," he whispered. "It is better to be alone. If I talked like Art Wilson the boys would understand me but they wouldn't understand what I've been thinking down here."

In Winesburg, as in all Ohio towns of twenty years ago, there was a section in which lived day laborers. As the time of factories had not yet come, the laborers worked in the fields or were section hands on the railroads. They worked twelve hours a day and received one dollar for the long day of toil. The houses in which they lived were small cheaply constructed wooden affairs with a garden at the back. The more comfortable among them kept cows and perhaps a pig, housed in a little shed at the rear of the garden.

With his head filled with resounding thoughts, George Willard walked into such a street on the clear January night. The street was dimly lighted and in places there was no sidewalk. In the scene that lay about him there was something that excited his already aroused fancy. For a year he had been devoting all of his odd moments

(**Pool Room** *ed* < pool room

These laborers in Clyde would have been Irishmen, brought in starting in the 1850s to build and work on the area railroads.

Concerning Belle Carpenter

to the reading of books and now some tale he had read concerning life in old world towns of the middle ages came sharply back to his mind so that he stumbled forward with the curious feeling of one revisiting a place that had been a part of some former existence. On an impulse he turned out of the street and went into a little dark alleyway behind the sheds in which lived the cows and pigs.

For a half hour he stayed in the alleyway, smelling the strong smell of animals too closely housed and letting his mind play with the strange new thoughts that came to him. The very rankness of the smell of manure in the clear sweet air awoke something heady in his brain. The poor little houses lighted by kerosene lamps, the smoke from the chimneys mounting straight up into the clear air, the grunting of pigs, the women clad in cheap calico dresses and washing dishes in the kitchens, the footsteps of men coming out of the houses and going off to the stores and saloons of Main Street, the dogs barking and the children crying—all of these things made him seem, as he lurked in the darkness, oddly detached and apart from all life.

The excited young man, unable to bear the weight of his own thoughts, began to move cautiously along the alleyway. A dog attacked him and had to be driven away with stones, and a man appeared at the door of one of the houses and swore at the dog. George went into a vacant lot and throwing back his head looked up at the sky. He felt unutterably big and remade by the simple experience through which he had been passing and in a kind of fervor of emotion put up his hands, thrusting them into the darkness above his head and muttering words. The desire to say words overcame him and he said words without meaning, rolling them over on his

An Awakening

tongue and saying them because they were brave words, full of meaning. "Death," he muttered, "night, the sea, fear, loveliness."

George Willard came out of the vacant lot and stood again on the sidewalk facing the houses. He felt that all of the people in the little street must be brothers and sisters to him and he wished he had the courage to call them out of their houses and to shake their hands. "If there were only a woman here I would take hold of her hand and we would run until we were both tired out," he thought. "That would make me feel better." With the thought of a woman in his mind he walked out of the street and went toward the house where Belle Carpenter lived. He thought she would understand his mood and that he could achieve in her presence a position he had long been wanting to achieve. In the past when he had been with her and had kissed her lips he had come away filled with anger at himself. He had felt like one being used for some obscure purpose and had not enjoyed the feeling. Now he thought he had suddenly become too big to be used.

When George got to Belle Carpenter's house there had already been a visitor there before him. Ed Handby had come to the door and calling Belle out of the house had tried to talk to her. He had wanted to ask the woman to come away with him and to be his wife, but when she came and stood by the door he lost his self assurance and became sullen. "You stay away from that kid," he growled, thinking of George Willard, and then, not knowing what else to say, turned to go away. "If I catch you together I will break your bones and his too," he added. The bartender had come to woo, not to threaten, and was angry with himself because of his failure.

When her lover had departed Belle went indoors and

(self assurance *ed*
< self-assurance

Concerning Belle Carpenter

ran hurriedly upstairs. From a window at the upper part of the house she saw Ed Handby cross the street and sit down on a horse block before the house of a neighbor. In the dim light the man sat motionless holding his head in his hands. She was made happy by the sight and when George Willard came to the door she greeted him effusively and hurriedly put on her hat. She thought that, as she walked through the streets with young Willard, Ed Handby would follow and she wanted to make him suffer.

For an hour Belle Carpenter and the young reporter walked about under the trees in the sweet night air. George Willard was full of big words. The sense of power that had come to him during the hour in the darkness in the alleyway remained with him and he talked boldly, swaggering along and swinging his arms about. He wanted to make Belle Carpenter realize that he was aware of his former weakness and that he had changed. "You'll find me different," he declared, thrusting his hands into his pockets and looking boldly into her eyes. "I don't know why but it is so. You've got to take me for a man or let me alone. That's how it is."

Up and down the quiet streets under the new moon went the woman and the boy. When George had finished talking they turned down a side street and went across a bridge into a path that ran up the side of a hill. The hill began at Waterworks Pond and climbed upward to the Winesburg Fair Grounds. On the hillside grew dense bushes and small trees and among the bushes were little open spaces carpeted with long grass, now stiff and frozen.

As he walked behind the woman up the hill George Willard's heart began to beat rapidly and his shoulders straightened. Suddenly he decided that Belle Carpenter

To ease mounting upon and dismounting from horses, nineteenth-century homes and businesses often (con't below)

sight *ms* < sight,

provided "horse-blocks," built-up stepped platforms in front of the premises.

upward *ed* < upwards

An Awakening

was about to surrender herself to him. The new force that had manifested itself in him had, he felt, been at work upon her and had led to her conquest. The thought made him half drunk with the sense of masculine power. Although he had been annoyed that as they walked about she had not seemed to be listening to his words, the fact that she had accompanied him to this place took all his doubts away. "It is different. Everything has become different," he thought and taking hold of her shoulder turned her about and stood looking at her, his eyes shining with pride.

Belle Carpenter did not resist. When he kissed her upon the lips she leaned heavily against him and looked over his shoulder into the darkness. In her whole attitude there was a suggestion of waiting. Again, as in the alleyway, George Willard's mind ran off into words and, holding the woman tightly, he whispered the words into the still night. "Lust," he whispered, "lust and night and women."

George Willard did not understand what happened to him that night on the hillside. Later, when he got to his own room, he wanted to weep and then grew half insane with anger and hate. He hated Belle Carpenter and was sure that all his life he would continue to hate her. On the hillside he had led the woman to one of the little open spaces among the bushes and had dropped to his knees beside her. As in the vacant lot, by the laborers' houses, he had put up his hands in gratitude for the new power in himself and was waiting for the woman to speak when Ed Handby appeared.

The bartender did not want to beat the boy, who he thought had tried to take his woman away. He knew that beating was unnecessary, that he had power within himself to accomplish his purpose without using his fists.

tightly, *ed* < tightly

Concerning Belle Carpenter

Gripping George by the shoulder and pulling him to his feet, he held him with one hand while he looked at Belle Carpenter seated on the grass. Then with a quick wide movement of his arm he sent the younger man sprawling away into the bushes and began to bully the woman who had risen to her feet. "You're no good," he said roughly. "I've half a mind not to bother with you. I'd let you alone if I didn't want you so much."

On his hands and knees in the bushes George Willard stared at the scene before him and tried hard to think. He prepared to spring at the man who had humiliated him. To be beaten seemed to be infinitely better than to be thus hurled ignominiously aside.

Three times the young reporter sprang at Ed Handby and each time the bartender, catching him by the shoulder, hurled him back into the bushes. The older man seemed prepared to keep the exercise going indefinitely but George Willard's head struck the root of a tree and he lay still. Then Ed Handby took Belle Carpenter by the arm and marched her away.

George heard the man and woman making their way through the bushes. As he crept down the hillside his heart was sick within him. He hated himself and he hated the fate that had brought about his humiliation. When his mind went back to the hour alone in the alleyway he was puzzled and stopping in the darkness listened, hoping to hear again the voice outside himself that had so short a time before put new courage into his heart. When his way homeward led him again into the street of frame houses he could not bear the sight and began to run, wanting to get quickly out of the neighborhood that now seemed to him utterly squalid and commonplace.

woman *ms* < woman,

Handby *ed* < Hanby

"QUEER"

Concerning Elmer Cowley

FROM HIS SEAT on a box in the rough board shed that stuck like a burr on the rear of Cowley & Son's Store in Winesburg, Elmer Cowley, the junior member of the firm, could see through a dirty window into the print shop of the *Winesburg Eagle*. Elmer was putting new shoe laces in his shoes. They did not go in readily and he had to take the shoes off. With the shoes in his hand he sat looking at a large hole in the heel of one of his stockings. Then looking quickly up he saw George Willard, the only newspaper reporter in Winesburg, standing at the back door of the *Eagle* print shop and staring absent-mindedly about. "Well, well, what next," exclaimed the young man with the shoes in his hand, jumping to his feet and creeping away from the window.

A flush crept into Elmer Cowley's face and his hands began to tremble. In Cowley & Son's Store a Jewish traveling salesman stood by the counter talking to his father. He imagined the reporter could hear what was being said and the thought made him furious. With one of the shoes still held in his hand he stood in a corner of

Store *ed* < store

(print shop *ed*
(< printshop
shoe laces *ed* < shoelaces

(print shop *ed*
(< printshop
next, *ms* < next!

Store *ed* < store

Concerning Elmer Cowley

the shed and stamped with a stockinged foot upon the board floor.

Cowley & Son's Store did not face the main street of Winesburg. The front was on Maumee Street and beyond it was Voight's Wagon Shop and a shed for the sheltering of farmers' horses. Beside the store an alleyway ran behind the Main Street stores and all day drays and delivery wagons, intent on bringing in and taking out goods, passed up and down. The store itself was indescribable. Will Henderson once said of it that it sold everything and nothing. In the window facing Maumee Street stood a chunk of coal as large as an apple barrel, to indicate that orders for coal were taken, and beside the black mass of the coal stood three combs of honey grown brown and dirty in their wooden frames.

The honey had stood in the store window for six months. It was for sale as were also the coat hangers, patent suspender buttons, cans of roof paint, bottles of rheumatism cure, and a substitute for coffee that companioned the honey in its patient willingness to serve the public.

Ebenezer Cowley, the man who stood in the store listening to the eager patter of words that fell from the lips of the traveling man, was tall and lean and looked unwashed. On his scrawny neck was a large wen, partially covered by a grey beard. He wore a long Prince Albert coat. The coat had been purchased to serve as a wedding garment. Before he became a merchant Ebenezer was a farmer and after his marriage he wore the Prince Albert coat to church on Sundays and on Saturday afternoons when he came into town to trade. When he sold the farm to become a merchant he wore the coat constantly. It had become brown with age and was cov-

Store *ed* < store

(Wagon Shop *ed* < wagon shop

(Main Street *ed* < main street

Anderson models the Cowley & Son Store on Clyde's B. F. Rogers shoe-repair shop, later Mann & Shaw Coal & Feed Store, at 106 East Buckeye Street.

cure, *ms* < cure

wen, *ms* < wen

Prince Albert of Saxe-Coburg-Gotha (1819–1861), consort to England's Queen Victoria, wore and popularized a style of men's dark-wool dress coat that was double-breasted and knee-length.

"Queer"

ered with grease spots, but in it Ebenezer always felt dressed up and ready for the day in town.

As a merchant Ebenezer was not happily placed in life and he had not been happily placed as a farmer. Still he existed. His family, consisting of a daughter named Mabel and the son, lived with him in rooms above the store and it did not cost them much to live. His troubles were not financial. His unhappiness as a merchant lay in the fact that when a traveling man with wares to be sold came in at the front door he was afraid. Behind the counter he stood shaking his head. He was afraid, first that he would stubbornly refuse to buy and thus lose the opportunity to sell again; second that he would not be stubborn enough and would in a moment of weakness buy what could not be sold.

In the store, on the morning when Elmer Cowley saw George Willard standing and apparently listening at the back door of the *Eagle* print shop, a situation had arisen that always stirred the son's wrath. The traveling man talked and Ebenezer listened, his whole figure expressing uncertainty. "You see how quickly it is done," said the traveling man who had for sale a small flat metal substitute for collar buttons. With one hand he quickly unfastened a collar from his shirt and then fastened it on again. He assumed a flattering wheedling tone. "I tell you what, men have come to the end of all this fooling with collar buttons and you are the man to make money out of the change that is coming. I am offering you the exclusive agency for this town. Take twenty dozen of these fasteners and I'll not visit any other store. I'll leave the field to you."

The traveling man leaned over the counter and tapped with his finger on Ebenezer's breast. "It's an opportunity and I want you to take it," he urged. "A friend of

---

store, *ms* < store

(print shop *ed*
  < printshop

Before World War II, men's dress shirts were often made or bought without collars; collars were separate items that had to be buttoned into place over shirt neckbands.

Concerning Elmer Cowley

mine told me about you. 'See that man Cowley,' he said. 'He's a live one.'"

The traveling man paused and waited. Taking a book from his pocket he began writing out the order. Still holding the shoe in his hand Elmer Cowley went through the store, past the two absorbed men, to a glass show case near the front door. He took a cheap revolver from the case and began to wave it about. "You get out of here," he shrieked. "We don't want any collar fasteners here." An idea came to him. "Mind, I'm not making any threat," he added. "I don't say I'll shoot. Maybe I just took this gun out of the case to look at it. But you better get out. Yes sir, I'll say that. You better grab up your things and get out."

here, *ms* < here!

The young store keeper's voice rose to a scream and going behind the counter he began to advance upon the two men. "We're through being fools here!" he cried. "We ain't going to buy any more stuff until we begin to sell. We ain't going to keep on being queer and have folks staring and listening. You get out of here."

(store keeper's *ed* < storekeeper's

here. *ms* < here!

The traveling man left. Raking the samples of collar fasteners off the counter into a black leather bag, he ran. He was a small man and very bow-legged and he ran awkwardly. The black bag caught against the door and he stumbled and fell. "Crazy, that's what he is— crazy!" he sputtered as he arose from the sidewalk and hurried away.

In the store Elmer Cowley and his father stared at each other. Now that the immediate object of his wrath had fled, the younger man was embarrassed. "Well, I meant it. I think we've been queer long enough," he declared, going to the show case and replacing the revolver. Sitting on a barrel he pulled on and fastened the shoe he had been holding in his hand. He was waiting

show case *ms* < showcase

"Queer"

re-awaken *ed*
< reawaken

for some word of understanding from his father but when Ebenezer spoke his words only served to re-awaken the wrath in the son and the young man ran out of the store without replying. Scratching his grey beard with his long dirty fingers, the merchant looked at his son with the same wavering uncertain stare with which he had confronted the traveling man. "I'll be starched," he said softly. "Well, well, I'll be washed and ironed and starched."

starched. *ms*
< starched!

tracks *ms* < track

Elmer Cowley went out of Winesburg and along a country road that paralleled the railroad tracks. He did not know where he was going or what he was going to do. In the shelter of a deep cut where the road, after turning sharply to the right, dipped under the tracks he stopped and the passion that had been the cause of his outburst in the store began to again find expression. "I will not be queer—one to be looked at and listened to," he declared aloud. "I'll be like other people. I'll show that George Willard. He'll find out. I'll show him."

him. *ms* < him!

The distraught young man stood in the middle of the road and glared back at the town. He did not know the reporter George Willard and had no special feeling concerning the tall boy who ran about town gathering the town news. The reporter had merely come, by his presence in the office and in the print shop of the *Winesburg Eagle*, to stand for something in the young merchant's mind. He thought the boy who passed and re-passed Cowley & Son's Store and who stopped to talk to people in the street must be thinking of him and perhaps laughing at him. George Willard, he felt, belonged to the town, typified the town, represented in his person the spirit of the town. Elmer Cowley could not have believed that George Willard had also his days of unhappiness, that vague hungers and secret unnamable de-

print shop *ed*
< printshop

Store *ed* < store

Concerning Elmer Cowley

sires visited also his mind. Did he not represent public opinion and had not the public opinion of Winesburg condemned the Cowleys to queerness? Did he not walk whistling and laughing through Main Street? Might not one by striking his person strike also the greater enemy— the thing that smiled and went its own way—the judgment of Winesburg?

Elmer Cowley was extraordinarily tall and his arms were long and powerful. His hair, his eyebrows, and the downy beard that had begun to grow upon his chin were pale almost to whiteness. His teeth protruded from between his lips and his eyes were blue with the colorless blueness of the marbles called "aggies" that the boys of Winesburg carried in their pockets. Elmer had lived in Winesburg for a year and had made no friends. He was, he felt, one condemned to go through life without friends and he hated the thought.

Sullenly the tall young man tramped along the road with his hands stuffed into his trousers pockets. The day was cold with a raw wind, but presently the sun began to shine and the road became soft and muddy. The tops of the ridges of frozen mud that formed the road began to melt and the mud clung to Elmer's shoes. His feet became cold. When he had gone several miles he turned off the road, crossed a field and entered a woods. In the woods he gathered sticks to build a fire by which he sat trying to warm himself, miserable in body and in mind.

For two hours he sat on the log by the fire and then, arising and creeping cautiously through a mass of underbrush, he went to a fence and looked across fields to a small farm house, surrounded by low sheds. A smile came to his lips and he began making motions with his long arms to a man who was husking corn in one of the fields.

chin ed < chin,

Marbles for playing children's games were sometimes made of colorful banded stone, agate stone—hence "aggies."

trousers ed < trouser

woods ed < wood
woods ed < wood

(*farm house ed*
(*< farmhouse*
(*farm house, ms*
(*< farmhouse*

"Queer"

In his hour of misery the young merchant had returned to the farm where he had lived through boyhood and where there was another human being to whom he felt he could explain himself. The man on the farm was a half witted old fellow named Mook. He had once been employed by Ebenezer Cowley and had stayed on the farm when it was sold. The old man lived in one of the unpainted sheds back of the farm house and puttered about all day in the fields.

Mook the half wit lived happily. With child-like faith he believed in the intelligence of the animals that lived in the sheds with him, and when he was lonely held long conversations with the cows, the pigs, and even with the chickens that ran about the barn yard. He it was who had put the expression regarding being "laundered" into the mouth of his former employer. When excited or surprised by anything he smiled vaguely and muttered: "I'll be washed and ironed. Well, well, I'll be washed and ironed and starched."

When the half witted old man left his husking of corn and came into the woods to meet Elmer Cowley, he was neither surprised nor especially interested in the sudden appearance of the young man. His feet also were cold and he sat on the log by the fire, grateful for the warmth and apparently indifferent to what Elmer had to say.

Elmer talked earnestly and with great freedom, walking up and down and waving his arms about. "You don't understand what's the matter with you so of course you don't care," he declared. "With me it's different. Look how it has always been with me. Father is queer and mother was queer too. Even the clothes mother used to wear were not like other people's clothes, and look at that coat in which father goes about there in town, thinking he's dressed up too. Why don't he get a new one. It

half *ed* < half-

(farm house *ed*
< farmhouse

half *ed* < half-
child-like *ed* < childlike

(barn yard *ed*
< barnyard

half *ed* < half-
woods *ed* < wood

you *ed* < me

queer *ms* < queer,

up *ms* < up,
one. *ms* < one?

Concerning Elmer Cowley

wouldn't cost much. I'll tell you why. Father doesn't know and when mother was alive she didn't know either. Mabel is different. She knows but she won't say anything. I will, though. I'm not going to be stared at any longer. Why look here, Mook, father doesn't know that his store there in town is just a queer jumble, that he'll never sell the stuff he buys. He knows nothing about it. Sometimes he's a little worried that trade doesn't come and then he goes and buys something else. In the evening he sits by the fire upstairs and says trade will come after a while. He isn't worried. He's queer. He doesn't know enough to be worried."

evening *ms* < evenings

The excited young man became more excited. "He don't know but I know," he shouted, stopping to gaze down into the dumb, unresponsive face of the half wit. "I know too well. I can't stand it. When we lived out here it was different. I worked and at night I went to bed and slept. I wasn't always seeing people and thinking as I am now. In the evening there in town I go to the post office or to the depot to see the train come in and no one says anything to me. Everyone stands around and laughs and they talk but they say nothing to me. Then I feel so queer that I can't talk either. I go away. I don't say anything. I can't."

half *ed* < half-

evening *ms* < evening,
town *ms* < town,
in *ms* < in,

The fury of the young man became uncontrollable. "I won't stand it," he yelled, looking up at the bare branches of the trees. "I'm not made to stand it."

Maddened by the dull face of the man on the log by the fire, Elmer turned and glared at him as he had glared back along the road at the town of Winesburg. "Go on back to work," he screamed. "What good does it do me to talk to you?" A thought came to him and his voice dropped. "I'm a coward too, eh?" he muttered. "Do you know why I came clear out here afoot? I had to tell some-

someone *ms* < some one

"*Queer*"

one and you were the only one I could tell. I hunted out another queer one, you see. I ran away, that's what I did. I couldn't stand up to someone like that George Willard. I had to come to you. I ought to tell him and I will."

someone *ms* < some one

Again his voice arose to a shout and his arms flew about. "I will tell him. I won't be queer. I don't care what they think. I won't stand it."

half *ed* < half-

Elmer Cowley ran out of the woods leaving the half wit sitting on the log before the fire. Presently the old man arose and climbing over the fence went back to his work in the corn. "I'll be washed and ironed and starched," he declared. "Well, well, I'll be washed and ironed." Mook was interested. He went along a lane to a field where two cows stood nibbling at a straw stack. "Elmer was here," he said to the cows. "Elmer is crazy. You better get behind the stack where he don't see you. He'll hurt someone yet, Elmer will."

At eight o'clock that evening Elmer Cowley put his head in at the front door of the office of the *Winesburg Eagle* where George Willard sat writing. His cap was pulled down over his eyes and a sullen determined look was on his face. "You come on outside with me," he said, stepping in and closing the door. He kept his hand on the knob as though prepared to resist anyone else coming in. "You just come along outside. I want to see you."

George Willard and Elmer Cowley walked through the main street of Winesburg. The night was cold and George Willard had on a new overcoat and looked very spruce and dressed up. He thrust his hands into the overcoat pockets and looked inquiringly at his companion. He had long been wanting to make friends with the young merchant and find out what was in his mind.

Concerning Elmer Cowley

Now he thought he saw a chance and was delighted. "I wonder what he's up to? Perhaps he thinks he has a piece of news for the paper. It can't be a fire because I haven't heard the fire bell and there isn't anyone running," he thought.

In the main street of Winesburg, on the cold November evening, but few citizens appeared and these hurried along bent on getting to the stove at the back of some store. The windows of the stores were frosted and the wind rattled the tin sign that hung over the entrance to the stairway leading to Doctor Welling's office. Before Hern's Grocery a basket of apples and a rack filled with new brooms stood on the sidewalk. Elmer Cowley stopped and stood facing George Willard. He tried to talk and his arms began to pump up and down. His face worked spasmodically. He seemed about to shout. "Oh, you go on back," he cried. "Don't stay out here with me. I ain't got anything to tell you. I don't want to see you at all."

For three hours the distracted young merchant wandered through the residence streets of Winesburg blind with anger, brought on by his failure to declare his determination not to be queer. Bitterly the sense of defeat settled upon him and he wanted to weep. After the hours of futile sputtering at nothingness that had occupied the afternoon and his failure in the presence of the young reporter, he thought he could see no hope of a future for himself.

And then a new idea dawned for him. In the darkness that surrounded him he began to see a light. Going to the now darkened store, where Cowley & Son had for over a year waited vainly for trade to come, he crept stealthily in and felt about in a barrel that stood by the stove at the rear. In the barrel beneath shavings lay a tin

Hern's *ms* < Hearn's

residence *ed* < resident

"Queer"

box containing Cowley & Son's cash. Every evening Ebenezer Cowley put the box in the barrel when he closed the store and went upstairs to bed. "They wouldn't never think of a careless place like that," he told himself, thinking of robbers.

Elmer took twenty dollars, two ten dollar bills, from the little roll containing perhaps four hundred dollars, the cash left from the sale of the farm. Then replacing the box beneath the shavings he went quietly out at the front door and walked again in the streets.

The idea that he thought might put an end to all of his unhappiness was very simple. "I will get out of here, run away from home," he told himself. He knew that a local freight train passed through Winesburg at midnight and went on to Cleveland where it arrived at dawn. He would steal a ride on the local and when he got to Cleveland would lose himself in the crowds there. He would get work in some shop and become friends with the other workmen. Gradually he would become like other men and would be indistinguishable. Then he could talk and laugh. He would no longer be queer and would make friends. Life would begin to have warmth and meaning for him as it had for others.

The tall awkward young man, striding through the streets, laughed at himself because he had been angry and had been half afraid of George Willard. He decided he would have his talk with the young reporter before he left town, that he would tell him about things, perhaps challenge him, challenge all of Winesburg through him.

Aglow with new confidence Elmer went to the office of the New Willard House and pounded on the door. A sleep-eyed boy slept on a cot in the office. He received no salary but was fed at the hotel table and bore with

A "local" train stops at all stations on its route, not at just major terminals; a "through" train serves only major stations.

Concerning Elmer Cowley

pride the title of "night clerk." Before the boy Elmer was bold, insistent. "You wake him up," he commanded. "You tell him to come down by the depot. I got to see him and I'm going away on the local. Tell him to dress and come on down. I ain't got much time."

The midnight local had finished its work in Winesburg and the trainsmen were coupling cars, swinging lanterns and preparing to resume their flight east. George Willard, rubbing his eyes and again wearing the new overcoat, ran down to the station platform afire with curiosity. "Well, here I am. What do you want? You've got something to tell me, eh?" he said.

Elmer tried to explain. He wet his lips with his tongue and looked at the train that had begun to groan and get under way. "Well, you see," he began, and then lost control of his tongue. "I'll be washed and ironed. I'll be washed and ironed and starched," he muttered half incoherently.

Elmer Cowley danced with fury beside the groaning train in the darkness on the station platform. Lights leaped into the air and bobbed up and down before his eyes. Taking the two ten dollar bills from his pocket he thrust them into George Willard's hand. "Take them," he cried. "I don't want them. Give them to father. I stole them." With a snarl of rage he turned and his long arms began to flay the air. Like one struggling for release from hands that held him he struck out, hitting George Willard blow after blow on the breast, the neck, the mouth. The young reporter rolled over on the platform half unconscious, stunned by the terrific force of the blows. Springing aboard the passing train and running over the tops of cars, Elmer sprang down to a flat car and lying on his face looked back, trying to see the fallen man in the darkness. Pride surged up in him. "I showed

"Queer"

him," he cried. "I guess I showed him. I ain't so queer. I guess I showed him I ain't so queer."

THE UNTOLD LIE

Concerning Ray Pearson

RAY PEARSON and Hal Winters were farm hands employed on a farm three miles north of Winesburg. On Saturday afternoons they came into town and wandered about through the streets with other fellows from the country.

quiet *ms* < quiet,

Ray was a quiet rather nervous man of perhaps fifty with a brown beard and shoulders rounded by too much and too hard labor. In his nature he was as unlike Hal Winters as two men can be unlike.

Ray was an altogether serious man and had a little sharp featured wife who had also a sharp voice. The two, with half a dozen thin legged children, lived in a tumble-down frame house beside a creek at the back end of the Wills farm where Ray was employed.

Hal Winters, his fellow employee, was a young fellow. He was not of the Ned Winters family, who were very respectable people in Winesburg, but was one of the three sons of the old man called Windpeter Winters who had a sawmill near Unionville, six miles away, and who was looked upon by everyone in Winesburg as a confirmed old reprobate.

People from the part of Northern Ohio in which Winesburg lies will remember old Windpeter by his

Concerning Ray Pearson

unusual and tragic death. He got drunk one evening in town and started to drive home to Unionville along the railroad tracks. Henry Brattenburg, the butcher, who lived out that way, stopped him at the edge of the town and told him he was sure to meet the down train but Windpeter slashed at him with his whip and drove on. When the train struck and killed him and his two horses a farmer and his wife who were driving home along a nearby road saw the accident. They said that old Windpeter stood up on the seat of his wagon, raving and swearing at the onrushing locomotive, and that he fairly screamed with delight when the team, maddened by his incessant slashing at them, rushed straight ahead to certain death. Boys like young George Willard and Seth Richmond will remember the incident quite vividly because, although everyone in our town said that the old man would go straight to hell and that the community was better off without him, they had a secret conviction that he knew what he was doing and admired his foolish courage. Most boys have seasons of wishing they could die gloriously instead of just being grocery clerks and going on with their humdrum lives.

But this is not the story of Windpeter Winters nor yet of his son Hal who worked on the Wills farm with Ray Pearson. It is Ray's story. It will, however, be necessary to talk a little of young Hal so that you will get into the spirit of it.

Hal was a bad one. Everyone said that. There were three of the Winters boys in that family, John, Hal, and Edward, all broad-shouldered big fellows like old Windpeter himself and all fighters and woman-chasers and generally all-around bad ones.

Hal was the worst of the lot and always up to some

Anderson has located the fictional Unionville, Ohio, where the real Green Springs would be, six miles southwest of Clyde.

(broad-shouldered *ed*
< broad shouldered

The Untold Lie

devilment. He once stole a load of boards from his father's mill and sold them in Winesburg. With the money he bought himself a suit of cheap, flashy clothes. Then he got drunk and, when his father came raving into town to find him, they met and fought with their fists on Main Street and were arrested and put into jail together.

Hal went to work on the Wills farm because there was a country school teacher out that way who had taken his fancy. He was only twenty-two then but had already been in two or three of what were spoken of in Winesburg as "women scrapes." Everyone who heard of his infatuation for the school teacher was sure it would turn out badly. "He'll only get her into trouble, you'll see," was the word that went around.

And so these two men, Ray and Hal, were at work in a field on a day in the late October. They were husking corn and occasionally something was said and they laughed. Then came silence. Ray, who was the more sensitive and always minded things more, had chapped hands and they hurt. He put them into his coat pockets and looked away across the fields. He was in a sad distracted mood and was affected by the beauty of the country. If you knew the Winesburg country in the fall and how the low hills are all splashed with yellows and reds you would understand his feeling. He began to think of the time long ago, when he was a young fellow living with his father, then a baker in Winesburg, and how on such days he had wandered away to the woods to gather nuts, hunt rabbits, or just to loaf about and smoke his pipe. His marriage had come about through one of his days of wandering. He had induced a girl who waited on trade in his father's shop to go with him and something had happened. He was thinking of that afternoon

---

and, *ed* < and

Before mechanized corn harvesting, mature corn stalks were cut and bunched into upright shocks to dry; when cool autumn weather came, workers used their hands to pull off and discard the dried husks (shucks) covering the ears of corn.

time *ms* < time, ago, *ms* < ago

Concerning Ray Pearson

and how it had affected his whole life when a spirit of protest awoke in him. He had forgotten about Hal and muttered words. "Tricked, by Gad, that's what I was, tricked by life and made a fool of," he said in a low voice.

Tricked, *ed* < Tricked

As though understanding his thoughts, Hal Winters spoke up. "Well, has it been worthwhile? What about it, eh? What about marriage and all that?" he asked and then laughed. Hal tried to keep on laughing but he too was in an earnest mood. He began to talk earnestly. "Has a fellow got to do it?" he asked. "Has he got to be harnessed up and driven through life like a horse?"

(worthwhile *ed* < worth while

Hal didn't wait for an answer but sprang to his feet and began to walk back and forth between the corn shocks. He was getting more and more excited. Bending down suddenly he picked up an ear of the yellow corn and threw it at the fence. "I've got Nell Gunther in trouble," he said. "I'm telling you, but you keep your mouth shut."

Ray Pearson arose and stood staring. He was almost a foot shorter than Hal, and when the younger man came and put his two hands on the older man's shoulders they made a picture. There they stood in the big empty field with the quiet corn shocks standing in rows behind them and the red and yellow hills in the distance, and from being just two indifferent workmen they had become all alive to each other. Hal sensed it and because that was his way he laughed. "Well, old daddy," he said awkwardly, "come on, advise me. I've got Nell in trouble. Perhaps you've been in the same fix yourself. I know what everyone would say is the right thing to do, but what do you say? Shall I marry and settle down? Shall I put myself into the harness to be worn out like an old horse? You know me, Ray. There can't anyone break me

everyone *ed* < every one

anyone *ms* < any one

The Untold Lie

but I can break myself. Shall I do it or shall I tell Nell to go to the devil? Come on, you tell me. Whatever you say, Ray, I'll do."

Ray couldn't answer. He shook Hal's hands loose and turning walked straight away toward the barn. He was a sensitive man and there were tears in his eyes. He knew there was only one thing to say to Hal Winters, son of old Windpeter Winters, only one thing that all his own training and all the beliefs of the people he knew would approve, but for his life he couldn't say what he knew he should say.

At half-past four that afternoon Ray was puttering about the barn yard when his wife came up the lane along the creek and called him. After the talk with Hal he hadn't returned to the corn field but worked about the barn. He had already done the evening chores and had seen Hal, dressed and ready for a roistering night in town, come out of the farm house and go into the road. Along the path to his own house he trudged behind his wife, looking at the ground and thinking. He couldn't make out what was wrong. Every time he raised his eyes and saw the beauty of the country in the failing light he wanted to do something he had never done before, shout or scream or hit his wife with his fists or something equally unexpected and terrifying. Along the path he went scratching his head and trying to make it out. He looked hard at his wife's back but she seemed all right.

She only wanted him to go into town for groceries and as soon as she had told him what she wanted began to scold. "You're always puttering," she said. "Now I want you to hustle. There isn't anything in the house for supper and you've got to get to town and back in a hurry."

Ray went into his own house and took an overcoat

(barn yard *ed*
< barnyard

(farm house *ed*
< farmhouse

you've *ms* < you-ve

Concerning Ray Pearson

from a hook back of the door. It was torn about the pockets and the collar was shiny. His wife went into the bedroom and presently came out with a soiled cloth in one hand and three silver dollars in the other. Somewhere in the house a child wept bitterly and a dog that had been sleeping by the stove arose and yawned. Again the wife scolded. "The children will cry and cry. Why are you always puttering?" she asked.

Ray went out of the house and climbed the fence into a field. It was just growing dark and the scene that lay before him was lovely. All the low hills were washed with color and even the little clusters of bushes in the corners by the fences were alive with beauty. The whole world seemed to Ray Pearson to have become alive with something just as he and Hal had suddenly become alive when they stood in the corn field staring into each other's eyes.

The beauty of the country about Winesburg was too much for Ray on that fall evening. That is all there was to it. He could not stand it. Of a sudden he forgot all about being a quiet old farm hand and throwing off the torn overcoat began to run across the field. As he ran he shouted a protest against his life, against all life, against everything that makes life ugly. "There was no promise made," he cried into the empty spaces that lay about him. "I didn't promise my Minnie anything and Hal hasn't made any promise to Nell. I know he hasn't. She went into the woods with him because she wanted to go. What he wanted she wanted. Why should I pay? Why should Hal pay? Why should anyone pay? I don't want Hal to become old and worn out. I'll tell him. I won't let it go on. I'll catch Hal before he gets to town and I'll tell him."

anyone *ed* < any one

Ray ran clumsily and once he stumbled and fell down. "I must catch Hal and tell him," he kept thinking and

The Untold Lie

although his breath came in gasps he kept running harder and harder. As he ran he thought of things that hadn't come into his mind for years—how at the time he married he had planned to go west to his uncle in Portland, Oregon—how he hadn't wanted to be a farm hand, but had thought when he got out west he would go to sea and be a sailor or get a job on a ranch and ride a horse into western towns shouting and laughing and waking the people in the houses with his wild cries. Then as he ran he remembered his children and in fancy felt their hands clutching at him. All of his thoughts of himself were involved with the thoughts of Hal and he thought the children were clutching at the younger man also. "They are the accidents of life, Hal," he cried. "They are not mine or yours. I had nothing to do with them."

Darkness began to spread over the fields as Ray Pearson ran on and on. His breath came in little sobs. When he came to the fence at the edge of the road and confronted Hal Winters, all dressed up and smoking a pipe as he walked jauntily along, he could not have told what he thought or what he wanted.

Ray Pearson lost his nerve and this is really the end of the story of what happened to him. It was almost dark when he got to the fence and he put his hands on the top bar and stood staring. Hal Winters jumped a ditch and coming up close to Ray put his hands into his pockets and laughed. He seemed to have lost his own sense of what had happened in the corn field and when he put up a strong hand and took hold of the lapel of Ray's coat he shook the old man as he might have shaken a dog that had misbehaved.

"You came to tell me, eh?" he said. "Well, never mind telling me anything. I'm not a coward and I've already made up my mind." He laughed again and jumped back

Concerning Ray Pearson

across the ditch. "Nell ain't no fool," he said. "She didn't ask me to marry her. I want to marry her. I want to settle down and have kids."

Ray Pearson also laughed. He felt like laughing at himself and all the world.

As the form of Hal Winters disappeared in the dusk that lay over the road that led to Winesburg, he turned and walked slowly back across the fields to where he had left his torn overcoat. As he went some memory of pleasant evenings spent with the thin-legged children in the tumble-down house by the creek must have come into his mind, for he muttered words. "It's just as well. Whatever I told him would have been a lie," he said softly, and then his form also disappeared into the darkness of the fields.

DRINK

Concerning Tom Foster

TOM FOSTER came to Winesburg from Cincinnati when he was still young and could get many new impressions. His grandmother had been raised on a farm near the town and as a young girl had gone to school there when Winesburg was a village of twelve or fifteen houses clustered about a general store on the Trunion Pike.

What a life the old woman had led since she went away from the frontier settlement and what a strong, capable little old thing she was. She had been in Kansas, in Canada and in New York City, traveling about with her husband, a mechanic, before he died. Later she went

Clyde, Ohio, began as Hamer's Corners, first settled in the 1820s. On the Maumee and Western Reserve Turnpike, the Hamer's Corners area, bounded by the turnpike, Main Street, and Maple Street, lost being the town center when in the 1850s a railroad crossing moved new development just to the southwest.

was. *ms* < was!

Canada *ms* < Canada,

Drink

to stay with her daughter who had also married a mechanic and lived in Covington, Kentucky, across the river from Cincinnati.

Then began the hard years for Tom Foster's grandmother. First her son-in-law was killed by a policeman during a strike and then Tom's mother became an invalid and died also. The grandmother had saved a little money, but it was swept away by the illness of the daughter and by the cost of the two funerals. She became a half worn-out old woman worker and lived with the grandson above a junk shop on a side street in Cincinnati. For five years she scrubbed the floors in an office building and then got a place as dish washer in a restaurant. Her hands were all twisted out of shape. When she took hold of a mop or a broom handle the hands looked like the dried stems of an old creeping vine clinging to a tree.

The old woman came back to Winesburg as soon as she got the chance. One evening as she was coming home from work she found a pocket book containing thirty-seven dollars and that opened the way. The trip was a great adventure for the boy. It was past seven o'clock at night when the grandmother came home with the pocket book held tightly in her old hands and she was so excited she could scarcely speak. She insisted on leaving Cincinnati that night, saying that if they stayed until morning the owner of the money would be sure to find them out and make trouble. Tom, who was then sixteen years old, had to go trudging off to the station with the old woman bearing all of their earthly belongings done up in a worn-out blanket and slung across his back. By his side walked the grandmother urging him forward. Her toothless old mouth twitched nervously, and when

(pocket book *ed*
< pocket-book
dollars *ms* < dollars,

(pocket book *ms*
< pocketbook

Concerning Tom Foster

Tom grew weary and wanted to put the pack down at a street crossing she snatched it up and if he had not prevented would have slung it across her own back. When they got into the train and it had run out of the city she was as delighted as a girl and talked as the boy had never heard her talk before.

All through the night as the train rattled along, the grandmother told Tom tales of Winesburg and of how he would enjoy his life working in the fields and shooting wild things in the woods there. She could not believe that the tiny village of fifty years before had grown into a thriving town in her absence and in the morning when the train came to Winesburg did not want to get off. "It isn't what I thought. It may be hard for you here," she said and then the train went on its way and the two stood confused, not knowing where to turn, in the presence of Albert Longworth, the Winesburg baggage master.

But Tom Foster did get along all right. He was one to get along anywhere. Mrs. White, the banker's wife, employed his grandmother to work in the kitchen and he got a place as stable boy in the banker's new brick barn.

In Winesburg servants were hard to get. The woman who wanted help in her housework employed a "hired girl" who insisted on sitting at the table with the family. Mrs. White was sick of hired girls and snatched at the chance to get hold of the old city woman. She furnished a room for the boy Tom upstairs in the barn. "He can mow the lawn and run errands when the horses do not need attention," she explained to her husband.

Tom Foster was rather small for his age and had a large head covered with stiff black hair that stood straight up. The hair emphasized the bigness of his head. His

woods *ms* < wood

absence *ms* < absence,

said *ms* < said,

Drink

imaginable *ms*
< imaginable,

voice was the softest thing imaginable and he was himself so gentle and quiet that he slipped into the life of the town without attracting the least bit of attention.

One could not help wondering where Tom Foster got his gentleness. In Cincinnati he had lived in a neighborhood where gangs of tough boys prowled through the streets, and all through his early formative years he ran about with tough boys. For a while he was messenger for a telegraph company and delivered messages in a neighborhood sprinkled with houses of prostitution. The women in the houses knew and loved Tom Foster and the tough boys in the gangs loved him also.

He never asserted himself. That was one thing that helped him escape. In an odd way he stood in the shadow of the wall of life, was meant to stand in the shadow. He saw the men and women in the houses of lust, sensed their casual and horrible love affairs, saw boys fighting and listened to their tales of thieving and drunkenness unmoved and strangely unaffected.

thieving and *ms, Pr*
2–*Pr* 7 < thieving,

Once Tom did steal. That was while he still lived in the city. The grandmother was ill at the time and he himself was out of work. There was nothing to eat in the house, and so he went into a harness shop on a side street and stole a dollar and seventy-five cents out of the cash drawer.

The harness shop was run by an old man with a long mustache. He saw the boy lurking about and thought nothing of it. When he went out into the street to talk to a teamster Tom opened the cash drawer and taking the money walked away. Later he was caught and his grandmother settled the matter by offering to come twice a week for a month and scrub the shop. The boy was ashamed but he was rather glad too. "It is all right to be ashamed and makes me understand new things," he said

ashamed *ms* < ashamed,
glad *ms* < glad,

Concerning Tom Foster

to the grandmother, who didn't know what the boy was talking about but loved him so much that it didn't matter whether she understood or not.

For a year Tom Foster lived in the banker's stable and then lost his place there. He didn't take very good care of the horses and he was a constant source of irritation to the banker's wife. She told him to mow the lawn and he forgot. Then she sent him to the store or to the post office and he did not come back but joined a group of men and boys and spent the whole afternoon with them, standing about, listening and occasionally, when addressed, saying a few words.

As in the city in the houses of prostitution and with the rowdy boys running through the streets at night, so in Winesburg among its citizens he had always the power to be a part of and yet distinctly apart from the life about him.

After Tom lost his place at Banker White's he did not live with his grandmother, although often in the evening she came to visit him. He rented a room at the rear of a little frame building belonging to old Rufus Whiting. The building was on Duane Street, just off Main Street, and had been used for years as a law office by the old man who had become too feeble and forgetful for the practice of his profession but did not realize his inefficiency. He liked Tom and let him have the room for a dollar a month. In the late afternoon when the lawyer had gone home the boy had the place to himself and spent hours lying on the floor by the stove and thinking of things. In the evening the grandmother came and sat in the lawyer's chair to smoke a pipe while Tom remained silent, as he always did in the presence of everyone.

Often the old woman talked with great vigor. Some-

words. [¶] *ms* < words. [no ¶]

everyone *ms* < every one

Drink

times she was angry about some happening at the banker's house and scolded away for hours. Out of her own earnings she bought a mop and regularly scrubbed the lawyer's office. Then when the place was spotlessly clean and smelled clean she lighted her clay pipe and she and Tom had a smoke together. "When you get ready to die then I will die also," she said to the boy lying on the floor beside her chair.

Tom Foster enjoyed life in Winesburg. He did odd jobs, such as cutting wood for kitchen stoves and mowing the grass before houses. In late May and early June he picked strawberries in the fields. He had time to loaf and he enjoyed loafing. Banker White had given him a cast-off coat which was too large for him, but his grandmother cut it down, and he had also an overcoat, got at the same place, that was lined with fur. The fur was worn away in spots, but the coat was warm and in the winter Tom slept in it. He thought his method of getting along good enough and was happy and satisfied with the way life in Winesburg had turned out for him.

The most absurd little things made Tom Foster happy. That, I suppose, was why people loved him. In Hern's Grocery they would be roasting coffee on Friday afternoon, preparatory to the Saturday rush of trade, and the rich odor invaded lower Main Street. Tom Foster appeared and sat on a box at the rear of the store. For an hour he did not move but sat perfectly still, filling his being with the spicy odor that made him half drunk with happiness. "I like it," he said gently. "It makes me think of things far away, places and things like that."

One night Tom Foster got drunk. That came about in a curious way. He never had been drunk before, and indeed in all his life had never taken a drink of anything

Grocery *ms < grocery*

The drunkenness of the character Tom Foster is based on the story of Bronson Gobe (who sometimes called himself Jack Gobe), a youth who lived as did Anderson at 735 North Cass Street, in Chicago, and who was at least once brought home drunk by policemen.

Concerning Tom Foster

intoxicating, but he felt he needed to be drunk that one time and so went and did it.

In Cincinnati, when he lived there, Tom had found out many things, things about ugliness and crime and lust. Indeed he knew more of these things than anyone else in Winesburg. The matter of sex in particular had presented itself to him in a quite horrible way and had made a deep impression on his mind. He thought, after what he had seen of the women standing before the squalid houses on cold nights and the look he had seen in the eyes of the men who stopped to talk to them, that he would put sex altogether out of his own life. One of the women of the neighborhood tempted him once and he went into a room with her. He never forgot the smell of the room nor the greedy look that came into the eyes of the woman. It sickened him and in a very terrible way left a scar on his soul. He had always before thought of women as quite innocent things, much like his grandmother, but after that one experience in the room he dismissed women from his mind. So gentle was his nature that he could not hate anything and not being able to understand he decided to forget.

And Tom did forget until he came to Winesburg. After he had lived there for two years something began to stir in him. On all sides he saw youth making love and he was himself a youth. Before he knew what had happened he was in love also. He fell in love with Helen White, daughter of the man for whom he had worked, and found himself thinking of her at night.

That was a problem for Tom and he settled it in his own way. He let himself think of Helen White whenever her figure came into his mind and only concerned himself with the manner of his thoughts. He had a fight,

Indeed *ms* < Indeed, anyone *ms* < any one

Drink

a quiet determined little fight of his own, to keep his desires in the channel where he thought they belonged, but on the whole he was victorious.

And then came the spring night when he got drunk. Tom was wild on that night. He was like an innocent young buck of the forest that has eaten of some maddening weed. The thing began, ran its course, and was ended in one night, and you may be sure that no one in Winesburg was any the worse for Tom's outbreak.

In the first place the night was one to make a sensitive nature drunk. The trees along the residence streets of the town were all newly clothed in soft green leaves, in the gardens behind the houses men were puttering about in vegetable gardens, and in the air there was a hush, a waiting kind of silence very stirring to the blood.

Tom left his room, on Duane Street, just as the young night began to make itself felt. First he walked through the streets, going softly and quietly along, thinking thoughts that he tried to put into words. He said that Helen White was a flame dancing in the air and that he was a little tree without leaves standing out sharply against the sky. Then he said that she was a wind, a strong terrible wind, coming out of the darkness of a stormy sea, and that he was a boat left on the shore of the sea by a fisherman.

That idea pleased the boy and he sauntered along playing with it. He went into Main Street and sat on the curbing before Wacker's Tobacco Store. For an hour he lingered about, listening to the talk of men, but it did not interest him much and he slipped away. Then he decided to get drunk and went into Willy's Saloon and bought a bottle of whiskey. Putting the bottle into his pocket, he walked out of town wanting to be alone to think more thoughts and to drink the whiskey.

place *ms* < place,

room, *ms* < room
Street, *ed* < Street

sea, *ed* < sea

Wacker's Tobacco
Store *ed* < Wracker's
tobacco store
about, *ed* < about
Saloon *ed* < saloon

town *ms* < town,

Concerning Tom Foster

Tom got drunk sitting on a bank of new grass beside the road about a mile north of town. Before him was a white road and at his back an apple orchard in full bloom. He took a drink out of the bottle and then lay down on the grass. He thought of mornings in Winesburg and of how the stones in the graveled driveway by Banker White's house were wet with dew and glistened in the morning light. He thought of the nights in the barn when it rained and he lay awake hearing the drumming of the rain drops and smelling the warm smell of horses and of hay. Then he thought of a storm that had gone roaring through Winesburg several days before and, his mind going back, he relived the night he had spent on the train with his grandmother when the two were coming from Cincinnati. Sharply he remembered how strange it had seemed to sit quietly in the coach and to feel the power of the engine hurling the train along through the night.

Tom got drunk in a very short time. He kept taking drinks from the bottle as the thoughts visited him and when his head began to reel got up and walked along the road going away from Winesburg. There was a bridge on the road that ran out of Winesburg north to Lake Erie and the drunken boy made his way along the road to the bridge. There he sat down. He tried to drink again, but when he had taken the cork out of the bottle he became ill and put it quickly back. His head was rocking back and forth and so he sat on the stone approach to the bridge and sighed. His head seemed to be flying about like a pin wheel and then projecting itself off into space and his arms and legs flopped helplessly about.

At eleven o'clock Tom got back into town. George Willard found him wandering about and took him into the *Eagle* print shop. Then he became afraid that the

print shop *ed* < printshop

Drink

drunken boy would make a mess on the floor and helped him into the alleyway.

The reporter was confused by Tom Foster. The drunken boy talked of Helen White and said he had been with her on the shore of a sea and had made love to her. George had seen Helen White walking in the street with her father during the evening and decided that Tom was out of his head. A sentiment concerning Helen White that lurked in his own heart flamed up and he became angry. "Now you quit that," he said. "I won't let Helen White's name be dragged into this. I won't let that happen." He began shaking Tom's shoulder, trying to make him understand. "You quit it," he said again.

For three hours the two young men, thus strangely thrown together, stayed in the print shop. When he had a little recovered George took Tom for a walk. They went into the country and sat on a log near the edge of a woods. Something in the still night drew them together and when the drunken boy's head began to clear they talked.

"It was good to be drunk," Tom Foster said. "It taught me something. I won't have to do it again. I will think more clearly after this. You see how it is."

George Willard did not see, but his anger concerning Helen White passed and he felt drawn toward the pale, shaken boy as he had never before been drawn toward anyone. With motherly solicitude, he insisted that Tom get to his feet and walk about. Again they went back to the print shop and sat in silence in the darkness.

The reporter could not get the purpose of Tom Foster's action straightened out in his mind. When Tom spoke again of Helen White he again grew angry and began to scold. "You quit that," he said sharply. "You haven't been

print shop *ed* < printshop

woods *ed* < wood

toward *ms* < towards
toward *ms* < towards
anyone *ed* < any one

print shop *ed* < printshop

Concerning Tom Foster

with her. What makes you say you have? What makes you keep saying such things? Now you quit it, do you hear?"

Tom was hurt. He couldn't quarrel with George Willard because he was incapable of quarreling, so he got up to go away. When George Willard was insistent he put out his hand, laying it on the older boy's arm, and tried to explain.

"Well," he said softly, "I don't know how it was. I was happy. You see how that was. Helen White made me happy and the night did too. I wanted to suffer, to be hurt somehow. I thought that was what I should do. I wanted to suffer, you see, because everyone suffers and does wrong. I thought of a lot of things to do, but they wouldn't work. They all hurt someone else."

everyone *ms* < every one

someone *ms* < some one

Tom Foster's voice arose and for once in his life he became almost excited. "It was like making love, that's what I mean," he explained. "Don't you see how it is? It hurt me to do what I did and made everything strange. That's why I did it. I'm glad too. It taught me something, that's it, that's what I wanted. Don't you understand? I wanted to learn things, you see. That's why I did it."

arose *ms* < arose,

glad *ms* < glad,

DEATH

Concerning Doctor Reefy
and Elizabeth Willard

THE STAIRWAY LEADING up to Dr. Reefy's office, in the Heffner Block above the Paris Dry Goods Company, was but dimly lighted. At the head of the stairway

Company *ed* < Store

Death

hung a lamp with a dirty chimney that was fastened by
a bracket to the wall. The lamp had a tin reflector, brown
with rust and covered with dust. The people who went
up the stairway followed with their feet the feet of many
who had gone before. The soft boards of the stairs had
yielded under the pressure of feet and deep hollows
marked the way.

At the top of the stairway a turn to the right brought
you to the doctor's door. To the left was a dark hallway
filled with rubbish. Old chairs, carpenters' horses, step
ladders and empty boxes lay in the darkness waiting for
shins to be barked. The pile of rubbish belonged to the
Paris Dry Goods Company. When a counter or a row
of shelves in the store became useless, clerks carried it
up the stairway and threw it on the pile.

Doctor Reefy's office was as large as a barn. A stove
with a round paunch sat in the middle of the room.
Around its base was piled sawdust, held in place by heavy
planks nailed to the floor. By the door stood a huge
table that had once been a part of the furniture of
Herrick's Clothing Store and that had been used for dis-
playing custom-made clothes. It was covered with books,
bottles and surgical instruments. Near the edge of the
table lay three or four apples left by John Spaniard, a
tree nursery man who was Doctor Reefy's friend, and
who had slipped the apples out of his pocket as he came
in at the door.

At middle age Doctor Reefy was tall and awkward.
The grey beard he later wore had not yet appeared, but
on the upper lip grew a brown mustache. He was not a
graceful man, as when he grew older, and was much
occupied with the problem of disposing of his hands
and feet.

On summer afternoons, when she had been married

(carpenters' *ms*
< carpenter's

Company. *ed* < Co.

*Carpenters often use
paired trestles ("horses")
as frames to hold up
boards being shortened
or shaped for use in
construction.*

(nursery man *ed*
< nurseryman

*A nurseryman named
French did live in Clyde,
Ohio, in Anderson's
youth.*

Concerning Doctor Reefy and Elizabeth Willard

many years and when her son George was a boy of twelve or fourteen, Elizabeth Willard sometimes went up the worn steps to Doctor Reefy's office. Already the woman's naturally tall figure had begun to droop and to drag itself listlessly about. Ostensibly she went to see the doctor because of her health, but on the half dozen occasions when she had been to see him the outcome of the visits did not primarily concern her health. She and the doctor talked of that but they talked most of her life, of their two lives and of the ideas that had come to them as they lived their lives in Winesburg.

In the big empty office the man and the woman sat looking at each other and they were a good deal alike. Their bodies were different as were also the color of their eyes, the length of their noses and the circumstances of their existence, but something inside them meant the same thing, wanted the same release, would have left the same impression on the memory of an onlooker. Later, and when he grew older and married a young wife, the doctor often talked to her of the hours spent with the sick woman and expressed a good many things he had been unable to express to Elizabeth. He was almost a poet in his old age and his notion of what happened took a poetic turn. "I had come to the time in my life when prayer became necessary and so I invented gods and prayed to them," he said. "I did not say my prayers in words nor did I kneel down but sat perfectly still in my chair. In the late afternoon when it was hot and quiet on Main Street or in the winter when the days were gloomy, the gods came into the office and I thought no one knew about them. Then I found that this woman Elizabeth knew, that she worshipped also the same gods. I have a notion that she came to the office because she thought the gods would be there but

Death

she was happy to find herself not alone just the same. It was an experience that cannot be explained, although I suppose it is always happening to men and women in all sorts of places."

———————

On the summer afternoons when Elizabeth and the doctor sat in the office and talked of their two lives they talked of other lives also. Sometimes the doctor made philosophic epigrams. Then he chuckled with amusement. Now and then, after a period of silence, a word was said or a hint given that strangely illuminated the life of the speaker, a wish became a desire, or a dream, half dead, flared suddenly into life. For the most part the words came from the woman and she said them without looking at the man.

Each time she came to see the doctor the hotel keeper's wife talked a little more freely and after an hour or two in his presence went down the stairway, into Main Street, feeling renewed and strengthened against the dullness of her days. With something approaching a girlhood swing to her body she walked along, but when she had got back to her chair by the window of her room and, when darkness had come on and a girl from the hotel dining room brought her dinner on a tray, she let it grow cold. Her thoughts ran away to her girlhood with its passionate longing for adventure and she remembered the arms of men that had held her when adventure was a possible thing for her. Particularly she remembered one who had for a time been her lover and who in the moment of his passion had cried out to her more than a hundred times, saying the same words madly over and over: "You dear! You dear! You lovely dear!" The words she thought expressed something she would have liked to have achieved in life.

then, *ed* < then

stairway, *ms* < stairway
Street, *ed* < Street

and, *ed* < and

Concerning Doctor Reefy and Elizabeth Willard

In her room in the shabby old hotel the sick wife of the hotel keeper began to weep and putting her hands to her face rocked back and forth. The words of her one friend, Doctor Reefy, rang in her ears. "Love is like a wind stirring the grass beneath trees on a black night," he had said. "You must not try to make love definite. It is the divine accident of life. If you try to be definite and sure about it and to live beneath the trees, where soft night winds blow, the long hot day of disappointment comes swiftly and the gritty dust from passing wagons gathers upon lips inflamed and made tender by kisses."

Elizabeth Willard could not remember her mother who had died when she was but five years old. Her girlhood had been lived in the most haphazard manner imaginable. Her father was a man who had wanted to be let alone and the affairs of the hotel would not let him alone. He also had lived and died a sick man. Every day he arose with a cheerful face, but by ten o'clock in the morning all the joy had gone out of his heart. When a guest complained of the fare in the hotel dining room or one of the girls who made up the beds got married and went away, he stamped on the floor and swore. At night when he went to bed he thought of his daughter growing up among the stream of people that drifted in and out of the hotel and was overcome with sadness. As the girl grew older and began to walk out in the evening with men he wanted to talk to her, but when he tried was not successful. He always forgot what he wanted to say and spent the time complaining of his own affairs.

In her girlhood and young womanhood Elizabeth had tried to be a real adventurer in life. At eighteen life had so gripped her that she was no longer a virgin, but, although she had a half dozen lovers before she married

virgin, *ms* < virgin

Death

Tom Willard, she had never entered upon an adventure prompted by desire alone. Like all the women in the world, she wanted a real lover. Always there was something she sought blindly, passionately, some hidden wonder in life. The tall beautiful girl with the swinging stride who had walked under the trees with men was forever putting out her hand into the darkness and trying to get hold of some other hand. In all the babble of words that fell from the lips of the men with whom she adventured she was trying to find what would be for her the true word.

Elizabeth had married Tom Willard, a clerk in her father's hotel, because he was at hand and wanted to marry at the time when the determination to marry came to her. For a while, like most young girls, she thought marriage would change the face of life. If there was in her mind a doubt of the outcome of the marriage with Tom she brushed it aside. Her father was ill and near death at the time and she was perplexed because of the meaningless outcome of an affair in which she had just been involved. Other girls of her age in Winesburg were marrying men she had always known, grocery clerks or young farmers. In the evening they walked in Main Street with their husbands and when she passed they smiled happily. She began to think that the fact of marriage might be full of some hidden significance. Young wives with whom she talked spoke softly and shyly. "It changes things to have a man of your own," they said.

On the evening before her marriage the perplexed girl had a talk with her father. Later she wondered if the hours alone with the sick man had not led to her decision to marry. The father talked of his life and advised the daughter to avoid being led into another such muddle. He abused Tom Willard, and that led Eliza-

Concerning Doctor Reefy and Elizabeth Willard

beth to come to the clerk's defense. The sick man became excited and tried to get out of bed. When she would not let him walk about he began to complain. "I've never been let alone," he said. "Although I've worked hard I've not made the hotel pay. Even now I owe money at the bank. You'll find that out when I'm gone."

The voice of the sick man became tense with earnestness. Being unable to arise, he put out his hand and pulled the girl's head down beside his own. "There's a way out," he whispered. "Don't marry Tom Willard or anyone else here in Winesburg. There is eight hundred dollars in a tin box in my trunk. Take it and go away."

anyone *ms* < any one

Again the sick man's voice became querulous. "You've got to promise," he declared. "If you won't promise not to marry, give me your word that you'll never tell Tom about the money. It is mine and if I give it to you I've the right to make that demand. Hide it away. It is to make up to you for my failure as a father. Sometime it may prove to be a door, a great open door to you. Come now, I tell you I'm about to die, give me your promise."

Sometime *ed* < Some time

In Doctor Reefy's office, Elizabeth, a tired gaunt old woman at forty-one, sat in a chair near the stove and looked at the floor. By a small desk near the window sat the doctor. His hands played with a lead pencil that lay on the desk. Elizabeth talked of her life as a married woman. She became impersonal and forgot her husband, only using him as a lay figure to give point to her tale. "And then I was married and it did not turn out at all," she said bitterly. "As soon as I had gone into it I began to be afraid. Perhaps I knew too much before and then perhaps I found out too much during my first night with him. I don't remember.

"What a fool I was. When father gave me the money

Death

and tried to talk me out of the thought of marriage I would not listen. I thought of what the girls who were married had said of it and I wanted marriage also. It wasn't Tom I wanted, it was marriage. When father went to sleep I leaned out of the window and thought of the life I had led. I didn't want to be a bad woman. The town was full of stories about me. I even began to be afraid Tom would change his mind."

The woman's voice began to quiver with excitement. To Doctor Reefy, who without realizing what was happening had begun to love her, there came an odd illusion. He thought that as she talked the woman's body was changing, that she was becoming younger, straighter, stronger. When he could not shake off the illusion his mind gave it a professional twist. "It is good for both her body and her mind, this talking," he muttered.

The woman began telling of an incident that had happened one afternoon a few months after her marriage. Her voice became steadier. "In the late afternoon I went for a drive alone," she said. "I had a buggy and a little grey pony I kept in Moyer's Livery. Tom was painting and repapering rooms in the hotel. He wanted money and I was trying to make up my mind to tell him about the eight hundred dollars father had given to me. I couldn't decide to do it. I didn't like him well enough. There was always paint on his hands and face during those days and he smelled of paint. He was trying to fix up the old hotel, make it new and smart."

The excited woman sat up very straight in her chair and made a quick girlish movement with her hand as she told of the drive alone on the spring afternoon. "It was cloudy and a storm threatened," she said. "Black clouds made the green of the trees and the grass stand out so that the colors hurt my eyes. I went out Trunion

Concerning Doctor Reefy and Elizabeth Willard

Pike a mile or more and then turned into a side road. The little horse went quickly along uphill and down. I was impatient. Thoughts came and I wanted to get away from my thoughts. I began to beat the horse. The black clouds settled down and it began to rain. I wanted to go at a terrible speed, to drive on and on forever. I wanted to get out of town, out of my clothes, out of my marriage, out of my body, out of everything. I almost killed the horse, making him run, and when he could not run anymore I got out of the buggy and ran afoot into the darkness until I fell and hurt my side. I wanted to run away from everything but I wanted to run toward something too. Don't you see, dear, how it was?"

Elizabeth sprang out of the chair and began to walk about in the office. She walked as Doctor Reefy thought he had never seen anyone walk before. To her whole body there was a swing, a rhythm that intoxicated him. When she came and knelt on the floor beside his chair he took her into his arms and began to kiss her passionately. "I cried all the way home," she said, as she tried to continue the story of her wild ride, but he did not listen. "You dear! You lovely dear! Oh you lovely dear!" he muttered and thought he held in his arms not the tired-out woman of forty-one, but a lovely and innocent girl who had been able by some miracle to project herself out of the husk of the body of the tired-out woman.

Doctor Reefy did not see the woman he had held in his arms again until after her death. On the summer afternoon in the office when he was on the point of becoming her lover a half grotesque little incident brought his love-making quickly to an end. As the man and woman held each other tightly heavy feet came tramping up the office stairs. The two sprang to their feet and stood listening and trembling. The noise on

uphill *ed* < up hill

anymore *ed* < any more

toward *ms* < towards

anyone *ms* < any one

arms *ed* < arms,

tired-out *ms* < tired out
forty-one, *ed* < forty-one

Death

(Company *ed*
< Store Co.

the stairs was made by a clerk from the Paris Dry Goods Company. With a loud bang he threw an empty box on the pile of rubbish in the hallway and then went heavily down the stairs. Elizabeth followed him almost immediately. The thing that had come to life in her as she talked to her one friend died suddenly. She was hysterical, as was also Doctor Reefy, and did not want to continue the talk. Along the street she went with the blood still singing in her body, but when she turned out of Main Street and saw ahead the lights of the New Willard House, she began to tremble and her knees shook so that for a moment she thought she would fall in the street.

The sick woman spent the last few months of her life hungering for death. Along the road of death she went, seeking, hungering. She personified the figure of death and made him now a strong black-haired youth running over hills, now a stern quiet man marked and

him *ed* < him,

scarred by the business of living. In the darkness of her room she put out her hand, thrusting it from under the covers of her bed, and she thought that death like a living thing put out his hand to her. "Be patient, lover," she whispered. "Keep yourself young and beautiful and be patient."

On the evening when disease laid its heavy hand upon her and defeated her plans for telling her son George of the eight hundred dollars hidden away, she got out of

room, *ms* < room

bed and crept half across the room, pleading with death for another hour of life. "Wait, dear! The boy! The boy! The boy!" she pleaded as she tried with all of her strength to fight off the arms of the lover she had wanted so earnestly.

Concerning Doctor Reefy and Elizabeth Willard

Elizabeth died one day in March, in the year when her son George became eighteen, and the young man had but little sense of the meaning of her death. Only time could give him that. For a month he had seen her lying white and still and speechless in her bed and then one afternoon the doctor stopped him in the hallway and said a few words.

The young man went into his own room and closed the door. He had a queer empty feeling in the region of his stomach. For a moment he sat staring at the floor and then jumping up went for a walk. Along the station platform he went and around through residence streets past the high school building, thinking almost entirely of his own affairs. The notion of death could not get hold of him and he was in fact a little annoyed that his mother had died on that day. He had just received a note from Helen White, the daughter of the town banker, in answer to one from him. "Tonight I could have gone to see her and now it will have to be put off," he thought half angrily.

Elizabeth died on a Friday afternoon at three o'clock. It had been cold and rainy in the morning but in the afternoon the sun came out. Before she died she lay paralyzed for six days unable to speak or move and with only her mind and her eyes alive. For three of the six days she struggled, thinking of her boy, trying to say some few words in regard to his future, and in her eyes there was an appeal so touching that all who saw it kept the memory of the dying woman in their minds for years. Even Tom Willard who had always half resented his wife forgot his resentment and the tears ran out of his eyes and lodged in his mustache. The mustache had begun to turn grey and Tom colored it with dye. There was oil in the preparation he used for the purpose and the tears,

March, *ms* < March

bed *ms* < bed,

went *ms* < went,

Parts of the character Elizabeth Willard are based on Anderson's mother, Emma Smith Anderson, who died in Clyde, Ohio, on May 10, 1895, and whose death freed Sherwood to leave Ohio for his first adventure in Chicago.

Death

catching in the mustache and being brushed away by his hand, formed a fine mist-like vapor. In his grief Tom Willard's face looked like the face of a little dog that has been out a long time in bitter weather.

George came home along Main Street at dark on the day of his mother's death and, after going to his own room to brush his hair and clothes, went along the hallway and into the room where the body lay. There was a candle on the dressing table by the door and Doctor Reefy sat in a chair by the bed. The doctor arose and started to go out. He put out his hand as though to greet the younger man and then awkwardly drew it back again. The air of the room was heavy with the presence of the two self-conscious human beings, and the man hurried away.

The dead woman's son sat down in a chair and looked at the floor. He again thought of his own affairs and definitely decided he would make a change in his life, that he would leave Winesburg. "I will go to some city. Perhaps I can get a job on some newspaper," he thought and then his mind turned to the girl with whom he was to have spent this evening and again he was half angry at the turn of events that had prevented his going to her.

In the dimly lighted room with the dead woman the young man began to have thoughts. His mind played with thoughts of life as his mother's mind had played with the thought of death. He closed his eyes and imagined that the red young lips of Helen White touched his own lips. His body trembled and his hands shook. And then something happened. The boy sprang to his feet and stood stiffly. He looked at the figure of the dead woman under the sheet and shame for his thoughts swept

sheet *ed* < sheets

Concerning Doctor Reefy and Elizabeth Willard

over him so that he began to weep. A new notion came into his mind and he turned and looked guiltily about as though afraid he would be observed.

George Willard became possessed of a madness to lift the sheet from the body of his mother and look at her face. The thought that had come into his mind gripped him terribly. He became convinced that not his mother but someone else lay in the bed before him. The conviction was so real that it was almost unbearable. The body under the sheet was long and in death looked young and graceful. To the boy, held by some strange fancy, it was unspeakably lovely. The feeling that the body before him was alive, that in another moment a lovely woman would spring out of the bed and confront him, became so overpowering that he could not bear the suspense. Again and again he put out his hand. Once he touched and half lifted the white sheet that covered her, but his courage failed and he, like Doctor Reefy, turned and went out of the room. In the hallway outside the door he stopped and trembled so that he had to put a hand against the wall to support himself. "That's not my mother. That's not my mother in there," he whispered to himself and again his body shook with fright and uncertainty. When Aunt Elizabeth Swift, who had come to watch over the body, came out of an adjoining room he put his hand into hers and began to sob, shaking his head from side to side, half blind with grief. "My mother is dead," he said, and then forgetting the woman he turned and stared at the door through which he had just come. "The dear, the dear, oh the lovely dear," the boy, urged by some impulse outside himself, muttered aloud.

someone *ms* < some one

sheet *ms* < sheets

him, *ed* < him

Death

dollars *ed* < dollars,

As for the eight hundred dollars the dead woman had kept hidden so long and that was to give George Willard his start in the city, it lay in the tin box behind the plaster by the foot of his mother's bed. Elizabeth had put it there a week after her marriage, breaking the plaster away with a stick. Then she got one of the workmen her husband was at that time employing about the hotel to mend the wall. "I jammed the corner of the bed against it," she had explained to her husband, unable at the moment to give up her dream of release, the release that after all came to her but twice in her life, in the moments when her lovers Death and Doctor Reefy held her in their arms.

SOPHISTICATION

Concerning Helen White

IT WAS EARLY evening of a day in the late fall and the Winesburg County Fair had brought crowds of country people into town. The day had been clear and the night came on warm and pleasant. On the Trunion Pike, where the road after it left town stretched away between berry fields now covered with dry brown leaves, the dust from passing wagons arose in clouds. Children, curled into little balls, slept on the straw scattered on wagon beds. Their hair was full of dust and their fingers black and sticky. The dust rolled away over the fields and the departing sun set it ablaze with colors.

In the main street of Winesburg crowds filled the stores and the sidewalks. Night came on, horses whinnied, the clerks in the stores ran madly about, children became

Concerning Helen White

lost and cried lustily—an American town worked terribly at the task of amusing itself.

Pushing his way through the crowds in Main Street, young George Willard concealed himself in the stairway leading to Doctor Reefy's office and looked at the people. With feverish eyes he watched the faces drifting past under the store lights. Thoughts kept coming into his head and he did not want to think. He stamped impatiently on the wooden steps and looked sharply about. "Well, is she going to stay with him all day? Have I done all this waiting for nothing?" he muttered.

George Willard, the Ohio village boy, was fast growing into manhood and new thoughts had been coming into his mind. All that day, amid the jam of people at the fair, he had gone about feeling lonely. He was about to leave Winesburg to go away to some city where he hoped to get work on a city newspaper and he felt grown up. The mood that had taken possession of him was a thing known to men and unknown to boys. He felt old and a little tired. Memories awoke in him. To his mind his new sense of maturity set him apart, made of him a half tragic figure. He wanted someone to understand the feeling that had taken possession of him after his mother's death.

There is a time in the life of every boy when he for the first time takes the backward view of life. Perhaps that is the moment when he crosses the line into manhood. The boy is walking through the streets of his town. He is thinking of the future and of the figure he will cut in the world. Ambitions and regrets awake within him. Suddenly something happens; he stops under a tree and waits as for a voice calling his name. Ghosts of old things creep into his consciousness; the voices outside of himself whisper a message concerning the limitations of life.

lustily— *ed* < lustily,

fair *ed* < Fair,

half *ed* < half-

streets *ms* < street

Sophistication

From being quite sure of himself and his future he becomes not at all sure. If he be an imaginative boy a door
is torn open and for the first time he looks out upon the
world, seeing, as though they marched in procession
before him, the countless figures of men who before his
time have come out of nothingness into the world, lived
their lives and again disappeared into nothingness. The
sadness of sophistication has come to the boy. With a
little gasp he sees himself as merely a leaf blown by the
wind through the streets of his village. He knows that
in spite of all the stout talk of his fellows he must live
and die in uncertainty, a thing blown by the winds, a
thing destined like corn to wilt in the sun. He shivers
and looks eagerly about. The eighteen years he has lived
seem but a moment, a breathing space in the long march
of humanity. Already he hears death calling. With all
his heart he wants to come close to some other human,
touch someone with his hands, be touched by the hand
of another. If he prefers that the other be a woman, that
is because he believes that a woman will be gentle, that
she will understand. He wants, most of all, understanding.

When the moment of sophistication came to George
Willard his mind turned to Helen White, the Winesburg
banker's daughter. Always he had been conscious of the
girl growing into womanhood as he grew into manhood.
Once, on a summer night when he was eighteen, he
had walked with her on a country road and in her presence had given way to an impulse to boast, to make
himself appear big and significant in her eyes. Now he
wanted to see her for another purpose. He wanted to
tell her of the new impulses that had come to him. He
had tried to make her think of him as a man when he
knew nothing of manhood and now he wanted to be

Once, *ed* < Once

Concerning Helen White

with her and to try to make her feel the change he believed had taken place in his nature.

As for Helen White, she also had come to a period of change. What George felt, she in her young woman's way felt also. She was no longer a girl and hungered to reach into the grace and beauty of womanhood. She had come home from Cleveland, where she was attending college, to spend a day at the fair. She also had begun to have memories. During the day she sat in the grand-stand with a young man, one of the instructors from the college, who was a guest of her mother's. The young man was of a pedantic turn of mind and she felt at once he would not do for her purpose. At the fair she was glad to be seen in his company as he was well dressed and a stranger. She knew that the fact of his presence would create an impression. During the day she was happy, but when night came on she began to grow restless. She wanted to drive the instructor away, to get out of his presence. While they sat together in the grand-stand and while the eyes of former school mates were upon them, she paid so much attention to her escort that he grew interested. "A scholar needs money. I should marry a woman with money," he mused.

Helen White was thinking of George Willard even as he wandered gloomily through the crowds thinking of her. She remembered the summer evening when they had walked together and wanted to walk with him again. She thought that the months she had spent in the city, the going to theatres and the seeing of great crowds wandering in lighted thoroughfares, had changed her profoundly. She wanted him to feel and be conscious of the change in her nature.

The summer evening together that had left its mark on the memory of both the young man and woman

fair *ms* < Fair

(grand-stand *ed*
(< grandstand

fair *ed* < Fair

(school mates *ed*
(< schoolmates

Helen White may be based on a young woman of Clyde, Ohio (daughter of a Dr. Luse), who came home from an eastern music school each summer, beautifully dressed and seeming too grand for the attentions of the town youths.

Sophistication

had, when looked at quite sensibly, been rather stupidly spent. They had walked out of town along a country road. Then they had stopped by a fence near a field of young corn and George had taken off his coat and let it hang on his arm. "Well, I've stayed here in Winesburg—yes. I've not yet gone away but I'm growing up," he had said. "I've been reading books and I've been thinking. I'm going to try to amount to something in life.

"Well," he explained, "that isn't the point. Perhaps I'd better quit talking."

The confused boy put his hand on the girl's arm. His voice trembled. The two started to walk back along the road toward town. In his desperation George boasted. "I'm going to be a big man, the biggest that ever lived here in Winesburg," he declared. "I want you to do something, I don't know what. Perhaps it is none of my business. I want you to try to be different from other women. You see the point. It's none of my business I tell you. I want you to be a beautiful woman. You see what I want."

The boy's voice failed and in silence the two came back into town and went along the street to Helen White's house. At the gate he tried to say something impressive. Speeches he had thought out came into his head, but they seemed utterly pointless. "I thought—I used to think—I had it in my mind you would marry Seth Richmond. Now I know you won't," was all he could find to say as she went through the gate and toward the door of her house.

On the warm fall evening as he stood in the stairway and looked at the crowd drifting through Main Street, George thought of the talk beside the field of young corn and was ashamed of the figure he had made of himself. In the street the people surged up and down like cattle confined in a pen. Buggies and wagons al-

(Winesburg—yes.
 I've *ms* < Winesburg—
   yes—I've

boasted. *ms* < boasted,

(know you *ms, Pr* 2–
 Pr 7 < know that you

Concerning Helen White

most filled the narrow thoroughfare. A band played and small boys raced along the sidewalk, diving between the legs of men. Young men with shining red faces walked awkwardly about with girls on their arms. In a room above one of the stores, where a dance was to be held, the fiddlers tuned their instruments. The broken sounds floated down through an open window and out across the murmur of voices and the loud blare of the horns of the band. The medley of sounds got on young Willard's nerves. Everywhere, on all sides, the sense of crowding, moving life closed in about him. He wanted to run away by himself and think. "If she wants to stay with that fellow she may. Why should I care? What difference does it make to me?" he growled and went along Main Street and through Hern's Grocery into a side street.

George felt so utterly lonely and dejected that he wanted to weep but pride made him walk rapidly along, swinging his arms. He came to Wesley Moyer's Livery and stopped in the shadows to listen to a group of men who talked of a race Wesley's stallion, Tony Tip, had won at the fair during the afternoon. A crowd had gathered in front of the barn and before the crowd walked Wesley, prancing up and down and boasting. He held a whip in his hand and kept tapping the ground. Little puffs of dust arose in the lamp light. "Hell, quit your talking," Wesley exclaimed. "I wasn't afraid, I knew I had 'em beat all the time. I wasn't afraid."

Ordinarily George Willard would have been intensely interested in the boasting of Moyer, the horse man. Now it made him angry. He turned and hurried away along the street. "Old Windbag," he sputtered. "Why does he want to be bragging? Why don't he shut up?"

George went into a vacant lot and, as he hurried along, fell over a pile of rubbish. A nail protruding from an

murmur *ms* < murmer

Grocery *ed* < grocery

Wesley *ed* < Westley
Livery *ed* < livery barn

Wesley's *ed* < Westley's
fair *ms* < Fair

Wesley *ed* < Westley

lamp light *ed* < lamplight
Wesley *ed* < Westley

horse man *ed*
< horseman

Windbag *ms*
< wind-bag,

and, *ed* < and

Sophistication

empty barrel tore his trousers. He sat down on the ground and swore. With a pin he mended the torn place and then arose and went on. "I'll go to Helen White's house, that's what I'll do. I'll walk right in. I'll say that I want to see her. I'll walk right in and sit down, that's what I'll do," he declared, climbing over a fence and beginning to run.

On the veranda of Banker White's house Helen was restless and distraught. The instructor sat between the mother and daughter. His talk wearied the girl. Although he had also been raised in an Ohio town, the instructor began to put on the airs of the city. He wanted to appear cosmopolitan. "I like the chance you have given me to study the background out of which most of our girls come," he declared. "It was good of you, Mrs. White, to have me down for the day." He turned to Helen and laughed. "Your life is still bound up with the life of this town?" he asked. "There are people here in whom you are interested?" To the girl his voice sounded pompous and heavy.

Helen arose and went into the house. At the door leading to a garden at the back she stopped and stood listening. Her mother began to talk. "There is no one here fit to associate with a girl of Helen's breeding," she said.

Helen ran down a flight of stairs at the back of the house and into the garden. In the darkness she stopped and stood trembling. It seemed to her that the world was full of meaningless people saying words. Afire with eagerness she ran through a garden gate and, turning a corner by the banker's barn, went into a little side street. "George! Where are you, George?" she cried, filled with nervous excitement. She stopped running, and leaned

and, *ed* < and

Concerning Helen White

against a tree to laugh hysterically. Along the dark little street came George Willard, still saying words. "I'm going to walk right into her house. I'll go right in and sit down," he declared as he came up to her. He stopped and stared stupidly. "Come on," he said and took hold of her hand. With hanging heads they walked away along the street under the trees. Dry leaves rustled underfoot. Now that he had found her George wondered what he had better do and say.

underfoot ed < under foot

At the upper end of the fair grounds, in Winesburg, there is a half decayed old grand-stand. It has never been painted and the boards are all warped out of shape. The fair grounds stands on top of a low hill rising out of the valley of Wine Creek and from the grand-stand one can see at night, over a corn field, the lights of the town reflected against the sky.

grounds ed < ground

grounds ed < ground

corn field ed < cornfield

George and Helen climbed the hill to the fair grounds, coming by the path past Waterworks Pond. The feeling of loneliness and isolation that had come to the young man in the crowded streets of his town was both broken and intensified by the presence of Helen. What he felt was reflected in her.

grounds ed < ground

In youth there are always two forces fighting in people. The warm unthinking little animal struggles against the thing that reflects and remembers, and the older, the more sophisticated thing had possession of George Willard. Sensing his mood, Helen walked beside him filled with respect. When they got to the grand-stand they climbed up under the roof and sat down on one of the long bench-like seats.

There is something memorable in the experience to be had by going into a fair grounds that stands at the edge of a Middle Western town on a night after the

grounds ed < ground

Sophistication

annual fair has been held. The sensation is one never to be forgotten. On all sides are ghosts, not of the dead, but of living people. Here, during the day just passed, have come the people pouring in from the town and the country around. Farmers with their wives and children and all the people from the hundreds of little frame houses have gathered within these board walls. Young girls have laughed and men with beards have talked of the affairs of their lives. The place has been filled to overflowing with life. It has itched and squirmed with life and now it is night and the life has all gone away. The silence is almost terrifying. One conceals oneself standing silently beside the trunk of a tree and what there is of a reflective tendency in his nature is intensified. One shudders at the thought of the meaninglessness of life while at the same instant, and if the people of the town are his people, one loves life so intensely that tears come into the eyes.

In the darkness under the roof of the grand-stand, George Willard sat beside Helen White and felt very keenly his own insignificance in the scheme of existence. Now that he had come out of town where the presence of the people stirring about, busy with a multitude of affairs, had been so irritating the irritation was all gone. The presence of Helen renewed and refreshed him. It was as though her woman's hand was assisting him to make some minute re-adjustment of the machinery of his life. He began to think of the people in the town where he had always lived with something like reverence. He had reverence for Helen. He wanted to love and to be loved by her, but he did not want at the moment to be confused by her womanhood. In the darkness he took hold of her hand and when she crept close put a hand on her shoulder. A wind began to blow and

(over-flowing *ed*
  < overflowing

(re-adjustment *ed*
  < readjustment

Concerning Helen White

he shivered. With all his strength he tried to hold and to understand the mood that had come upon him. In that high place in the darkness the two oddly sensitive human atoms held each other tightly and waited. In the mind of each was the same thought. "I have come to this lonely place and here is this other," was the substance of the thing felt.

In Winesburg the crowded day had run itself out into the long night of the late fall. Farm horses jogged away along lonely country roads pulling their portion of weary people. Clerks began to bring samples of goods in off the sidewalks and lock the doors of stores. In the Opera House a crowd had gathered to see a show and farther down Main Street the fiddlers, their instruments tuned, sweated and worked to keep the feet of youth flying over a dance floor.

In the darkness in the grand-stand Helen White and George Willard remained silent. Now and then the spell that held them was broken and they turned and tried in the dim light to see into each other's eyes. They kissed but that impulse did not last. At the upper end of the fair grounds a half dozen men worked over horses that had raced during the afternoon. The men had built a fire and were heating kettles of water. Only their legs could be seen as they passed back and forth in the light. When the wind blew the little flames of the fire danced crazily about.

George and Helen arose and walked away into the darkness. They went along a path past a field of corn that had not yet been cut. The wind whispered among the dry corn blades. For a moment during the walk back into town the spell that held them was broken. When they had come to the crest of Waterworks Hill they stopped by a tree and George again put his hands on

Most towns in the nineteenth century featured "opera houses," meeting halls large enough for staging dramatic or musical events but seldom actual grand operas. In Clyde, (con't below)

farther *ed* < further

Terry's Hall (called also Terry's Opera House), capable of seating five hundred people, occupied the upper floor of 110 South Main Street.

other's *ms* < others

grounds *ed* < ground

Sophistication

the girl's shoulders. She embraced him eagerly and then again they drew quickly back from that impulse. They stopped kissing and stood a little apart. Mutual respect grew big in them. They were both embarrassed and to relieve their embarrassment dropped into the animalism of youth. They laughed and began to pull and haul at each other. In some way chastened and purified by the mood they had been in they became not man and woman, not boy and girl, but excited little animals.

became *ed* < became,

It was so they went down the hill. In the darkness they played like two splendid young things in a young world. Once, running swiftly forward, Helen tripped George and he fell. He squirmed and shouted. Shaking with laughter, he rolled down the hill. Helen ran after him. For just a moment she stopped in the darkness. There is no way of knowing what woman's thoughts went through her mind but, when the bottom of the hill was reached and she came up to the boy, she took his arm and walked beside him in dignified silence. For some reason they could not have explained they had both got from their silent evening together the thing needed. Man or boy, woman or girl, they had for a moment taken hold of the thing that makes the mature life of men and women in the modern world possible.

DEPARTURE

Concerning George Willard

YOUNG GEORGE WILLARD got out of bed at four in the morning. It was April and the young tree leaves were just coming out of their buds. The trees along the residence streets in Winesburg are maple and the seeds are winged. When the wind blows they whirl crazily about, filling the air and making a carpet underfoot.

George came downstairs into the hotel office carrying a brown leather bag. His trunk was packed for departure. Since two o'clock he had been awake thinking of the journey he was about to take and wondering what he would find at the end of his journey. The boy who slept in the hotel office lay on a cot by the door. His mouth was open and he snored lustily. George crept past the cot and went out into the silent deserted main street. The east was pink with the dawn and long streaks of light climbed into the sky where a few stars still shone.

Beyond the last house on Trunion Pike in Winesburg there is a great stretch of open fields. The fields are owned by farmers who live in town and drive homeward at evening along Trunion Pike in light creaking wagons. In the fields are planted berries and small fruits. In the late afternoon in the hot summer, when the road and

(downstairs *ed*
< down stairs

summer *ms* < summers
summer, *ed* < summer

Departure

the fields are covered with dust, a smoky haze lies over the great flat basin of land. To look across it is like looking out across the sea. In the spring, when the land is green, the effect is somewhat different. The land becomes a wide green billiard table on which tiny human insects toil up and down.

spring, *ms* < spring
green, *ed* < green

All through his boyhood and young manhood George Willard had been in the habit of walking on Trunion Pike. He had been in the midst of the great open place on winter nights when it was covered with snow and only the moon looked down at him; he had been there in the fall when bleak winds blew and on summer evenings when the air vibrated with the song of insects. On the April morning he wanted to go there again, to walk again in the silence. He did walk to where the road dipped down by a little stream two miles from town and then turned and walked silently back again. When he got to Main Street clerks were sweeping the sidewalks before the stores. "Hey you, George. How does it feel to be going away?" they asked.

Hey you, *ed* < Hey, you

The west bound train leaves Winesburg at seven forty-five in the morning. Tom Little is conductor. His train runs from Cleveland to where it connects with a great trunk line railroad with terminals in Chicago and New York. Tom has what in railroad circles is called an "easy run." Every evening he returns to his family. In the fall and spring he spends his Sundays fishing in Lake Erie. He has a round red face and small blue eyes. He knows the people in the towns along his railroad better than a city man knows the people who live in his apartment building.

returns *ms* < returned

George came down the little incline from the New Willard House at seven o'clock. Tom Willard carried his bag. The son had become taller than the father.

Concerning George Willard

On the station platform everyone shook the young man's hand. More than a dozen people waited about. Then they talked of their own affairs. Even Will Henderson, who was lazy and often slept until nine, had got out of bed. George was embarrassed. Gertrude Wilmot, a tall thin woman of fifty who worked in the Winesburg Post Office, came along the station platform. She had never before paid any attention to George. Now she stopped and put out her hand. In two words she voiced what everyone felt. "Good luck," she said sharply and then turning went on her way.

Post Office *ed* < post office,

When the train came into the station George felt relieved. He scampered hurriedly aboard. Helen White came running along Main Street hoping to have a parting word with him, but he had found a seat and did not see her. When the train started Tom Little punched his ticket, grinned and, although he knew George well and knew on what adventure he was just setting out, made no comment. Tom had seen a thousand George Willards go out of their towns to the city. It was a commonplace enough incident with him. In the smoking car there was a man who had just invited Tom to go on a fishing trip to Sandusky Bay. He wanted to accept the invitation and talk over details.

George glanced up and down the car to be sure no one was looking, then took out his pocket book and counted his money. His mind was occupied with a desire not to appear green. Almost the last words his father had said to him concerned the matter of his behavior when he got to the city. "Be a sharp one," Tom Willard had said. "Keep your eyes on your money. Be awake. That's the ticket. Don't let anyone think you're a greenhorn."

looking, *ed* < looking

pocket book *ed* < pocketbook

anyone *ms* < any one

After George counted his money he looked out of the

Departure

window and was surprised to see that the train was still in Winesburg.

The young man, going out of his town to meet the adventure of life, began to think but he did not think of anything very big or dramatic. Things like his mother's death, his departure from Winesburg, the uncertainty of his future life in the city, the serious and larger aspects of his life did not come into his mind.

He thought of little things—Turk Smollet wheeling boards through the main street of his town in the morning, a tall woman, beautifully gowned, who had once stayed overnight at his father's hotel, Butch Wheeler, the lamp lighter of Winesburg, hurrying through the streets on a summer evening and holding a torch in his hand, Helen White standing by a window in the Winesburg Post Office and putting a stamp on an envelope.

The young man's mind was carried away by his growing passion for dreams. One looking at him would not have thought him particularly sharp. With the recollection of little things occupying his mind he closed his eyes and leaned back in the car seat. He stayed that way for a long time and when he aroused himself and again looked out of the car window the town of Winesburg had disappeared and his life there had become but a background on which to paint the dreams of his manhood.

Smollet *ms* < Smallet

(overnight *ed*
  < over night
(Wheeler, *ed*
  < Wheeler
(Winesburg, *ed*
  < Winesburg
(Post Office *ed*
  < post office

SELECT BIBLIOGRAPHY

BIBLIOGRAPHIES

Modlin, Charles E., Hilbert H. Campbell, and Kenichi Takada. "Sherwood Anderson: Additions to the Bibliography." *Studies in Bibliography* 39 (1985): 166–168.

Rogers, Douglas G. *Sherwood Anderson: A Selective Annotated Bibliography.* Metuchen: Scarecrow Press, 1976.

Sheehy, Eugene P., and Kenneth A. Lohf. *Sherwood Anderson: A Bibliography.* Los Gatos: Talisman Press, 1960.

White, Ray Lewis. *The Merrill Checklist of Sherwood Anderson.* Columbus: Charles E. Merrill, 1969.

_____. "A Checklist of Sherwood Anderson Studies, 1959–1969." *Newberry Library Bulletin* 6 (July 1971): 288–302.

_____. *Sherwood Anderson: A Reference Guide.* Boston: G. K. Hall, 1977.

_____. "Sherwood Anderson: Fugitive Pamphlets and Broadsides, 1918–1940." *Studies in Bibliography* 31 (1978): 257–263.

_____. "*Winesburg* in Translation." *Ohioana Quarterly* 19 (Summer 1976): 58–60.

Select Bibliography

_____. "Sherwood Anderson." *Bibliography of American Fiction: 1866–1918.* Edited by James and Gwen L. Nagel. New York: Facts on File, 1993: 50–54.

BY ANDERSON

BOOKS

Windy McPherson's Son. New York and London: John Lane, 1916; revised edition New York: B. W. Huebsch, 1922; London: Jonathan Cape, 1923.

Marching Men. New York and London: John Lane, 1917.

Mid-American Chants. New York and London: John Lane, 1918.

Winesburg, Ohio. New York: B. W. Huebsch, 1919; London: Jonathan Cape, 1922.

Poor White. New York: B. W. Huebsch, 1920; London: Jonathan Cape, 1921.

The Triumph of the Egg. New York: B. W. Huebsch, 1921; London: Jonathan Cape, 1922.

Horses and Men. New York: B. W. Huebsch, 1923; London: Jonathan Cape, 1924.

Many Marriages. New York: B. W. Huebsch, 1923.

A Story Teller's Story. New York: B. W. Huebsch, 1924; London: Jonathan Cape, 1925.

Dark Laughter. New York: Boni & Liveright, 1925; London: Jarrolds, 1926.

The Modern Writer. San Francisco: Gelber, Lilienthal, 1925.

Sherwood Anderson's Notebook. New York: Boni & Liveright, 1926.

Tar: A Midwest Childhood. New York: Boni and Liveright, 1926; London: Secker, 1927.

Select Bibliography

A New Testament. New York: Boni and Liveright, 1927.

Alice [and] The Lost Novel. London: Elkin Mathews & Marrot, 1929.

Hello Towns! New York: Horace Liveright, 1929.

Nearer the Grass Roots [and] Elizabethton. San Francisco: Westgate Press, 1929.

The American County Fair. New York: Random House, 1930.

Perhaps Women. New York: Horace Liveright, 1931.

Beyond Desire. New York: Horace Liveright, 1932.

Death in the Woods. New York: Horace Liveright, 1933.

No Swank. Philadelphia: Centaur Press, 1934.

Puzzled America. New York and London: Charles Scribner's Sons, 1935.

Kit Brandon. New York and London: Charles Scribner's Sons, 1936; London: Hutchinson, 1937.

Plays: Winesburg and Others. New York and London: Charles Scribner's Sons, 1937.

A Writer's Conception of Realism. Olivet: Olivet College, 1939.

Home Town. New York: Alliance Book Corporation, 1940.

Sherwood Anderson's Memoirs. New York: Harcourt, Brace, 1942.

LETTERS AND DIARIES

Letters of Sherwood Anderson, edited by Howard Mumford Jones in association with Walter B. Rideout. Boston: Little, Brown, 1953.

Sherwood Anderson / Gertrude Stein: Correspondence and Personal Essays, edited by Ray Lewis White. Chapel Hill: University of North Carolina Press, 1972.

Select Bibliography

Letters to Bab: Sherwood Anderson to Marietta D. Finley,
1916–33, edited by William A. Sutton. Urbana: University of Illinois Press, 1985.

The Sherwood Anderson Diaries, 1936–1941, edited by
Hilbert H. Campbell. Athens: University of Georgia Press, 1987.

Sherwood Anderson's Love Letters to Eleanor Copenhaver
Anderson, edited by Charles E. Modlin. Athens: University of Georgia Press, 1989.

Sherwood Anderson's Secret Love Letters: For Eleanor, A
Letter a Day, edited by Ray Lewis White. Baton Rouge:
Louisiana State University Press, 1991.

EDITIONS AND COLLECTIONS

The Sherwood Anderson Reader, edited by Paul Rosenfeld.
Boston: Houghton Mifflin, 1947.

The Portable Sherwood Anderson, edited by Horace Greg-
ory. New York: Viking Press, 1949.

Winesburg, Ohio, intro. by Malcolm Cowley. New York:
Viking Press, 1960; New York: Penguin Books, 1976.

Sherwood Anderson: Short Stories, edited by Maxwell
Geismar. New York: Hill and Wang, 1962.

Mid-American Chants: 6 Midwestern Chants by Sherwood
Anderson / 11 Midwest Photographs by Art Sinsabaugh,
note by Edward Dahlberg. Highlands, N.C.: Nan-
tahala Foundation, 1964.

Winesburg, Ohio: Text and Criticism, edited by John H.
Ferres. New York: Viking Press, 1966.

Return to Winesburg, edited by Ray Lewis White. Chapel
Hill: University of North Carolina Press, 1967.

Sherwood Anderson's Memoirs: A Critical Edition, edited
by Ray Lewis White. Chapel Hill: University of North
Carolina Press, 1969.

Select Bibliography

A Story Teller's Story: A Critical Text, edited by Ray Lewis White. Cleveland: Press of Case Western Reserve University, 1969.

Tar: A Midwest Childhood—A Critical Text, edited by Ray Lewis White. Cleveland and London: Press of Case Western Reserve University, 1969.

The Buck Fever Papers, edited by Welford Dunaway Taylor. Charlottesville: University Press of Virginia, 1971.

Sherwood Anderson / Gertrude Stein: Correspondence and Personal Essays, edited by Ray Lewis White. Chapel Hill: University of North Carolina Press, 1972.

Marching Men: A Critical Text, edited by Ray Lewis White. Cleveland and London: Press of Case Western Reserve University, 1972.

The "Writer's Book" by Sherwood Anderson: A Critical Edition, edited by Martha Mulroy Curry. Metuchen: Scarecrow Press, 1975.

France and Sherwood Anderson: Paris Notebook, 1921, edited by Michael Fanning. Baton Rouge: Louisiana State University Press, 1976.

Sherwood Anderson: The Writer at His Craft, edited by Jack Salzman, David D. Anderson, and Kichinosuke Ohashi. Mamaroneck: Paul P. Appel, 1979.

The Complete Works of Sherwood Anderson, 21 vols., edited by Kichinosuke Ohashi. Kyoto: Rinsen Book Company, 1982.

The Teller's Tales, edited by Frank Gado. Schenectady: Union College Press, 1983.

Sherwood Anderson: Early Writings, edited by Ray Lewis White. Kent: Kent State University Press, 1989.

Certain Things Last: The Selected Short Stories of Sherwood Anderson, edited by Charles E. Modlin. New York: Four Walls Eight Windows, 1992.

Select Bibliography

Winesburg, Ohio: A Norton Critical Edition, edited by Charles E. Modlin and Ray Lewis White. New York: W. W. Norton, 1996.

ABOUT ANDERSON

BIOGRAPHIES

Dinsmoor, Mary Helen. "An Inquiry into the Life of Sherwood Anderson as Reflected in His Literary Works." Thesis, Ohio University, 1939.

Phillips, William Louis. "Sherwood Anderson's *Winesburg, Ohio:* Its Origins, Composition, Technique, and Reception." Dissertation, University of Chicago, 1949.

Schevill, James. *Sherwood Anderson: His Life and Work.* Denver: University of Denver Press, 1951.

Sutton, William A. *The Road to Winesburg: A Mosaic of the Imaginative Life of Sherwood Anderson.* Metuchen: Scarecrow Press, 1972.

_____. "Sherwood Anderson's Formative Years (1876–1913)." Dissertation, Ohio State University, 1943.

Townsend, Kim. *Sherwood Anderson.* Boston: Houghton Mifflin, 1987.

Williams, Kenny J. *A Storyteller and a City: Sherwood Anderson's Chicago.* DeKalb: Northern Illinois University Press, 1988.

CRITICAL STUDIES

Anderson, David D. *Sherwood Anderson: An Introduction and Interpretation.* New York: Holt, Rinehart, 1967.

Bruyère, Claire. *Sherwood Anderson: L'Impuissance Créatrice.* Paris: Klincksieck, 1985.

Select Bibliography

Burbank, Rex. *Sherwood Anderson.* New York: Twayne Publishers, 1964.

Chase, Cleveland. *Sherwood Anderson.* New York: R. M. McBride, 1927.

Fagin, Nathan Bryllion. *The Phenomenon of Sherwood Anderson.* Baltimore: Rossi-Bryn, 1927.

Papinchak, Robert Allen. *Sherwood Anderson: A Study of the Short Fiction.* New York: Twayne Publishers, 1992.

Weber, Brom. *Sherwood Anderson.* Minneapolis: University of Minnesota Press, 1964.

White, Ray Lewis. *Winesburg, Ohio: An Exploration.* Boston: Twayne Publishers, 1990.

COLLECTIONS OF ESSAYS

Anderson, David D., ed. *Critical Essays on Sherwood Anderson.* Boston: G. K. Hall, 1981.

_____, ed. *Sherwood Anderson: Dimensions of His Literary Art.* East Lansing: Michigan State University Press, 1976.

Appel, Paul P., ed. *Homage to Sherwood Anderson: 1876–1941.* Mamaroneck: Paul P. Appel, 1970.

Campbell, Hilbert H., and Charles E. Modlin, eds. *Sherwood Anderson: Centennial Studies.* Troy: Whitson Publishing, 1976.

Crowley, John W., ed. *New Essays on* Winesburg, Ohio. Cambridge: Cambridge University Press, 1990.

Ohashi, Kichinosuke, ed. *Sherwood Anderson.* Guide to 20th Century English and American Literature 8. Tokyo: Kenkyusha, 1968.

Rideout, Walter B., ed. *Sherwood Anderson: A Collection of Critical Essays.* Englewood Cliffs: Prentice-Hall, 1974.

Select Bibliography

White, Ray Lewis, comp. *The Merrill Studies in* Winesburg, Ohio. Columbus: Charles E. Merrill, 1971.
_____, ed. *Sherwood Anderson: Essays in Criticism.* Chapel Hill: University of North Carolina Press, 1966.

SPECIAL JOURNALS

American Notes & Queries 15 (September 1976).
Midwestern Miscellany 12 (1984).
Midwestern Miscellany 23 (1995).
Newberry Library Bulletin Ser. 2, No. 2 (December 1948).
Newberry Library Bulletin 6 (July 1971).
Shenandoah 13 (Spring 1962).
Story 19 (September–October 1941).
Twentieth Century Literature 23 (February 1977).
Winesburg Eagle: The Official Publication of the Sherwood Anderson Society 1 (November 1975–).